Award-winning author **Louisa George** has been
an avid reader her whole life. In between chapters
she's managed to train as a nurse, marry her
doctor hero and have two sons. Now she writes
chapters of her own in the medical romance,
contemporary romance and women's fiction
genres. Louisa's books have variously been
nominated for the coveted RITA® Award and
the New Zealand Koru Award, and have been
translated into twelve languages. She lives in
Auckland, New Zealand.

Louisa Heaton lives on Hayling Island,
Hampshire, with her husband, four children and
a small zoo. She has worked in various roles in
the health industry—most recently four years
as a Community First Responder, answering
999 calls. When not writing Louisa enjoys other
creative pursuits, including reading, quilting and
patchwork—usually instead of the things she
ought to be doing!

Also by Louisa George

Reunited by the Nurse's Secret

A Sydney Central Reunion miniseries

Ivy's Fling with the Surgeon

Rawhiti Island Medics miniseries

Resisting the Single Dad Next Door

Also by Louisa Heaton

Snowed In with the Children's Doctor
Single Mum's Alaskan Adventure

Yorkshire Village Vets miniseries

Bound by Their Pregnancy Surprise

Discover more at millsandboon.co.uk.

WINNING BACK HIS RUNAWAY WIFE

LOUISA GEORGE

FINDING FOREVER WITH THE FIREFIGHTER

LOUISA HEATON

MILLS & BOON

First published in Great Britain 2024
by Mills & Boon, an imprint of HarperCollins*Publishers* Ltd,
1 London Bridge Street, London, SE1 9GF

www.harpercollins.co.uk

HarperCollins*Publishers* Macken House, 39/40 Mayor Street Upper, Dublin 1, D01 C9W8, Ireland

Winning Back His Runaway Wife © 2024 Louisa George

Finding Forever with the Firefighter © 2024 Louisa Heaton

ISBN: 978-0-263-32158-6

05/24

This book contains FSC™ certified paper
and other controlled sources to ensure responsible forest management.

For more information visit www.harpercollins.co.uk/green.

Printed and Bound in the UK using 100% Renewable Electricity
at CPI Group (UK) Ltd, Croydon, CR0 4YY

WINNING BACK HIS RUNAWAY WIFE

LOUISA GEORGE

MILLS & BOON

To Flo Nicoll, the best editor any writer could ask for.

Thank you for taking a chance on me and for encouraging and supporting my writing dreams.

And to the Mills and Boon Medical Romance team.

Thank you so much for bringing me into your family and making my writing dreams come true!

CHAPTER ONE

FIVE YEARS AGO Charlotte Rose would have cherished this moment.

This...exact...moment: clipping the most adorable, smiling baby into her car seat after a night of nine hours' sleep—nine whole hours! And she was only six months old. Baby Stella was a veritable miracle of cuteness overload. Climbing into the driver's seat and heading across the city she loved to a job she adored: part-time emergency doctor at busy Auckland Central hospital. And enjoying the whole Auckland summer vibe of sunshine, sparkling waterfront views and, today, surprisingly little traffic.

Five years ago, Charlotte would have thought this scenario would make her life utterly complete: a baby; the perfect job with hours to suit; being back in her beloved hometown. But here she was, wishing everything could be different.

From the back seat baby Stella made a little hiccupping noise. Charlotte's heart jolted, knowing that specific sound was a precursor to... Oh, yes: here it came, loud and heart-wrenching, not just a cry but a full-on bawl.

Smiling, Charlotte glanced in her mirror and cooed, 'Stella, Stella, sweetie. Please don't cry. Hush. Hush.'

The baby had been fed, nappy-changed and had a toy to play with for the short drive. Maybe she'd dropped it. Ah, well, it would have to wait.

Charlotte switched the talkback radio station to something with upbeat music, hoping that would soothe her precious cargo. Sure enough, Stella blinked, mouth open. A pause….? A reprieve…? Yes…? Yes…?

Then she inhaled deeply and started with that heart-breaking sound again.

No.

'Stella, darling. Please don't cry. It's all going to be okay.' *Please let it all be okay.*

Charlotte sighed, wondering whether she should pull over, find the dropped toy and give Stella a quick cuddle because, yes, she was a softie who would rather cradle a baby than let it cry. And why not? Babies didn't understand timetables and deadlines. Didn't know about having to go to work. One quick smooch wouldn't hurt. Maybe Stella needed a drink or a snack.

She spied a good parking spot across the other side of the traffic lights. She cooed some more as they sat idling at the front of the car line, waiting at the intersection until the lights turned green. Then she headed across…

A shadow whooshed across her line of vision. Her neck and upper body jerked as she felt an impact, as if she were a rag doll being shaken. Then her car was shunted from the side, across the road, out of control.

What the hell?

Panic made her hands shake, made her limbs weak and her heart race. She managed to turn her head to work out what the hell was going on. The front of a huge truck was glued to her door. There was a screech of tires. The stench of burning rubber. The crunch of metal on concrete. A looming lamp post.

And a very quiet baby.

CHAPTER TWO

'MATE, MIA'S FRIENDS *loved* you. She said to tell you that any time you fancy coming over again for a break we can organise a double date...'

'Thanks, but no.' Lewis Parry laughed but jumped in to shut his colleague up. Being on holiday for two weeks with Brin and his family on Rāwhiti Island had been amazing. They'd gone fishing, swimming and diving. They'd eaten what they'd caught from the ocean and drunk the local craft beer. 'I had a great holiday and I've come back to work feeling refreshed and relaxed. In my experience, a relationship would put a swift end to that kind of vibe.'

'Just saying...' Brin put up his hands. 'I thought the same, but find the right woman and it all clicks into place.'

Been there. Done that. And it all fell apart.

'I'm thinking you got lucky.' Lewis finished up his electronic notes from their last call out and slipped the tablet into the glove box. Sometimes he wished he worked in wide open spaces rather than the confines of an ambulance with a newly ordained and far too enthusiastic matchmaker as sidekick.

'You have to make your own luck, mate.' Brin grinned. 'Hey, maybe you'll make some luck at the fundraiser on Saturday night. Lots of hospital staff will be there...' He winked and nudged Lewis's arm.

Great. Brin's happily settled so he thinks we all have to be.

The radio crackled.

'Code Red. R Four. MVA. Female driver. Baby passenger. Ponsonby Road and Picton Street intersection.'

Lewis was immediately grateful for the spotlight shifting from his woeful love life to their jobs.

'Ten-two. Unit Four responding. Over,' he radioed back to control. Then he turned to Brin. 'A baby? Damn. Let's get a move on.'

As they approached the accident scene, it was obvious that a truck had ploughed into the side of an old blue sedan which had then been shunted into a lamp post. The car's rear driver's side door had been totalled and the driver's door buckled and dented enough to impede opening. The passenger-side doors rear and front were dented but openable. He assessed the area for safety as he jumped from the van: no evidence of spilt petrol or oil.

The truck driver was sitting on the side of the road, head in hands.

Lewis called out, 'You okay? Do you need help?'

Face pale and wan, the man shook his head. 'Help the others. I'm… I'm okay. My brakes… I kept pressing on them but they didn't…'

'Thanks, man. We'll come back to you and check you over.' The man was walking and talking: he could wait. Lewis turned to Brin. 'I'll check the driver, you check the baby.'

'On it.' Brin nodded and peeled off to the far side of the car.

The driver's window was smashed and Lewis had a partial view of the person in the driving seat as he tried to tug open the distorted door. She had her head turned away, looking into the back seat. Her shoulders were shaking, and she was saying something he couldn't quite hear. Her hair—a beautiful shade of russet red—was tied into a low ponytail.

Red...

Charlie?

A long-forgotten ache slammed into his gut, mingling with memories he'd tried to keep at bay for five years. Memories that flashed through his mind: red hair entwined with flowers and a gossamer veil; red hair splayed on a pillow as they'd made love. A tight ponytail, shoulders shuddering as she'd walked away, suitcase in hand—the last image of her as she'd left him.

No, it couldn't be Charlie. He shook himself. She lived in London. But funny-weird how, even though she lived on the opposite side of the world, he sometimes thought he saw her at the beach, in a crowded street or in a shopping mall.

It was never her.

Focus, man.

Her screams were becoming clearer now. 'The baby! Is the baby okay? *Please.* Please get the baby.'

Definitely not Charlie. There were no babies in her life; there couldn't be. But as she turned to look at him, her blue eyes red-rimmed and imploring, cheeks streaked with running mascara, his gut folded in on itself. It felt as if the world had stopped turning. It was her, with her mesmerising eyes and perfect mouth.

His wife.

Ex-wife.

'Charlie?'

'Lewis?' Her chest caved forward then, and her face crumpled. 'Oh, my God, Lewis, thank God it's you. You've got to help me. Please, get the baby. She's too quiet.'

Damn. Was it her baby? He pushed the spike of hurt away. 'It's okay, Charlie. My colleague's opening the door now. He'll check your baby. What's her name?'

'St… Stella,' Charlie stuttered through gulps of air. 'Is she okay? Please make sure she's okay.'

'It's okay, it's okay, I can hear her fussing,' He lowered his voice and crouched to talk to her. Charlie was his patient now. Their past had nothing to do with this. He needed to be the paramedic, despite his shaking hands. *Damn.* She'd always had this effect on him: taking his breath away, tipping his world sideways. 'She doesn't look hurt at all. The car seat kept her safe. My colleague Brin will look after Stella. I'm here for you. Tell me, where do *you* hurt?'

The front airbag hadn't activated. It was an old car, and probably didn't even have side bags.

'I don't know.' She looked down at her trembling hands and his eyes followed: no wedding ring. There was no ring at all where her platinum bands used to be. 'I think… I'm okay. My chest hurts a little. And my shoulder…it's not bad. Probably from the seatbelt.'

'I bet. You want me to take a look?'

She edged sideways away from him and for a moment he thought she was recoiling at his suggestion, but in fact she was making room in the tight space. 'I think it's just bruised. Yes, look—check.'

Her gaze caught his and for a moment his need to look after her almost overwhelmed him, even after all these years apart. Even after she'd walked away.

He drew his gaze from hers. Just looking at her made his heart sore. He couldn't bear to see her hurting too, and he reached in and moved the soft fabric of her blouse away from her shoulder. Her familiar perfume of rose and sweet citrus hung in the air, spinning him back in time. 'Ouch. Yes, it's red raw. You're going to have a nasty bruise there. Do your ribs hurt?' He quickly moved his hand away and closed down more memories that assaulted his brain.

She blinked up at him and something flickered across her eyes: gratitude? He wasn't sure. She gave him a shoddy attempt at a smile. 'Only if I move.'

'So, stay still. What about your feet? Legs?' He could see bent metal close to her knees but not around her feet. It was a miracle she hadn't been badly hurt.

'They're okay, not hurt. I'm just wedged in by the door. Oh, Lewis, I need to get to work. But I need… I can't leave Stella. I can't take her to nursery. Not now after this.'

Work? She lived here now?

'Oh, no, you don't.' He peered into the car and tried to get a better view of her body so he could assess for any more injuries. 'We need to get you out of this vehicle and checked out at the hospital. You're in shock. You could be hurt and not even realise—whiplash, for example.'

'Hey.' Brin came round to this side of the car, a baby cradled in his arms. 'Someone needs their mama.'

Charlie's face filled with love and panic. 'Is she…?'

Brin grinned. 'She seems fine, love. A little bewildered by all the drama, but absolutely fine. I'll give her a proper check in a minute, but thought you'd want to see her first.'

'Thank God.' Relief flooded Charlie's face as she reached through the cracked window and stroked little Stella's head. 'I'm sorry, baby. I love you. You're okay. You're okay.'

The baby gurgled and giggled, her arms stretched out to be held by her mother. But Charlie smiled through her tears and shook her head. Lewis recognised the brave face she'd spent a good eighteen months out of their four-year marriage trying to put on as she cooed, 'Hey, hey, baby. I'm a bit stuck. I'll hold you when I can get out of here.'

Lewis's gut hollowed out.

Charlie and a baby: all they'd ever wanted.

But how? It didn't matter, right? She'd got the baby she'd so desperately wanted…just with another guy.

He tugged again at the door and breathed out in relief at the sound of a siren. 'Sounds like help is on its way. We'll get you out in no time.'

'The car is wrecked.' She shook her head.

'Thank God it was just the car, right?'

She put her head on the steering wheel. 'Ugh. Lucy's going to kill me.'

'It's Lucy's car?'

'Yes. I haven't had time to find one for me yet.' She slowly sat up and rubbed her shoulder. 'And I don't even know what happened. How the hell am I going to explain this?'

So she hadn't been back long enough to buy herself a car. Why was she back? And why did he care? Why did it matter? They were ancient history. She'd been so unhappy back then she'd fled to the other side of the world without him. What mattered now was that she and her baby were safe and unhurt.

'Truck driver said his brakes failed.'

'Oh. I guess it could have been much worse.' She closed her eyes and swallowed, as if imaging what worse would look like.

'Do you want me to call her—Lucy? Your parents? Call… someone else?' She'd moved on, right? Was Stella's father still in the picture?

'No!' Her eyes flashed pure panic for a brief moment, then she relaxed. 'No, it's fine. I'll call Lucy when I'm done at the hospital.'

'Okay…' He thought about asking her more about some significant other she might need to call, but thought better of it. It wasn't his business.

But she was still looking at him. 'Look, Lewis, I need to explain…'

'Like I said, the truck driver seems to be taking responsibility.' He got the feeling she wasn't referring to the accident, but he didn't want to get into anything deeper here. She had a family now; she'd moved on. Just as he had…*kind of.* Sure, he'd thought he had, but the ache at seeing her again had blindsided him. 'Honestly. We just need to get you safe. The firies are almost here; I can hear the sirens. They'll lever the door open, then we can take you and your baby to Central.'

She put her hand to her head. 'Ugh. A patient at my own workplace. That sucks.'

'You're working there?'

'Yes. I came back a few weeks ago. It's a long—'

'Hey, Lewis. Missy's getting a bit antsy.' Brin handed him the baby who was now wriggling and fretting—not quite crying but it was a definite overture before the big crescendo. 'Can you have a go at soothing her? She might like your face better than mine.'

'Damn right she will,' Lewis quipped with a smile that he didn't feel as he took baby Stella into his arms. She was a good weight, about six months old, maybe seven. Same shock of red hair as her mother. She was healthy; cute as a damned button.

He cleared his throat as it had become surprisingly raw all of a sudden. 'Um…hey, you. Look who's here. She's right here. And she wants to give you a cuddle, but she's stuck in the car. So you're stuck with me.'

Little Stella gazed up at him and tapped his nose with her little fist. She had huge navy eyes which were swimming with tears. Lewis's heart contracted. *No.* He did not want to feel anything. Not the hurt he'd felt at Charlotte leaving. Not the tug towards her that was as natural as breathing. Not the softening, or the care. He did not want those things again—ever.

This was not Charlie's and his baby, but his chest hurt, his throat burning as he held her. Panicked, he turned to hand her back to Brin, but he was over checking on the truck driver.

So, there he was, holding his ex-wife's much-wanted baby with feet feeling like clay and his chest like a vice around his heart. A weird and unexpected start to a Monday morning.

''Scuse me, mate.' A fire fighter in full yellow uniform was standing behind him holding the metal 'jaws of life' hydraulic rescue tool. 'Give us some room, yeah?'

'Sure.' Lewis swallowed back all the emotion rattling through him and rocked the baby up and down, pulling faces at her to try make her laugh. Maybe she was scared at seeing her mummy stuck in the car. Maybe this kind of thing traumatised a kid. Or maybe she was too young for it to make a difference.

He only knew of his own experiences—that what adults did and said, or neglected to do and neglected to say, had a lasting effect. So he turned away from the car and showed Stella the seagull sitting on top of the damaged lamp post, the flowers on the grass verge and an aeroplane high in the sky.

'You're a natural.'

What?

He whirled round to see Charlotte standing in front of him. Her face was damp from tears, her expression soul-deep sad and her cheeks now red with a blush. 'Um… I said, you're a natural. With the baby, I mean.'

He didn't know what to say; he did not want to go over old history. Talking about the past didn't change what had happened. Better to hold his guard and keep schtum.

And…there was the root of all their problems. He'd spent

the last five years mentally unravelling their unravelling. Perhaps…*maybe*…he could have said more back then instead of keeping it all balled up inside him instead of trying to bolster her up to his own detriment and feeding her…not lies, exactly, but little wishes he'd wanted to be true. He should have ditched the stoicism and just been outright, totally, unequivocally honest.

But he'd thought he was doing the right thing. He'd done what he'd learnt to do: biting back his own truths, because no one wanted to hear your problems. No one wanted to hear how you feel.

She held out her hands for her baby, which he gave her gladly. Her eyes roamed her daughter's face, then her body, as if checking for signs of injury. 'There you are. You're okay, you're just perfect.' Then she smooched the little girl's face with kisses. When she seemed satisfied all was okay, she turned back to Lewis. 'Brin says we have to go to hospital, and I think I should get Stella checked out. I mean, I'm okay, but I want to be sure about her.'

'Of course. Very wise. Get your neck and shoulder checked too.'

'Are you…in the back of the ambulance? Will you be there…with us?' Worry nipped at her features.

He shook his head. 'I'm driver today.'

Her eyebrows rose. 'Oh.'

He couldn't identify the emotion behind that word. Relief that they wouldn't be in an enclosed space together or disappointment? Why did he hope it was the latter? Oh, poor, pathetic heart.

She left you, mate. Reel it in.

Brin, oblivious to *everything*, laughed and opened the

back doors of the ambulance. 'He thinks I'm too Perez to be a paramedic.'

She frowned as she climbed into the back of the van. 'Perez?'

'He's a Formula One racing-car driver.' Lewis found a smile. 'Trust me, it's safer this way.'

Trust me.

Another knife to his heart.

Trust me to listen, to support. To grow with you. To be flexible. To change as we change.

Yet he'd done none of those things, although he'd tried damned hard. It just hadn't been enough, apparently.

It was all too late now anyway.

He turned and walked to the front of his van, readying himself to take her to the hospital, her place of work. The place he visited on a very regular basis. The place where he was going to see her daily, probably more than that, handing over patients, sharing the lunchroom space, the café and the corridors.

Up until today he hadn't realised how easier his life had been, knowing she was at the other side of the world and that he wouldn't bump into her here in Auckland. Or how much effect she would still have on him even after five years apart.

But Charlotte Rose was back and she was going to haunt his working days now, as well as his nights.

CHAPTER THREE

TELLING LUCY ABOUT the accident was one of the worst things Charlie had ever done, even though they were both just fine—apart from Charlie's chest and shoulder bruising. But she'd broken the news gently and reassured her sister that they were both okay.

Lucy shrugged the blankets off her knee and slowly sat up from her prone position on the couch, taking Stella in her arms. 'Poor baby. A car crash? What an adventure.'

'An adventure? I wish I had your slant on things. I'm supposed to be here to help you, not cause even more stress.' But, when she looked at her sister, Charlie saw the pain she was hiding. The worry lines that made her look older than her thirty-eight years: the dark rings under her eyes; the slack skin from her weight loss—a direct result of the disease inside her—and the medication that was poisoning her and curing her in equal measure.

Lucy sighed. 'You're being a massive help. You know I couldn't have gone through this on my own. I'm so grateful you came back. Hell, you gave up your whole London life for me and Stella. Come sit down, Charlie. You look terrible, so pale and shocked. I'll get the kettle on.'

'No, I'm fine, really. Just a bit bruised and heart sore. I'd hate anything to happen to Stella, especially if it was on my watch. Sit.' She mock-glared at her sister, who was supposed to be resting. 'You stay here, and I'll get the kettle on. Maybe we can go sit outside in the sun for a while.'

'Oh, yes please. And let's have the ginger biscuits. I'm starving.'

'That's great. The nausea has settled, then?'

'I'm trying to ignore it.' Lucy shook her head and smiled wanly. 'I need to keep my strength up for this little one.'

'That's why I'm here to help.' Charlie sat down next to her sister.

Lucy's eyes glistened with tears, showing a rare chink in her 'I'll be fine' armour. 'I love you. Thank you.'

'I love you too.' Charlie circled her arms round her older sister and hugged her gently, so glad she'd come back to help her.

She'd been away too long, licking her own wounds after her infertility diagnosis and failed marriage, and had only barely acknowledged her family's attempts to connect. But getting that call from a terrified Lucy had been the shake-up Charlie had needed. Lucy hadn't wanted to spoil their parents' overseas charity-work trip of a lifetime, as they'd no doubt have rushed back to help out, so the first person she'd called was her sister. Charlie had jumped at the chance to walk this cancer journey with her.

And she was not going to lambast Lucy's ex-boyfriend for not stepping up to help look after his child. It was none of her business, and his loss. But the way Lucy was handling things now was impressive.

'I don't understand how you can be so upbeat when you must be knackered after the chemo.' One round down, six more to go…. maybe…hopefully…and a long road to recovery.

'Hey, I feel like crap, yes. But I choose to be positive. Look, I still have my hair. And my sense of humour.' Lucy pulled a funny face, although they both knew that the hair would be gone soon. Charlie just hoped Lucy could maintain her sunny outlook through the gruelling treatment. Lucy sighed and snuggled her daughter. 'It could all have been worse.'

'That's what I said to Lewis—'

'Oh my God, you saw Lewis?' Lucy's eyes widened. 'You kept that quiet.'

'I thought it was more important that I told you about the accident than the attending paramedic.'

'But, wow, imagine that. You have an accident and the paramedic is your ex-husband. Thank God you parted agreeably.'

'Yeah. Imagine.' She hadn't gone into a lot of detail with her family about the reasons for her marriage break-up, although they knew it had been to do with her infertility.

But she hadn't been aware her sister thought it had been an agreeable split. In truth, they'd barely been speaking. Communication had dwindled over months until they'd been more like distant flatmates than married partners. But there hadn't been any raging arguments or outward bitterness, just sadness that they hadn't been able to make it as a couple. Sadness that Charlie had taken a long time to shake off.

In truth, she hadn't known what to say about seeing Lewis. Their meeting was inevitable, given where she now worked, and she'd thought she'd prepared herself for seeing him in the flesh. But nothing could have equipped her for the onslaught of emotions—happiness and bone-deep sadness—that had accompanied the panic of being in an MVA and the relief at having him, of all people, help her.

'How did it go? What was he like?'

Still gorgeous.

Through the haze of panic, fear and, yes, some pain, she hadn't been immune to his beautiful, soulful brown eyes and dazzling smile. He'd always taken her breath away with that smile. And the way he'd gently examined her shoulder, the look in his eyes filled with emotion, had made her heart squeeze. She remembered the way he used to look at her, with such affection and love, then…disappointment. Although he'd never admit it.

'I was just glad he was there. He's very good at his job and made me feel a lot better—very professional. He checked Stella over. Distracted her from anything that might have scared her.'

'Did you talk? You know, about what happened?'

'We didn't talk about anything, Luce. I was his patient, then I was taken to hospital and he left to go to his next call-out.'

Lucy frowned. 'Not even a brief conversation?'

'About what? How? He was busy and working. You'd never have known we even knew each other, never mind been married.'

'Still tight-lipped about his feelings, then.' Lucy laughed hollowly.

'Yeah. Strong and silent and infuriating. And I'm feeling a bit…battered.' Not just physically, but emotionally, even though she had no right to feel that at all.

But he'd never told her his true feelings about their break-up or her infertility. He'd always been an enigma. His expressions had betrayed his emotions, but he would refuse to talk about the way he felt. Oh, he'd told her he loved her and cherished her; about how much he'd cared; that he believed in her, that she was amazing… But getting him to talk about raw things, core-deep things? He'd rather have stuck pins in his eyes. He'd thought it was stoicism to keep quiet about difficult issues but in the end it was just intractability.

Was he married now? Had he a family of his own? Had he made it work with someone else? That thought hurt her too much for her to dwell on.

She looked at her little niece, fast asleep in her mother's arms, and her heart twinged.

'He held her, Lucy. He looked so right with a baby in his arms. It clarified everything—I did the right thing by leaving him so he could have that in his future. Even though he would never admit I did us both a favour.' It had almost broken her to see him hold Stella and remind her of the dreams they'd once shared. And she'd told him he was a natural parent. Oh, God, why had she said that? But she'd been so wrong-footed at seeing him, and him cooing over the baby, the words had tumbled out of her.

Lucy patted Charlie's arm. 'Oh, honey. I can imagine how it must have felt seeing him with a baby in his arms.'

'I think… I don't know if I managed to set him straight or not, it's all a bit blurry. But I think he believes Stella is *my* baby.'

'Yikes.' Her sister pulled a face. 'Awkward.'

'Very. It all seemed too much to explain all at once—why I'm here, who Stella belongs to and why she was in my car… your car. Your very wrecked car.' Charlie winced at the thought of dealing with all of the insurance stuff now. 'See? It's a lot. Plus, I didn't want to tell him about your illness without checking in with you first. I know you're still coming to terms with it all and it's not common knowledge.'

'Tell whoever you like. It's not a secret. Except Mum and Dad, obviously. I'm not ready for their reaction yet. I need to be stronger for their panic than I feel right now.'

Their parents would drop everything if they knew Lucy was sick, even their dream trip. 'Okay, well, if it comes up I'll set Lewis straight about why I'm back.' To look after Lucy and Stella—not…repeat, *not*…to pine after the man she'd left. Or pine about what they'd once had before the sex on schedule, the failed pregnancy tests and the medical tests and scans.

Okay, enough now.

Time to put thought into action. She stood up and headed towards the kitchen. 'Right, then, let's get that tea made.'

'Thanks, hun.' Lucy grimaced. 'It's so weird, having you look after me.'

Charlie hovered in the kitchen doorway. 'Why?'

'Because I'm the older sister. I'm supposed to look after you.'

'You always have. Very well.' Too much, if she was being honest. There was eight years between Lucy and her, so she'd had a big sister to look out for her from day one. A very devoted big sister.

Born to older parents, Charlie had always felt she might have been a 'Band-Aid' baby to help heal a possible rift between her mother and father. A child to make everyone happy again, another focus. And, given that Lucy had never wanted to follow in the family footsteps as a doctor, there'd been a lot of pressure on Charlie to fulfil her parents' expectations, and a lot of attending to Charlie's every need.

By the time she'd graduated from medical school, and then married and moved in with Lewis, she hadn't had a day living on her own or fighting her own battles—being herself. She'd always been Lucy's kid sister, the formidable Dr Rose's daughter, Lewis's wife. She'd been well taken care of but smothered too. It hadn't been until she'd settled on her own in London that she'd realised just how much she'd leaned into that.

Not any more. 'Sit back and rest; it's my turn to look after you.'

She'd deal with the Lewis problem later. *If* she could get him out of her head. But, after seeing him up close, having him touch her with such tenderness and care, getting him out of her head was proving a lot more difficult than she'd thought.

'Eighty-two-year-old gentleman: Henry Gerald Woods. Slipped on wet lino in the kitchen at home last night. Couldn't get himself back up and had to wait for his carers to come in this morning. Complaining of severe pain in his right hip. Blood pressure eighty over fifty at presentation, now ninety-four over sixty-seven. Slightly hypothermic at thirty-four point nine degrees when found, rising steadily now. IV zero point nine percent normal saline in situ. Pain score eight out of ten initially, but has come down to five after morphine administration. We brought his medications in. Takes daily fluid tablets and beta blockers.' Lewis handed his patient's tablets over to the A and E triage nurse.

'Thanks, we'll take over from here,' she said, and smiled at Henry as they lifted him from the portable trolley onto the hospital gurney. 'Hello, Henry. Back again so soon? What on earth have you been up to this time?'

'See you, mate.' Lewis nodded at Henry, one of their 'frequent flyers' who insisted on independent living whilst also refusing to wear the alert necklace that would bring help quickly when needed. 'Don't go giving these lovely nurses any of your cheek, okay?'

'You're just jealous of my charisma,' Henry joked, just audible around the confines of his oxygen mask.

'To be fair, our man Lewis here has plenty of charisma. He just keeps it well hidden.' Brin laughed and opened the cubicle curtain for Lewis to step into the hustle and bustle of the A and E logistics area.

Lewis's heart immediately started its staccato rhythm of anxiety and, unexpectedly, excitement. Was Charlie here? He glanced around the large open space. She was not at the work stations in the centre of the room; not obviously in the corridor. He couldn't hear her voice coming from one of the cubicles. Couldn't see her giveaway red locks.

Hot damn, he'd never been on the lookout for a glimpse of her and her gorgeous hair in here before. In fact, because she'd been doing her medical rotations when they'd been married, they'd never worked in the same department until now—today.

Yesterday, to be factually correct, but he'd earlier overheard one of the nurses saying that the new emergency doctor had been involved in a car crash and that she was mostly unharmed and had come back this morning. So far, he'd managed three visits here over his shift and he hadn't seen anything of her. Now he was clocking off, he could breathe again. The chances of seeing her now were slim to nil.

Until tomorrow. When he'd be on high alert all over again.

'Lewis?' Brin's tone was brisk and he was frowning. 'I said, do you want to go sort the van out and I'll grab us some takeaway coffees?'

'Sure.' The sooner he got out of here, the sooner he'd stop looking for her.

Brin's frown deepened. 'You seem a bit distracted today. You okay?'

'Never better.' Lewis nodded, determined to stay focused on the job. He hadn't thought it necessary to tell Brin about his relationship status with the new emergency doctor, but no doubt he'd have to soon enough. 'Cheers, yes. Trim flat white, please, and one of those giant chocolate-chip cookies. Meet you at the van.'

Once in the ambulance bay, he took a deep breath of the fresh, sea-salted air and was just about to climb into the back of the van to tidy up when he caught a flash of red hair. A figure was walking towards the hospital entry, moving stiffly with her head down, right next to where he was standing.

She lifted her head. Their gazes tangled. *Damn.* Now she'd seen him, neither of them could avoid the inevitable, awkward small talk.

'Um… Hi, Lewis.' She inhaled as she approached, a hesitant smile hovering on her lips.

And, damn it, if he couldn't help thinking about the way she tasted. *Don't. Just don't.*

Now there was no urgency of injury assessment or need to rescue, as there had been yesterday, he was able to take a longer look at her. She was still achingly beautiful with her huge blue eyes, pale Celtic skin, that gorgeous kissable mouth and blush-pink lips. But she was thinner, her cheekbones more pronounced, and there were little lines around her eyes when she smiled. She hadn't done a lot of that with him in the later years of their marriage, but he'd seen them there yesterday when she'd hugged her baby. He swallowed. 'Hey, Charlotte.'

'*Charlotte?* Not Charlie?' A pause. Clearly, she was finding this as difficult as he was. 'Okay, yes. I guess we're at that point, right?'

Which point, exactly? They'd breached breaking point a long time ago. His gut clenched as he cleared his throat. 'I was just being polite.'

In truth, 'Charlie' was the woman he'd adored. Using her formal, full name 'Charlotte' gave him emotional space.

'I know…exactly. It's just, you never called me Charlotte.' She shook her head and her eyes darkened, as if she was carrying the world on her shoulders. 'Okay, so, while I have the chance, I want to thank you for what you did for me yesterday.'

'No problem. I was just doing my job. How are you?'

She shrugged her right shoulder and winced. 'Sore, as expected, and bruised. But I'll live.'

His innate immediate response was to put his arms round her and tell her to rest up, that he'd look after her, but they weren't in that space any more. Things between them had broken. Instead, he found what he hoped was a benign smile and said, 'So take it easy, okay? No heavy lifting.'

She nodded, her expression difficult to read. 'Okay. Thank you.'

He was just about to turn away but then had another thought. 'And your baby—Stella? She's okay?'

Her features softened at the mention of Stella. She clearly loved her daughter very much. 'Yes, she's fine. No issues at all. In fact, I've just been to check on her at the hospital creche.'

Oh, God, this was all too painful. He needed not to be here with her. 'Good to hear. Right, well, I've got to get on, you know...'

'Wait, Lewis. I need to explain.' Her hand touched his wrist, stopping him from turning away. He felt warmth on his skin from a gesture that was almost too intimate. Her skin was soft, her grip light with delicate bones, beautiful hands. But he didn't, couldn't, draw attention to the gesture because that would make things even more awkward.

'No, look, you don't have to explain anything. It's not my business.' Nevertheless, the ache to know everything was surprising and deep. That Charlie had a family was a shock, and it wasn't just the 'who with?', but the *'how?'*.

She looked at her fingers on his and her eyes widened. Grimacing, she lifted her hand and shoved it into her scrubs pocket. 'Um... Stella isn't my baby. She's my niece—Lucy's daughter.'

'Ah.' *Okay*...he'd jumped to conclusions. Something in his

chest shifted and eased a little. 'Okay.... Lucy. Of course, Lucy's baby. I see.'

Charlie shook her head. 'No, I don't think you do. I've come home because Lucy is sick.' Her eyes flickered closed briefly as if she was finding it hard to say the words. 'Breast cancer.'

His gut knotted. 'God, I'm sorry. And with a young baby too. That's terrible. Is she...is she going to be okay?'

'It's early days with the chemo, but the odds are good. I'm helping her look after Stella, and of course I'm trying my best to look after Lucy too, but you might remember that that's not always easy.'

Of course; he remembered that the two sisters had had a difficult dynamic at times. Lucy had always been slightly domineering, a bit meddlesome but well intentioned. Charlie used to complain that her family was trying to be the third spoke in her marriage, in her life.

The Roses were a tight unit: a doting sister and helicopter parents. They'd always been in each other's business, with entangled lives...in a good way, mostly. He'd kind of envied them that closeness which was so very, very different from his own family. His parents had never lived in the same town, never mind the same house. He hadn't heard from his dad...ever. And he wasn't exactly sure where his nomad mother was; last time he'd heard, she was in Invercargill but planning to leave there because it was too cold. That was, what, six months ago? She wasn't great at keeping in touch, regardless of how many times he texted or called.

But at least he had a good bond with his twin brother, Logan. If Logan had been ill, Lewis would have done the same as Charlie and given up his life to look after his sibling. 'Of course I remember. You were joined at the hip growing up. Maybe she'll let you look after her, for a change. *Maybe?*'

'I wish.' Charlie seemed to relax a little, knowing he understood her dilemma. 'She's hellbent on doing everything, but she's so tired. Looking after a baby is knackering enough without cancer treatment too. But that's why I took a part-time job here—so I can fit my work around my life for a change. To be honest, I'd prefer not to be working at all while I look after her, but someone needs to pay the bills, right?'

'Right, of course. I hope she has a speedy recovery.' So Charlie hadn't had a sudden change of heart about her ex and rushed back for him. Not that he'd thought that but…maybe his pathetic heart had hoped? Yeah, he didn't want to admit to a fleeting hope. 'And your parents? Are they okay too?'

He had to ask, right? He couldn't exactly have a half-conversation about her family. But this was just about the most awkward he'd ever felt: asking guarded, polite questions about people he'd known, loved and spent many happy times with of the woman he'd rocked into; whose hair he'd held when she'd vomited after a fun night out and too many drinks; with whom he'd laughed; with whom he'd planned his whole life. Now she was like a stranger, with a completely different life.

'They're fine. Retired now, but doing charity work in Uganda. We haven't told them about Lucy's diagnosis because they'd rush back. You know what they're like; they need to be in the thick of our lives and it's a bit stifling. I can't tell you how relieved we were when they decided to travel, just doing things for themselves, you know? Lucy didn't want them to cut their time in Uganda short so I just told them I'd decided to come home for a while to spend time with my sister.'

She suddenly looked flustered, shaking her head and rolling her eyes. 'God, I don't know why I'm telling you all this. You're busy; you should probably go. What am I saying? I'm busy too. And I'm going to be late back to work. I'm sorry, Lewis.'

'Don't, Charlotte. Don't apologise.' He was amused by her fluster, glad she'd been able to let off some steam and talk about her sister's illness. 'Give my regards to Lucy.'

'I will. Thanks.' She looked a little relieved and smiled. Had she been worried about how this whole interaction would go? Had she thought he might bring up their past? Because, hell, there was a lot to unpick there. But maybe it was best to keep it firmly in the past.

He found himself smiling too, despite the weirdness of everything. 'Take care, Charlotte…um… Charlie. See you around.'

'Yes. Undoubtedly.' She smiled properly then, a full-blown mega-watt smile that did something to his chest. He hadn't realised just how much he'd been looking forward to seeing that smile again. How much the ache for her was still embedded in his DNA.

Then he watched her walk away.

The story of my life.

There was no way he'd let himself fall for her again. She'd broken his heart once and, if he wasn't careful, she could do it again.

CHAPTER FOUR

CHARLIE TOOK A seat at the empty round table in the fund-raiser venue, not entirely happy to be here when she should have been at home looking after her sister and her niece. But Lucy had made her come, waving her off with a big smile, a sigh and a promise to call if she felt poorly.

'You need to get out more,' Lucy had said. 'You can't spend your whole life stuck within these four walls with me. You need some friends, Charlie.'

'I go out to work and to the supermarket,' Charlie had replied, as if grocery shopping was the most exciting thing in the world. 'I want to be here.'

'And I need you to go out. You're making me feel guilty, hogging you all the time when you should be building a social life now that you've come home. You're too young to be spending all your waking hours around sick people.' Lucy had smiled her wan smile and sighed. 'Go to that comedy night you were talking about the other day, have fun then come home and tell me all about it. I want to live a normal Saturday night vicariously.'

I need you to go out. Just like that, Charlie had read between the lines. Lucy was grateful to have Charlie here to help, but spending all this time together was as stifling as their home had been growing up. Lucy wanted things to feel normal instead of staring down the barrel of sickness and uncertainty. So here Charlie was, hoping the comedy part of the night would give her something to laugh about so she could retell it all to Lucy and make her giggle too.

A chatting, laughing group of people entered the large events centre and scanned the room for their table. Charlie recognised them: Patience and Arno, two staff nurses from work, followed by a couple of junior doctors who had recently joined the team, Seung and Mei. Charlie stood up and waved. 'Here! We're over here.'

Patience waved back and started to make her way over with the doctors, while Arno nodded, then turned to speak to people behind him: a woman she didn't know, who was holding hands with one of the paramedics that seemed to spend their life in the A and E department, and behind them...

Lewis.

No. Her belly tightened.

No.

Charlie slid down in her seat. Did the Emergency department have so few people keen to make up a table of eight that they'd had to invite the visiting paramedics too? The last thing she wanted to do was spend the evening with him. That had been her normal once upon a time but it wasn't now. Hadn't been for five years and, judging by the way her body prickled at the sight of him, her instinctive reaction at seeing him was one of excitement and anticipation.

No. Please, no. She was supposed to be building a new life. Despite him being nice to her, he was probably just being polite. He probably hated her. He probably had a wife and kids.

How to act with him in the company of colleagues and friends? Did they acknowledge they knew each other more than people thought they did, or pretend they were strangers?

She patted the space next to her and indicated to Patience

to come and sit down. But she wasn't quick enough, embroiled as she was in air kisses with her colleagues, to see that all the seats were being taken except for the one on the other side of her. And there was only one person left still standing.

'Lewis, hi.' She gave him a tight smile. 'Looks like this is your seat.'

'This is awkward,' he whispered, as if feeling her embarrassment. 'Sorry. There isn't anywhere else.'

So he was approaching this head-on. She nodded, her throat tight. 'It's okay. I'm sure we can get through one evening.'

'Of course. I don't think anyone here knows about our past so let's just keep it that way, right? Let's just forget about everything and try have a good time.' He caught her gaze and… *oh, dear*…those brown eyes had her all tangled up inside.

Forget everything? What was he saying? She could never forget being married to Lewis: their courtship, the wedding, the dreamy honeymoon, the laughter, the fun…the sex. *Oh*, the sex.

But it wasn't meant to be. They'd tried to make it work and failed. She'd walked away in the end, desperate for some space from the sadness of it all. She'd left him, taken a job on the other side of the world, and the guilt of doing that still stung. Should she have stayed and tried harder? Could they have worn the difficulties they'd faced if they'd stuck it through? He probably did hate her, but how would she know? He'd agreed they separate, but he hadn't told her how he felt about any of it.

So what could she do now but agree to keep everything civil? Just civil, as if they were mere colleagues. She nodded. 'Sure. I don't want to bring the mood down either. Deal.'

'Drink?' He reached for one of the bottles of wine on the table and hovered it over her glass.

'Absolutely. Thanks.'

Lewis poured their drinks and sat down, his knee knocking against hers. He grimaced and shifted away but she was left with his scent lingering in the air: his favourite cologne and something that was uniquely Lewis. It was as familiar to her as her morning coffee aroma.

But she needn't have worried about any further awkwardness because he was immediately embroiled in a conversation with Dr Mei beside him. And Patience engaged Charlie in a conversation about the emergency department politics then introduced her to the other paramedic, Brin—of whom she'd seen lots but didn't know—and his girlfriend Mia.

Apparently Mia was a nurse practitioner at a local GP practice. She told Charlie that Brin was Irish but had settled here now. They had a little girl called Harper. They spent half their lives on Rāwhiti Island and they'd recently been there with the guy sitting next to her—Lewis. Did Charlie know him?

Remembering their deal, Charlie simply nodded at that and redirected her conversation to their holiday with him. *Had he been there with a significant other—a wife, girlfriend?* Of course she didn't ask that, even though she was suddenly very keen to know the answer. Had he found someone else? She tried to read between the conversation lines…she was getting good at that these days…but it was just *Lewis this, Lewis that…*

He was such good fun, apparently: a talented fisherman; a good friend; a dab hand at the barbecue; great with kids. He babysat their daughter sometimes. He was a real good guy.

Her heart felt raw. She knew that, of course, more than any of them. A good guy with a heart of gold…

Eventually Lewis rolled his eyes at Brin and told him to stop with the ego massaging but Brin just grinned. 'Ah, man. I'm just telling Charlie here how it is.' Brin turned back to her.

'I see you're here on your own tonight, Charlie. Do you have a partner? Family?'

They all looked at her then and her mouth felt as dry as a husk. 'Um… No to both—'

'What is this?' Lewis interrupted, jumping to her aid like he used to, his voice imbued with humour, but Charlie knew him better. Knew it was forced. 'I'm sure Charlie doesn't need an interrogation.'

Brin shrugged and shot his friend a curious look. 'Being friendly, is all. Getting to know the new doc in town.'

Charlie didn't need Lewis's help any more. She'd grown up a lot while she'd been in London and could fight her own battles. She smiled at them both. 'No worries at all. I've no partner, no kids. I'm from Auckland but I've been away for a few years. Now I'm back.'

'And we're glad to have you.' Brin raised his glass and looked at Lewis. He made some sort of face, pigging his eyes at him as if to encourage him to say something.

Lewis shook his head tightly… There was something going on between these two—some in joke or something. In the end, Lewis cleared his throat and said almost robotically, 'Hey. Yes. We're glad you're here.'

Yet she didn't think he was glad at all. He didn't want anyone to know about their shared past. He'd physically shifted away from her when he'd sat down. He'd glared at any suggestion of being too friendly towards her.

The lights dimmed and the comedienne took to the stage. She was funny, and told some great stories that almost distracted Charlie from the fact she was sitting here in the dark next to her ex-husband who clearly wanted to be anywhere but next to her. But they were all crammed in round the table. He was so close, and she was acutely aware of him. Once upon a time they'd have held hands at an event like this, played foot-sie under the table. He'd have slid his arm around the back of her chair, absentmindedly playing with her hair or massaging her shoulder. She'd have leant into him and he'd have kissed the top of her head.

Even now his leg kept pressing against hers as they shifted position in their seats, but that was more because they'd been shunted together than by desire. But she was wrapped in his scent, mesmerised by his hands as they played with the stem of his wine glass. She'd always loved his hands and his long, slender fingers.

Her gaze roamed the place where his wedding band had once sat. They'd bought their rings from a high street chain because they hadn't been able to afford anything too swanky. But they'd loved their choices—a simple band for him and stacked engagement and wedding rings for her. There wasn't even a white line on his finger any more. Time and the sun had filled in the place where his ring used to be.

She looked at her own hands then. Her wedding-ring finger was empty too; there were no tan lines around where the platinum ring had been. It was all so long ago. She'd kept the rings, though, at the bottom of her jewellery box. There'd been something so desperately sad about getting rid of them. Even after the divorce had come through, she kept them as a reminder that once she'd been in love and been loved. That she'd planned an idyllic future...until the dream had fallen apart due to her damned useless uterus.

It was a great relief when, during the interval, they were all encouraged to bid on items in a silent auction. Charlie jumped up and took some well-needed breathing space, walking down the side of the room, reading the details of the silent-auction items. She wrote her name and her bid on a few of them, then made her way back to her seat. The table was empty and she could see most of her colleagues standing in a queue to bid in the auction too.

But where was…? 'Hey.'

Ah. Lewis was here, taking his seat next to her again. His tone was flat, as if he was pushing himself to talk to her and fill in the yawning conversational gap.

'Hi.' She turned to speak to him and smiled to try and soften the atmosphere. 'I managed to bid on a few things—a couple of spa packages for Lucy for when she's feeling up to having some nice treatments, and the paddling pool for Stella. You?'

'I'm sure Lucy would love to be pampered when she's up to it.' He shrugged. 'There's not much there for guys, to be honest, but I'm bidding on the dinner at that fancy restaurant, Marcel's.'

'Is it good? I'm a bit out of the loop when it comes to restaurants here.'

'I don't know.' He gave another shrug. 'I've been wanting to try it for a while.'

'Oh.' Fleetingly she wondered whether he was planning to take a date there. And then her competitive streak got the better of her. 'Well, I was the last one to bid on that, so don't you dare outbid me.'

His eyebrows rose. And there…just there…she saw a glimpse of the old Lewis in the glimmer of a smile playing across his lips and the spark of tease. 'Or…what?'

'Or…' She jumped up, throwing him a gauntlet she thought he might not refuse, because he never could resist a dare. 'I'll just have to bid higher than you.'

'Not likely.' He jumped up too and started towards the table that held the restaurant auction. And just like that they were back seven years playing, competing, laughing.

'Don't you dare, Lewis Parry!' She dashed ahead of him but he scooted in front of her as they both arrived at the table at the same time. They reached out, their hands entwining as their fingers curled round the pen. For the briefest moment, she felt a skitter of electricity through her skin, arrowing towards her heart. But she wasn't going to let go of the pen for love nor money.

'Mine!' He looked at her, pulling a face and laughing. 'Mine. Mine.'

Back in the halcyon days of their relationship, they'd watched *Finding Nemo* and had laughed so hard at the seagull scene where the birds fought for fish shouting, 'Mine, mine, mine!' Every time they'd seen a seagull after that, they'd mimicked the word over and over, dissolving into fits of laughter.

Her heart flooded with something... Nostalgia, or just muscle memory? She laughed at his victorious expression: *I win*. 'I think not, Mr Parry. *Mine*. I was here first.'

'Hey hey, children. Now, now.' A voice behind them made them jump apart.

They turned to see Brin grinning at them both. 'This is for charity, it's not WWE wrestling. Truce?'

They looked at each other and she saw Lewis trying to stifle more laughter as much as she was. In the end, she couldn't hold it in, and chuckled. 'We were a bit petty, weren't we?'

'Nothing like a bit of healthy competition.' Lewis grinned back. 'I'm still going to beat you.'

'Not a chance, Lewis. Not a chance.'

Brin looked from one to the other, frowning at first, but the frown slowly dissolved as the moments ticked by. He was clearly cooking up something. 'I have an idea—hear me out. It's not guaranteed that either of you will win, cos there are plenty of others bidding on this auction too, but if one of you does win…why don't you share the prize?'

'What?' Charlie and Lewis said to Brin at the same time, both wide-eyed.

'Genius, yes?' Brin laughed.

Charlie could think of other words to describe the suggestion: meddlesome, idiotic, dangerous. If she was spending this evening looking at Lewis's wedding-ring finger, and trying to prise information out of him when he clearly wasn't interested, then she needed to spend less time with him, not more.

Hell, she wasn't interested in her ex-husband…was she?

No. Working with him was just a new dynamic she had to get used to. She'd need to work out a new normal. Besides, someone else could easily outbid them. She looked at Brin, then at Lewis, and they both stared back expectantly. And now she couldn't exactly say no, could she? That would just seem rude. 'Okay…maybe.'

'Oh.' Lewis scrunched his nose as he thought—playful Lewis replaced again with the earlier, more detached one. 'Well. Um… I guess…maybe too.'

Huh. Don't hold back on the enthusiasm, matey. His reluctance bit deep.

Brin nodded. 'Nice. Good. I'll take that as two yesses.'

Now was her chance to find out Lewis's relationship status. She looked up at him. 'Shouldn't you check with your partner first?'

Lewis frowned, confused, then he shook his head and threw Brin a wry look. 'This is all your fault, *partner*. So, I'm not asking permission. I may well kill you later, though.'

Yikes. But he was at least smiling a little. So perhaps he didn't find the prospect of dinner with her so odious. And… was that Lewis's way of telling her he was single? Okay, dinner might be a good idea—maybe they could clear the air and stop all this awkwardness around them whenever they met.

They wandered back to their table and the evening continued, but Charlie was a little blindsided about what she'd just agreed to. She couldn't get it out of her head: dinner with Lewis?

Dinner with Lewis...after everything they'd been through? After their divorce? What in the actual hell had she been thinking when she'd said yes?

The comedienne finally started going through the silent auction and announcing the winners. Charlie stood and waved at the applause for her generous bid on one of the spa packages. She also won the paddling pool for Stella.

Then came the announcement for dinner at Marcel's. The comedienne cleared her throat. 'Now for the last auction item of the night. We're very lucky to have Marcel, the restaurant owner, here with us tonight. His father was an in-patient at the hospital a couple of weeks ago, and Marcel was so impressed with the care given that he has decided to add an extra-special treat for the person who wins the bid for dinner at his restaurant...'

'Ooh? Wonder what it is?' Brin gave Lewis and Charlie a thumbs-up. 'Maybe a bottle of champagne too?'

She shook her head. 'Won't be me. I'm never that lucky.'

Lewis laughed. 'Well, I'm always up for a free bottle of champagne.'

'Not just dinner...but also a night for two in the luxury of the Quay Hotel. Time for some rest and relaxation or...' the comedienne winked suggestively '...whatever you fancy doing in a very swanky hotel for the night. I know I wouldn't want to just sleep between those eight-hundred-thread-count sheets...'

Charlie glanced at Lewis. He was looking right at her.

A night in a hotel…together…between the sheets. Something inside her flickered to life. And something in his eyes told her he was thinking the same thing. His gaze softened yet heated at the same time. She knew that look. She had basked in it many, many times. His eyes were molten and, in return, her insides melted. Heat shot through her. Her body thrummed.

One night with him…

He was so close. Close enough to touch, to kiss. And she'd seen the old Lewis a few moments ago, laughing and playing, uninhibited by disappointment or sadness. She had a sudden ache to run her fingers across his jaw, to press her mouth against his.

Whoa. Really? But then, the physical side of their relationship had never been the problem. Their desire for each other had been insatiable.

Did he feel the same need?

No. No. No.

He looked away and shook his head, as if giving himself a good telling off. *So maybe, yes, yes, yes?* He had been thinking the same thing!

The ache inside her intensified. She ran her fingers round the stem of her wine glass, hoping the cool condensation would bring her some relief. Hoping like hell that neither of them won that prize.

'And the winner of this amazing prize is… Drum roll, please…' The whole room erupted with people banging the tables. 'Lewis Parry!'

'Oh?' His chest inflated as he sucked in air. His eyebrows rose and then he nodded at her. 'Okay. Okay, looks like we're doing this.'

She watched him walk across the room with his long legs and confident stride. The years had been good to him; he looked fitter, stronger, even more gorgeous.

And so off-limits.

She'd broken everything. It had been her fault, in the end. Doing the right thing by him had meant breaking her own heart too. But she cheered as he stepped onto the stage and shook hands with the famous Marcel.

He collected the vouchers, chatted with some other members of the audience then returned to the table as everyone was starting to put on coats to leave. The night was over.

He helped her with her denim jacket and then handed her the hotel information. 'Hey, you can have the hotel room, I don't want it.'

She looked down at the pamphlet. It was indeed a very fine-looking place and, oh, so tempting. 'No thanks. I'll need to be back for Lucy, in case she needs me. You take it.'

'No, Charlie. You should take it. You're doing a lot for your sister; you deserve a good night's sleep.'

'If you don't take it, I'll give it away.' She laughed. 'Maybe to your partner in crime?'

His gaze flicked to Brin, ahead of them in the crowd milling towards the exit, and he laughed. 'Not a chance. He doesn't know about our past. I think he was trying to…you know…'

'Get us together?' She watched Lewis's reaction. 'Bit of a stirrer?'

He shook his head, a little guarded, and rolled his eyes. 'He's got a good sense of humour, for sure. One of these days it's going to get him into trouble. Right, I'll book the restaurant. Friday? Saturday? I can do either. I'm on early shifts this week.'

With a roll of his eyes, he showed he was clearly still reluctant. And yet they were planning a dinner out. 'Feel free to take someone else, Lewis.'

'Oh, no, you don't. You had a deal,' chipped in Brin, who had obviously overheard bits of their conversation. 'Both of you go, or I'll take Mia. I do love a free dinner, and a hotel room. You can babysit instead of a lovely meal. Yes, please.'

'Funny guy.' Lewis flicked his thumb towards Brin and shook his head. Then he leaned closer to Charlie and lowered his voice. 'Truth is, I only bid one cent more than you anyway.'

'What? You little...' She laughed and gasped at the whisper of his breath across her skin. 'Anything to win, right?'

'You know me.' His eyebrows rose and he stopped walking.

'I certainly do.' Her gaze landed on his mouth and joy fizzed through her as she watched him laugh. It was so refreshing, so damned lovely to see. She'd missed it, missed him. Missed *them*. Oh, God. She hadn't realised how confusing seeing him again, being with him, would be.

Maybe they needed this dinner to clear the air. *Yes—excellent idea.* 'I'm on call Friday night but Saturday works. Then you can have a nice lie-in on Sunday morning in your swanky hotel room—not that I'd be jealous at all.'

Sunday morning—their favourite time for sex. Long, lazy mornings in bed on the rare occasions they'd both had Sundays off. It was a ritual they'd enjoyed almost until the end—uncomplicated, leisurely, exploring each other. She remembered the touch of his fingers and the press of his body on her, over her, inside her...the way he'd tasted. Her body tingled in awareness. He was still so damned close.

His breath hitched and he cleared his throat, and she was fairly sure he was remembering all their Sunday mornings too.

'Cool,' he said. 'Saturday it is.'

Which meant she had precisely one week to stop thinking about Lewis in bed. And to start thinking of him as purely and only her colleague.

CHAPTER FIVE

SO OUT OF NOWHERE, and after five years apart, he was going out to dinner with his ex-wife—*tomorrow*.

If anyone had told him last week, last month or even last year he'd be doing this, he'd have laughed in their face. But, yeah, dinner.

He was finishing up a few days on early shift so hadn't seen much of Charlie, except in passing in the corridor and twice at a patient handover surrounded by the team—certainly not long enough for a chat.

It had given him enough time to put some well-needed space and perspective on the whole thing. Dinner was a good idea. A chance to catch up on everything and smooth the transition from not seeing each other for a very long time to working together a few times a week. To work out how to be, with her back in his life. It wasn't as if he could avoid it, so he needed a plan to get through it.

He wandered across the hospital ambulance shared car park towards his car, planning a quick ride home, a speedy shower and then heading to his niece's birthday party.

'Lewis!' A female voice behind him had him turning round.

He spotted luscious red curls coming towards him, bobbing between the cars: *Charlie*, her hand raised in a wave.

His heart did a weird leap as all the perspective faded away and he was back to the other night, imagining her in bed. In his bed, for Sunday morning sex—his favourite time of the week.

He couldn't have stopped the smile if he'd tried. 'Hey, we have to stop meeting like this.' *Yeah. Corny as hell.*

'I know, right? Who would have thought the work car park would be our new rendezvous place?' She laughed, but her smile was sad and her eyes were red-rimmed.

His gut knotted the way it always did when Charlie was anything other than happy, as if it was his own personal mission to put a smile back on her face.

But that had been before. Now, he needed to keep some emotional distance before he got all bent out of shape with trying to make her happy. That wasn't his job any more. She'd walked away, but not before telling him he needed to focus on himself and not on her. That she didn't want or need his platitudes.

But, still, she looked upset and he couldn't ignore that. 'You okay?'

She shrugged, her eyes weary. 'Sure.'

She didn't look okay at all. He nodded towards the creche. 'Just been to see Stella?'

'Actually, just on my way to pick her up. I'm done working for the day.'

'And she's okay?' At her nod, he frowned. 'So, what's up? You look upset.'

'Oh, I'm just tired.' She waved her hand wearily in front of her face. 'Lucy had a bad night with pain and vomiting. She refuses to let me get up if Stella wakes, but she's so weak after her chemo, so I make sure to get up too. For some reason, Stella was agitated just after midnight, and around two-thirty, and then again at four-eighteen precisely. Not that I was clock-watching.' She rolled her eyes.

'Could be teething. Is she drooling more than usual? Pink cheeks?' Then he smacked his head with his palm. 'Duh. You're talking to a doctor, Lewis.'

She laughed. 'Always happy for advice. What do you know about teething?'

'Logan had hellish sleepless nights with both Lily and Lola, remember?'

'Oh, yes, of course. I'd forgotten about your brother's kids. We babysat them that time and couldn't calm Lily down at all. I thought she didn't like me.'

'She loved you.'

We all did.

His heart twinged. When Charlie had fled to London, she'd left a hole in his family. She'd not just been his wife, but an auntie and sister-in-law too. He hadn't told Logan she was back…that was going to be an interesting conversation. 'Teething—a whole new dynamic to test you, just when you think you're getting into a routine.'

Charlie chuckled. 'Yes, it's probably just her teeth coming through. She's definitely unsettled. I hope she's not feeding off our worries over Lucy's diagnosis. Kids are funny like that.'

'Sure are. Logan used to cool teething rings and let them suck on them. Said it worked a treat.' It made him sad to think they could talk about other people's child-rearing woes but not their own. And he knew damned well just how much a parent's anxiety, worry or neglect could have an effect. He'd lived it, breathed it. His mother had barely hidden her struggles with her twin sons.

You ruined my life. I could have been something if you two hadn't come along.

Of course, looking back, he knew it had been more her struggles with her own mental health than anything to do with their behaviour, but at the time it had been devastating. 'I'm sure you're doing all the right things to shield her from any upset.'

Charlie sighed. 'Oh, I hope so. But it's a vicious circle sometimes. If Lucy's upset, then Stella seems more grizzly. And of course if Stella's awake, then so is Lucy. And so am I. I've come to work for the rest.' She laughed wryly.

'It's a lot.'

'It certainly is. I'm never going to admit it to Lucy, because she needs my help, not my gripes, but I didn't realise babies were such hard work.' She pressed her lips together, wincing. 'Oh…sorry.'

Her eyes caught his and their shared past flickered into view.

He recalled the doctor's gentle words. *I'm so sorry, but it is impossible for you to carry a child. There may be other options you could explore…*

It embarrassed Lewis to admit it now, but he hadn't wanted to consider other options back then. His whole focus had been to try to stop Charlie from hurting, hiding his own grief at losing his dream of being a father and helping her get through: throwing the bundle of unused pregnancy tests away when she wasn't looking; deleting the ovulation app from her phone; helping her in the way he'd *thought* she'd needed to be helped and giving no attention to the fact he needed help too. Of course, she'd noticed these things missing and had called him out, saying he needed to face his own grief and not try to protect her from hers.

And, in hindsight, he wondered whether this had tipped her over the edge, pushed her into her decision to leave.

He shook his head. 'It's fine, honestly. But, yes, I've heard

the first six months are the worst. Until the second six months.'
He chuckled.

She groaned. 'Gee, you're filling me with confidence.'

'Hey, you'll cope. Just like when you did your medical rotations and had those horrific weekends on call.' He winked,
knowing how she'd managed to work but had been too exhausted to do anything else at the end of the weekends. He'd
been the cook, the cleaner and the cheerleader. Hell, he'd always been her cheerleader...until it hadn't worked for her any
more. She hadn't wanted to hear how much he loved her, how
things were going to be okay, because they'd both known they
weren't. 'But with a new job, a sick sister plus a grizzly baby:
that's a triple whammy.'

'All the while you just fake it till you make it, right?' She
flashed a fake smile, then a real one. Her eyes lit up and she
just glowed. Or it could have been the way the setting sun lit
up her face and hair in golden hues.

Either way, she was still so beautiful—older now but no
less stunning. Just looking at her made his heart swell and his
body prickle. He swallowed, trying to dampen the tingles firing across his skin and the tightening in his groin. 'And we
are champion fakers, right? You remember Matt and Claire's
wedding?'

'Oh, hell, yes. The traffic down to Tauranga was terrible.
We were so late for the wedding that we met the bride and
groom as they were coming out of the chapel...married.' She
pulled a face: *woops*.

'And we pretended we'd watched the whole ceremony.' He
laughed at the memory, parroting the way they'd greeted the
new Mr and Mrs Sinclair. *'Congratulations, lovely service.'*

'Lovely service...' She laughed, putting on a cute, posh En-
glish accent. *'Just lovely.* They never knew we hadn't seen

any of it and were just throwing confetti like we'd been there the whole time.'

'Faking pros, see? You can do it. You've got this.' Words he'd said over and over to her, from when they'd first started dating in the final year of school until that very last day when she'd told him she absolutely couldn't do it any more. That she *hadn't* got this. She didn't have a functioning uterus. She didn't have a child-filled future. She had no answers. That he was blinkered and no amount of positivity would get them through.

But he'd always believed in her. She believed she could do anything. And when her belief in herself had withered, he'd soldiered on, bolstering her up, thinking that was the way to show his love. Because that was what had always been missing in his life: no one had ever the hell said it to him. Not his mother, not the many random relatives they'd been sent to stay with in the school holidays and not even his brother.

But Charlie...yeah. She'd never actually said it when they'd been together but he'd always *felt* her belief in him: bone-deep; soul-deep.

Until she'd left.

He shook his head, coming back to reality with a bump. Because if thoughts about what she'd done to him weren't a warning call, he didn't know what was. He should have left then. He could have made an excuse and gone—hell, he was going to be late for Lola's birthday tea and that would not go down well with his brother.

But Charlie was still laughing and, he now realised, he was still acutely drawn to her, circling her like she was the god-damned sun.

'So don't be surprised if I fall asleep in my soup tomorrow night,' she quipped.

'Charming.' He fake-coughed. 'I hope my conversation is a little more riveting than that.'

'Well, I didn't want to say, but…' she joked, one eyebrow raised, her mouth all cocky and impudent as she fake-yawned.

And did she step closer? She was fingertip-distance away. He could see the flecks of silver in her eyes. The freckles she hated and he'd always loved. The laughter on her mouth and at the corners of her eyes. His first love—right here.

'You called me a lot of things over the years, Charlie Jade Rose.' He grinned and his gaze connected with hers. 'But boring was never one of them.'

'No.' She squared up to him, capturing his gaze, her pupils dilating and softening. Something white-hot fired there, igniting something scalding inside him. 'Definitely not boring.'

She was looking at him the way she had last week at the comedy night, eyes misted, body tilting towards him, all turned on and trembling. He *knew* that look. He knew her, and what she wanted.

Did she want him? Was he imagining it?

Did she want…?

He took a breath, but couldn't get enough oxygen into his lungs and drew his eyes away from hers. Everything was getting tangled up inside him. He looked away, then back. This time his gaze landed on her mouth. He wanted to kiss her. How the hell could he want to kiss her, after everything? But…he did. It was like an ache that had never really abated, only now rekindled, a hundred times more intense.

He took a step back before he did something stupid, like reach out and slide his mouth over hers. 'Look, I should go…'

'Sure.' But she didn't move.

How did a person greet and leave an ex-wife? Especially when there was this atmosphere of heat. There had been so much intimacy shared before, and now there was this five-year fissure. But they'd straddled it a little and were forging something like a collegial relationship at worst, a friendship at best.

Okay, he was freaking turned on as all hell. Should he give her a hug or an air-kiss goodbye? A nod didn't seem enough. A hug would be too much…for him.

He leaned to kiss her cheek, trying to be platonic when platonic was not the way he felt.

The touch of his mouth on her skin sent his pulse into orbit. She smelt insanely delicious, and it felt as if her cheek was pressing against his mouth rather than the other way round. Maintaining skin contact, she turned her cheek until her mouth was centimetres from his.

His whole body buzzed. He should have moved back, away from her touch, but he couldn't.

'Lewis…' It was more of a tremble than a word and it connected with his gut, his groin, his skin, throbbing and beating inside him until the world around them faded to nothing and all he could see was her face—so compassionate, so beautiful, so familiar. *Charlie…*

And he couldn't have stopped it if he'd tried. He slid his fingers into her silken hair, cupped the back of her neck and slid his mouth softly over hers.

She shivered and moaned, her body trembling under his touch. Her eyes flickered closed. Her breath stuttered.

'Lewis…' she whispered against his mouth. 'I missed you.'

'*God,* Charlie. I never stopped missing you.' That was the truth of it.

He pulled her against him, relishing the press of her body against his. Two pieces of a jigsaw slotting neatly and perfectly together. She raised her arms and framed his face with her hands, deepening the kiss. She tasted of fresh air and salty tears. Of Charlie from five years ago and something new… something intoxicating and exciting. There was no re-learning; it was as if they'd never stopped kissing. Had never had those five years apart.

His tongue slid into her mouth and she whimpered, which set him aflame. He wanted her, right here in the damned car park. But she pulled away and looked at him, her chest heaving. She just stared at him, her face a mix of sadness, surprise and heat. In those dark-blue eyes, he saw need and desire and he thought of all the things he wanted to do to her, with her, right now.

She opened her mouth to speak but his phone beeped.

He jumped and checked his phone: Logan. Could Lewis pick up some ice on the way over to the tea party?

Man, he loved his brother, but his timing was diabolical.

Although, also very wise.

Charlie was now studying her phone too as if she couldn't quite look him in the eye. Hell. What were they doing? The kiss was one road they should not have gone down. But then she shoved her phone into her bag and put her hand on his chest, looking up at him as if she was as confused as he was, and aching to be kissed again.

He shook his head and stepped well away. 'No. No. Just no, Charlie. We can't do this. *I* can't do this.'

Because he had to save them both here. They'd broken the good thing they'd once had. It could not be fixed back together with a kiss or a wish. It had taken him years to come to terms with his part in it all, get over her and move on.

She stepped back too, her expression half-regret and half-relief, but she was trembling as much as he was. 'Right. Yes. Okay. I've got to get Stella.'

He nodded, torn between wanting a repeat kiss and stopping this craving dead.

In the end, self-preservation won out. Once upon a time, she'd told him he had to stop putting her needs before his.

She was damned right.

And this time it was he who walked away and didn't look back.

CHAPTER SIX

DO NOT KISS HIM. Do not kiss him.

Lewis had made it very clear yesterday that kissing was not on his agenda and, while it stung…because it had been the most amazing kiss…he was right. Kissing was not a good idea.

But, hell, it had been inevitable. From the moment Charlie had seen him again after five years, she'd been assaulted by conflicting emotions—some sad, some funny, most hot—all about him and what they'd once had and lost. But the attraction was very much still there, simmering between them the way it always had.

But that was yesterday. Today, she'd convinced herself that they'd both needed some closure for the old part of their lives and the kiss had been the final full-stop on that.

So why they were still meeting up at Marcel's, she didn't know, but neither of them had cancelled so it appeared it was all still on. Well, he had paid an arm and a leg for it, so she guessed he didn't want to lose his money. As for her, well, it would be rude not to turn up after she'd agreed to accompany him as a friend. Besides, they really did need to get their relationship into civil territory, for a more congenial working environment as much as anything else.

And, of course, it was raining, with the promise of worse to come. Her umbrella had blown inside out twice since she'd climbed out of the taxi so now she was just holding it all limp and dripping above her head in a feeble attempt to keep maybe one strand of hair dry. But, as she approached the restaurant and caught her reflection in the window, she knew even that hadn't worked. Her trench coat was not, in fact, as advertised, waterproof. Her hair, which had been expertly and beautifully clipped up into a loose bun by her sister, was a flattened soggy mess, and her eyeliner and mascara were probably running down her face.

Lewis was standing in the restaurant doorway, hands shoved deeply into his jacket pockets, collar turned up, looking immaculate and, somehow, dry. He met her gaze with a little warmth—probably because he was resigned to coming tonight, so was making an effort to be cordial. 'Hey, Charlie. Quick, come inside; this weather is nuts.'

There was no kiss this time, not even an air-kiss. But he held the door open, she stepped inside the warm restaurant and was immediately assailed by the aroma of garlic, anise and something else exotic and delicious.

She shook her cold, wet hands and grimaced as water pooled at her feet. 'Ugh, sorry. Okay, I'm just heading to the bathroom to dry off. I must look a wreck.'

'No. You look amaz…' He swallowed and shook his head, taking her umbrella from her and putting it in a receptacle at the door. 'Okay, sure, of course. I'll find the table.'

Glumly, she stared at herself in the bathroom mirror. She'd been right: her hair needed drying and redoing and her mascara was now just two black smudges beneath her eyes—pretty much exactly the way she'd looked the day she'd left him. She'd been down and out, bedraggled, beaten up by elements out of her control. At least, that was how she'd felt back then.

But for some reason she wanted to show him, and show herself, that she'd put those days behind her. She was a different person from the one who'd gone to London. She was independent, capable and well put together...usually. She'd come to terms with her infertility and divorce, even though both stung when she dwelt on them too much. So she didn't dwell on them. There was no point looking back.

And yet here she was, looking back, going back. Wasn't it a sign of madness, repeating the same thing and expecting a different result? But this was just two friends catching up. That was all. No kissing allowed.

She quickly dried her hair under the hand drier, reapplied her make-up and slicked on her favourite lip gloss: *his* favourite lip gloss. *Whatever.* She just hadn't got round to finding one she liked better. *Honestly.* Well, you kept some things out of habit, right? And others purely for nostalgia.

She found him at a table overlooking the road and, beyond, the harbour. Water ran down the outside of the windows, distorting the reflections of people rushing through the early evening, car lights were fuzzy and the occasional blare of a car horn reminded her that driving in an Auckland downpour was dangerous.

As if she needed reminding about the dangers of cars. She rubbed her shoulder where the bruising was starting to fade from purple to yellow. Relaxing was difficult: not because she was in pain, but because she didn't know what to say or how to act. This felt intimate and yet disparate. They'd never been short on conversation before and now she was racking her mind, trying to think of the right things to say.

Trying not to think of that kiss.

Lewis frowned as he watched her movements. 'Does your shoulder hurt? Are you okay?'

'Oh, I'm fine, honestly. It's not so bad.' She rotated her shoulder forward and back to show him her range of movement. 'I was just thinking how nice and cosy it is in here, compared to outside.'

'There's flash-flooding forecast.' He laughed and then grimaced. 'I bet that's not easy to say after a couple of wines.'

'Flash flooding forecast,' she repeated, grateful that he'd broken the atmosphere with a joke. 'Maybe we should have some wine and see?'

As if on cue, Marcel appeared and shook their hands. 'Thank you, thank you, for bidding so much on the auction for the degustation dinner for two...'

What did he mean, *so much*? She glanced at Lewis for clarification. But Lewis just bugged his eyes at her to be quiet.

Marcel continued, 'I will throw in the wine match as a token of thanks.'

Lewis shook his head and smiled at the restaurant owner. 'Not necessary, honestly.'

'I insist.' Marcel reached for a bottle in an ice-bucket he'd brought with him and poured them a glass each of champagne. 'Bubbles to start. Are we celebrating anything tonight?'

They stared at each other.

Awkward.

How did they label this?

'Not really. Just—just two...um...old *friends*,' Lewis stammered, echoing the sudden panic inside her.

Old friends who happened to have been married and divorced. Old friends who had shared a searing hot kiss yesterday.

Marcel beamed. 'Well, old friends, have an excellent evening.'

Once he'd gone, Charlie leaned forward and whispered to Lewis, 'You said you'd paid one cent more than me. But I know I probably didn't bid enough to cover the cost of the meal.'

'Well, I may have embroidered the truth a little. All in a good cause—it's for the hospital cancer unit, right?' He sat back and regarded her, his arms casually crossed. His sultry gaze reached into her soul and something inside her flipped and danced. He'd always had a knack of disarming her just by looking at her. 'How are you doing, Charlie? I mean, *really*—how are you?'

She inhaled and thought about everything she was juggling at the moment and how it all seemed far away from here and now. 'I'm okay, I think. Yes, I'm good.'

'Good. Because I know you're under a lot of pressure.'

'It's nothing I can't handle.' She flashed him a wry smile because only yesterday she'd been bleating on about how it was all so difficult. But today she felt as if she could manage her way through being a decent sister, a good auntie and an efficient and compassionate doctor.

He smiled. 'You had a better sleep last night?'

'After we gave Stella the cooled teething ring, which worked like magic—thanks for the tip—we slept all night.' Apart from replaying that mind-warping kiss over and over before she'd fallen asleep, and immediately on waking.

His eyes flitted to her mouth and she wondered if he was remembering their kiss too or whether he'd put it to the back of his mind. She'd tried, but it was here now at the front, and she couldn't stop thinking about it.

He cleared his throat. 'Do we…um…need to talk about yesterday?'

Ah, so he had been thinking about it. And, even though she'd agreed they wouldn't do it again, her cheeks heated at the memory. 'No. No, we don't. I agree with you—we can't go back, Lewis. It's all done and gone.'

He nodded. 'And we don't want any awkwardness tipping over into our work, do we?'

Of course. This was just two people catching up after a long five years, trying to be normal. Trying to clear the air because they were colleagues. But here was the thing: Lewis never dealt with things like this head-on. He always shied away from conflict or difficult conversations but they were facing this awkward moment and he was totally in control. Maybe she wasn't the only one who'd changed, at least a little. 'No. No, we don't. I'd hate for anything to affect how we work together.'

'Okay, then. It's good that we agree.' He held up his glass, those soft, dark eyes capturing her gaze. God, he was so good to look at. He tipped his glass to hers. 'So…to friends and the future.'

'And flash-flooding forecasts.' She clinked his glass and laughed. 'Okay, tell me, what the heck have you been doing these last five years?'

'Not a lot, you know; just plodding along.'

He'd been promoted three times, apparently, but she wasn't surprised. He was damned good at his job.

He'd bought a house. Travelled to Laos, Cambodia and Singapore and had hiked in Australia. Been on three stag weekends and attended four of their mutual friends' weddings, which she'd decided not to come home for, because of so many reasons…mainly, Lewis.

He'd become an uncle to another girl, now three in total: Lola, Lily and Luna. Luna had been a surprise, but also a joy. Logan had said it was their last, but Lewis wasn't so sure. He'd spent yesterday afternoon at Lola's eighth birthday party, a tie-dye party, but he'd chosen not to wear his pink-and-orange

T-shirt tonight. Then they'd cooked pizzas in Logan's outdoor pizza oven for the birthday tea.

All that, straight after the hotter than hot kiss.

How had he managed to function in public after that? She'd been a trembling wreck and had needed a lie down before being able to look her sister in the eye, while keeping the kiss a secret, close to her chest. Because why tell her something that might worry her, or excite her, when it had been a mistake?

She shook her head and tried to put thoughts of Lewis's mouth to the back of her mind. 'What is it with your family and names starting with L? I'm sure this wasn't a thing a few years ago.'

He laughed and shrugged. 'Don't ask me. Neither of our parents have L names, it's just something Logan's decided to do with his kids.'

'You obviously married the wrong sister, then. Should have been Lucy. She'd have fit right in.' She laughed, but stopped short when she saw his expression suddenly change from light to dark. His gaze dipped to his glass, then back to her. He paused a beat, then two.

She wished she could take it back but it was too late.

'I definitely married the right sister, Charlie.' He held her gaze and it felt simultaneously like a knife lancing her chest and her heart weakening. He'd thought he'd chosen well, but she'd left him. Would he have been better off with Lucy, with someone else? Would he have been happy?

She couldn't bear to think of him married to another woman, and yet, she'd been the one who'd filed for divorce. Torn apart by grief for her future, she'd wanted to make a positive move for a fresh start, for both of them. Perhaps if she'd stood on her own two feet from an earlier age, had made that stand for herself instead of letting everyone else take care of her, she might have been stronger at fighting for her marriage too.

She didn't know how to answer him, so scrambled around to change the subject. 'So, you bought a house? That's impressive, especially with house prices these days.'

'Yes.' Pride glittered in his eyes now. 'I finally managed to get a mortgage. All grown-up, right? It's a do-up, but it's all mine. It's in Grey Lynn.'

All mine.

They'd been saving to buy their own house and had almost made enough for a deposit when everything had fallen apart. She shook herself and ignored the hurt slicing through her. They weren't going back that far, just covering the last five years. 'Oh! Lucy lives in Ponsonby. We must be almost neighbours.'

They shared address details; they were close but not quite neighbours.

'Walking distance, though. That's funny—I thought Lucy lived in Titirangi.' His eyebrows rose. 'It's weird, isn't it, that when a relationship breaks up you lose touch with people you were once close with?'

'I know. It's like a part of you is shirred off. I often wondered about Logan and your friends and, well…' *You.* Her throat felt scratchy—too much nostalgia. 'Anyway, after her split with Tony, Lucy moved to Grey Lynn.'

'They're not together any more? I didn't want to ask…you know…' He grimaced and shrugged again.

'Because *I'm* here looking after her, not him?'

'And because it's none of my business.'

It was once.

'Lucy wouldn't care if I told you; she's very open about

it. Basically, he didn't want kids and bolted when Lucy fell pregnant.'

'What a guy.' He shook his head and took another drink of wine. There'd never been a big friendship between Lewis and Tony but they had met up at family gatherings. She tried not to think about the gaps that existed now, the empty places at the table whenever, if ever, the Rose family got together. Conversely, she'd also lost Lewis's twin brother and the cosy friendships they'd once all shared.

'Yes, well, Mum and Dad moved in with Lucy to help her for the first four weeks of Stella's life until Lucy pushed them to go to Uganda.'

Marcel arrived with the *amuse bouche*, which was a divine nibble of goat's cheese panna cotta and gone in one delicious mouthful. But she took the brief conversation hiatus to settle her emotions. Splitting with him had been the right decision at the time, so there was no point reliving the pain of getting used to life without him.

He looked up from his plate and smiled, much more re-laxed than she was, especially now they'd agreed not to kiss again. 'What about you, Charlie? How have the five years been for you?'

'Oh. Work, mainly. Yes, work with a few weekend city breaks to places in Europe. I went to the Edinburgh Fringe a couple of times. Spent a fortnight in France. But, yeah, work… I couldn't afford to buy a flat in London on a single doctor's salary, so I rented. But that did make it easier for me to leave.'

'You enjoyed it over there?'

'Oh, yes. London is amazing. There's always something to do, new things popping up all the time. There's a real buzz—' She was interrupted by the drum of heavy rain on the window. It sounded like rapid gunfire: *rata-tata-rata*. Then it became louder and harder—hail now too. The cars in the street had slowed and somehow the night sky had got even darker. 'Looks like the flash-flooding forecast was right.'

'Got to love Auckland summer weather.' He shook his head, smiling. 'Do you think you'd ever have come home if it hadn't been for Lucy's illness?'

'Um…well… I have been back a couple of times, actually. Just briefly, for Christmas.' But she hadn't contacted him because she'd thought it would hurt too much, for herself and for him.

'Oh.' His eyes widened with a flash of disappointment. 'Yes, Christmas. Of course.'

'You don't think Mum and Dad would have let me get away with not being here for five years?'

'No. That is very true. Your parents would have hated not seeing you at Christmas.' He cleared his throat, not very good at hiding his emotion. Did he miss her at Christmas, on every birthday? Did he remember their anniversary and light a candle in memory of what they'd once had, the way she did?

He shook his head. 'Right. I wonder where that next course is?'

He turned and nodded at Marcel who came running over, took away their plates and poured them a small glass of Riesling to pair with their starter of prosciutto and pickles, accompanied by the most divine olive and rosemary focaccia she'd ever tasted.

Soon enough, Marcel was back with their fish course, then slow-roasted lamb plus a half-glass of Sangiovese, while she chatted with Lewis about the differences in hospital emergency rooms between London and Auckland, about baby girls, seeing as they had those in common, and about recent movies they'd seen.

They didn't talk about whether either of them had had any other relationships or about their feelings or their shared past.

And, while it was a good catch-up, the shared past was glaringly the elephant in the room, there in every look and every word. Because they couldn't escape it, could they? But at some point they needed to face it, even if only to put it to rest.

They were both distracted momentarily by the blare of a car horn outside. The rain still hammered against the window, making them raise their voices to be heard.

'And now you're back.' He smiled and she thought he might actually be okay with her being here. At least, now they'd had this chance to talk.

She found herself smiling too. Who would have thought she'd be sitting here doing this with Lewis? 'Yes, I'm back.'

He turned his warm gaze back to her. 'In a high-level job you must have worked hard to get. Well done. You always were a high flyer.'

'Thanks.' He'd always been her cheerleader, and she'd always let him be. Until the end, when she'd realised he was using his support of her to abnegate his own emotional needs. 'Well, I had to negotiate hard for the part-time bit, but I've promised to increase my hours once Lucy feels better. I'm not that desperate mess I was back then; I can manage full time just fine under normal circumstances. I just want to be able to give Stella and Lucy my time and attention.'

Um...like you are right now?

She pushed away her guilt at leaving them at home. Lucy had all but shoved her out of the door anyway.

'You were never a mess, Charlie, just messed up by grief and disappointment. There's a difference.' He paused for a beat, his eyes roving over her face, her mouth. 'I hope I've changed too. I'd have done things differently.'

What did he mean? 'You would...?'

Her words were stolen by another blare of a horn, so long and so loud, they could hear it from their table.

CHAPTER SEVEN

'WHAT THE HELL? Did you hear that?' Lewis tore his eyes away from Charlie's exquisite features and tried to listen to the street noises, trying to zone out the restaurant chatter.

The horn sounded again, then there was shouting.

He glanced at Charlie and she nodded, clearly reading his mind. Something bad had happened and they were duty-bound, and *needed*, to go and help. He jumped up and rushed to the door, pausing only for a moment to hold it open for her.

'Over there!' He pointed to a small crowd at the other side of the road. The traffic had come to a standstill so they quickly jogged across.

'Excuse me. 'Scuse me. I'm a paramedic and Charlie is a doctor. Can someone tell us what's happened?' He gently squeezed through the huddle of strangers to find a young woman, soaked through with rain, kneeling in the road and talking to an elderly gentleman, who was lying on the ground, pale, shocked and obviously in pain.

The young woman looked up at him and blinked through the rain. 'This is Graham. He was running across the road, trying to dodge the traffic, and suddenly collapsed. I don't know if he tripped or what, but he hit the ground with a real bump. And now he tells me he's got back and arm pain.'

'Okay, thanks.' Charlie turned to the crowd as Lewis knelt

to assess the man. Had it been a trip or a collapse? 'Has anyone called an ambulance?'

The woman nodded. 'Yes, I did.'

'Great, thank you. We've got this now.'

'Brilliant.' She turned to Graham. 'Graham? Graham, this is a paramedic. He's going to help you.'

'And, lucky for us all, we've a doctor here too,' Lewis said to Graham as Charlie knelt in a puddle to start her examination. He turned to the crowd as he stripped off his jacket and laid it over the man in an attempt to keep him warm.

'Can someone ask in the restaurants for a blanket? We need to keep our friend here as warm and dry as possible. And can someone please redirect the traffic? Otherwise we'll be snarled up from here to Hamilton. You…perfect.' He pointed to a guy who was filming everything on his mobile phone; best to keep him occupied with something else. 'Please put that away. I'm sure our friend here doesn't want this all over the Internet. And can someone else please keep an eye out for the ambulance and direct them here? Right…' He turned back to Charlie. 'How are we doing?'

'Graham's got a blinding headache, but is managing to tell me where else he's got pain. He's trying not to move and I think that's a very good idea.' She looked up at Lewis and nodded, water dripping off her nose, and she blinked more rain out of her eyes. But she focused and he read between the lines. Graham had a possible head and neck injury but was conscious and responsive, all of which were good signs. 'Pain in his right wrist. Swelling and accompanying grazes on his elbow, palm and forehead. What was that…?' She looked back at their patient. 'What's that? Chest pain.'

He watched her fingers go instinctively to Graham's radial pulse point. She looked up warily. 'Thready. Weak. Irregular.'

Not good. Did he have a history of heart problems? 'Anyone here with Graham?' Lewis asked the now-diminishing crowd.

No one answered. The poor guy was on his own. And that meant there was no information.

'Graham? Graham, can you hear me? Damn. Graham?' Charlie's voice grew louder. 'Graham.' She put her hands to the man's carotid artery and shook her head. Then she put her face close to the man's lips and shook her head again. 'Lewis, cardiac arrest...'

After checking his airway, she tipped Graham's head back, lifted his chin, pinched his nose and put her mouth over his, then blew twice.

Lewis watched for Graham's chest to rise and fall with Charlie's breaths then he knelt alongside Graham, placed the heel of his hand over the centre of the man's chest and started compressions, counting quickly. 'One, two, three...'

'Hey! Can you go look for an AED...defibrillator...please?' Charlie called to a passer-by. 'Ask in a shop. The museum. Any public space.'

'Twenty-nine, thirty...' Lewis called and she blew again twice.

Lewis nodded and started compressions again. 'One, two, three...'

'Where's that ambulance?' Charlie stood and peered down the car-blocked road. 'Can someone please provide some privacy? Stand here and here...' She directed three people, totally in command. But then, this was her turf.

And it was his. He huffed out, 'Twenty-nine, thirty.'

He leant back as she did mouth-to-mouth again. 'I can hear a distant siren but it's probably stuck in this snarled traffic.'

'Then we don't give up.'

'We don't give up.' Lewis nodded as he took her in. Her

face was set and determined, her tone positive but guarded. Her hair was stuck to her cheeks, her clothes completely saturated. But her eyes blazed with a resolve bordering on stubbornness. She would not give up.

And she was quite possibly the most beautiful he'd ever seen her.

They did not give up. Not when the crowd began to disperse. Not when the hail started again, hitting them like pellets of ice on their faces and hands. Not when the paramedics finally arrived—Emma and Raj, Lewis's colleagues. Not until Graham had pads attached to his chest and had been shocked twice then bundled into the ambulance and taken away.

Lewis watched the ambulance drive away, wishing he could be in there, giving the drugs and doing the hard yards to keep Graham alive. But he was also glad he was here, with Charlie, sharing this most profound experience.

She was talking to someone in the crowd, thanking them for their help. As she said goodbye, she turned, caught his eye and walked over to him, the friendly smile she'd put on for the bystander slipping to reveal her real thoughts. She inhaled deeply then blew out slowly. 'We did our best, right?'

He grimaced. 'We did.'

They both knew the odds of Graham being alive when he arrived at the emergency department were slim to none. And, even though they lived and breathed this kind of scenario every day, and had both learnt to deal with loss and the fragile human condition, he wanted to put his arms round her and hold her close. Because this was different. This was them against the odds and the elements.

It seemed they could work in perfect harmony even if they couldn't live in it.

Couldn't: past tense. Could never again, he reminded himself. Their chance was over. They were different people now, and still bruised from what had happened before. It would be madness to try get any of it back.

We don't give up.

You stay.

But they had given up on themselves. They'd stopped talking, stopped kissing, stopped being *them*. They'd become disparate people living under the same roof.

He'd stayed. But staying hadn't helped, had it? He'd thrown all his energy into making her feel better and had ignored his own needs. He'd pushed them aside and refused to talk about how he felt.

And it had all been for nothing, because how could she have stayed with someone who'd refused to acknowledge there was a problem, especially when the problem ended up being him?

He should have been open to talking about adoption or surrogacy, but he hadn't been able to see past her pain, and had thought talking about alternatives to her carrying a child would be even more painful.

God, he didn't know, even now, whether she'd thought about those options since, once the rawness had faded. Maybe in time, if they'd stuck it out, they'd have reached a place where they could have talked about that. The thought made his heart ache. So many missed opportunities because they'd been enmeshed in so much grief.

She shook her head and then her arms, and laughed as water sprayed and sluiced onto the ground. 'Ugh. I am completely soaked.'

'So I see.' He laughed and his gaze grazed her wet top which showed the outline of her bra.

Lace...

Something deep inside him flared. *Stop*. But how could

he help it? She was freaking beautiful. Not just because she looked amazing, all dishevelled and undone, but because she didn't care about getting wet and cold for the sake of someone who needed her skills.

'Ah.' She tugged her jacket around her breasts and then put her palm on his chest. Even though they were both cold, her touch was warm and steady, unlike his heart. 'You didn't even have a jacket on. Wow, your heart is beating very fast, Lewis.'

'Cardiac compressions can do that to a guy.' As could the tender touch of a beautiful woman. And the thought of what was beneath her lacy bra.

'Mr Parry!' It was Marcel calling from across the road, outside the restaurant. He ducked between the now slow-moving cars making his way towards them. 'Thought you might be still here.'

Lewis glanced at the restaurant. The closed sign hung in the window. 'Hi. Yes, sorry we had to dash off like that. There was a medical emergency and we had to help.'

'Not a problem. How is he?'

Lewis sighed. 'Touch and go, to be honest.'

'Well, thank you for being there for him, especially on a night like this.' Marcel held up a brown paper carrier bag. 'You missed your dessert but I've packed it up for you. Plus some sticky wine to go with it.'

'Sticky?' Charlie frowned. He could feel her shivering next to him.

The restaurant owner laughed. 'Dessert wine—thick and sweet and delicious. You'll like it.'

'You know, I've never tried dessert wine.' Charlie beamed at Marcel. 'Thank you.'

'Yes, thank you, Marcel. That's very kind.' Lewis took the

paper bag and thought if it got any more soggy it might not last the trip back to the hotel, only a couple of streets away.

Once Marcel had returned to his restaurant, Charlie looked at her phone. 'I'm freezing. I'm going to call a cab and go home.'

No. Lewis's gut contracted. He wasn't ready to let her go, because they hadn't really talked, had they? They'd only just started to unpack things before Graham's emergency had interrupted everything. But they were both soaked and cold. It was probably a good idea to end the night now, before he read too much into the warmth of her palm on his chest and the way she sometimes looked at him with regret, sadness and… desire. 'Sounds good.'

But a frown formed as she looked at the car-hire app, her teeth chattering now. 'Is there something else going on tonight—a gig or big sports game? Because I can't seem to get any take-up on my ride home. *Oh*… It's not even responding now. I've just got the swirl of doom on my screen. Maybe the app's down, or my phone's drowned.'

'I'll give it a go.' He pulled out his phone, trying to keep his own shivering under control. 'Nope, nothing. Look, my hotel is literally two streets away. Why don't you come up to my room, dry off and wait until the app's working again? Or wait until the alcohol's worn off enough for me to be safe to drive you.'

'Go to your hotel?' Her gaze tangled with his and, despite the shivering and teeth chattering, her eyes misted the way they'd always used to when she'd been all turned on. 'I… I don't know, Lewis.'

But he knew it wasn't just a question of whether they should go together, it was a question of what might happen. Because the warmth of her palm was good. The desire in her eyes was better.

The flare of need inside him threatened to overwhelm him. But they'd agreed, nothing was going to happen.

Nothing could happen.

CHAPTER EIGHT

GO TO HIS HOTEL?

Charlotte's head filled with all the things that could happen in a hotel room with Lewis. They had form, right? Back when they'd been married, a hotel room had always meant sex. They had a relationship history of many hotel rooms and lots of good times. History that should not be repeated.

And yet, that kiss yesterday had been…hot. And needed, and like some kind of switch that had flipped her world upside down. Because she couldn't deny that she wanted to do it again…and again…and again. So going to his hotel would be dangerous. 'I… I don't know, Lewis.'

He blinked as rain ran in rivulets down his cheeks, then he pulled her into a doorway out of the rain. 'Because what? You think I'll make a move? No way, Charlie. We agreed, right?'

'Yes, we agreed.' Although, up close with him in a doorway, she was currently regretting that agreement.

Stop it.

His eyes widened. 'So, where's the harm? We are both completely soaked and shivering. That is not good. What if you're waiting for half an hour for a cab? I don't want you getting hypothermia on my watch.'

The harm was, she didn't think she could keep her promise if she was in a hotel room with him. But she *was* freezing and completely drenched and he was holding up the soggy restaurant takeaway bag saying, 'There's pudding too.'

And she'd always been a sucker for dessert. 'Oh, okay. Just until I'm dry and warm.'

'Come on, then.' He stretched out his hand and she grabbed it and ran with him through the Auckland streets to his hotel. She was holding Lewis's hand. And it felt so instinctively right and good.

But when they entered the hotel and he had to retrieve his room key from his wallet, he let go, pausing for a moment as he looked at her, then at their hands. 'Sorry. Habit, I guess.'

'It's okay. It helped us get here quicker, that's all. I'm not sure I'd have kept up with you otherwise. You're very fit, Lewis.'

'I try.' He grinned and she followed him into the lift, her heart sagging, but knowing he was right. Kissing and hand-holding were not on the agenda. The question she had to ask herself, then, was…what was really on the agenda here? Because she could have waited for a cab, or even got a bus. She could have taken her share of the dessert home and given half to Lucy.

But all questions were forgotten when she walked into the penthouse suite he'd been given. The walls were dark slatted wood, the furnishings made of the softest cream leather and the curtains were a lovely, soft taupe linen. It was all very top-end and luxurious. 'Wow. This is seriously expensive and very, very swanky. I bet it's a great view on a fine day.'

'When I checked in this afternoon, I could see right out over the harbour bridge and up to the North Shore,' he said. But all they could see now was the rain lashing against the floor-to-ceiling windows. 'It's also got an outside fire pit, but that's a bit redundant tonight. Go hop in the shower; I'll plate this up. You want a hot drink too?' He pulled out a drawer in a console. 'There's a kettle and coffee and tea here.'

She was so cold, her body had gone from shivering to bone-rattling and her fingers were numb. 'Can you see if they've got hot chocolate?'

He grinned and his eyes grew wide and wicked. 'Hot chocolate, dessert wine *and* pudding—now you're talking. I'll see what I can do. Go—shower.'

The shower was glorious, with high-end shower gel, shampoo and conditioner and a rain shower-head. *This* rain was going to be hot and healing. Although she probably should have a cold shower if she was going to get through dessert with Lewis.

She scrubbed and shampooed herself and then wrapped her hair in a thick towel and drew a fluffy white robe round her naked body. When she went back into the bedroom, she found him standing by the console, stirring a cup of something that smelt delicious. He'd changed out of his wet clothes and was now in a dry pair of shorts and T-shirt. He glanced up as she approached, his eyes warm and soft as he smiled. 'Feel better?'

That smile was so good, it made her insides tingle. 'Oh, yes. I've stopped shivering, and these towels are *so* fluffy. Your turn.'

He shook his head. 'It's okay. I'll just finish making the hot drinks.'

'Lewis, please. You must be freezing.'

'No. You…' He looked as if he was about to say something more but closed his mouth. 'As it happens, I am cold, actually. Can you finish off stirring these? I won't be long.'

You…what? Had he been about to put her needs above his again? But he hadn't, had he? He'd stopped himself. *Interest-*

ing. It was a small thing, but the second time she'd noticed he'd put his needs first. That was good; he needed to do that.

She could hear him singing in the bathroom like he used to at home. Always the same tune, Rihanna's *Umbrella.* Which was pretty appropriate right now.

But...*home.* Her gut tightened in sadness. They'd loved that little rented cottage in Parnell. they'd made it theirs with the pieces of furniture they'd carefully chosen from second-hand shops. It had been hard leaving that place too, hard leaving him.

She heard the water running and imagined him in there, and wondered how the last five years had changed his body. She'd met him at high school and had watched with delight as he'd grown from lanky, sporty teenager to a man. She'd encouraged him to follow his dream of being a paramedic and celebrated when he got accepted on the course and when he'd graduated top of the class.

He'd kept himself fit for his job by running, swimming and gym work. She'd always loved the hard ridges of his muscles, the way she'd felt so safe and wanted in his arms. The way he'd looked at her as they'd made love.

She recalled the words he'd whispered to her on their wedding night: *I promise I'll always love you, Charlie. Whatever happens. I don't want a life without you. Ever.*

But, even so, she'd forced him to have one. Tears threatened, prickling the back of her eyes. Her heart hurt.

God, Lewis...

The door lock clicked and she swallowed back her regret and sadness. She must not show him how she felt. Which was...what exactly? Mixed up. *Turned on.* More... All the feelings, all the things.

Was she just hankering for what they'd once had? She didn't

know. But something new beat inside her and she couldn't ignore it. She also didn't know what the hell to do with it, because it seemed to be beating louder and harder every second she spent with him.

He came out of the bathroom in a cloud of steam, dressed again in his shorts and T shirt and, disappointingly, not just with a small towel at his waist.

Had she really been hoping for that?

Yes, she had. She'd been secretly hoping to see him half-naked.

All naked, actually.

Oh, God, she had it bad. Why hadn't she stayed, tried harder?

She settled on the comfortable chair next to the little coffee table in the middle of the room, tucked her feet up under her bottom and cradled her mug, relishing the scent and taking little sips just for something to take her focus away from Lewis. 'This is delicious.'

'Excellent.' He grabbed his cup and drank, leaning against the console. His eyes widened. 'Wow. It really is. Everything in here is next level.'

'I wanted to say, you did good before, Lewis—with the CPR. In all our years together, I never actually saw you working. You're very professional. Amazing.'

'That's high praise from an emergency doctor; thanks. You too.' He rubbed his hair dry with a hand towel. 'It wasn't easy kneeling on wet tarmac trying to save someone's life. But you didn't hesitate.'

'Of course not. And neither did you. But I think I've got gravel burns on my knees.' She examined them: just a little bruising. She looked up and caught him looking at her legs too. 'Do you still love your job?'

'Absolutely. There is nothing I'd rather do for work.' His gaze moved to her face. 'You? Emergency medicine was always on your radar. Are you glad you chose it?'

'Hell, yes. I love the urgency and the adrenalin rush. And I love helping people.'

'You always did.' He thought for a moment. 'I wonder how Graham's doing.'

'I don't have great hopes, I'm afraid.'

Lewis's eyebrows rose as he sat down opposite her. 'I'll ask at work tomorrow.'

'Or I could.' She bugged her eyes at him and chuckled.

He laughed and scrubbed a hand through his tousled hair. 'This is so weird. Who would have thought I'd be working with you? And be *here* in a hotel room with you?'

She glanced down at her towelling robe. Half-naked in a hotel room; once upon a time, he'd have slipped his hands in between the robe folds and made some sexy comment.

She tightened the tie at her waist. 'Well, who else would you like to be in a hotel room with? Please don't tell me you still have a crush on Amanda Seyfried?'

'Oh, *Mamma Mia*.' He made a 'chef's kiss' gesture, bringing his thumb and two fingers to his mouth and flaring them out. 'There's just something about her I can't let go of. She was in the best movies of my youth.'

'Um…you were late teens when *Mamma Mia* came out.' She laughed. She'd always ribbed him about his love for the actress who'd played the starring role in the movie. She knew him so well—*had* known him so well—and suddenly she wanted to fill the important gaps in her knowledge of him, even though some of his answers might hurt her. 'Have you…um…dated anyone since…you know…? Is it okay to ask?'

'Sure.' He blinked, obviously a little taken aback. 'I guess we were bound to get round to this conversation at some point. I've been out with a couple of women, yes.'

Why had she asked him that when any answer other than *no* would stab her heart? 'Oh? And...?'

He shrugged and sat back. 'Didn't work out. You?'

'A couple of dinner dates, nothing more. When I got to London I decided to throw myself into my job. Seemed a lot easier than getting into another relationship.'

'So nothing serious?' He drained his hot chocolate, his expression one that said, 'seriously, you haven't had sex for five years?'

'Nothing much at all. It took a long time to come to terms with everything. I didn't feel I had a lot to offer someone.'

He put his cup down and frowned at her. 'Please, Charlie. For God's sake. You've got so much to offer anyone.'

'Oh, I'm not saying it to get sympathy. Just, most guys our age are looking to settle down and I couldn't commit to anything. Not after...you.'

He inhaled sharply, took a moment, then leaned forward and touched her hand. 'Charlie, I'm sorry I broke it. I didn't give you what you needed. I thought I was saying and doing the right things but in hindsight...' His voice trailed off but he kept on looking at her. Kept his hand on hers.

'Hell, even I didn't know what I needed, so don't beat yourself up about that.' She shook her head. So here they were, suddenly in the thick of it. There was so much they needed to unpack, and yet at the same time she wondered if they should venture into their past at all. Because it might only drum up the old arguments and they'd be no further on, except five years older. '*I* left, Lewis. I broke it. Me and my stupid uterus.'

'Don't ever say that. Nothing about you is stupid, Charlie. Nothing at all.' His jaw set as he looked at her. And in his expression she saw so many tangled emotions that mirrored hers: confusion, desire, affection. Fear…yes, fear, because they were treading new territory here. Forging something out of the ashes of their marriage… *friendship?*

Everything was loaded with the weight of their break-up and there needed to be some honesty before anything, including their fledgling friendship, could grow. And here tonight, after they'd shared something so momentous as trying to save a life, it felt right to do a deep dive.

She rested her cup on her knee and tried to explain her version of what had happened after she'd left. 'I had some counselling, you know. Talked myself silly going round and round. But eventually I came to terms with why I was so devastated by it all.'

She didn't know why she'd suddenly blurted out that particular thing but it felt right to say something, to show him and herself that she'd tried to understand everything.

He frowned. 'Because the infertility was a shock. Because it was cruel, Charlie.'

'Yes.' *The* infertility—not *your* infertility. Lewis generally chose his words carefully. Maybe he still didn't see it as just *her* problem. She didn't know how to feel about that. 'And because I felt as if I let everyone down.'

'Whoa. No way.' He raised his palm. 'That wasn't it at all. I didn't feel let down. I hurt for you—with you.'

'I know, but I could see in your eyes how you pretended you were okay about it but, deep down, you weren't. You couldn't have been okay with it. You had this idea of what a perfect family looked like…'

'Sure. I always wanted a family, you know that. Especially after my crappy childhood, being shunted from pillar to post because my mum didn't actually want or like children, and my dad never, ever being in the picture. I missed not having a dad like other kids. I missed my mum a lot too.'

He hauled in a breath. 'In my head, I had this blueprint of a family: two kids, two parents; probably something I'd seen on TV. But if I ever did it I wanted to get it right. I wanted to have what Logan and I never had, what Logan is creating with Alice and the girls. Is that such a bad thing—to want to love your own child? To have a tight bond? To be *present*?'

'Not at all. You deserve to have that, Lewis.' She took a breath, her chest constricting. 'But when I couldn't do that you still said everything would be okay, everything was fine. It was like you weren't listening or understanding the situation.' She watched his expression, hoping she wasn't hurting him all over again. Because they were actually talking about this—really *talking*—for the first time.

But he just smiled sadly. 'I wanted you to believe in yourself the way I believed in you.'

Her heart squeezed. 'And I just felt trapped by impossible dreams I couldn't fulfil.'

His expression hollowed out to one of shock and uncertainty. '*Trapped* by me?'

She drew her gaze away from him, swallowing down the raw lump in her throat. 'By you, by my parents, by other people's expectations: to carry on the family doctoring tradition; bear the grandchildren my parents desperately wanted; provide the family you so desperately deserved to have. Your mother wasn't there for you when you grew up, Lewis. You scratched a family out of distant relatives. You and Logan clung to each other and you both deserved to grow something good for yourselves. Logan has done that; you need that too. But I couldn't… can't…do that for you. And no amount of you telling me everything was going to be fine was going to magically make things what they weren't.'

He swallowed as he digested her words. 'You were struggling; I was trying to make it better for you.'

'I know. And you did. *You did.*' She ached to soothe away the hurt they'd both endured during that rocky time. 'But rightly or wrongly I felt as if there was a sheen of facade, a brave face rather than an honest one. You never told me how you *felt* about it all. It was like trying to talk to a rock.'

'I was trying to *be* a rock for you—staunch and solid. If I said it was all okay, it would be. If I said we'd get through it, we would. I was trying to be a support. Have you any idea how hard it is to see someone you love cry every day for eighteen months? To endure endless painful tests and investigations? And to have nothing…*nothing*…you can do to help them? To see them closed off, hibernating under the duvet, refusing to come out, to *live*? Then to see the anger rip through them, to come home to broken plates and slashed cushions? To not know which Charlotte I was actually coming home to? Depressed Charlotte, angry Charlotte, numb Charlotte…'

He shook his head, eyes sad. 'I tried; God help me I did. I knew you were hurting so badly but I didn't know what else to do, other than try make you believe things would be okay.'

Her lips trembled and she pressed them together. Because she had been that person—she wasn't now, but she had been. Torn apart by despair, she'd allowed her emotions to engulf her. 'I was devastated and I took it out on you. But I could see you were broken too. You just wanted to hide that from me.'

His dark-brown eyes blazed then. 'Damn right I did. I was protecting you. I didn't want to make you feel worse by adding my feelings to the mix.'

'And that…right there. That's why I had to go, Lewis. We'd

always talked openly about having kids. You were thrilled when Logan had his. You were, and I'm sure still are, an amazing uncle. But, when it came to us, you couldn't admit how disappointed you were. You clammed up. You refused to talk about your feelings.

'But I saw it. I tried to get through to you. I pushed you because I didn't want you to resent me further down the track. But the more I pushed, the more distant you became. Then I got angry…with you and the unfairness of having our plans taken away. And then I stopped trying. In the end, it felt like were living separate lives. We both deserved more than that.'

He shook his head, his eyes flickering closed for a beat. When he looked up at her again, he saw fathomless sadness there. 'I'm so sorry. I thought saying that everything would be okay was what you wanted to hear. And I realise I was wrong; I see that now. I've thought about it so much over the years and I get it. But back then I loved you so much, Charlie. I just wanted you to stop hurting.'

Loved: past tense. But, hell, what else could she expect? That he'd held a torch for her these last few years? That he'd put his life on hold until she decided to come back? No. But the loss of it reverberated through her, core-deep.

She reached out and stroked her fingertips across his jaw, because this was so profound, so damned deep, she couldn't sit there and not touch him. She needed to feel the physical connection as well as the emotional one. 'You know what? I don't even know what I wanted to hear back then except for, *I'm sorry, Mrs Parry, we made a mistake. Of course you can have a baby.*'

'I wish that had happened, Charlie. I really do. More than anything.' His eyes glistened. 'And I'm sorry I got it so wrong.'

She moved her hand from his cheek and knitted her fingers with his. 'Oh, we were so young, Lewis. And blindsided at the news. I'd always had everything given to me on a plate. I had you, my doting parents and a loving sister, and you all conspired to keep me happy and boost my ego and soothe my journey through life. God knows why.'

'Because we loved you, Charlie. Plain and simple.'

Loved: there it was again. 'And I'd had it so easy up until then. I'd never failed at anything before and didn't know how to cope with it all.'

'And I refused to discuss some things. I refused to acknowledge how I felt.'

'Which was?' She waited, wondering if he had enough personal growth and faith in her to be honest. 'How did you feel about what *you'd* lost?'

'You want me to say those things? That I was broken up that I couldn't be a dad? That it hurt whenever I saw pregnant women, or when I held little Lola? It hurt that I'd never have that; I'd never get to watch my son play football.'

'Or do ballet?' She smiled, because it was never going to happen for her, but if it did for Lewis...if someone was lucky enough to find him and keep him...then he needed to be open to all opportunities for his kids.

'Or ballet. I didn't say those things because I didn't want you to hurt more.' He exhaled a long breath, then looked her full in the eyes. He hesitated and closed his eyes briefly. When he opened them, he nodded sadly. 'I was gutted, if I'm honest. Absolutely broken.'

Finally.

She let go of the breath she felt she'd been holding for nearly six and a half years, since that day at the doctor when they'd got the terrible news. Finally, he was being honest. *Finally.*

She felt hollowed out, as broken as he was describing, but also felt relief too. This was a breakthrough for them.

Tears sprang in her eyes and she fisted them away. 'I'm sorry, Lewis. So sorry we couldn't fulfil your dream. But thank you for telling me the truth.'

'I should have done it a long time ago.'

The dream hadn't fallen apart because of her uterus. The dream had fallen apart because they'd been unable to deal with that. 'Were we too young? Was that it? Too disconnected from each other or too immature to deal with such big personal issues?'

Her parents had never wanted them to get married so young. It had almost been a case of 'told you so' when she'd left him. *You should have listened to us; we know what's best for you.*

'We did the best we could at the time. Two hurting people who didn't know what to do.' He brought her hand to his mouth, kissing it gently, the way he used to back when things between them had been a whole lot better. She shivered at the touch of his lips on her skin. There was something so intimate in such a small gesture, it almost overpowered her.

She needed some space before she crawled into his lap and kissed him properly again, long and hard. She took a deep breath, then another, trying to find her equilibrium again. She slipped her hand from his, found a smile and made it real… for Lewis. 'Hey, you know what's going to make us both feel better?'

'I'm all ears.' He smiled, the glistening eyes dry now.

'Marcel's pudding. And what about that wine? It would be a shame not to have it.'

You were supposed to be leaving, Charlie.

But she needed some light relief before going home and facing Lucy's questions.

One little taste...*of the wine.*

'Excellent idea, Dr Rose.' He looked relieved to be chartering less difficult territory as he jumped up to find plates, arrange the dessert items on a large one and then pull a piece of card out of the bag. 'There's a copy of the menu here. Looks like these are mini almond-and-espresso cannoli, and chocolate-and-salted-caramel bom...boloni...bomboloni.' He stumbled over the Italian word, then brought the plate to the little coffee table. 'That must be these little doughnut-shaped things. And...mini cheesecake.'

'Oh, *yes*!' Charlie fist-pumped the air. 'I'm going to go for the chee—'

'Cheesecake first? Your favourite, right?' He laughed and handed her a glass of the wine he'd just opened. 'Try it with some of this.'

There was a new ease to the atmosphere now—breathing space, an understanding. Things felt brighter inside her, as if the weight of nearly seven years...the difficult last two of their marriage and five apart...was lifting.

She bit into the cheesecake, which was light and yet rich, followed by a mouthful of the wine. 'Oh, okay, it's sweet, all right. Oh. Wow.' She blinked and swallowed. 'Okay. There's a lot going on there. That's...different.'

He grinned. 'Yes, but what do you think?'

'It's like drinking jam. Winey jam. Jammy wine.' She laughed. 'Is it strong?'

He examined the bottle. 'Only fourteen and a half percent.'

'Hmm. Strong enough.' She had another mouthful. 'Okay, I'm getting used to it. It's nice—yummy, actually.

'Let me try again then, ahem: flash-flooding forecast. Flash flooding florecast.' She giggled. 'Imagine me after more than one glass.'

'Lightweight.' He leaned forward across the little table to pick up a mini cannoli at the same time she did. Their noses almost touched. He inhaled sharply as he captured her gaze. *'God.'*

'What?' Her forehead brushed against his. He smelt of expensive shampoo. He smelt good. She was acutely aware of him so close, so here, so... Lewis.

'Your laugh. Your smile...' He ran the back of his fingertips down her cheek. 'Jeez, Charlie.'

She closed her eyes and tried to swallow away the rush of desire but found herself curling towards his fingers and his heat.

'Lewis,' she whispered, every cell in her body straining for his touch.

No. They'd agreed. But he was so damned irresistible.

She drew away, picked up a *bombol...* doughnutty thing... and held it to his mouth. He took a bite and sighed. 'Oh, my God. You have got to try this.' He took the leftover half from her fingers and held it to her lips. 'Try it, Charlie. Bomboloni is "the bomb". This is the best thing you'll taste all night.'

I hope not.

She opened her mouth and bit into the bomboloni. Salted caramel and chocolate cream burst onto her tongue, sweet, salty and delicious. 'Oh, God, that is heaven.'

He edged away slightly and looked at her, cupping her cheek with his palm. 'No, darling. You are.'

The world stopped turning right then and shrank to that room, that night, that man. She swallowed then cleared her throat. 'But, Lewis... We said...' She didn't have the fight in her to say any more. She wanted it—wanted him.

He shrugged. 'Hey, I'm trying here, I promise. But you are so damned gorgeous. I tried to not be attracted to you. I tried not to notice how amazing you looked when you arrived at the restaurant. I tried not to look at your gorgeous nipples through your wet top. I'm trying to be platonic but I'm failing…badly.'

She gasped at his words, her body tingling with the rush of need rippling through her, and laughed as she remembered her restaurant entrance: dripping wet with a useless umbrella held over her soggy hair. 'I was drenched.'

'You looked beautiful to me.'

She curled her fingers round his wrist. His pulse beat fast and furious against her fingers. 'Please, Lewis. Don't try bolster me up. I know I looked a mess.'

'I'm telling you the truth, Charlie. I like you all undone.' His eyes flickered closed briefly, as if he was wrestling with his self-control. Clearly he failed, as he whispered, 'I particularly like the way you're looking at me right now.'

She swallowed, her grip on her own self-control weakening with every word he said. 'Like how?'

'Like you want to kiss me.'

CHAPTER NINE

HE DIDN'T WAIT for her answer. He knew his Charlie—knew when she was turned on, knew how to make her so. Knew when she needed to be kissed, and right now she needed it as much as he did.

He stood up and strode towards her, framing her cheek with his palm as he bent and slid his lips over hers. She gripped his shoulder and moaned, whispering his name like a sacred psalm. 'Lewis. Lewis. *Lewis...*'

She closed her eyes and sank into the kiss, sliding her tongue into his mouth and deepening their connection even more.

His pulse sky-rocketed. Need heated him. *She* heated him. This evening had been so intense, the embers of what they'd once had crashing back into full, incandescent life. The raw honesty was something only they could share. No one else had experienced the things they'd been through, and there was a new and deeper connection, so much swelling emotion between them—he and his amazing wife.

Ex-wife... The thought fleetingly assailed him and threatened to douse the desire coursing through him. But he pushed away all the pain and hurt from the past. She was here, she wanted him and, right now, he wanted this new version of her. She was sexier, more beautiful, more fun than he remembered and the way she was looking at him stoked the fire prickling over his skin, under his skin and deep in his belly.

There was only one way this could go. The kiss started soft and slow, achingly familiar and yet different too. He felt a new, heightened thrum of desire between them, the frank honesty lacing their connection and tightening it. He'd never wanted a woman as damned much as he did right now.

She tasted of jammy wine and chocolate; of the past and the now—this moment, this woman.

Charlie. The first woman he'd ever loved. The only woman he'd ever loved.

He needed to explore her, to feel her tight against him, so he broke the kiss and offered his hand. She took it, standing up and stroking her palm across his chest. He kissed the top of her head, her forehead, her nose. He imprinted the new things he noticed into his memory banks: the scent of high-end shower gel; little laughter lines at the corners of her eyes. 'I can't get enough of you, Charlie. Stay the night?'

Her teeth worried at her bottom lip as she stared up at him, those beautiful blue eyes glittering with need but also concern. 'Lucy… She might be worried.'

Not a refusal, just hesitation.

'Call her, then—see if she's okay. Then stay.' His lips were on her throat and he murmured the words against her skin. 'I want you so much. I need this, Charlie, and I think you do too.'

'I do. But…' She kissed him again, long and slow. Then she pulled away, picked up her bag from the floor and rummaged for her phone. 'Hang on a second.'

She wrote a text and showed it to him, smiling, before sending it.

Luce, hey. Just checking in. Got stuck in rain downpour and now drying off at Lewis's hotel. Car hire apps are down. Might not be back until morning.

'Excellent. Might as well keep busy while we wait for her reply.' He tipped her chin so he could kiss her again. This time it was a slow burn kiss, backlit with a lightning show from the midnight sky. They were literally on top of the world, the forces of nature outside amplifying the potency of their passion in the penthouse.

Her hands slid down his back and pulled him tightly against her. She pressed against him and, when he slid his leg between hers, she moaned and rubbed her core against it. Her eyes flashed pure sex as she looked at him. 'God, Lewis, I want you so much.'

'You drive me crazy.' His body flooded with a deep, long-forgotten hunger as he slid his hand into the folds of her robe, finding her nipple and stroking until the tight bud peaked. Then he cupped her breast, relishing the soft silk of her skin and the misting of her eyes as he stroked and caressed.

Her phone beeped.

'Damn.' She reached for it, tutted then giggled. Then she showed him her sister's response:

You should change professions, sis. Novelist would be good. Fiction is your strong suit. You could just have told me you were having sex. Lucky thing. I would say be careful but you're a grown adult and you never listen to me anyway. See you in the morning. Have a good night.

He guffawed. 'Your sister has the measure of you.'

'Of you, more like.' She shook her head.

'Me? How? I'm just looking after you until the car hire app works.' He made to look all innocent, when he actually felt the complete opposite: desperate for her; carnal, base.

'Sure you are. Come here.' Laughing, she tugged at the neck of his T-shirt and brought him closer. Her hands were trembling.

He stilled and tilted her chin, looking deep into her eyes. 'You're shaking. Are you sure about this, Charlie?'

'I'm more sure about this than anything ever in my life.' She frowned. 'You have to ask?'

'Yes, I do. This…it's a lot.'

'It is. And I don't know what it means. I just know that I want it now. I want *you* now. Tonight.' She kissed his throat. 'I have no idea what it'll mean tomorrow, though.'

'That we're two grown adults who make rash decisions based on intense sexual craving and a deep sense of nostalgia, fuelled by adrenalin from a recent intense CPR situation?' Laughing, he slid his hand down to her thigh and whispered, 'Basically, I want to be deep inside you, Charlie. And damned quickly.'

'You've got such a way with words.' She giggled then put her arms round his neck and kissed his throat. 'Intense sexual craving…huh? I like the sound of that. Now, where were we?'

'I think…we were about here…' Her towelling robe had slipped down one shoulder, revealing her breast, and he slid his hand across the naked nipple and watched desire and delight heat her face. But when he looked back at her body he was jolted by the yellow-black bruising across her shoulder. He shuddered. 'I hate to see you so bruised, Charlie. I don't want to hurt you. Tell me to stop any time.'

'I'm not made of paper, Lewis. I'm a tough old cookie these days.' She kissed his jaw, then his mouth. By the time she pulled away, he was fairly sure she was sure. But he very gently kissed the bruising, making sure not to hurt her.

She smiled. 'You're just a softie at heart, aren't you?'

He growled as his erection pressed against her core. 'Soft?'

'Hard. So hard.' Her body tensed as she moaned and writhed against him, her hands sliding into his hair. 'God, that's so… good.'

'Yes. It is. But actually…' He slipped his hands behind her knees and picked her up.

She screeched. 'Lewis Parry, what the actual hell?'

'Got to do this properly.' It wasn't exactly far. Three strides and he was laying her down on the plush, soft comforter, her hair splayed on his pillow, copper against white. Just as he remembered. Just as he'd dreamt of so many times.

He lay next to her, propped his head up on his hand and cupped her face for more kisses. He untied the robe and let the fabric fall open. Emotion caught in his throat. 'You are so beautiful, Charlie.'

She smiled at him. 'I want to see you too. All of you.'

He knelt and reached for the hem of his T-shirt but she stopped him. 'Wait. I want to undress you.'

'Be my guest.' He laughed, but then stopped as he watched her still trembling hands tug at the hem.

'You sure you're okay, Charlie?'

'I'm better than okay. I'm just… I don't know. Nervous. Excited.'

'It's me—no need to be nervous.'

'But we've both changed so much over five years. Oh, Lewis, when I think about how much we've missed out on—'

'Don't.' He interrupted her. 'Don't over-think. Just go with this.'

'Intense sexual craving, right?' She knelt up, tugged his T-shirt over his head then ran her fingertips across his chest. 'Wow. You've kept up the gym work, then?'

Pride punched his gut. Okay, yes, he shouldn't care how he looked, but he liked that she still found his hard-worked-for body sexy. She traced over his nipples and giggled when he winced. 'Still ticklish?'

'I guess so.' But his throat was dry and he wasn't laughing any more. The atmosphere was too thick with need, their scent and…anticipation. As her fingers explored his pecs, making her way south towards his erection, he hauled in a stuttering breath, trying hard to rein in the overwhelm of pure lust. He wanted her so much that, if those fingers went anywhere near his groin, he'd explode. So he gently pushed her back on the bed and kissed her again, tracing his own fingertip path down her belly.

He slid his fingers between her legs and she gasped. 'Yes. Yes.'

He slipped his fingers inside her, revelling in her pleasure as she rocked against his hand. A few thrusts had her arching her back, guttural moans filling the room. He found her nub and rubbed slowly.

'Oh. Oh, please, Lewis. I need you. Now…' she managed through snatched, breathless kisses. He felt her tighten, stroking her to a wonderful hot, slick mess of moaning.

'Whoa. You really do want it.'

'Yes. Now.' But then she was pulsing around his fingers and kissing him greedily. 'Please.'

He held her as her orgasm rocked through her, waiting until she rode the crescendo. He kissed her long and hard. But she reached for him and stroked his length, and he held his breath, garnering whatever flimsy thread of control he had left.

'Condom….wallet….' He shook his head then smacked the bed with his palm. 'Damn. They've probably expired.' He grimaced and explained, 'It's been a while.'

But she beamed up at him and stroked his cheek. 'Hey, have you forgotten? There's zero chance of pregnancy. And I haven't had sex with anyone for a long time. Not…since you. I'm good.'

Not since him… His heart squeezed. And *God*, yes—no babies. That had been the core of their problem. But this was now, this was new. 'It's been a long while for me too.'

She pulled him closer and rubbed her wet heat against his erection. 'I want you inside me. I want you, Lewis.'

And he couldn't hold back any longer. He rolled on top of her and gently pushed her legs apart, positioning himself at her entrance. Then he nudged inside her.

God. She was so ready for him. So…*much*. He inhaled sharply and withdrew because it was too much, too fast.

'No! Don't stop.' She moaned. 'Please.'

He thrust into her again, deeper, harder.

'Yes. Please.' She wrapped her legs around his backside, ramping up the rhythm with the rock of her hips. 'This is so good.'

He brushed her damp hair from her face and kissed her. Their gazes locked and he slowed the rhythm. He couldn't take his eyes from her. She was achingly beautiful and here in his arms. She stared up at him as if he was a freaking god or something—the way she used to, back when they'd had so much future to look forward to.

When they could make each other feel this good, how had it all gone so wrong?

Tears slipped down her cheek.

'Hey.' He kissed them away one by one. 'Don't cry. This is…perfect. You are perfect, Charlie. You're beautiful. *Man*, you are so beautiful, it makes my heart hurt.'

'Oh, Lewis.' She gripped him and hiccupped out a sob, then laughed…all of which mirrored the same confused emotions whirling round his body. She fisted the tears away. 'I'm sorry, I can't help it. It's just, I never thought this could happen. It's so good. I love the way you feel inside me. But it's all just so much.'

'I know. I know. I know.' He pressed his lips to her cheek, then captured her mouth in a searing hot kiss as he thrust into her, faster and harder. Bright light flashed in front of his eyes, in his brain, in his body.

'Lewis.'

He'd never thought he'd hear his name on her lips again.

'Lewis. Yes… *Yes...*' Her tears were coming thick and fast now as he felt her clench and contract around him, then shudder her release in a cry. And his world balled tight into this moment, this woman—this beautiful, amazing woman taking him over the edge too.

For a few long minutes he lay there, cradling her in his arms, dazed, satisfied and happy for the first time in a very long time. It wasn't that they'd rewound, but that they'd built something new out of intense sorrow and confusion.

'Lewis, I'm sorry.' She kept her arms around him, holding him tightly against her. 'I'm sorry.'

He didn't know what she meant. Sorry that she was crying? Sorry that she'd left? Sorry that she'd come back and tipped his world upside down?

But he held her tight and stroked her hair, feeling her heat, feeling her chest heave against him, the wet of her tears on his arm. Then slowly…slowly…she settled. But he kept on holding her closely, not wanting to let her go. *Again.*

She was back and somehow he'd allowed her to creep under his skin, to make him want her, to hope for things they couldn't have—impossible dreams. A future? That was crazy talk, after everything they'd been through before.

And yet…his heart couldn't separate this feeling from the feeling he'd had before it had all started going wrong.

Hope.

He knew then without a doubt that he was going to lose his heart to her all over again.

If he didn't do something about it…fast.

CHAPTER TEN

HOTEL ROOMS HAD always meant sex.

It hadn't felt like *just* sex, though. It had felt consequential in some way: meaningful.

She'd cried, for God's sake. It had all been too much for her poor heart to take. It seemed unreal, as if their problems, their divorce, had somehow magically fallen away.

And yet she couldn't allow any wishful thinking here. She couldn't let this be more than two people having a good time for one night. She couldn't pretend that the last five years hadn't happened—she had left him and broken both their hearts. She'd sent him papers to sign. She'd cried her heart out every night for eighteen months.

It was six-forty-two in the morning and the summer sun was already peeping through the blinds. Charlie had fallen asleep snuggled into the crook of Lewis's arm—fitting exactly the way she'd fitted before—a deep, satisfying sleep that she hadn't experienced for a long time. Then she'd woken suddenly, not quite sure where she was.

When reality hit, guilt did too. She should be with Lucy, not there. She'd got carried away with her own needs and wants instead of putting her sister first.

Should she sneak out and leave him sleeping? His eyes were closed, his long, dark lashes something any woman would be envious of. His hair was tousled. Would he be as confused as she was? She could leave now and avoid what could be an embarrassing conversation trawling through regret and recrimination about being here together. Although she'd had the best time, and would not regret that one night with Lewis.

'Morning,' he whispered against her throat as his warm hand snaked across her naked belly. He tugged her closer to him, her back tight against his chest, spooning her. 'You slept.'

She relaxed back against the pillows. There was no sneaking out now. 'I did.'

'You also snored.' He laughed.

She pushed back gently against his shoulder. 'I did not.'

'Okay, more a purr than a snore. But you were out like a light.'

She turned over, about to say she was going to grab a shower and head off, but he smiled, and her belly quivered and tingled in response. She would not regret last night. And she could not resist him now. 'I need to go…soon.'

'I know.' His nose wrinkled as he pulled a face.

It made good sense to leave now; it would alleviate some of her guilt if she got home this early in the morning, and hopefully found her sister and niece still sleeping, and it would give her much-needed emotional space to work out exactly what she felt about making love with Lewis.

But she did not want to leave. 'Maybe in five minutes?'

He edged away a little. 'Look, if you need to go, that's fine.'

'Whoa. Are you trying to get rid of me?' *God*, he regretted this. He regretted her staying.

But he frowned and shook his head. 'Of course not. I just know you want to get back to Lucy.' He raised himself up on his elbow, threading his fingers through her hair and rubbing a strand against his cheek. 'You know, I always loved your hair. I'm glad you didn't change it or dye it some random colour.'

Was he remembering their wedding night too, when he'd unclipped her hair, let it fall over her shoulders, nuzzled his face into it and told her how much he loved her? She'd forgotten how much he'd adored her hair back then. 'I've been sorely tempted to change it over the years. This colour runs in the family. Stella's got it too.' She grimaced. 'Poor kid.'

'Why? It's the most beautiful colour I've ever seen.'

'Not when you're in primary school and everyone calls you Carrot Top and other less nice nicknames. It's the kind of colour you grow into and only appreciate when you're older.'

'Tell me who they were and I'll… I'll sort them out for calling you names.' He flexed his biceps. 'I have a certain set of skills.'

'Sort them out? No need, Mr Bodyguard. Stand down.' She stroked his arm, laughing. 'I love it now and I don't care what anyone thinks.'

But with the thought of Stella her chest constricted and she wriggled out from under his arm. 'Look, I do really need to get back. Lucy… She pretends she's okay…'

Like you always did.

When would people start to treat her as if she was a grown adult and start being honest with her? When would they stop protecting her and let her protect them for a change? 'But I want to take the burden off her.'

'Sure.' He jumped out of bed and slipped on the robe she'd been wearing last night. 'Coffee first; I know you don't like to function without it.'

'You remember! I *can't* function without it.' She laughed. 'I need it IV'd in the mornings.'

He fiddled with the chrome coffee machine, then peered at the selection of purple, silver and gold coffee pods. 'Coming up. Hop in the shower and it'll be ready when you're done. You want me to give you a ride home?'

'That would be great. Thanks.'

Was he in a hurry to get rid of her—just being polite about the coffee and the shower when he really wanted her gone?

She went through to the bathroom and turned on the shower. Two minutes on her own, and she was immediately hit with all the questions she'd wilfully ignored last night.

A ride home...and then what? What did this mean? Were they back together? No. That would be...difficult, given what they'd been through before. The warm water didn't help soothe her confusion. Did it have to mean anything? It could just be two consenting adults having fun.

But then what?

Last night the answer to that question hadn't seemed important, but today she needed certainty. Oh, she was no good at this. How could she pretend it had just been casual sex when...well...when her heart's reaction was far from casual?

She dried and dressed in yesterday's clothes, used the hotel's freebie toothbrush and paste then went back into the main room. He was sitting at the coffee table, looking at his phone.

Her heart danced just to look at him. What was he thinking?

He looked up and pointed at two steaming cups of coffee. 'There you go. Ambrosia from the gods.'

'Thanks.' She grabbed a cup and had a sip. 'What have you got planned today? Anything fun?'

He glanced back at his phone. 'Just messaging Logan. I'm going to the beach with him and the family, then lunch at their place in Meadowbank. It's a sort of tradition now, whenever I get the weekend off—which isn't often. We hang out, and sometimes I even babysit.'

'It sounds lovely. It's good that you two are so close.' He

had made his brother's family, his own family. Made up for the lack of his own kids. Which, despite him being at odds to tell her it wasn't her fault, it was. And all of a sudden she felt a little *lost*....robbed, even...because she couldn't pretend they didn't have a break-up history mired in her infertility. Or that he still wanted a family she couldn't give him.

She needed to go.

'Okay, do you mind if we make tracks now? I really need to give Lucy a break from parenting duties. She needs to get her rest.' To add to the emotional rollercoaster, guilt shimmied down her spine. Being with Lewis, amazing as he was, wasn't what she was supposed to be doing. Lucy would forgive her, right? 'I feel bad about staying out overnight.'

He fleetingly frowned. 'Don't. She would have said if she needed you, right?'

'I'm not so sure. You're not the only one who hides their feelings, Lewis.'

'Hey, I'm trying here. You're not the only one who's done a lot of thinking over the last few years, Charlie. And some growing up too.' He ran his hand through his hair and then smiled. But there was something about it that was almost sad, as if he was contemplating something coming to an end. Maybe he was. 'I had a great night, Charlie. I'm glad you're back.'

Okay... This new honest and open Lewis, the Lewis who told her what he wanted and needed, was someone else— interesting and refreshing and so not what he used to be like. And yet she was waiting for the 'but', which should be a relief and would make things less difficult. But...at the same time... she liked him. Last night had been amazing.

Oh, she was all kinds of confused. 'I'm not sure you were very glad when you found me in that smashed-up car.'

'Okay, I'll admit I was shocked.' He laughed. 'And I understand about Lucy. She's the big sister, right? She feels responsible—like Logan does with me. Only thirty minutes' difference but sometimes he acts like it's thirty years.'

'She's always looked out for me, and has been one of my fiercest supporters. I think I took it for granted, *expected* the support even. It was too easy for me not to stand on my own two feet because I had my parents, Lucy and you to do the hard yards for me.'

'Hey, you got the brilliant exam results, not us.' He drained his cup.

'But you made sure I had nothing else to worry about. You made food or my parents brought us food parcels. My mother paid a cleaner every week to come spruce the house. I was a spoilt princess.'

'You weren't.' He cleared the empty coffee cups onto a little tray and carried them to the console. 'You were studying and learning your new job. It's not easy being a junior doctor.'

'Oh, I was spoilt, Lewis. I was also selfish and a little bit lazy. I didn't like being pampered by everyone but I couldn't bring myself to take control either. Then, when I moved to London, I... Well, I pushed *everyone* away—not just you. I only came back twice in five years and even then only briefly. I wouldn't even let my family visit me in London.' And she'd felt so very alone, but hadn't had any energy to give to anyone else, to answer their questions or even have a conversation about what was going on inside her head and her heart.

He leaned back against the console, legs crossed at the ankles. 'I had no idea. Why?'

'I don't know for sure. I think I needed some distance from everyone. Some space from everything I knew—a new direction. A new life with no pain in it. No reminder of what I couldn't do or who I was.' Until she'd realised she couldn't run away from herself or her feelings. She'd had to face them. 'But, again selfishly, didn't think how that might have affected my mum and dad. And Lucy.'

'You're being very hard on yourself. You'd been through a very difficult time; you were all over the place emotionally. I'm sure they understood.'

'I didn't give them a choice. But I can imagine how hurt they must have felt and worried about my mental wellbeing. I only stayed in cursory contact when necessary for the first couple of years. When Lucy called to tell me about her pregnancy, I didn't rush home to be with her for the birth; I just sent flowers and cooed over video calls. I missed some of Stella's firsts, and didn't help in those difficult early days. I wasn't here when Lucy found the lump. She didn't tell anyone until after Mum and Dad went away to do their charity work. She was facing all that on her own. There was a chasm between us and it was my fault.' Now it was time for her to give back. 'I'm trying to make amends for that.'

'I'm sure you don't need to. I am absolutely sure Lucy understands you just needed some alone time.' He smiled. 'But, what are you waiting for? Get your bag. I'll take you.'

'I can get a bus if you need to get to Logan's.'

He frowned. 'We're neighbours, remember? I won't let you get the bus when I practically drive past your house. I have to change and grab Lola's present anyway.'

'Oh, okay. If you insist.' She grabbed her bag, not ready for this intimate time with him to end, because she had no idea how they would navigate the 'what next?'

Twenty minutes later, they pulled up outside Lucy's home and Lewis twisted in his seat to talk to Charlie. The conversation from the hotel had been sparse and the atmosphere a little loaded, as if they both knew they needed to say something but didn't know what.

'Right, here you go.' He rubbed the back of his neck. 'Um… What do we do now?'

Awkward.

'I don't know. I came here to look after Lucy and Stella and then somehow here I am, doing the drive of shame.' She looked down at yesterday's clothes, and felt a belt of contrition tightening around her chest, but smiled nonetheless.

He stroked her hair, then palmed her cheek. 'Hey. There's absolutely nothing to be ashamed of. We're consenting adults. We were married once.' What had he said last night about grown adults and sexual craving? But there was something in his expression that gave her pause before he added, 'How about we catch up when we're both ready?'

What? When? Wasn't he ready either? Did he feel the same discombobulation?

Suddenly she felt a little out of her depth. They'd spent an intense few hours getting to the core of what had split them up, but they certainly weren't healed enough to lay their hearts wide open yet. And she shouldn't be doing this when she had so little time to give. It wasn't fair on him or on Lucy.

And it wasn't fair on her own heart. She didn't want to fall for him again and then lose him. She'd barely recovered from that before. 'Sure. Yes. I'm in a difficult space at the moment.'

'I get it: Lucy; Stella; the job… It's a lot. No problem. You know where I am and you have my phone number if you need me. But, in the meantime, no doubt I'll see you at work.' He nodded.

And she'd have the tease and temptation of seeing him… probably on every shift, trying to ignore the ache, the want and the need. But neither of them was in a position to make more of this. She sighed as her chest constricted. 'So, you're okay with this? You know…not making plans? Please—tell me the truth.'

He smiled wryly. 'Hey, don't stress. I have to get my head straight too. I did not expect any of last night to ever happen, so I'm just sort of…working through it. But, for the record, I had a good time—*great* time. And I'd like us to be friends, if that works for you.'

'Friends. Sure, I can do that.'

And wow: *just sort of working through it.* His honesty about his feelings was coming thick and fast. She squeezed his hand, but when he leaned in to kiss her cheek she turned her mouth to meet his. She couldn't resist kissing him again.

He hesitated, then groaned as their lips met. And, oh, how her body heated and responded to his kiss.

It was a while before they came up for air.

She chuckled, more in embarrassment at her lack of restraint than anything else. 'Okay, sorry. That was a very unfriend thing to do. But I couldn't resist just one last kiss. Right; friends from now?'

He chuckled, his eyes still filled with heat. 'Yeah. Friends from now. You want to synchronise watches or something?'

'No need; I think I'm good now. Right, I should go.' She opened the door and climbed out, but leaned back in through the window to add, 'I'll see you…some time. Thanks for a great night.'

'Yeah. Back at ya, Charlie.' He leaned across the passenger seat and smiled up at her.

Oh, those eyes. That mouth. That man.

Last night.

This kiss.

Oh, hell…the friend thing wasn't working very well at all.

CHAPTER ELEVEN

IT WAS A great night, Lewis thought as he jogged down the path to the beach. *Pinch me.*

Had it really happened—Charlie back in his arms? After their deep and raw conversation, so many emotions had been swimming through his veins. He hadn't been so honest or felt so close to anyone for a long time. Sex had been the natural conclusion—inevitable after that first stolen kiss.

And now what?

He wasn't sure how to navigate casual sex with his ex, or just being friends, or how to protect himself from falling for her again. Because, even though they'd straddled some of the niggly reasons why they'd split, some issues were still there, right? Big issues too. Besides, she'd made it clear she didn't want anything deep or involved.

So why the hell had he allowed last night to happen?

He spotted the girls in bright-pink bathers paddling in the shallows, with Logan helicoptering over them. Lewis watched them splash each other for a moment with a sting in his chest. Lucky Logan; he'd got it all: a lovely wife and three gorgeous kids. Lewis was thrilled for him; he was. After what they'd been through growing up, his brother deserved every scrap of happiness, every moment of family life with his precious girls.

But it didn't stop him craving that for himself, even now.

His brother met him with a bro hug of hand-slap and back-clap. 'Hey, you look bright-eyed and bushy-tailed. Early night?'

'Hmm.' Far from it, but he wasn't sure what to say. As far as Logan was concerned, Charlie had abandoned her husband... just like everyone else had over their early years. Logan was a stickler for staying and trying to work things through, just like Lewis. And Lewis hadn't yet found the head space or opportunity to tell Logan that Charlotte Rose was back.

Logan frowned at Lewis's non-committal response. 'What did you do, watch the game? Shame about the result, eh? It was a lousy night to be out anyway. There was flash-flooding on Tamaki Drive. You wouldn't think so now, though. It's a beaut of a day.'

Flash-flooding florecast.

God, she was beautiful. And his head was a mess. Images from last night kept flashing through his brain: her mouth; her smile; the tight press of her body. 'Actually, I went out with Charlie.'

Logan stepped back, almost falling over a sand castle, then stepped down into a deep hole. He staggered, then fell backwards onto the sand. 'Charlie? Your Charlie? Dr Charlie? Your wife?'

'Ex-wife.' Lewis held out his hand and hauled Logan upright.

Logan brushed the sand from his shorts. 'How? Why?'

'She's moved back to Auckland and we bumped into each other at work.'

Logan's eyes roamed Lewis face, assessing. 'And...?'

Siblings—they always wanted a piece of you. 'We had dinner.'

'So you're getting back together? Just like that?'

'We had dinner, Logan.' And great sex. 'No one said anything about getting back together.'

'Okay.' Logan's eyebrows rose and he blew out a slow breath. 'How was she? How are you?'

He thought of her underneath him—the way she'd looked at him as he'd entered her; the way she'd clung to him. The way tears had slipped down her cheeks, emotion spilling over. 'She's great, actually. Really good.'

'And you?' Logan peered closer at him. 'You look too happy about it and that gives me the heebie-jeebies.'

Lewis inhaled deeply. Happy? Confused, more like. 'Yeah. I'm not gonna lie. It was a shock to see her at first but we talked and…well… I'm okay… I think. We agreed to try be friends, seeing as we're likely going to be working together on occasion.'

'Friends?' His brother's eyes widened in shock. 'Be careful, bro. I remember how you were after she'd gone. I don't ever want to see you like that again.'

Lewis remembered too and no way was he going back to that darkness again. 'Don't worry, I can handle it. I'm in a good space now.'

'Yes. And it's good to see.' Logan shook his head and put his hand on Lewis's shoulder. 'But, with Charlie back, how long is that going to last?'

He had a point. Lewis had been broken into a million pieces when she'd left. 'I'm being careful. We're both older and wiser.' *Liar.* Last night he'd felt like a giddy teenager again, carried away with wild need.

'Do you…you know…?' Logan inhaled as his question trailed off.

'Know what?' Lewis frowned at his brother. Where was this going?

'Still love her?'

'Whoa. Get straight to the point, why don't you?' But

Logan had always talked about how he was feeling. He didn't hold back. He was open and honest; Lewis had got the other side of that coin. He preferred to keep everything inside so he could work it through. And, anyway, no one had ever cared what he thought about stuff. If he'd had a problem and wanted help from an adult, he might as well have shouted into the wind.

Except for Charlie… She'd pushed him to say things. And he was trying. He just wasn't sure if he trusted himself, or her…although after last night he wasn't sure. She hadn't given him false hope or led him on. They'd both consented and parted in agreement.

It had been a good night. He wanted to do it again.

But did he still *love* her? Absolutely not. She'd thrashed his heart. He couldn't do that to himself, never again.

Logan was still looking at him, waiting for a response. Lewis shook his head. 'Come on, man. It was one night.'

'Night?' His brother glared at him. 'You said dinner.'

Great. There was no getting out of this. 'We got caught in the rain doing a resus on some poor bloke who got run over in the middle of Quay Street, and then she couldn't get a taxi, and I had that hotel room booked…' He shrugged. Yeah, it did sound a likely story, now he thought about it, but he wasn't going to lie. 'So she spent the night, okay? It was probably closure for both of us. One night, then we can both properly move on.'

Because, in reality, it looked as if he hadn't fully moved on at all, no matter how much he told himself he had. He was healed, yes, but he hadn't been able to find happiness with anyone else.

Logan shot him a blunt look and was about to say something when Lily hurtled towards them. 'Uncle Lewis, piggy-back ride?'

'Please,' admonished Logan.

Lily beamed her toothy smile. '*Please,* Uncle Lewis?'

How could he resist? This could be the only chance at a family he ever got, these little poppets in pink. Plus, maybe it'd get him back in the good books with his brother. He bent down onto all fours. 'Okay, hop on, both of you. And be nice to each other.'

The little girls giggled and screeched as they scrambled onto his back with Lily in front and Lola at the back, complaining about being behind her little sister and giggling at the same time.

He crawled across the sand, ignoring the burn in his knees and palms...and in his heart. This was everything he'd dreamt of happening with Charlie: two little copper-headed kids, squirming and wriggling and laughing. Then Sunday lunch all together, maybe with Logan and his brood too—family time.

Charlie had thought that impossible and he'd been too distraught to argue. But there were options, right? Why hadn't they talked about adoption or surrogacy? Why had he been so closed to that idea five years ago?

But how could they talk about that now? They weren't in that space. She'd drawn her boundary and he had to respect that. Hell, he needed that line in the sand too.

So why the hell was he imagining happy families when nothing could be further from reality?

'Hey, there,' Charlie whispered as she opened the door to Lucy's bedroom to find her niece asleep on her sister's chest. Lucy's eyes were closed as she lay on the bed, her chest steadily rising and falling. She looked peaceful, which was lovely, given the stress she was under right now.

Charlie's heart squeezed. These two here were what was important. *But, oops...*

Charlie tiptoed backwards and closed the door as quietly as she could.

'Charlie? Charlotte, is that you?' came a strained whisper.

Charlie opened the door again and popped her head round. 'Hey, yes. Sorry, I didn't mean to disturb you.'

'Oh, don't worry. She's been napping for an hour now so it's probably time she woke up.' Lucy looked down at her daughter and smiled that soft mamma smile filled with adoration. 'She had a restless night.'

Charlie's chest ached with guilt. 'Oh, I'm sorry, I should have been here.'

'No, you should not. I told you to go. The least I can do is let you have a night out every now and then.'

Which did not erase the guilt at all. 'How are you feeling?'

'Yuck.' Lucy sat up, leaning back against the pillows, and hoisted a fast-asleep Stella higher on her chest. She looked worn out, but she smiled. 'But I don't want to talk about me. I want every little detail about your illicit night.'

To be honest, Charlie didn't know what to say, or how to feel. 'Oh, you know? It was nice.'

Lucy guffawed. 'You stay at a fabulous hotel with a gorgeous man and it's *nice*?'

'Well, we did have a medical emergency to deal with as well.' Her sex-induced tachycardia, as well as poor Graham.

Lucy rolled her eyes. 'Yeah, yeah. And it was raining and all the apps were down and there was absolutely nothing you could do except go to his hotel.' Lucy smiled softly. 'So what happened?'

Charlie shook her head and glanced down at her sleeping niece. 'No can do. Stella is far too young to hear this.'

'Oh? That good?'

Charlie plopped down on the bed next to her sister. 'Yes. *That* good.'

Lucy peered more closely at Charlie's face. 'And yet, you don't seem your usually happy self.'

Charlie pressed her lips together, because she was smiling inside; she really was. It had been un-freaking-believable but tinged now with 'what next?' and guilt at not being here. 'I'm not sure where we're at.'

'You're seeing him again?' Lucy frowned at Charlie's shrug. 'You're not seeing him again?'

'Undoubtedly I'll see him again. He brings in my patients. Our paths will cross many, many times.' The enormity of the potential emotional and personal fallout from last night finally hit her. Making love had muddied everything: distracted her from her commitment to looking after her family members; intruded into her work space and bruised her heart. 'We're friends, apparently. He's working things through.'

Lucy's eyes widened. 'He said that?'

'Yeah. But anyway…it doesn't matter. It's not a good time for me.'

Lucy's frown deepened. 'Because of me? Please don't let me stop you having fun. Watching you living a great life might be the only good thing I have left, after this little one, of course.' She kissed the top of her daughter's head.

'No.' Tears pricked Charlie's eyes. 'Don't say that.'

'It's true. We have to face up to it. My life is crappy and horrible and I'm scared to death. Let's just hope the medicine is working, okay?'

Charlie nodded and squeezed her sister's hand. 'Absolutely. It will. It *will*.'

'And I don't want to talk about it any more. It's all I ever seem to think about and it's not good for me. I need a distraction and, unfortunately for you, you're it.'

Lucy cupped Charlie's face with her Stella-free hand and sighed. 'I know this thing with Lewis is complicated; you have so much history. And I do not want you hurting like you did before or scurrying away overseas again. I should be telling you to be careful. To take your time. To figure out what *you* want. If it's just that one night, then great, you can tick that box. If it's more, then, you'll have to talk to him about it. Tell him what you want. Find out what he wants.'

'The same as he always did—kids.' Charlie exhaled slowly.

'So you talked about it?'

'No. But he's so close with Logan's girls. It's obvious.'

I was gutted, if I'm honest. Absolutely broken. His words rubbed a bruise in her chest wall.

'I don't suppose you talked about other options? Adoption? Fostering?'

'It wasn't that kind of conversation, Luce.'

Lucy brushed Charlotte's hair back from her forehead and smiled softly. 'Oh, sweetheart, I'm sorry.'

'Because, if he doesn't want that, we'd still have the same issues as before and I'm not ready to be rejected. Anyway, it was one night, Lucy. You are my number one focus.' She wrapped Lucy and Stella in a warm hug. 'Other than to see you get better, I have no idea what I want.'

How about a carefree, problem-free, happy, committed relationship with a gorgeous man? Lots of kids. *Love.*

'I don't want a life without you,' he'd said on their wedding night.

Yet he'd managed just fine—was thriving, in fact.

While her heart, it seemed, was still a fractured mess.

CHAPTER TWELVE

'THIS IS TIA, a twenty-seven-year-old woman who fell off her horse when she was trying to do a jump at speed. She fell forward over the horse's head; face and head took the brunt of the impact, as you can see by the grazing and swelling on her forehead and bruising around the eyes. Luckily, she was wearing a helmet, but a witness said she was possibly unconscious for a few minutes. Glasgow coma scale was thirteen on initial assessment but fifteen now.' Lewis glanced up at the group of medics he was handing over to and momentarily froze.

He hadn't seen Charlie come in. He certainly hadn't realised she was standing right in front of him, her startling blue eyes watching him as she listened intently. Her hair was piled on top of her head in a gorgeously messy bun with stray, loose tendrils framing her pretty face. Lip gloss highlighted her perfect Cupid's bow. His brain immediately rewound to the night in the hotel: the heat, the touch, the intensity of it all; the honesty.

No.

He shook himself. He was not going there. He was doing his job. Charlie was a friend, that was all. 'She also has swelling and pain in her upper right arm, right hip and right knee. She's had ketorolac for pain relief, which is working well.'

'Hi, Tia. My name is Charlie. I'm one of the doctors here. Good to hear Lewis's magic medicine is working.' Charlie flashed him a smile that reached deep into his heart and tugged it in a way not so much friendly, more sexy, then fixed back on their patient. 'I'll need to ask you a few more questions and examine you again, so I'm sorry if it seems as if we're repeating ourselves.'

He stepped back and let her do her stuff. He couldn't begin to count how many handovers he'd given over the course of his career, but he'd felt like a blathering idiot every time he'd done one in front of Charlie in the past few days.

He was so aware of her. Aware of her eyes on him and of the memories from years ago bolstered by the memories of Saturday night. Memories of the mind-blowing kisses, and her beautiful naked body. Of him finally opening up, as if a pressure valve had been released inside him, giving him hope and making him...what? *Exposed.* All of these messy emotions didn't stop him doing his job—he'd never let anything get in the way of that—but they didn't make it easy.

He stepped away out of the cubicle, eager to put distance between himself and his ex-wife. Maybe one day he would come to work and feel platonic vibes about her.

Today was not that day.

Keen to leave, Lewis found Brin at the nurses' station, chatting to some of the medical team. 'Hey, Brin, ready to go?'

Brin nodded. 'Sure. But I'm parched and it's my turn for coffees again. So, I'll go grab them and meet you in the van.'

'Great.' That would give Lewis some time to breathe and get his head straight after seeing Charlie. He turned to leave but came face to face with her as she stepped out from behind the cubicle curtain.

She looked surprised and a little embarrassed now it was just the two of them. She gave him a half-smile. She was guarded, unsure. 'Hey...um...friend.'

'Hey, Charlie. How's things?' Was it his imagination or had

there been extra emphasis on the word 'friend', as if she was feeling the same discombobulation he was? The memory of their night together filled the air, unacknowledged, loaded.

'Good.' She nodded. 'Yes. I'm good.'

He waited for her to ask him how he was, but nothing came, so he said, 'And Lucy? Stella?'

'They're okay.'

'Right. Good.' He wasn't sure what to say next. She wasn't exactly encouraging conversation but she wasn't making moves to leave either. They'd shared a very intimate night together... hell, a marriage of four years and longer than that in a relationship... but friends? It seemed it didn't come naturally. Maybe they couldn't have a relationship that didn't involve the emotional and physical. *Ouch*. That didn't bode well for their future professional relationship.

Because what he wanted was to whip her into his arms and kiss her right here in the emergency room. Take her to his bed and make long, slow, sweet love to her. Wake up with her in the morning, lots of mornings.... *Every* morning...

Hot damn. He couldn't let these emotions take hold. He shoved his hands into his pockets and rocked back on his heels, trying to be nonchalant when his body felt the opposite. 'Cool. Well, I should be going.'

'Yeah. Me too.' But she paused, a smile flickering as something seemed to occur to her. 'Oh, I almost forgot. Did you hear about Graham?'

'Graham?' For a moment he was confused, then he realised. 'Oh, yes, our CPR man. No, I haven't had the chance to ask after him.'

'He's actually hanging in there. In Intensive Care, but improving. Apparently, it was touch and go for a while, but he pulled through. We did good, Lewis.'

And, with that, the tension between them seemed to diminish. Maybe it was because they were in safe territory talking about work. Or maybe because they'd been reminded of how good they could be together. 'That's great news. I'm so pleased. I might pop up to see him if I get a chance.'

'Yeah.' She nodded, her eyes brighter now. 'Just goes to show that things don't always end up the way you think they might.'

Tell that to my pathetic, hopeful heart.

'Go us.' He raised his palm and she high-fived it.

'The dream team.' Her smile was worth all the awkward tension.

'Hey, you two.' Brin was striding towards them carrying two takeaway cups. 'I've just had Mia on the phone and she wondered if you'd like to come for a barbecue at the weekend?'

Lewis wasn't sure whether Brin meant the two of them generally or *together*. His meddling was getting a little out of control. He glanced at Charlie, and she looked as uncomfortable as he felt at the invitation, so before he replied Lewis narrowed his eyes in a question to his colleague. 'What's the occasion?'

Brin rolled his eyes. 'Sorry, should have been clearer—house warming. It's a little overdue, but Mia's sister-in-law and family are coming over for the weekend, so we thought it'd be a good opportunity to throw a party.'

Which meant there'd be others there, it wouldn't be just a double date kind of thing. Lewis exhaled and agreed to come, because refusing the invitation would be out of character and would probably engender more questions from his co-worker, not fewer. 'Sure thing, sounds good. Let me know what to bring.'

But Charlie shook her head. 'No, sorry. Thanks, anyway, but I need to look after Lucy.'

Brin frowned. 'Your daughter?'

'Sister.' She smiled tightly. At the mention of Lucy, her body language had become guarded and taut. Looking after her family was taking a toll and Lewis wondered how he could ease that burden. Then he remembered he was not getting involved.

Brin smiled. 'No worries. Bring her too.'

'Okay, I'll ask her. Thanks.' Charlie's gaze darted to Lewis. It seemed she was checking if that was okay by him. He nodded. He could hardly refuse, could he? She looked back at Brin. 'She's got a baby, six months old: is it okay to bring her too?'

Brin grinned. 'That's no problem. Mia loves babies. We've got a little one too. Bring them all. The more the merrier. Stay an hour, stay all evening, whatever works.' Brin nodded at Lewis and handed him a warm takeaway cup. 'Okay, boss. I'll be in the van clearing up. Take your time.'

As they watched him walk away, Lewis heaved a sigh. 'Geez, I am so sorry about him.'

She laughed. 'It's fine. He's just being friendly.'

'Or meddling. Looks like we're not going to be let out of this. You good with it?'

'Yes. I guess. It's actually nice to be invited out somewhere and hopefully make some friends. I haven't had much of a chance to meet many people or catch up with my old Auckland mates.' Her eyebrows rose and he wondered if she was alluding to *their* old Auckland mates, joint school friends with whom she'd lost touch with living so far away, while he'd done his best to stay in contact. She shrugged. 'I'll ask Lucy to come, because she could use cheering up. With the chemo, she's not keen on going out and mingling too much. Her immune system's not great.'

'I could pick you all up…' The words were out of his mouth before he realised what he was saying. Not only would he be up close with Charlie in a car, but he'd have to see Lucy again after the messy divorce from her little sister. How would he navigate that? But he couldn't sit by and see them worry or struggle when he might be able to help somehow. 'It would save you driving your little broken car or using public transport, which is a greater risk for catching infections. And if it's all too much for her then I can run her home any time, no worries.'

Her smile widened. 'That would be lovely.'

'That's what friends are for, right?' This time he made himself *feel* the emphasis on the word 'friend'.

'Yeah. I guess.' She put her hand on his arm, sending sparks of need firing across his skin, arrowing to his chest and lower... way lower. He thought about the way she tasted, and the soft sounds she'd made when he'd slid inside her, and the sparks in his belly threatened to burst into flame. 'Thanks, Lewis.'

He tried to push back all sexy thoughts of her. 'No worries. I just have to put on my big boy pants to face your older sister. Otherwise, everything is golden.'

'She won't bite.' She chuckled. 'She always liked you. She knows I was the one who left.'

'Hmm. The jury's still out on that. You were heartbroken and I couldn't fix it. That was my job, right?' He imagined what Logan might say whenever—*if ever*—he got to see Charlie again.

'Oh, Lewis, it was never your job to fix my broken heart. I'm responsible for my own emotions.' She patted his arm and he realised just how much she'd changed in the intervening years since their break-up. Back then, she'd have allowed him to wade in and try to fix everything. Now she was self-determined and fiercely autonomous. It suited her, a lot. She grinned. 'Don't worry. If I say you're generously being our taxi driver, she'll be fine with it. She just wants me to be happy.'

'And are you?' It was the million-dollar question. It was probably unfair to ask, really, given what she was going through.

She closed her eyes briefly, then exhaled long and slowly. 'That's too big a question for work time. I'm loving spending time with my family. I have a great job and…ahem…*interesting* friends and colleagues.' She shot him a knowing smile. 'But ask me again in a few months, when Lucy's treatment's finished. That's all I can think of at the moment. When she gets the all-clear, I'll be deliriously happy.'

If ever there was a sign they needed to be platonic more than ever, this was it. Because he realised he wanted her to say, yes, she was happy they'd spent the night together. That they'd found each other again. That there was still something between them. Which was pathetic wishful thinking on his part, and also very selfish. Charlie was conflicted and busy and had other people she needed to put ahead of herself, and therefore ahead of him. He nodded. 'Sure. I get it.'

'And I mean thanks for understanding, Lewis. For sticking to the plan. You know…being friends. Not asking for more. And, on the other hand, for not ghosting me. I'm not sure which would be harder to deal with.' Her hand was still on his arm and the way she was looking at him, as if she was truly grateful, made him want to wrap his arms round her and hold her close. To soothe her worries and make her feel better. But that wasn't his job any more.

'I would never ghost you, Charlie. We're too old and wise to play those kinds of games.' He couldn't help smiling. 'Thank God you're not a mind-reader, is all.'

She blinked, then her smile grew into a grin, sexy and loaded. 'Lewis! Not you too?'

'Me what?' He was all mock-innocence.

She leaned closer so no one else could hear. 'Struggling with the aftermath of the other night?'

'I can't get it out of my head.' This close, he could see deep into her eyes. He saw the tease she was fighting, the need for affection. He was struggling with his need to protect her too, to be the one to solve all her problems and to have the answers. She hadn't wanted them five years ago and she certainly wouldn't want them now. But he couldn't help wanting to erase all her pain.

He needed to keep this growing connection between them under control if he was going to get out whole.

He took a sip of coffee and remembered that Brin was waiting for him. 'Look, I'd better go. Let me know if you want me to pick you all up. Otherwise, I'll see you at Brin's. I'll message you his address.'

Then he flashed her a quick smile and left, balling up his emotions and stuffing them deep inside, exactly where they should have stayed the moment he knew she was back.

It was silly to be nervous. It was a barbecue—friends from work—that was all.

But, the moment Lewis's car pulled up outside, her heart jumped into a very weird tachycardic rhythm she was fairly sure no cardiologist had ever seen on a heart trace.

Stop it.

As he crunched up the gravel path, she started to feel a little dizzy due to her jumpy heart rate and anticipatory nerves.

Ridiculous.

The rap on the door made her jump, even though she was expecting it.

'Lucy! We're heading off,' she called up the stairs. And received a muffled grunt in return. Then she took a deep breath and opened the door.

Hell... He looked good today in his untucked white linen shirt and duck-egg-blue shorts. His dark hair was casually tousled as always and there was a smattering of stubble on his jaw. His lovely soulful brown eyes glittered as he smiled. 'Taxi for Dr Rose?'

'Hey. Thanks so much for this.'

After holding off asking him to pick them all up, she'd capitulated at Lucy's urging: 'He has a much bigger car and it'll be so much more comfortable for us all.'

That was before Lucy had decided not to join them after all.

Laughing, Charlie hauled the car seat from the ground and handed it to him. 'Could you take this? You have to put the seat belt through the back.'

'Got it.' He grinned. 'Three nieces; I know the drill.' Then he disappeared down the path and into the car. She was mesmerised by the rhythm of his steps, the way he turned and winked at her, as he'd used to when they'd been happily married, and the cute smile that seemed to reach to her uterus and stroked. Which was damned unfair, given she had a non-functioning uterus and no amount of stroking would make it work.

But, oh, he was lovely. Her body prickled with awareness. Was he more lovely now than five years ago? He seemed more centred, wiser, happier in himself. He seemed confident. He was definitely better in so many ways. It was only when he backed out of the back passenger door that she realised she'd been staring at his backside for far longer than anyone would consider acceptable. If staring at a hunk of man's backside was acceptable at all… *Oops*.

'Come on, lovely,' she cooed at little Stella and picked her up from the travel cot they used as a playpen in the lounge. 'Time to be sociable.'

She was glad they were going to be surrounded by friends new to her, so temptation could stay at bay. And also frustrated that they would be surrounded by friends, so temptation could stay at bay. Oh, life was so complicated these days.

She yelled upstairs again. 'Bye, Luce. Please call me if you need anything.'

She waited for a reply. There came some splashing then a long sigh. 'Have fun, girls.'

'Car seat is in,' Lewis said as he walked back up the path. But he frowned as she pulled the door closed behind her. He ran up to take Stella's change bag out of Charlie's hands. 'Hey, give that to me. Where's Lucy?'

'In the bath. And she's not coming out for anyone or anything, apparently.' Charlie giggled. 'She has a glass of her favourite rosé, scented candles, some chocolate-covered ginger and a new romance novel to devour. She's not up to seeing anyone, but she is up to pampering herself. I told her I'd bring Stella with us so she can relax.'

'Great idea.' After he put the changing bag into the car boot, he took Stella from her arms as naturally as anything, then he beamed at the baby, swinging her high in the air until she giggled. 'Hello, little one. Yes, it's me, Lewis. We have met, but you probably don't remember. Yes, that's my chin. Yes, it's scratchy.' He shot Charlie a smile. 'She's a feisty little thing.'

'She needs to be, for her mum's sake.'

'It's difficult, for sure. But she won't understand what's going on.' His smile flattened a little, his eyes filling with warmth and worry. Then he turned another full-beam grin on Stella. 'Okay, missy. Let's get you plugged in so we can all go party.'

Charlie's breath caught in her throat. Lewis was gorgeous when he was just being himself but, smiling and laughing with a baby in his arms, he was devastating.

She'd tried to keep her distance, had not encouraged anything past polite conversation at work. Yet here she was, about to get into a car with him, go to a party and play. Once upon a time, playing with Lewis had been her most favourite thing.

Maybe it still was…

'Hey!' Brin grinned as he tugged open the front door twenty minutes later. 'Come in! Come in! Glad you could make it. Hello, little one.' He tickled Stella under her chin as he walked them through to a bright, smart-looking kitchen. 'This must be…?'

He glanced at Charlie. She smiled and bounced Stella up and down in her arms. 'Stella, my niece.'

'Something you guys have in common, then. Nieces.' Brin threw Lewis a look of encouragement and nodded towards Charlie with raised eyebrows, as if to say, *get in, lad. Make a move.*

She rolled her eyes at Lewis in solidarity. He smiled and mouthed the word, 'Sorry.' Somehow, their joint reaction at Brin's unsubtle matchmaking attempts was bringing them closer together. *Go figure.*

'Girls, yes, so many girls, including your Harper.' Lewis shook his head as he put a large bowl of delicious-looking caprese salad, gourmet sausages and halloumi cheese onto the kitchen counter. 'Where's Mia, and Harper?'

Brin gestured towards the back door. 'Outside. Come and look at our new back yard, mate. You're going to love it.'

'Huh?' Lewis frowned again and they all followed Brin outside to a neat back garden with a large wooden deck, built-in pizza oven and huge gas barbecue. Lewis's eyes widened. 'Ah, you got it? Lucky man. Yes, tasty.'

Brin preened in the sunshine. 'Back home in Ireland it's always hit and miss for barbecue weather. But here, it's pretty much always a hit. Thought I'd get the best one I could.'

Lewis lovingly ran his fingers over the chrome and cooed the way he had at Stella. 'She's a beauty. I have serious barbecue envy.'

'Men!' Laughing, Charlie looked round the little crowd of people for some female cavalry and noted Mia walking towards her. 'Hello. Thank goodness you're here. I was starting feel pressured into have a conversation about the benefits of gas barbecues over charcoal and boast about how many burners mine has.' Charlie puffed out her chest and flexed her left bicep.

'Men! Good to see you again, Charlie.' Mia laughed and gave her a hug. 'Let's leave them to their barbecue adoration. My daughter's around here somewhere. She's so excited to be having a party. And who is this?' She stroked Stella's hand.

'This is my niece, Stella. We left Mum relaxing in the bath at home. She needed some time off.'

Mia raised her eyebrows and groaned in delight. 'Oh, lucky lady.'

'Yes.' *Not lucky at all.* 'I was wondering if it would be okay to put Stella down for a nap somewhere in about an hour or so?'

'No problem at all. We've got a travel cot. I can put that up in Harper's room and she can nap in there.'

'I don't want to put you to any trouble.'

'Not at all. There are a few babies and kids coming, so it'll be put to good use.' Mia glanced at the kitchen door and smiled at a couple walking into the garden. 'Excuse me while I go welcome my other guests. I'll be back in a minute. Help yourself to a drink.' Mia pointed to a table with glasses and a large cool box filled with ice, bottles of wine, beer and soft drinks.

'Yes. Sure.' Although, she wasn't sure how she was going to manage that with a baby in her arms. She'd have to wait until Lewis came to her rescue. Her heart crumpled a little. Her knight in shining armour had always been exactly that. Too much. Too long ago.

She didn't have to wait long. While Lewis turned sausages on the barbecue, Brin brought her a glass of wine then steered her towards the newly arrived couple standing with Mia. He introduced her to Carly and Owen, who lived on Rāwhiti Island, and their boy Mason. Owen shook her hand. 'Your name's familiar. Maybe our paths have crossed?'

'I'm working in A and E at Auckland Central at the moment. Emergency registrar.'

'Ah. That must be it. I've probably had a discharge letter from you for some of my patients.' It turned out that Owen was a doctor too. He used to have a practice in the city but now worked full-time on the island. Charlie remembered that Mia was a practice nurse working for a GP partnership just up the road.

'Is there anyone here who isn't a medic?' Charlie laughed, then lost her breath as she saw Lewis heading over towards them. His smile was so warm and friendly, and she thought back to the days when they used to host parties like this. When he'd casually wrap his arm around her waist as they chatted, just the way Brin was doing to Mia now.

Lewis kissed Carly and shook hands with Owen. It seemed they all knew each other very well, leaving Charlie feeling just a little out of the loop.

Owen stood back and looked Lewis up and down. 'Hey, looking sharp, man.'

'All that training,' Brin quipped.

'Oh? Training for what?' Charlie asked. Lewis hadn't mentioned any training or event, although they had been distracted by other things recently: making love, navigating a fledgling friendship and kissing, mostly.

Her core heated at that thought and she drew her gaze from his sharp-looking body and made faces to entertain Stella, who was getting heavy and restless on her hip.

Brin put his hand on Lewis's shoulder and spoke in an extremely proud fatherly tone. 'This guy is a machine. We did the vertical challenge as a work team and you should have seen him go.'

'What's a vertical challenge?' Charlie asked. 'Sounds painful.'

'Running up fifty-one levels of the Sky Tower, and he left us all for dust. Which was pretty favourable, as it happens, because it meant we made a mint for charity too. He's a bona-fide legend.' Brin's eyes flitted to Charlie and she got the distinct impression he was saying all of this for her benefit.

But, yes, he was indeed a legend. Because not only was he super-fit for work but he used his skills, strength, spare energy and even money to support charities: first the silent auction, now the vertical challenge. *Impressive.*

But then, she knew that already. She caught Lewis's eye and he shook his head, clearly embarrassed at all the praise, but laughing. His gaze locked on hers and he rolled his eyes, as if to say, *this guy, huh?*

It was time to put poor Brin to rights, for the truth to be told at last. She cleared her throat. 'Yes, Lewis has always been devoted to being fit for his job—running, gym work, swimming. I used to call him an exercise junkie.'

Brin frowned and glanced from Lewis to Charlie. '*Always*? How do you…? Did you two know each other before you started working together?'

'You could say that.' She licked her lips and glanced at Lewis to make sure it was okay for her to explain their relationship. He nodded and smiled encouragingly. 'We were married once.'

'What?' Brin's expression turned from interest to shock to a full-on blush. He smacked his forehead with his palm. 'Here I was pushing you two together, thinking you both needed… company.' He coughed. 'I am so sorry.'

'Don't worry. It's okay, honestly.' She looked directly at Lewis and her tummy tumbled in delight and confusion. 'We're friends now.'

'Right. Wow, okay. Well, friends is good at least. Because that could have made for a mighty awkward barbecue otherwise.' Brin inhaled, then turned to Lewis, bugging his eyes at his friend. 'And you were going to tell me when, *partner*?'

'Now seemed like a good time.' Lewis laughed. 'I'm sorry to let you find out this way but you did kind of deserve it.'

'Jeez, mate. I am mortified.' Brin shook his head, but chuckled. '*Mortified.*'

'It'll wear off. Have another beer. Seriously, we're good, aren't we, Charlie?' Lewis looked over at Charlie and his laugh died away as his gaze settled on Stella wriggling. 'Whoa, little one, fancy giving your auntie a break? She's got a sore shoulder and you're probably not helping.'

'Thanks.' Charlie eased out the muscles in her neck as she passed the baby over to him to hold. 'She's getting a bit grizzly.'

He frowned at Stella, as if trying to solve a maths equation. 'Something to eat, maybe?'

'It's not long since she had a snack but we could try another one, I guess.'

He jiggled Stella up and down on his hip, blowing raspberries at her in a vain attempt to make the little girl laugh, to no avail. He grimaced. 'Raspberries usually work with my girls. Maybe she's tired?'

My girls. Her heart melted as he referenced Lily, Lola and Luna. 'Maybe. Mia said I could put her down in Harper's room.'

Lewis nodded. 'Great idea. You take her up and I'll grab her changing bag from the kitchen. We can give her some milk and see if it helps her drop off?'

So they really were the dream team now. 'Sure. Yes, thanks. The powder's in a little pot and you need to heat—'

'The milk carefully. And test the temperature on the back of my hand. I know.' He winked. 'I've got this. Go.'

Oh, Lewis. Her throat was suddenly raw and scratchy. She felt dejected that she couldn't give him the gift of fatherhood that he craved and was perfect for, yet her heart lifted to have him want to share this with her. She was a good auntie and would always hold Stella very close to her heart. She blinked back the stab of tears as she took Stella from him, feeling his heat and strength as he passed the baby over. Then she walked upstairs on wobbly legs, trying to put her attraction and sadness into a metaphorical box and leave it there.

She'd thought she'd got over the sadness years ago. And she could generally deal with it if it raised its head. She'd had therapy; she knew there was no surmounting the facts of her body's limits. There was no point in wishing for impossible things.

But it was the attraction that continually derailed her. She wanted him in so many ways.

And it was dangerous, making her reckless.

Making her forget all her promises to keep away.

CHAPTER THIRTEEN

LEWIS CAREFULLY OPENED the door into the dimly lit bedroom, and then paused, rooted to the spot.

Charlie was sitting in a nursing chair, cradling Stella and singing softly, a nursery lullaby. She was stroking the baby's head, staring lovingly down at her, while Stella's little fist bumped against Charlie's arm as she grizzled and fussed.

His chest hurt at the sight. Charlie was beautiful, that was all, stunning. And he hated that she would never get to hold her own child. He swallowed and tried to clear the lump in his throat.

'Hey,' he whispered, stepping into the room and closing the door against the loud, happy chatter of the party downstairs. 'Here's her bottle.'

'Thanks.' She looked up at him and smiled, taking the warm bottle and offering it to Stella. The baby immediately started to suck greedily. 'Oh, you were hungry, weren't you? I can't keep up with you.'

He watched Stella's breathless sucks. 'Yep, that definitely seems to be the answer.'

'I can't believe how much this baby eats.' She laughed. 'Hey, go down and talk to your friends. You don't have to stay here with me.'

Leaving them both here would be a wise thing to do, but he couldn't tear himself away. This was so intimate, so exactly what they'd dreamt about. It was too lovely to leave. He would just indulge himself for a few minutes and play that game of 'what if?'; what might have been; pretend they didn't have a million obstacles from their past pressing in on them. Just a few more moments.

'It's okay. I'll wait. You might need something else. How about a glass of wine? A plate of food?'

'No need. I'm fine, thanks.' She glanced at Stella and then back at him with an adorable smile. 'I think we've managed to get her off.'

'Sometimes it's the simplest of things, right? Peace and quiet and a full belly. That certainly works for me.'

'I remember. My mum used to say she'd never met anyone who ate as much as you did.' Charlie laughed. She was looking at him so fondly, the tension of the last few days gone from her face. The tension of their last two heart-breaking years together completely erased. She looked young and bright and ethereal in the orange glow from the night light.

He decided to focus on Stella because there was no good in doing or thinking anything else. And because the obstacles of the present threatened now too. 'There were a lot of new faces for her to take in down there; she might have been a bit overwhelmed.' He bent in front of Charlie and the milk-drunk baby. 'You want me to pop her in the cot?'

'Thanks. Yes. She's little but she's getting heavier every day.'

He slid his hands under the sleeping babe, very gently deposited her onto the cot mattress and covered her with a blanket. This whole scenario felt surreal: the warmth; the baby; Charlie. It was *cosy*.

He turned back to look at her. 'Are you ready to go back down?'

She wrinkled her nose and shook her head. 'Not quite.'

He sighed. 'I get it. Sometimes all those new faces are overwhelming for adults too. I'm sorry you don't know many people here.'

'It's fine. I want to make friends and all yours seem lovely. I just need a minute to catch my breath.' She giggled softly. 'Oh, my God, did you see poor Brin's face? I felt bad that I told him about our connection like that.'

'Poor Brin nothing.' Lewis chuckled. Making sure Stella was fast asleep and their voices wouldn't wake her, he slid down the wall and sat on the floor next to Charlie's chair. 'He's been trying to get us together since he set eyes on you. For some reason he seems to think we're a good fit.'

'For *some* reason?' She laughed hollowly. 'Maybe he sees us the way we used to see each other?'

Oh, the delicious, poignant naivety of youth. No one had ever been in love as much as they had. No one could possibly have known how it felt to be them, falling deeper and deeper, as if they'd been unbeatable for ever. He smiled at the memories bombarding his brain. 'I liked those days, back when we were starting out—dating, our wedding day...'

'Yes. Good times.' Her tone was as wistful as he felt. 'You remember when we were in sixth form and just started seeing each other, how I used to sneak out from home in the middle of the night and climb through your bedroom window?' She laughed. 'Good job you had a bungalow.'

'And when your parents found out and grounded you, I sneaked into your bedroom instead...via a tree-climb and a drain pipe. Almost broke my neck on more than two occasions.'

'We didn't care. It added to the drama of our...' She put her hand to her chest and swayed softly from side to side, then whispered, almost as if she couldn't bring herself to say the word, 'Love'.

Love that had shattered under pressure. He tried for a lighter note. 'You remember when Uncle Paul tripped and almost fell onto our uncut wedding cake?'

'And we all held our breath when his hand flew out as he careened towards the table. Luckily he righted himself before disaster struck.' She laughed. 'And Logan's best man speech. He was so funny.'

Lewis tutted at the memory of his brother spilling too many of Lewis's boyhood antics. 'I could have killed him at times.'

'Oh, everyone thought it was hilarious. Then all the brides-maids did a flash-mob dance and you...*you* knew all about it and never told me.' She nudged his leg with hers. 'We had the best wedding, Lewis.'

He felt the punch of pride now in his solar plexus as much as he had that day so long ago. The first time he'd seen her as she'd stepped into the little church, the sun haloing her from behind, had taken his breath away. 'I felt like I was the luckiest damned man in the world. I couldn't believe you'd chosen me.'

'Oh, Lewis. I was the lucky one.' Her hand slid down by the side of the chair next to him and he couldn't stop himself from taking her palm and stroking it. Then he slipped his fingers between hers. He heard her breathing hitch, felt a shift in the atmosphere, but she didn't let go.

They sat for a few minutes in silence. He listened to Stella's even breaths and his more staccato ones. He wondered what was going on in Charlie's head.

Then she inhaled and said, 'Lewis, can I ask you something?'

He dared not hope or think what it might be. 'Sure.'

'If it wasn't for me having to look after Lucy would you want a rerun of the other night?'

Yes. God, yes.

'If things weren't complicated? If we had no past? If we'd just met, two strangers?' Maybe here in the dark they could be honest about the way they felt because, in the real world, they couldn't admit that these feelings were growing.

She squeezed his hand. 'Or if none of the bad stuff had happened. Yes.'

'Then, yes. I wouldn't just want a rerun, I'd want more, Charlie.'

'Oh, God.' Silence lingered for a beat, then two. Then she breathed out. 'Me too.'

The baby stirred, a little cry that had him glancing over to the cot. He held his breath, wondering if he needed to go to her, but she seemed to settle on her own. His gaze drifted to a little device above the bed. 'Damn. Check the monitor—make sure it's not on.' The last thing they needed was an audience downstairs listening to their intimate confessions.

'I can't see a light on. We're good.' Charlie sighed and paused. 'Lewis…'

'Yes?'

There came another pause, then, 'The harder I try to keep away from you, the more I struggle.'

'*Charlie*. Please.' He closed his eyes and tried to control his stuttered exhale. It was too much; too much for him to handle. His heart hammered and his chest felt hollowed out. Because what did 'what if?' matter if they couldn't act on it? Being honest was a mistake. Staying up here was a mistake.

And yet he wanted it. He wanted her, wanted it all, so much that it was a physical ache he could not erase.

He was at risk here—serious risk. He'd tried so hard to

make things work before, and then had watched her walk away, and it had left him broken. He couldn't let her do it again, no matter how much he wanted her. So he slipped his fingers out from hers. 'Okay. Well, I'd better go see if Brin needs help with the barbecue.'

Then he forced himself to stand up and walk away.

Because, if he didn't leave right then, he would something they both might regret.

'This is baby Leo Hudson. Eight months old.' Lewis's voice sounded uncharacteristically strained as he lifted the fitting baby onto the trolley in the resus room. Sick babies did that to Charlie too. It didn't matter how long she'd been doing this job, or how many kids she treated, poorly babies tugged hard at every thread of maternal instinct she had.

She looked up into Lewis's eyes and her heart ached and jumped. She had an intense urge to reach for him and soothe away the pain in his eyes, but she refused to allow herself to be derailed from this emergency. This little one needed all their focus so they could fit the diagnosis jigsaw puzzle together. She nodded for him to continue.

'No medical history of note. Normal vaginal delivery at thirty-nine weeks. Generally well, but has been grizzly and snotty the last couple of days. Parents reported seeing some unusual twitching and jerking that has not stopped for a good hour and has worsened. No history of epilepsy or previous seizures. Airway is patent, oxygen administered, blood glucose normal. Temperature a little high at thirty-eight point one. IO Midazolam administered en route with no effect. Mum's just outside. Dad's followed in the car with two older children.'

'Thanks, Lewis. Arno,' she called to one of the senior nurses. 'Page Paeds, please—*urgently*. Tell them we have a status epilepticus. Someone please go talk to Mum and explain that we're doing all we can and I'll come talk to her when I get a chance.'

'I've explained some,' Lewis said. 'I'll go have a word in a minute. She said she'd wait in reception until her husband got here, but she's frantic with worry.'

'Understandable. Thanks. Take one of the nurses too; they'll be able to bring her in to see Leo once we've got him stable.' She knew Lewis would have built some rapport when he had attended the emergency. *Eight months old*—not much older than Stella. She could only imagine the way the mum was feeling, but she'd be in good hands with Lewis.

She grabbed the tiny oxygen mask and held it over the baby's mouth while she started her assessment. 'He's tachycardic with poor peripheral perfusion, pupils unreactive. Can I have a temperature reading please? And let's try another bolus of Midazolam.'

She was aware of Lewis's presence as they worked on the infant. By some miracle in the back of a moving ambulance, he'd managed to get IV access into Leo's tiny veins. He'd explained everything to the little baby, even though Leo wouldn't have a clue what was happening. It was comforting to have an extra pair of hands helping.

Then suddenly he wasn't there any more and she missed his strength and solid steadiness next to her. Was it her imagination that he was avoiding her? Every time he'd been in the department recently he'd barely glanced her way. Sure, he'd done his job professionally and efficiently, just as he was doing now, but there was no friendly chit chat afterwards. Maybe the closeness they'd shared on Saturday night had scared him away. Maybe she was over-thinking, and being a tad too sensitive. He was a busy man after all, and why would he specifically choose to chat to her at work?

Or maybe she was falling harder and quicker than she'd thought. Because, it had been six days since their heart-to-heart in Harper's bedroom and she'd burned every moment since just to see him again.

After she'd handed over to the paediatrics team, she stepped outside to get a breath of fresh air. From the back door of the emergency department she could see the hospital nursery and felt a pull to go and see Stella. Lately she'd been spending quite a lot of her break time with her niece and she realised it wasn't just to keep Stella happy: it fed something inside Charlie too.

She saw Seung walk by and called over, 'Hey, I'm well past due my break. Just popping over to the nursery. I'll be back soon as.'

'No worries.' Seung waved. 'Paeds are sorting Leo out. Arno's with Mum and Dad, and they're having a cup of tea before they all go up to Peter Pan Ward. Everywhere else is quiet.'

'Hush! Do not say that. Don't! You'll jinx us.' She waved back and headed across the car park for some serious snuggles with her favourite six-month-old.

But it wasn't Stella or Leo on her mind right now. It was Lewis. It felt as if she would never get used to working with him. Ever since the barbecue, all her shifts since had coincided with his. Which meant she couldn't get away from her admission in that darkened room: she was struggling to keep away from him and, in an ideal world, she'd want more and take more.

And she would never forget the tender stroke of his hand, the way she'd wanted to sink into another kiss with him or the deep yearning she had to be in his arms, in his bed, in his life.

Yes, back in his life, which would be a one-way ticket to heartbreak.

She'd been both glad and sad when he'd gone back down to the party, because she'd been feeling so mixed up she hadn't known what to do. So she'd stayed upstairs for as long as she could without appearing impolite to her hosts, until Mia had come looking for her and coaxed her down for some food. Of course, somehow she'd ended up sitting next to Lewis, and the rest of the evening had been pure torture.

Every time she'd looked round, he'd been there with his smile, his dark eyes glittering. She'd caught his scent on the air and felt the whisper of his breath as he laughed. And with every second she spent with him the torture had intensified. They both knew the truth of their need but she knew they could not, would not, *should not* act on it—not again.

It had almost been a relief for him to drop her home, her hands mercifully too full of baby and bags to reach for him and tug him close. A relief to close the door behind her and be free of his tempting presence. Yet here he was, every day in her space, at her place of work, tempting and torturing her. And, of course, there he was now, in her direct path, putting something into the boot of his car.

She closed her eyes and took a moment to erase any give-away facial expressions, trying to act normally instead of jumping into his arms. 'Hey, Lewis.'

'Hey. Finished up for the day?' He was standing right where they'd had their first 'this time round' kiss. Her body flushed at the memory. Since then they'd vowed not to get involved and yet had shared a wonderful night together. They'd admitted feelings for each other, but agreed they couldn't act on them again.

No wonder she was confused.

She found him a smile. 'Not yet. I've got another couple of hours to go. Just going to see Stella in my break time. I feel a need to hug her.' She didn't want to admit to the rest of her work colleagues that she'd been shaken up dealing with a sick baby, but she knew Lewis would understand.

'Yep, I get that. Sometimes a hug works wonders.' He nodded. 'How's the little lad doing?'

It seemed she didn't even need to explain why she had the urge to see her niece. 'We managed to stop the fitting. He's on his way up to the ward now and stabilised, but it'll be a while until we know what's causing the seizures.'

He stepped closer, his expression concerned. 'You okay, though?'

'Yep.' She blew out a breath. 'You know how it is, sick kids are hard to deal with sometimes.'

'Yeah. I dread the day I get a call out for Lola, Lily or Luna.'

She shuddered. 'Here's hoping that will never happen.'

'Indeed. It was bad enough that I had to attend your accident. It's always worse when you know the person involved.'

She hadn't actually given any thought to how he must have felt seeing her potentially injured, only to how he'd felt seeing her in the flesh again. 'Well, I for one am very glad it was you.'

'Don't you dare do that to me again.' He gave her a rueful smile.

'I'll try not to. Once is enough.' Then she remembered something that would make his smile grow. 'Oh, I had a call from the High Dependency Unit this morning. Graham's been transferred out of ICU and has been asking to see us.'

'Really?' It was lovely to see the genuine and huge smile bloom on his face, all trace of worry defused. 'I never get to see patients once they're out of my hands.'

'I was thinking about popping up there after my shift ends. Maybe we could go together?' It made sense, didn't it?

But his expression clouded. 'Oh. I don't know...'

'We're going to see a patient, Lewis. I'm not going to...' *Oh, hell. How to broach this?* 'Not going to say more of the things I said on Saturday.'

'Oh. Right.' He breathed out, looking a little taken aback and also relieved. 'No, me neither. I guess I could come with you. I'm off for the next couple of days so it would save me coming back into town to visit him. And, to be honest, I do really want to see the guy that survived CPR in the pouring rain.'

Flash-flooding florecast.

'Me too.' Grinning at the memory of what they'd done after saving Graham's life, she checked the time. 'Say, two and a half hours?'

'Sure. I've got paperwork to catch up on anyway so I could do that until you're ready.' He slammed the boot closed. 'I'll meet you outside HDU.'

Despite everything she'd promised herself, her tummy tumbled at the thought of seeing him again so soon. 'Can't wait.'

'Me neither. It'll be good to see him. Enjoy the Stella hugs. Say hi from me. See you soon, Charlie.' He turned and flashed her a look that was filled with the kind of promise that had her knees turning to jelly.

It's not a date, silly woman. He couldn't wait to see Graham, not to see her.

It was the way things were going to be. Had to be—two colleagues doing colleague-type things. Friends doing friend-type things. Because, upstairs at Brin's in that little dark room, she'd found the courage to tell him what she wanted and he'd let go of her hand and walked away, telling her through his actions that he was still too bruised, or hurt, to try again. Or that he was protecting himself...*from her*...and that thought made her heart hurt.

But it didn't stop the wish for the hugs she so badly needed to come from him. Or the senseless hope for the promise of more.

Because she couldn't ignore it any longer: she wanted more. Wanted more chats about their day and the shared patients they saw; more time with him; more kisses, more hugs; more *everything* with Lewis.

And that was going to be her downfall.

CHAPTER FOURTEEN

His HEART TRIPPED as he found Charlotte outside HDU. She'd changed out of her scrubs into a pretty pale-pink summer dress and white cardigan. Her hair hung loosely around her shoulders. *God,* he loved her hair. And she was carrying chocolates he recognised from the hospital shop in the lobby downstairs. It was so sweet she'd had the forethought to do that.

She beamed at him, excitement clear in her expression. 'Hey, Lewis.'

'Hey.' His immediate instinct was to reach out his hand for her to hold but he reined it in. So far, since Saturday, his avoidance tactics had been working. The less time he spent with her, the better. But, the moment she'd invited him to see the guy they'd worked on together, he'd folded. He knew he'd have folded at some time. He just couldn't keep away from her. It seemed as though she was a magnetic force he was destined to spin around.

He gestured to the door. 'Should we?'

'Indeed.' Her smile was infectious.

He buzzed the intercom and they were let in by the ward clerk, who showed them to Graham's bed. He was sitting upright, propped up by pillows. His arm was in a sling, his bruised chest dotted with sticky heart-monitor pads and he had a nasal cannula taped to his cheek delivering oxygen. His frail-looking features lit up as they approached and he raised his good arm in a small wave.

'Graham, hello.' Lewis gently shook the man's hand. 'I'm Lewis and this is Charlie. We're the paramedic and doctor who just happened to be in the right place at the right time a couple of weeks ago. Well, you're certainly looking better than the last time we met.'

'I hope so.' Graham's voice was weak even though he was clearly on the mend. 'Sorry if I don't recognise you, but I can't remember much of it.'

Lewis smiled. 'That's absolutely fine. You were a bit out of it.'

Understatement of the year.

Charlie sat down next to the bed. 'It was a hell of a night. All that rain didn't help. But we're so glad to see that you're out of the woods. Hope you feel up to eating these soon.' She handed Graham the box of chocolates.

'Thank you. I hope so too.' Graham nodded. He looked first at Charlie and then at Lewis, as if committing them to memory. 'They tell me that you two saved my life.'

Lewis glanced over at Charlie. 'Well, we did our best to keep your heart going until we could hand you over to the team. You're obviously one hell of a fighter, Graham.'

'You need to be these days. But I'm glad you two were on my side.' He laughed, which brought on a coughing fit. His monitor started to beep and a nurse came running over. She tutted and frowned, but her tone was jolly. 'Graham, honestly. What do I keep telling you about overdoing things?'

'I'm fine. I'm fine.' He waved her away weakly then looked at Charlie. 'I want you to know how much I appreciate what you both did. I owe you my life.'

'It's our pleasure. We were lucky to be there to help.' She

smiled at him and patted his hand. 'Now, we don't want to put you under any more stress or tire you out, so we'll say good bye for now. We'll pop back again soon and, in the meantime, keep getting better, Graham.'

The old man smiled and nodded, exhaustion bruising his eyes. 'What a lovely couple you are. Thank you again.'

Couple. It seemed as though everyone thought they should be or could be a couple...except the couple themselves.

Lewis glanced at Charlie. Her cheeks bloomed red, which was interesting, because she'd handled telling Brin the truth about their relationship so easily the other day. She scrunched up her nose as she smiled. 'Just doing our jobs. Get well soon, Graham.'

Lewis's heart felt lighter as they walked out of the ward and Charlie's smile was wide, her eyes dancing with light as she said, 'That was lovely.'

'Always great to meet a success story,' he agreed. But it was the happy glow in Charlie's eyes that was making his heart thump more quickly, not pride in doing his job well. She looked almost ethereal in that flowing dress. All he wanted to do was capture her mouth and taste that smile.

They wandered through the hospital and out into the car park, chatting about success stories and the weird and unusual cases they'd seen. So far, so collegial.

But once out in the car park she stopped, her expression morphing from animated to cautious. 'Lewis?'

His heart started to hammer against his chest. Where was this going? 'Yes?'

'Look, I just want you to know that you don't have to avoid me at work.'

'What do you mean?' He knew exactly what she meant.

She looked stricken. 'It just feels as if every time we meet on the department, you're very keen to make a quick retreat from my presence.'

Damn right he was keen not to spend any time with her. It was self-preservation, really. The more time he spent with her, the more torture it became. He *wanted* her…always. 'No. That's not it, Charlie…'

'Okay, maybe I'm being sensitive then. Sorry, forget I mentioned it. It's just… Oh, look, never mind.' Her brightness and elation of a few minutes ago now flattened, she turned away.

Now he felt as if he was gaslighting her, just because he wanted to protect his own heart from further damage, and he couldn't do that. He reached out and touched her shoulder. 'Wait, Charlie. I'm sorry. You're right: I have been trying to spend less time in the emergency department, if I can.'

'Oh?' She turned back to him, looking hurt. 'Because of me?'

Ugh. He'd been trying to be honest with her as much as he could. She kept asking him, pushing him to tell her how he was feeling, and she was showing him how, so why couldn't he do it?

He took a breath. 'Um…okay. So, what we said on Saturday… It's been playing on my mind—occupying it, actually.' He smiled but he knew it had a hint of wariness in it. 'I'm confused, if I'm honest. You coming back has thrown me for six. I need some space to get my head round everything. More for my benefit than yours.'

Her frown deepened. 'That makes me feel so many things, Lewis. I'm upset that you feel you have to actively avoid me and I'm so…so sad we can't be friends. Especially after what we said on Saturday.' She swallowed, her eyes large and soft. 'I thought I was doing okay, you know? But, the truth is, I'm not okay. I miss the closeness we once had. Sometimes, I just want to talk to you.'

As with today; after attending to a sick baby, she'd needed a hug and had had to get it from her niece, not from him.

'Oh, Charlie.' His heart felt as if it were turning inside out. He hated to see her upset, and because of something he'd done. Before he could stop himself, he'd pulled her into his arms. He stroked her hair as she lent her head against his chest. 'I'm here for you. Talk to me any time you want.'

She looked up at him and smiled almost shyly. Then she turned her head away, holding him tight, hugging him to her. As they stood there in that desolate car park, he felt the rise and fall of her chest and heard the soft sound of her breath. Awareness prickled through him. Something changed in the atmosphere around them, like a buzz of electricity sparking through him. His skin tingled at each pressure point where his body touched hers.

Her head nuzzled against his chin. He closed his eyes, trying to force away the urge to kiss her again, trying to wish away the growing erection between them. But she made a little sound in her throat and in the next moment all his fight was snapped into a thousand pieces, leaving just desire and heat winding through him.

'Sometimes I want more, Lewis. Sometimes I don't want to talk at all.' Her mouth was close to his ear, her warm breath tickling his skin. He turned his face to hers and she was so close, so very close. 'Just touch. And… I know that's not fair, because I can't give you what you want…the family you want.'

Right now, *she* was all he wanted. All he'd ever wanted. Her pupils were huge and her breathing fast. Her eyelids fluttered closed as her fingers stroked his back. Her hot body pressed against him in all the right places, her breasts against his chest, her core against his growing erection.

Then he couldn't control anything any longer. He walked her back towards his car and pressed her against it, capturing her mouth in his. 'Charlie. God, Charlie...'

Next he was kissing, kissing and kissing her, telling her in his kisses exactly what he wanted: that he couldn't bear to see her confused or upset; that he couldn't keep holding back; that he'd rather die than not be able to slide inside her, to hold her, to drown in her kisses.

'I had to avoid you because all I want to do is this.' He dragged his lips from hers, framing her face with his palms. 'You are the only woman I've ever wanted, Charlie. My Charlie Rose.'

He kissed her again, long, slowly and sensuously, and she whimpered...or was it him?

'I love the way you kiss me. I love...' She suddenly pulled back, shaking and breathless. 'Shoot. I...um... I have to go pick up Stella from nursery.'

I love... You...? Was that what she'd been about to say?

No. No. No. That was not where they were heading. He couldn't allow it full-stop. She'd loved him last time, but not enough to stay. Not enough to try and make things work. She loved his kisses, that was all.

'Yeah. I should go too.' His voice was gravelly as reality hit him hard. Firstly, they were kissing in the staff car park where anyone could see them. And secondly, and far more importantly, they'd stepped right over that line again. Blurred everything into a kiss, into hot need, into something from which he didn't know he could disentangle himself.

She swallowed, her hand on her chest as if trying to calm down her racing heart. 'And I need to check on Lucy too. She had another dose of chemo last week, so this week is where she starts to feel yuck again.'

'Of course. Of course.' He watched her walk away, feeling the pull to walk with her, to stay by her side. To talk whenever she needed him to, to listen, to soothe and to kiss.

But he couldn't ask where this was going or what this blurring of boundaries might mean. Couldn't put her in that situation to make rational choices when she was so involved with caring for her family. And he had no idea himself what could happen next, only that with every new moment spent with her…every kiss, every touch and with every *I love*…he was drawn back under her spell.

And he didn't know if he could fight it any more. Even though he had to, if he was going to get out sane.

She tried to keep away. She spent about thirty-two solid hours tending to Lucy's and Stella's every need when she wasn't at work. She focused on helping them get through this difficult week and tried to put Lewis to the back of her mind.

It was a futile exercise, of course. Because when she wasn't holding Lucy's hair back as she vomited, or changing Stella's nappy, cooing her to sleep, cajoling her to eat or reading her a picture book, the only thing she thought about was Lewis.

She still wanted him.

She wanted him right now, standing outside his house, wondering if she had actually gone mad with need, desire or… whatever it was that she refused to put a name to. Because if she acknowledged the depth of her feelings she'd have to walk away. So she told herself it was lust and possibly loneliness. That both those things could be easily remedied by sex, by friendship, maybe a combination of the two.

Friends with benefits—would he agree to that?

She pressed the doorbell and heard the echoing ring inside. She waited. Her heart thudded as she craned to hear thumping footsteps.

Nothing.

She pressed the bell again and waited. Maybe he wasn't here after all. Maybe he was fast asleep and couldn't hear the bell. Maybe he knew it was her and was choosing to ignore her, like a sensible person, not lust-drunk, would.

Eventually she turned away and started to walk down the path.

'Charlie?'

She whipped round, her breath stalling in her chest as the sight of him, in an old grey T-shirt and tight black boxer shorts made her feel dizzy with need. Could he look any sexier?

'Charlie?' His face crumpled as he reached out his hand, immediately worried. 'What's wrong?'

Her courage started to fail her. But she had to say something. 'Can I come in?'

'Sure.' He opened the door wider and let her walk in front of him into his lounge, switching on the wall lights, bringing a warm, soft glow. 'What's happened? Is everything all right?'

She turned to look at him, her heart pounding in her ears. 'Everything is fine. Don't worry.'

'Is Lucy okay? Stella?'

'Yes.' She smiled at his concern. 'Calm down, Lewis. They're fine. They're fast asleep.'

He shook his head. 'So, why are you here?'

Such a bad idea after all. She sighed and chuckled. 'It never used to be this difficult. For God's sake, do I have to spell it out? This is the adult woman version of sneaking out of my house in the middle of the night.'

He gasped, then laughed…more of a groan. 'Charlie Jade Rose—this is a booty call? What the hell?'

'What can I say? I wanted to see you. I couldn't sleep and wondered if you couldn't either.'

'As it happens, I was wide awake.' He met her gaze, suddenly heated. 'Thinking about you, actually.'

Thinking about what, exactly? 'You took your time answering the door.'

He ran his hand through his hair, eyes wide. 'I didn't think for a minute that it could be you. I thought it was kids messing about.'

She took a breath, thinking about what they used to get up to in his bedroom, in *their* bedroom, back when things had been fun. 'Maybe we could be.'

He swallowed and grinned. Clearly he remembered too. 'Charlie…' His voice was guttural, base.

It was probably meant to be a warning. A reminder of everything they'd agreed. But it sounded like the sexiest growl she'd ever heard.

'So, tell me to go if you're not…up for it…' She stepped towards him, or he stepped towards her; she wasn't sure. But suddenly he was up close, his forehead against hers, his hand snaking round her waist.

'How did you know my address?'

'Is it very lame to say I remembered from way back when we were checking to see if we were neighbours?' She chuckled. 'Plus, your car is parked in the drive.'

'Ah.' He nodded, swallowing hard as he looked her up and down, his gaze landing on her mouth. 'Doesn't take a genius, then.'

'And you're worrying about details and I'm standing here wanting you. Does my seduction technique need work?' She raised her eyebrows in question as she snaked her arms around his waist. 'It never used to fail me. You used to welcome me with a kiss and take me straight to bed.'

The cloud of hesitation that seemed to have been hovering over him dissipated. He laughed, his fingers trailing over her cheek. 'You have a seduction technique?'

'Hey, you.' She giggled. 'I can seduce.'

'Really? Interesting. Tell me when you're starting.' Tongue in cheek, he grinned, pretending to be immune to her advances when the tent in his boxer shorts told her he very much wasn't immune at all.

But he did have a point: she actually had to do or say something. Shrugging off her coat, she revealed her matching black lace bra and panties. God, she'd taken such a risk coming here in the middle of the night dressed like this. But it could be worth every threaded breath, every second-guess, every kiss, every touch, every stroke of his fingertips against her skin. Every second spent in his arms. 'You're telling me you hadn't thought about Sunday morning sex?'

'It's still…' His eyes darted to the wall clock. 'Oh, wait. Yes, Sunday morning. *Charlie*…'

Then his mouth found hers in a greedy, desperate kiss. He palmed her breast and she reached for his pants, each of them stripping each other in a haze of clumsy, desperate hunger.

Still kissing her as if he never wanted to let go, he tugged her to the bedroom and laid her on the bed. She reached for him, stroking her fingers down his length. He was so hard…. for her.

After this, she would go.

Sunday morning sex—just sex. Just friends and sex, and that was all.

She swallowed back the rawness in her throat. Whatever

label they put on it, it was hot and irresistible. She put aside their promises, ignoring the beat of anxiety at the back of her mind, and sank into this, with him—with Lewis.

He shuddered at her touch and groaned again. 'Jeez, Charlie. What you do to me…'

She whispered into his ear, 'Is what?'

'You turn me on so much.'

'Aha.' She slicked kisses across his throat. 'How?'

'You're supposed to be seducing me, right? Not the other way round.' He laughed and whispered, 'What do you want, Charlotte?'

'Oh, it's Charlotte now?' She laughed, then the laughter died in her throat as she thought about what she wanted.

I want you to hold me, to hug me. To be with me. I want you inside me. I want you to… I want you, Lewis. I want you, so much I can't breathe.

'I want to kiss you, Lewis. I want you to fill me. I want to ride you.'

'Jeez…' His breath stuttered on the inhale.

'Do you want that too?' She kissed his jaw, his bottom lip and his top lip, stroking him gently up and down, up and down… 'Tell me what you want.'

'I want to slide deep inside you. I want to feel you around me.' He turned onto his side and slid his hand between her legs, arrowing for her core and rubbing the sensitive spot right… *there.*

He stroked her, then slid his fingers inside her, making her squirm, contract and writhe against him. He was telling her what he needed. *Hell…* Sex had always been great with Lewis, but he'd never actually told her what he wanted. They'd just gone by feel and instinct before. It had been enough back then. She'd loved the way they'd made love. But this was next-level sexy. She was breathing so fast, she could barely get enough air into her lungs.

Her grip on him tightened and he groaned in delight. She was so dizzy with need she could barely form words. 'I want…'

'What else do you want, Charlie?'

'Everything.' She wanted this, wanted him. Wanted what they'd had years ago, before it had all gone wrong. Wanted this new thing they had going, this honesty, this need.

She'd only ever wanted him.

He lay back and lifted her onto his lap. *'God*, Charlie. I need to be inside you.'

Hot, electric need coursed through her and she knew she was hanging on the edge. One move, one thrust of him inside her, and she'd be undone.

'Now. Please. *Now.*' She straddled his thighs, his erection hard against her core. She positioned herself over him and lowered herself with a moan. And he was inside her again, rocking slowly, and it was so intense and perfect; perfectly intense.

She closed her eyes as their rhythm quickened, catching her breath in stuttered gasps. The pressure rising at her core sent flashes of sparks and light flickering across her skin, over her, inside her, deep and white-hot. She felt him ripple, heard him grind out her name and she clung on and rode with him until they were both crying out, mouths welded together in a messy, needy, hungry kiss.

Together. First and last.

Her Lewis. Her love. Her always.

CHAPTER FIFTEEN

IT TOOK SOME time for her breathing to steady and for her to feel emotionally anchored enough to climb off his thighs and snuggle against him. He wrapped his arms around her, hugging her the way she needed. If she was honest, that was what she'd come for, after all. Making love had been an accumulation of her need for him, all of him, but she'd needed to be with him because she'd simply been unable to keep away. She'd wanted *his* hug. Wanted his arms around her. She missed him.

'Sunday morning sex. The best ever.' He stroked her shoulder, his tone soft. 'Lucy didn't mind you coming out?'

'I didn't ask. It was the middle of the night, Lewis. They were both fine and well and fast asleep, and I'm not planning on staying long. No harm done. They won't even know I'm gone.'

'Oh. You're not staying?'

Feeling his frown against her neck, she turned round to look at him. 'Don't frown, Lewis. You know I have to go. It's just like old times, right? I have to be back in my bed before everyone wakes up. We have maybe another hour.'

'Makes it even more foolish to waste more time, then.' He pushed her hair back from her face and kissed her again. This time it was slow and tender and filled with so much emotion, it made her heart ache.

How could they be just friends when there was this much

emotion between them, this much connection? Was it too early to talk about what next? Yes, it was too early. She couldn't push him into a corner. Better to enjoy this silly, fun sex.

She broke the kiss and snuggled into the crook of his arm, closing her eyes, her head on his chest. He wrapped his other arm round her and she felt the strong, steady beat of his heart against her ribcage.

None of this felt silly. It felt consequential. Her heart had opened to him again. She stroked his forearm and closed her eyes. Being held like this made her feel as if nothing in the world could hurt her. She felt safe and secure. Nothing bad could happen in this haven of his strength, of their…their what? Their craving? Their need? Their love?

Love?

What?

Her eyes flickered open. Had she fallen in love with him again?

Had she ever stopped loving him?

Had she? She'd tried. She'd moved to the other side of the world to stop loving him but it hadn't worked. So the simple answer was no. And the most difficult, heart-wrenching answer was still…no. She'd always loved him and, instead of dimming, it was growing, glowing brighter and stronger. And she couldn't help it, she couldn't stop it.

And so what if…what if he didn't feel the same? What if…? She knew the 'what if?' Her stomach went into freefall.

Stupid, stupid, stupid Charlie.

He wanted kids and she couldn't have them—end of. That was the brutal truth. He would tell her it didn't matter. And she'd have to watch him coo at other people's babies and keep on pretending.

And her heart would break.

Oblivious to the sudden crisis in her heart, he lazily drew circles over her hip as he said, 'One thing I regret…well, I regret a lot of things about how we broke up…but we should have talked more…'

He didn't finish the sentence.

Completely alert now, she propped herself up on her elbow to look at him. 'What do you mean?'

His eyes were closed, but his breathing hitched. 'I was too closed off. But…' His voice trailed off again, as if he was rethinking the sentence or the whole conversation.

'But *what*, Lewis?'

He looked at her, eyes dark, haunted almost. Then he shook his head, as if shaking away his thoughts. 'It's… Ah, look, nothing. It's…too heavy for this time of night. You have to go soon, and that's okay.' He smiled but it was kind of sad. 'You have other commitments now.'

But…what?

Should we adopt? What about surrogacy? How about fostering? How about moving back in together? How about my giving up all my hopes and dreams for you? How about falling deeper in love? Were those the things he meant, those things he wasn't actually going to say again? The things he didn't want to talk about.

All the emotions were tangling up inside her and the only respite she ever seemed to have was when they were making love. For a few amazing minutes she could forget the past, but then it would barrel into her, along with all the reasons why they couldn't do this. 'Please, Lewis, I want to hear what you have to say.'

He rolled onto his back and stared up at the ceiling.

She waited, barely breathing.

He looked at her briefly, then away. 'We can't have kids.'

'*I* can't have kids, Lewis. You? You could probably have a whole football team of mini-mes if you wanted to.'

His eyes flashed at her words and that hurt her the most. He had options. He had a chance and he still wanted that; he could not refute the obvious minute flicker of hope at her words. But he shook his head. 'There are other ways to be happy, right?'

'Like what? Please don't say you'll give up your dream for me. Please don't give up your chance for a family, to be a dad. And please don't put that decision on me.'

He frowned. 'What do you mean?'

Okay, so they were going to talk about this. It felt as if a huge weight was crushing her chest. 'I don't want you to promise me something and then regret it down the line. Give me up for a woman who can give you children. I couldn't bear that.'

'Charlie. Please don't think like that. That's not what I'm saying. I'm saying you must never give up that hope.'

'Oh, the hope thing again?' She sighed, her heart hurting. They'd been down this road before. *Keep believing, Charlie. Everything's going to be okay.* Things had not been okay.

His jaw tightened. 'There are other things we could do.'

'Like get a dog?'

'Yes, if you want. But there's also adoption or surrogacy.' *Oh. Okay.*

Breathing out, she ventured, 'In New Zealand? The odds are very much against us. There aren't enough babies up for adoption and surrogacy has to be altruistic; it's not like we can pay someone to have a baby for us.'

But there was a chance. It wasn't impossible. A tiny flicker of hope fluttered in her chest. They were talking about this. *We*: he was talking about them as a couple. He was considering options.

Which meant things had gone too far already. Because no

amount of wanting him to say that he loved her, that nothing could come between them or that they had options, would change the facts. The same facts that had influenced their break-up. He still wanted a child of his own, regardless of what he said. She could see the longing every time he looked at a child or held a baby. And she couldn't give him one.

More than that…so much more…she wouldn't be able to bear seeing his realisation that he'd chosen the wrong woman. She couldn't risk him leaving her. That was something she'd never recover from. She was scared of the strength of her feelings for him and the vulnerability that instilled in her.

Because she loved him. She'd never stopped loving him. Hell, she'd adored him since sixth form and that love still burned strong inside her. But it was one thing to love him from a distance, another to love him up close…and wait for the truth to dawn on him that she would not be enough.

Her phone from downstairs intruded into the weighted silence. She held her breath and listened. 'Did you hear that?'

'Your phone?' He sat up.

'It's the early hours; everyone should be asleep. It's either Lucy or our parents.' Neither of them phoning at this time would be good news. 'I've got to go see who it is. It could be important.'

Throwing on his T-shirt, she ran down to the lounge, grabbed her phone from her bag and her heart constricted.

'It's Lucy,' she shouted up to Lewis. 'There must be something wrong. She never rings me.' She pressed the answer buttons and heard her sister's terrified cries. 'Charlie, please, where are you? I need you. Please come home. Please.'

'Wh-what's happened?' Charlie could only imagine something terrible.

A sob came, then another. 'Please just come home.'

'Of course. I'm on my way.' Her heart drummed against her ribcage as she turned to Lewis who was now standing in front of her, dressed in T-shirt and shorts. 'I've got to go.'

Face set in determination, he nodded. 'I'll grab your clothes. I'm coming with you.'

But she put her hand on his chest, shaking her head.

This was all her fault. She'd sneaked out instead of staying where she would have been all along. She'd given in to temptation, put her own needs first again. Her needs before those of Lewis…who would have been asleep still if she hadn't come booty calling. Her needs before those of her her sister and her niece.

Lewis's dark eyes bored into her. She knew him well enough to know he wanted to help and didn't like not being able to. Feeling helpless was something she'd experienced for a while; she knew exactly how it felt.

'No. No, Lewis. You can't come with me. I'm sorry.' She needed to be with her sister. Just the two of them, not with Lewis.

Not Lewis. Stark reality hit her hard: not Lewis…

They couldn't keep doing this and pretending everything would work out well. She couldn't keep bruising her heart. She had to, finally, put a stop to this. She shook her head again, not wanting to say things she knew she had to say. She'd said them all once before then she'd walked away.

He looked at her and a dozen questions ran across his gaze. She shook her head.

Don't make me say anything else. They'd got carried away.

But he squeezed her hand; either he didn't realise what she was trying to say or he didn't want to acknowledge it. 'Okay, you know where I am if you need me.'

'Thanks. But this is something I need to do on my own.'

Words she'd said before. She walked to the door and closed it behind her, heart aching, all on repeat.

It wasn't any easier the second time around.

She found Lucy bent over the toilet bowl, her eyes red-rimmed, her pale, too-thin body shaking inside her winter pyjamas. Fleecy pyjamas in the height of summer—poor Lucy was always cold these days. Charlie gasped, ran across the cold tiles and wrapped her arms round her sister's shoulders. 'Hey, girl. Lucy, what's wrong, darling?'

Her sister groaned. 'I've been attached to this loo for the last hour and I feel like absolute crap. But...' She held up a fistful of her beautiful Titian hair and her face crumpled. 'Worse than anything else, my hair's falling out, in clumps.'

The Rose crowning glory, the hair they'd hated and loved in equal measure growing up. They'd been warned it would happen after the chemo but it wasn't something they'd really talked about, maybe hoping they'd never have to face it. Charlie felt tears pricking her eyes but she forced them back. She would be her sister's tower of strength here. She would not cry. 'Oh, honey, I'm so sorry.'

Lucy sat back looking defeated and dejected. 'I wasn't ready for this to happen. I pretended I was going to be different to everyone else. I know I shouldn't care about how I look, but I do. I don't want to be bald. I don't want...any of this.'

Charlie's heart felt as if it were breaking from leaving Lewis amidst such confusion, and now seeing her sister in pieces. 'It's cruel, Lucy.'

'Yes, it is. I don't want this. I just want to be able to spend happy, lovely time with my daughter and my sister. Bloody cancer. And I'm ranting now too.' She gave a sniff and the faintest hint of a rueful smile. 'Sorry about that too.'

'You can rant and shout and scream all you need. None of this is fair, none of it. Not the lump or the cancer or the surgery or the chemo that makes you sick. And definitely not your beautiful hair. But if your hair's falling out, it means the medicine is working, right?'

'I suppose.' Lucy wiped her eyes with the back of her hand. 'I'm sorry if I gave you a fright. Were you at Lewis's house?'

Oh, Lewis... They hadn't finished their conversation and everything was up in the air. Neither of them had been brave enough to face the truth and say it. They'd grasped at one more chance to be together, to sink into each other's arms. 'Yes. I was only gone a couple of hours. I was about to head home anyway.'

'I'm sorry I interrupted your night.'

Charlie squeezed her sister in a warm hug. 'Never say sorry for what you're going through, Luce. I love you. *I'm* sorry I wasn't here when you needed me.'

'You are, hun. You're here all of the time. You work, sleep and look after me. I know that.'

She wiped her sister's forehead with a damp flannel then helped her to stand. 'I won't leave you again, I promise.'

But Lucy chuckled and put her head on Charlie's shoulder, leaning heavily on her as they walked slowly to her bedroom. 'Hey, don't make promises you can't keep.'

Charlie had tried to tell Lewis that, hadn't she? That good intentions were just that: good intentions. They weren't fixed in stone. Not that she'd ever leave her sister again to cope with this on her own, but she could. Just like Lewis could promise to stay with her and then leave when someone or something else came along. That was the risk, wasn't it, the risk with love? You put all your dreams into one person and hoped they'd stick with you. Hoped they'd stay.

Lucy slumped heavily on to her bed. Charlie lifted her sister's legs under the sheets and surreptitiously disposed of the fallen copper strands on her pillow. Her mind was made up. 'Well, obviously I'll be at work some of the time, but I'll be here for you, Lucy. Always. Lewis... Well, Lewis is only going to be a friend from now on. A proper friend, nothing more.'

'Don't put yourself second. Live your life, Charlie. You have so much to give.'

Not the right things for Lewis, though.

'I'm here. I'm not going anywhere.'

But he'd broached the subject of options, something they'd never managed to do five years ago. He'd brought it up. He'd been thinking about it.

I'm not going anywhere.

Why did she believe herself and not Lewis?

Because she knew that vows and promises could be broken by hardship and struggle. She knew, because she'd broken them herself.

So how could she trust anyone else to stay when she hadn't?

CHAPTER SIXTEEN

HE'D HANDLED IT BADLY. He'd clammed up right at the time when he should have been more open. But he hadn't known where they stood, especially after agreeing it had just been a friend thing, a booty call. Had it just been fun or was it more? Now it couldn't be anything, he realised that, because she'd be terrified of leaving her sister again.

He knocked on the front door, wondering whether this was a mistake. Charlie opened the door and peered out with wary, tired eyes. She was wearing cute shortie pyjamas, her hair was messy and, given that it was four o'clock in the afternoon, that was unusual. But she gave him a small smile. 'Hey. This is a surprise.'

'You left your purse. Thought I'd drop it by in case you needed it.' He held it out to her.

She opened the door a little further and took her purse from him. 'Thanks. It must have fallen out of my bag when I was in such a hurry to get back here.'

'Not surprising. You left in a whirl of panic. I thought I might see you at work to give it back to you, but they tell me you've been off for a few days.'

'Yes. I've taken a couple of carer's days.'

He should have known that, if they'd been involved in any way. But she hadn't answered his messages and hadn't sent any of her own. What was he meant to do with that—just walk away? Pretend that they hadn't made love or that they hadn't reconnected deeper and harder than before? 'I wanted to make sure you're okay. I don't want to come in, I just wanted to let you know I'm here for you. How's Lucy?'

Charlie's voice softened and she smiled sadly. 'She's trying to get some sleep. The chemo makes her sick and now her hair's falling out too.'

He looked at Charlie's messy beautiful hair and his gut lurched. 'Damn. I'm so sorry. You know there are charities that can help her feel better about the way she looks?'

'Yeah. I grabbed some leaflets from work last week. I just haven't got round to reading any of them yet.'

He watched as guilt flitted across her face. 'It's not a sin to want some relief for yourself too.'

'You mean sneaking out in the middle of the night?' Her eyebrows rose. 'Like a teenager?'

'Yeah. Time out.'

'Well, I'm not a teenager, Lewis. And nothing you can say will make me feel better about not being here when my sister needed me.' She shook her head and he knew that that conversation was dead in the water before it began.

A little cry came from inside the house.

'Ugh. Stella needs entertaining and we're both exhausted. Bless her.' She looked distraught, torn, sad and guilty all rolled into one. She turned round and called out, 'Hush, sweetie. It's okay, Stella baby, I'm coming.'

Here was something he could help with, at least. 'Do you want me to take her out for an hour, so you can get some rest?'

'Oh.' She blinked and looked sorely tempted but shook her head, raising her voice over the increasingly loud cries. 'Oh, well…no. No, thanks all the same.'

'You could do with some rest too, right? The carers need to be cared for.'

She pressed her lips together. The connection they'd had on Sunday morning was hanging by a thread. He could see she'd closed herself off. She was barely coping with her responsibilities here. Did she feel he was a responsibility too?

Finally, she nodded. 'Okay, yes. Thanks, Lewis. I owe you.'

'You owe me nothing. It's okay, I've got plenty of time. I'm on earlies this week.' Although he'd have moved heaven and earth to help her, taken carer's days off too if she'd needed him to, phoned in sick or given up his damned job. Because, regardless of what she told him, or how much he tried to convince himself otherwise, he was hard-wired to be her champion, her cheerleader and her supporter.

She opened the door wide and let him in. Stella was sitting in the play pen in the lounge, bawling her eyes out, so he picked her up and soothed her, rocking her against his chest. 'Hey, hey. Look at you, clever girl. You were sitting up all by yourself. What's the matter? Was no one here? Auntie Charlie was just talking to me. So much noise from one so little! What is it? There's no need to cry.'

As if by some miracle the little girl stopped crying and stared at him. She patted his cheek with her hand as she inhaled shuddering breaths, then she smiled.

He grinned back. 'That's better. Now, should we go for a walk, see what we can find at the park? Shall we go? Oh, butter wouldn't melt now, right?'

From behind him he heard a sharp intake of breath; or was it a strained, throaty cry…?

He turned to see Charlie striding towards him, arms outstretched for the baby. 'Actually, it's time for her nap. I'll take her for a quick walk round the block later.'

'I can do that. You look bushed.'

'No, Lewis.' Her tone was sharp enough to make him stop in his tracks.

Okay. She's tired and stressed.

He kissed Stella on the cheek and put her back into the playpen. Then he walked towards Charlie, his gut tightening in a knot. Her mouth was set in a line and he knew, just knew, that her tone wasn't just because she was tired and stressed; it was far more than that. He knew, soul-deep, this was the end.

Not again. Don't do this again.

He shook his head, not wanting her to say the words, not wanting to hear them. 'Before you say anything final, hear me out. I can wait… I will wait for you, Charlie. I'll wait as long as I have to until you're freed up a little.'

She walked to the front door, then outside, and he couldn't do anything but follow. She stopped on the path and turned to him. 'No, Lewis. You cannot wait for me. I don't know how long this will take. Lucy needs me and I need to take care of her. This isn't something you can fix for me.'

But I want to.

'No, I get that. But I can be here for you. I can help, or just be at the end of the phone.'

They'd never finished their important conversation.

She shook her head, resolute. 'I don't think that's a good idea. I'm not sure we can even stay friends, not the way things are between us.'

'You mean the way we're good together? The way we make each other feel? The way we keep coming back to each other even after everything that happened? We're divorced, Charlie. We've lived apart for five years and missed so much of each other's lives and yet none of that matters, none of it, because I believe in us.'

Her hand flew to her mouth. 'Please. Don't.'

'So you're going to walk way *again*?' His heart felt cleaved in two.

It wasn't supposed to have got this intense. He hadn't wanted to feel this much. He was meant to have protected himself from this very scenario. And yet here he was, trying to make her see sense again. Because he knew that they could have something very special, could be happy together, if they gave it a shot. If she did.

She swallowed, looking as hurt as he felt. 'Last time I had to go for *me*. I needed space to lick my wounds and come to terms with my infertility. This time it's for you.'

'For me? That's bull, Charlie.' He knew his tone was becoming sharp too and he tried to soften it. 'You haven't even asked what I want.'

'Because I already know. We were just about to talk about it, the other morning, right? Really talk about what we might do as a...couple. How you're willing to put your wants and needs second to mine. But we don't know if we can adopt, or find a surrogate. We don't know if we'd be lucky enough to be chosen to be parents. That's a very uncertain future for someone who's desperate to be a daddy.

'I don't want to wake up one morning and see regret in your eyes, Lewis. Regret that you made the wrong choice, and a realisation that you could have what you want with someone else. So we can't be a couple, Lewis. I won't let it happen. I won't let either of us take that risk. I don't want to have my heart broken again and I imagine you don't want that either.'

It was already breaking; couldn't she see that? She was breaking him, breaking this amazing thing they could have together. 'We don't walk away when things get tough, Charlie. We stay. We stay and we fight. I would never walk away.'

'I know. I know you'd try to stay to the bitter end. You'd fight and fight and fight.' She put her palm up. 'So please don't make this harder than it has to be. We both knew coming into it that there were huge barriers. Nothing can change facts, Lewis. I am not the right person for you.

'I'm okay with what life has thrown at me. I know I can be fulfilled and happy without having kids. I've come to terms with a child-free future. I am a fantastic auntie and godmother and a great doctor. I have so many amazing plans for travel, and for my life. I am whole and I am thriving. But, every time I see you with Stella, I see that longing ripple through you. I can't trust that you won't decide to leave me. And I couldn't live every day waiting for it to happen.'

'You don't believe it when I tell you I'll wait? That I'll stay? I'll be here for you, Charlie, always. But, hell you can't *trust* me?' That was the lowest blow. Even after everything he'd said and done, she didn't think he had staying power. 'You walked away last time, Charlie, not me.'

He knew he should be walking away now, relieved that she'd set him free. But his feet were lead, his limbs too heavy to move. He didn't feel free, he felt broken.

She put her hand on his arm. 'I know, more than anyone, how sometimes you have to escape for your own sanity. And I couldn't bear to see you do the same. I'm sorry, Lewis.'

'So am I.' He shook his arm and got her to take her hand away. If she touched him again, he'd fold. 'But I'm not sure how you can say you want to leave when you were talking about love only the other day.'

She blinked, shock flashing across her expression. 'When?'

'In the car park. When we were making out.' His heart had swollen in panic but also comfort and relief.

Her eyes widened as the memory hit her. 'Oh, Lewis. I said

"I love the way you kiss me". I love your smile, yes. I love lots of things about you—'

'But you don't love me enough to stay.'

She looked up at him, her eyes swimming with tears. Her mouth trembled and he could see she was trying hard not to cry. 'No, Lewis. That's the problem, don't you see? I love you too much to stay.'

Then she walked up the path and closed the door.

She was gone—again.

He stared at the red paint.

She did love him.

He rubbed his forehead with the heel of his hand then stalked up to the door to hammer on it. To tell her to come back out and that they'd sort it all. Make her believe that he'd stay. Make her understand.

But Lucy... Stella... He couldn't disturb them and add to her problems.

He heard the baby start to cry again and heard someone cooing in a cracked voice, then an adult sob.

Charlie. Come back.

He walked down the path then back up again.

How the hell could he convince her that this time they could work it through?

He kicked the doorstep and slumped down on it.

'Charlie,' he whispered. 'For God's sake.'

How would he survive seeing her every day at work? How would she survive seeing him? How would he cope hearing her voice, her laughter? How would he be able to hand over a patient when there was this chasm between them?

He put his head in his hands.

Oh, Charlie, why the hell are you doing this to us?

How would he ever get over her second time round?

* * *

'Who was at the door?' Lucy croaked as she sat down at the kitchen table. 'Did I hear someone?'

'It was Lewis.' Charlie put a bowl of home-made chicken soup in front of her sister, then sat down in front of her own food, but she had no appetite.

Lucy frowned. 'He didn't want to come in?'

'Oh, he did.' Charlie tried to control herself. She'd been stuffing back the tears the whole time she'd been playing with Stella, putting on that false happy voice as she'd read to her from the little cloth book, trying to get her to go to sleep. She'd pretended she was okay when she'd chopped the carrots and onions. She'd forced herself to hold back when she'd called Lucy down for dinner. 'I ended it.'

'What?' Lucy's sunken eyes fizzed with shock as she reached over the table for Charlie's hand. 'Why?'

Charlie put up her palm. 'Don't. Please don't. If you touch me or say one single nice thing, I'll cry.'

Lucy scraped her chair back, went over and wrapped her arms around Charlie. 'Cry all you want, sis. I'm here.'

But Charlie squeezed her eyelids closed, pressing back the threatening tears. 'I'm okay. It's for the best. It is.'

She had to keep telling herself that. She had to believe it. She needed to forget him.

Her gaze fell on the leaflets scattered on the console. Leaflets about a charity that ran programmes to support women going through chemotherapy and hair loss. About another one that did free counselling, one that provided wigs, another that accepted hair donations and another that raised money for cancer charities by running head shaves. There was help for everything Lucy was going through and more. Charlie determined to put all her focus on her sister to help her reach out for this available support.

Maybe then she might forget Lewis.

Fat chance, when she'd see him most days.

Maybe then things wouldn't hurt so much.

Fat chance, because real, honest, true love didn't fade, did it? She knew that already. She'd been there, trying to forget her marriage and Lewis for five years, and had learnt that she would not, could not, forget him. She loved him more now than ever before.

She cleared her throat and picked up the leaflets, unable to meet her sister's piercing and enquiring gaze. 'Hey, why don't we take a look through these? Maybe we can contact a couple of these places tomorrow?'

'Charlie, look at me. *Look at me.* Stop deflecting.' Lucy stepped back and peered at her. 'Oh, honey. You are so not okay.'

Charlie's throat felt raw and thick. She couldn't pretend to her sister that she was all right when she was actually falling to pieces. She was trying not to say the words again, because they were barbs in her heart, but they were stuck in her gullet and she couldn't say or swallow anything unless she set them free. 'I love him, Lucy.'

Lucy stroked Charlie's hair. 'I know you do. So I don't understand why you ended it. And, God, please don't say you did it because you're looking after me.'

'No. Not for you, for me. I wish we'd never started up again.' She shook her head. 'No. That's not true. It's been lovely, really lovely. I just wish it didn't all hurt this much.' It was twice as bad as last time because he'd changed, and so had she. They'd become wiser, bolder and more willing to share their feelings. He'd changed so much for the better.

Truth was, there was no better man than Lewis Parry. And she'd lost him again. The hurt and sadness swelled through her until it threatened to overpower her. She stood up on wobbly legs. 'Sorry. I'll be back in a minute.'

She flung back her chair, not wanting her sister to see her in such a state. Then she ran up to her room and flopped on her bed.

And finally gave in to the tears and grief.

CHAPTER SEVENTEEN

'COME ON, MATE, it's for charity.' Brin steered the van into the beach-side car park and pulled on the hand brake. 'The team are relying on you.'

Lewis shrugged, the lethargy that had been dogging him for the last two weeks feeling worse, not better. He stared at the ocean, choppy and churning today, kind of how he felt too: roiling, swirling, out of sorts. 'I don't feel like going out.'

'Which means you need to.' Brin nudged him, about to take a bite out of his chicken and cranberry pie. 'You can't keep moping around like this. To be brutally honest, you're becoming a bit of a tragic.'

'I'm not moping. Or tragic.' Lewis shook his head and stared at the soggy sandwich he'd brought with him for lunch. He missed her. He hated seeing her at work and feeling the awkwardness between them. Hated the short, patient-focused conversations, the sadness in her eyes, the pain. Hated hearing her laughter and not being part of the joke or the fun. 'I don't feel like being sociable.'

Brin turned to him. 'Well, you have to. You're Mr Charity. You run up buildings…you bid too much in auctions… You have to come with us.'

'I don't, actually.'

'No, mate. You don't have to do anything. You can just never go out again. Sit around all day like a bear with a sore head. Actually, I'd prefer it if you did actually snap or growl. I'm not a huge fan of this sullen apathy.' Brin took a mouthful of pie and they sat in a loaded silence.

Lewis put his uneaten sandwich back in the container. 'I'm not apathetic. I come to work, do my job.'

'Then go home again and do nothing. You know, I haven't heard you talking about your running or training recently. You haven't been to any of the team nights out. You just…exist.' Brin's expression softened. 'I'm worried about you.'

'No need.' But Brin was right. Ever since Charlie had closed that doo, Lewis had lost his sense of fun and humour. Not wanting to ruin the vibe, he'd skipped Lily's ballet concert and had got a rap from his brother for his absence.

Bad Uncle Lewis.

Bad colleague Lewis.

Bad friend Lewis.

Yeah, okay, so maybe he was feeling sorry for himself.

Brin fixed him with his gaze. 'You know you're going to have to try to forget her…or win her back.'

'Who?' He hadn't discussed Charlie with Brin, apart from telling him to back off with his matchmaking.

Brin chortled. 'You know who.'

'I can't win her back if she doesn't want me.'

'I saw the way she looked at you, mate. I heard…' Brin shook his head and winced. 'Oh, never mind.'

'Heard what?' Lewis's gut tightened.

'I heard you talking in Harper's room. The baby monitor was on.' Brin screwed up his face. 'Sorry.'

'What exactly did you hear?' Lewis cringed. They'd thought the monitor was off. They hadn't seen a light on it.

'Something about wanting more… Struggling to keep away

from you...' Brin's face bloomed red. 'As soon as I realised you were in there I turned the app off, honest.'

Lewis swore. 'Oh, God. Embarrassing.'

'Or witness to how much you care about each other.'

'Well, forget whatever you heard. She's broken it off. We're done.'

'And you're just going to take it? Not fight?' Brin frowned. 'Surely if you got back together so quickly there's something worth fighting for? Remember what I did when I fell love with Mia and decided to fight for her, for us?'

'Gave me notice on your job. Yeah, I remember. And also asked for the job back when you both admitted your feelings for each other.'

Charlie had told him she loved him. He hadn't done that. He hadn't told her the depth of his feelings. Maybe he should have. 'I don't think admitting anything is going to help.'

But there was a kernel of something bright and hopeful in his chest. She wanted him to open up, didn't she?

'Well, anything's worth a try, right?'

'I don't know.' Lewis checked the time. 'We need to head off.'

'Okay.' His colleague sighed heavily and handed him a leaflet that had been stuffed in the glove compartment with other detritus. 'Look, I don't want to sound like I'm nagging, but this is the biggest charity event of the season. Some of our team are having their heads shaved to support the cancer patients. It's the biggest money-raiser they have all year. You've got to come support us.'

'You're going to get your head shaved?' How had he missed that? But then, he'd not been focusing on anything except getting through work so he could go home and...okay...mope a bit.

'Yes, I told you.' Brin tutted and shook his head. 'Me and Emma and Raj.'

Lucy. Charlie had been distraught about Lucy losing her hair.

Charlie. He couldn't help them in person but he could do this—give money to the people that helped them.

For the first time in the last couple of weeks he felt the fog in his brain start to shift. He had a purpose. 'Okay.'

She did care for him. She loved him. And where there was love there was hope.

He'd go to the event then he'd go round and see her, try to get her to understand things from his point of view.

He'd let her go last time. This time he was going to fight a damned sight harder.

Charlie watched from the side of the stage as the compere announced the final event of the fund-raising evening. She'd kept a low profile backstage, because she hadn't felt like talking to anyone, but she kind of wished she'd had a couple of drinks, because what she was about to do scared her to death. But if Lucy was going through it then the least Charlie could do was show her support by doing it too.

She took a deep breath and headed to the back of the small queue of people waiting to go on stage.

'Charlie?'

She turned to the sound of a male voice, her heart jumping, then diving. 'Brin! Hi. Are you going for the big shave too?'

Brin was standing in front of her with a couple of other paramedics she recognised from work.

He ran his fingers over his short hair. 'Not that it'll make much difference to my head, but I've got quite a few sponsors, so hopefully it'll raise a bit of cash.'

'Good on you.' She tugged her hair out of the ponytail and ran her fingers through the strands, easing out any knots. It would make a massive difference to her, and the money she was going to raise would help the charity.

The compere called for the first three people to come up to the stage. She stood with Brin and watched them go. She heard the chatter and the audience clapping, the buzz of the razor.

Her heart quickened. Her stomach lurched. Was this a good idea? What would Lucy say? Or Lewis, when he saw her at work?

Oh, Lewis. She missed him so much.

The next three went. She closed her eyes and tried to steady her nerves.

There was more talking, and cheering this time. There was snipping and buzzing. Everyone's motivation and story was similar to hers. People were shaving their heads for loved ones who were going through treatments, in memory of people who had passed or for those who had got through and were living their full lives. People just wanting to help somehow.

'Good luck,' Brin called to her as he stepped on to the stage.

'You too.'

I'm going to need it. I also need a hug.

A Lewis hug in particular. She knew without a doubt that he'd hate her shaving off her hair, but would also support her one hundred percent. Because he was her supporter, her cheerleader. Always had been.

There wasn't a single minute of her day when she didn't miss him. For five long years she'd learnt to get along without him, but now—after only a few weeks back in his presence, in his arms and in his bed—she could not get him out of her mind. It was as if her body couldn't function without him but needed him to fully live, to breathe.

But it was for the best.

It was—for his best, not hers.

Then it was her turn. She stepped on to the stage, her legs shaking just a little. *Be brave.* This was only a shave; she wasn't going to endure anything like Lucy was.

She'd devoted every spare minute to looking after her sister and niece. Last week they'd got word that Lucy was responding better than expected to the treatment. There were still long days ahead but the news had given them all a lift. For the first time since she'd closed the door on any kind of relationship with Lewis, she'd felt positive.

But hell, she'd ached to call him and tell him the good news. To share their milestones with him. To share her life.

She sat down and looked out at the crowd. There must have been five hundred people in the auditorium but in the sea of faces only one stood out.

Lewis.

Her heart hammered. Lewis was here; of course he was. He was supporting his colleagues, as he always did. He was that kind of guy—good, kind and compassionate.

He was sexy, fun, gorgeous and lovable. So loved…

The microphone was thrust into her hands and she was asked about her motivation for doing this. She cleared her throat and her eyes locked with his. He hadn't known she'd be here, that was obvious. She shifted her gaze away from his shocked one to somewhere in the middle of the crowd, because she couldn't look at him without crying.

'I'm doing this to raise money for cancer care. My sister's going through a hard time with chemotherapy at the moment and I wanted to show her she wasn't on her own. To show her that she is loved and that no one going through cancer treatment need be alone. Believe that you are loved and that we will walk this journey with you. Whatever it takes, we'll stay by your side.'

We'll stay.

She hadn't. She'd left him when things had got tough, and had chosen to walk away instead of staying and fighting. Because she was scared of being left on her own—something she'd never been allowed to do—she'd made it happen. She'd got in there first. She'd chosen that path because staying and hoping *he* wouldn't leave her had been worse. She hadn't been able to bear watching him realise he'd made the wrong choice. Hadn't been able to bear seeing the disappointment on her parents' faces or on Lewis's.

There came a round of applause, then the hairdresser walked forward.

Heart thumping, Charlie looked over at the place where Lewis had been sitting, but he wasn't there. Had he walked out? He'd always loved her hair. Was he angry that she was shaving her hair off? Her throat filled with the swell of tears. She felt sure he'd somehow have managed to convince her not to do this.

Oh, Lewis.

'I want to donate my hair for wigs, please. It's not dyed and in good condition.'

'Great. It's lovely and long. I'll tie it back, because it's easier to cut off all in one go.' The hairdresser nodded and gathered Charlie's hair into ponytail. 'Are you ready?'

Was she? She took a deep breath, sad to her core that Lewis hadn't been able to sit and watch. 'Sure am.'

She listened to the *snip-snip* of the scissors close to her head, then the hairdresser held up her cut ponytail to the cheers and applause of the crowd. Then all she could hear was the thud-thud of her heart in her ears. Then the buzzing, first up the back.

'It's a bit cold.' She laughed nervously.

The hairdresser didn't answer. The crowd gasped.

'Do I look that bad?' Charlie asked.

'No. You look beautiful. You're always beautiful to me, Charlie.'

That voice. That tone. That man. *Lewis.*

She closed her eyes as she felt his fingers run over the tufts of hair she had left. Lewis was shaving her head. Her hands curled into fists as she tried to stop herself from crying. 'No. You can't do this. Stop. You love my hair.'

'I love you, Charlie Jade Rose. I love *you.* Your hair is icing.' He came to stand in front of her, crouched and looked her in the eyes. 'I'm not going anywhere. If you want to do this, then I want to help and support you. I love you. And if you love someone, you stay. You stay for the good and the bad. You stay.'

'You love me?'

No. No. No. No. That would make everything ten times worse.

'Of course, Charlie. I've never stopped. If it's possible, I love you more now than ever.'

'Then you have to leave now. Go. Please.' She grabbed his arm. 'Please. Don't make this any worse for me.'

'I'm not going anywhere.' He flicked the razor on and shaved one side, then the next. Then he took the microphone from the compere and said, 'Charlotte Rose, you are incredible. You have donated your lovely hair to be made into a wig so someone else can feel more like themselves when they're going through challenging times. And then you've allowed me to shave your hair completely off. You look...' he inhaled and shook his head, staring at her as if she was a model '…truly the most beautiful I have ever seen you.'

The audience gasped as one.

'How much have you raised?' he asked her.

He loves me. He thinks I'm beautiful. He's told me in front of all these people.

She couldn't believe what she was hearing. 'Um…for the charity? I think about fifteen hundred.'

'Brilliant.' He nodded. 'If you shave my hair, I'll double it.'

The crowd erupted in cheers, stamping their feet and clapping. The compere handed round orange buckets for donations and there was nothing she could do but change places.

She held the razor and took a breath. Because she couldn't allow herself to get all carried away like the audience. There were still insurmountable obstacles here. 'I love you, Lewis. I love you so much and I miss you. But there is no future for us. I've seen you with Stella. You need to be a dad.'

Not wanting to hear his answer, she set about shaving his head, starting at the back then the sides and then the top. In a few minutes she was done. And, hell, he looked beautiful too.

Just as she thought he'd given up on an answer, he took her razor-free hand. 'I love you, Charlie. Any way you are. With or without hair. With or without a baby, or a family. Nothing else matters. I love everything about you. I will always love you as you are, wholly, fully.'

She looked at the floor, at his hair mingling with hers and the drops of her tears. 'But…'

He put the microphone down and spoke directly to her. 'Listen to me, Charlie. You always told me I should put my needs first. Well, here I am, knowing what I need, standing up for what I need, telling you what I need.

'It's *you*, Charlie. *I need you.* If you want to explore surrogacy or adoption or any other options, then we can do exactly that. Whatever you want—whatever *we* want. We can talk about it; we can investigate it together. Because we do have options, being a parent isn't about blood ties, I know that from experience. And if children don't happen, then that will be absolutely fine too. We have four little girls who want our love. We can be the most doting auntie and uncle in the world. I have everything I need right here with you. I promise that *you* are all I need, Charlie. You *are* my family.'

She thought about Lucy, Stella and their little family of two. That was enough for her sister.

She thought about how she'd stayed with Lucy, not out of obligation but out of pure love. 'Don't put yourself second,' she'd told him and he'd promised her that nothing else mattered because he loved her so much. The same way she'd promised those things to Lucy because she loved her. She'd do anything for her, willingly and happily.

Was that how he felt—that selfless love for someone else, for *her*? No expectations, no conditions, just love.

She saw him now, doing this—shaving her head, having his head shaved. An act of true love, love that was inspiring and deep. He'd told her he loved her since high school and she'd loved him right back, even when she'd tried hard not to. That love had coddled her, fuelled her and now filled her with absolute joy. Their love was enduring and ever-lasting.

And, finally, she allowed herself to believe him. He would stay. Whatever happened, he would stay. And so would she. 'Oh, Lewis. I love you so, so much.'

But he bent down on one knee. 'So, Charlie Jade Rose...'

'Oh! What are you doing?' She blinked at him and then at the audience.

The crowd whistled and cheered. She heard the *thunk-thunk-*

thunk of coins being thrown into the buckets. Whatever else happened, they'd raised a lot more money for the charity than she'd hoped for. She smiled as she looked down at her beautiful man.

He took her hand. 'I thought, given that our wedding was the best ever, we might have a rerun. What do you think? Will you marry me, Charlie Rose, all over again?'

'Oh, yes. Of course. Yes!' She pulled him up and he took her into his arms—exactly where she was meant to be.

The crowd went wild.

One year later...

'Trying to co-ordinate four little bridesmaids and an eighteen-month-old flower girl is like herding cats.' Lucy grinned as she picked up Stella and smacked a kiss on her chubby cheek. 'Now, go with Lily. Let her help you throw the petals on to the path while Mummy walks in front of Auntie Charlie.'

'You are the best flower girl I could ask for.' Charlie kissed Stella goodbye and watched Lily take the toddler to their places in preparation for the wedding procession. Then she gave her sister a hug, her beautiful, happy and very healthy sister. 'Thank you.'

'No, thank you for asking her to be flower girl. She doesn't quite understand but she loves twirling in her pretty dress.' Lucy grinned. 'I love what you've done with your hair.'

Charlie patted the cornflowers entwined in her short pixie cut. 'Thanks. I'm going to keep it short, I think. It's a lot easier for work.'

'It suits you. And now we're all matchy-matchy.' She ran her fingertips over her short cut. The music began to play, the same tune they'd chosen for their first wedding. 'Now, where's Dad? Time to make your big entrance.'

Their parents had dashed back from Uganda two weeks after Charlie's head shave—and the moment Lucy had finally told them about her cancer—as both Lucy and Charlie had known they would. But they'd had their long-hoped-for overseas charity experience before moving in with Lucy and Stella and helping out. Somehow, they seemed to have mellowed a little, and only wanted to help, not domineer or take over.

And it had seemed an appropriate time then for a now homeless Charlie to move in with Lewis, and those empty seats at the dinner tables and social gatherings were filled again.

Their wedding was even better second time round. It was smaller, at the beach, with just family and a few close friends. Co-ordinating Lily, Lola, Luna, Harper and Stella all to stand still for the photos was the biggest and funniest challenge. Lewis wrapped his arms around Charlie's waist as they watched the girls skipping, jumping and wriggling and she leaned back against him.

'Five girls.' She laughed. 'Maybe one of our siblings will have a boy some time. You must be getting over all the pink.'

'What? I've got my football team all sorted. Lily's my star attacker, Lola's in goals and Luna's showing great potential in midfield. Harper's more thoughtful and watchful, plus she's tall…probably good at centre back.' They watched as Stella waddled towards her mum then plopped down on the sand. 'Stella might need a little more training.'

'Aw. She's only been walking a few months.'

'Got to get them when they're young.' He laughed, then squeezed Charlie tightly and kissed her cheek. His love for his girls shone and made her heart sing with love—even more love, if that were possible.

They'd applied to the adoption agency and had advertised for surrogates but no luck so far. That didn't matter; if it happened, it happened. If not, then…they had each other, the four blood-tied nieces plus Harper who, they'd all decided, must become an honorary niece. Their lives were full of babysitting and school concerts, loud and chaotic lunches and laughter. They were one big family.

'Are you happy?' Lewis whispered against her throat.

He'd asked her that not long after they'd reconnected and she'd told him to ask her again when Lucy had finished her treatment. 'More than I thought I ever could be. I'm married to my best husband. I can say that because I've had two now.' She grinned up at him. 'My sister's improving every day. We have the most amazing friends and family.'

As if on cue, best-man-again Logan ambled over. 'Hey, I'm sorry, but the weather forecast isn't great for the evening. We'll have to bring the chairs and tables inside the venue. It's going to rain.'

They'd planned an early-evening dinner outside at a long table under the trees. But Lewis grinned as he turned to Charlie. 'You know what that means?'

She laughed. 'Flash flooding?'

'I damned well hope so.' His eyes twinkled as they both remembered their night in the fancy hotel.

'Me too. I love you, Lewis Parry.'

'I love you too, Charlie. Always have and always will.'

And now she believed him, with all her heart.

* * * * *

FINDING FOREVER WITH THE FIREFIGHTER

LOUISA HEATON

MILLS & BOON

For Nick

CHAPTER ONE

THIS WAS THE perfect place. To rest. To recharge after a difficult and complicated shout. Here, halfway up Abraham's Hill, there was a clearing amongst the trees and she could look down upon the people in the park. Families sharing picnics. Children playing, giggling, chasing one another. Young couples sitting on the grass. Older ones holding hands, or feeding the birds gathered around their feet. The perfect place to stop thinking about the awful situations people often found themselves in and instead bask in the peace and serenity of happy, content, *safe* ones.

Hazardous Area Response Team paramedic Addalyn Snow yearned for the serenity of happy, content people, but often felt it was a condition that would always somehow be out of her reach. She wasn't bitter about it. It was something she had become resigned to. Her life was filled with drama, both at work and unfortunately, these last few years, at home.

Biting into her chicken salad wrap, she found her gaze captured by a young boy and a girl chasing each other around, laughing, and she didn't notice a dollop of garlic mayonnaise escape from her wrap until it landed on her uniform. She swore quietly and used her finger to wipe it up, licked it, then reached for the wipes that she kept in the glove compartment of her work vehicle. She was just rubbing at her uniform, hoping and praying that the mayo wouldn't stain, when she received a call.

'Three one four, this is Control. We have a report of a situation occurring at Finnegan's Hole in Bakewell. Possible tunnel collapse with multiple casualties. Cave rescue and fire brigade en route. Can you attend, over?'

'Control, this is three one four. Show as attending. ETA…' she glanced at her watch '…fifteen minutes, over.'

'Thank you, three one four.'

Addalyn looked about for a bin to throw the last part of her sandwich into, but the one near her car was already overflowing. So she just stuffed the rest of her sandwich into her mouth, closed the car door and started up the engine, activating the blue lights. She would use the siren when she reached built-up areas and traffic.

She felt some trepidation in her stomach. Finnegan's Hole was a popular potholing site with a narrow entrance. She'd attended a job there once before, as a new paramedic, when a potholer had gashed his leg open on a sharp rock formation. She could remember standing there, looking down at the cave entrance, and wondering why on earth anyone would be crazy enough to do potholing as a hobby. She'd never been fond of enclosed spaces herself, but hadn't realised the extent of this until she did her three-day-long confined space training in her quest to become a HART paramedic.

HART paramedics received extra training. They specialised in providing first responder care in areas considered more hazardous than those a conventional paramedic would operate in, often working alongside multiple other agencies.

Addalyn had worked hard to become a HART paramedic and she loved her job. It meant she had to think carefully about each and every decision. Each and every shout was completely different and no two work days were the same. She often worked long hours, but the best thing about that was that when she got home, exhausted and tired, it meant she could fall into bed and go right to sleep. When she woke up the cycle would begin again, so she didn't have to think too hard about the spaces in between when she was finished for the day and when she had to clock on again. It meant she didn't have to notice how alone she was. Or who she was missing. Or why.

And if those thoughts did creep in she silenced them with food, or the TV, or loud music pumping through her ears as she exercised to retain her fitness levels.

She knew how to push herself hard. It was what she had always done. Even as a child. And pushing hard, being determined not to let life beat her to a pulp, as it had tried in the last few years, was what kept her going.

Addalyn activated the sirens as she came upon traffic. There was always a lot of traffic in Derbyshire, even in rural areas such as Bakewell or Matlock. Her work covered the area of Derbyshire that contained the Peak District, and it was popular with tourists and walkers. And in this next job's case potholers. The Peak District had a lot of natural pothole formations. Nettle Pot, which was over a hundred and fifty metres deep, Poole's Cavern, a two-million-year-old limestone cavern, and the mighty Titan Cave, near Castleton, which was Britain's biggest cave.

She had to remain alert. Not all pedestrians saw the lights or heard the sirens. Nor all drivers. She had to be constantly alert for all the hazards that might come her way. It had become a learned skill. In life, as well as at work.

'Stay there…' she murmured to herself as a car appeared at a T-junction on her left, praying that the driver would see her and ease back to let her go past first. Thankfully, the driver saw her, and she raised a hand in thanks as she zoomed past.

Finnegan's Hole, her satnav instructed her, was halfway up a mountain on the other side of Bakewell. It was situated on the east face of Mitcham's Steps, another popular tourist attraction, because the hill there was like a stepped pyramid, with a viewing platform on the top. Finnegan's Hole had only been discovered in 1999, and from what she remembered reading, potholers were still mapping out its many caverns, twists and turns, deep into the earth.

A helicopter flew overhead and she became aware of other sirens ahead of her, and on one long stretch of road she saw the disappearing tail-end of a fire engine. It looked as if they might all arrive at the same time.

She radioed through to Control. 'Any update on the Finnegan's Hole job, Control? Do we know the number or types of casualties, over?'

'We do have an update for you. At least four trapped after a confirmed tunnel collapse. Mostly minor injuries, but one caver is said to be trapped beneath the rubble, over.'

'Any other information on that patient, over?'

'Patient is male and trapped about twenty feet beneath the surface, over.'

Addalyn shivered, imagining what that might look and feel like. Trapped beneath the ground, in the dark, in close quarters, dirt and muck in the air, maybe water... Torchlights flashing this way and that, sound echoing, reverberating around you. In pain. Trapped. Unable to move.

'Thanks, Control.'

Her thoughts immediately jumped back to her confined spaces training. She needed to be aware of the topography of the area they'd be working in, maybe find an expert on the tunnels if one was available. She'd have to think about the risk of further tunnel collapse, maybe gaseous emissions could be a danger, or an increase in water levels? Free-flowing solids? And all of this before she could even think about her patient. She knew nothing about him. He might have other medical conditions that she knew nothing about. A condition that would complicate her ability to attend him. And if he were trapped that far down, the big question was…would she have to go down there?

Her vehicle began to ascend the hill road on Mitcham's Steps, its engine roaring, easily taking her up the steep incline, smoothly and expertly. Some hikers were making their way down and moved to the side of the road to hug the verge as she passed.

She saw curious eyes and faces. Saw some stop to watch her pass, even one or two debating going back the way they'd come to watch the drama that was causing all these sirens to be heard, all these emergency vehicles to pass by.

Finnegan's Hole. One mile, she read on her satnav.

The sun was out, at least. It wasn't a grey, drizzly day. They'd have daylight and a bit of warmth to assist them.

When she arrived at Finnegan's Hole she parked and opened her boot to slip on her high-vis vest, her hard hat, and grab her equipment. As she closed the boot she became aware of a fire chief in a white hard hat approaching her. She recognised him. It was her father's friend Paolo. And seeing him walk towards her, in his fireman's garb, reminded her so strongly of how her father and brother had used to look that grief smacked her in the gut, as if she'd been swung at with a wrecking ball.

'Addy. Good to see you. Are you okay?'

She gave him a quick nod, not quite trusting herself to speak yet. It had been over a year, but it still felt so raw. Thankfully, Paolo seemed to understand, and he jumped straight to business.

'We've got seven in total, trapped from a tunnel collapse, and we have communications. Six of them are fine. Minor injuries, cuts, grazes, some bruises. But one potholer is trapped beneath the rubble. Attempts were made to lift off whatever rocks they could, but they had to stop because of risk of further collapse, and apparently there is one large boulder trapping his left leg. They say it doesn't look good. Almost crushed. Cave rescue is here, setting up, and we've got equipment going in right now to secure the cave roof.'

'Okay. Conditions down below?'

'Mixed. It's a tight squeeze, as I'm sure you know, but only a bare inflow of water. Trickles—nothing more. No gaseous emissions, so I don't think we need to worry about the risk of anything blowing up or catching fire. But they're panicking.'

'To be expected. Who have you got on your team that's good with small spaces?'

The chief smirked. 'You know they're all good.'

'What about Charlie?' She'd worked with Charlie before on an entrapment case.

'Off sick. But we do have Ryan Baker. He's new, but extremely good with stuff like this. Used to be in the army. Did a lot of tunnel work.'

'Then he's my guy. Get him in a harness and rope—he's coming in with me, once I've done the risk assessment.'

A new guy. That was good. He'd have no associations with her past.

The chief saluted and jogged off to talk to his team.

A tunnel guy. Army guy. Sounded good.

Addalyn went over to the mountain rescue team member who was co-ordinating his team with fire and rescue regarding the cave supports that were going in.

'How's it looking?'

'Nearly all the supports are in. Just setting up the lighting for you.'

'What can you tell me about this place?'

'It's pretty much what you'd expect. Lots of close quarters. Limestone, mostly. Some bigger caverns as you descend further. Atmosphere is moist.'

'Hazards?'

'There are some sharp rock formations. Stalagmites. Stalactites.'

'Biologics?'

'Nothing to concern you.'

'You're full of pleasant information.'

He smiled. 'I aim to please.'

'I'm going to lead the rescue. One of the fire crew is going in with me.'

'All right. We'll keep in touch with radio. You'll need one of these.' He passed her a hand radio that she slotted into her vest as he clipped her to a guide rope. 'Where's your other guy?'

'Here.'

She turned to give him a smile. A nod. To introduce herself by name, especially since they'd be in close quarters with one another. She liked firefighters. Had an affinity for them. Her father and brother had both been firefighters. She'd even thought that she would be one, too.

But Ryan Baker was not the sort of guy you just had a single glance at. He was not the type of guy you said hello to and then got on with what you were doing.

He was...different. Intense. Handsome.

Three danger zones that instantly made her heart thud painfully in her chest in an alert as his rich chocolate eyes bored into hers.

'Ryan? I'm Addalyn.'

She held out her hand for him to shake, aware of a tremor in her voice just as she felt a powerful feeling pass through her when he shook her hand and then let go, his dark eyes barely meeting hers.

'Nice to meet you.' He attached himself to the guide rope with strong, square hands.

An army guy. A tunnel guy.

A *firefighter* guy.

No. She wouldn't think about that.

The mountain rescue man gave her the thumbs-up. 'Lights are in. I've got two of my team who will meet you at cavern two. The tunnel collapse is just ahead of them.'

'All right.'

'Just follow the guide rope down. There will be cameras for you to use when you near the tunnel breach. Go in feet first. There's a small cavern about ten feet down, where you can move around and begin to crawl deeper in.'

'Perfect. Thank you.'

She eyed the small hole in the earth, that basically looked like it was the entrance to a badger sett or something. It didn't look like anything humans should be climbing down into, but she and Ryan would have to go. It was dark. Shadowy. It gave her the shivers, but she knew she could deal with it.

She took a step forward, then felt a hand on her arm.

'I'll go first,' suggested Ryan.

She looked at him and nodded briefly. Her heart was pounding so fast because of her claustrophobia, wasn't it? Nothing to do with him.

'I'll show you where to put your hands.'

She nodded. 'Thanks.'

He went in feet first, as instructed. Finnegan's Hole swallowed him up easily and he had no hesitation about heading into the dark. She watched him disappear.

People often joked that they wished the earth would swallow them up, but they wouldn't say it if they truly knew how it felt, she thought, following him down, her eyes taking a moment to adjust to the darkness. There were lanterns, as the mountain rescue guy had said, but they were spaced far apart and there were sections as they climbed down where the only light was provided by their head torches.

Her hands touched rock. Her boots found purchase on ledges and outcrops and her body scraped along the tunnel sides, where it got narrow. She tried to push images of this tunnel caving in on her away, knowing she needed to trust in the facts that she had been told: tunnel supports were in place.

Sounds began to carry towards her through the tunnels and caverns. Voices. Some shouting. Others trying to soothe and calm. The dripping of water. The echoes of everything.

Something skittered across the back of her hand and she yelled.

Ryan looked up at her. 'You okay?'

His concern for her was touching, but she was here to help someone. Not to be another person who would need rescuing. 'Fine.'

He squinted, as if deciding to trust that she was telling the truth.

'Honestly. I'm fine. Just not fond of spiders, that's all.'

'Stay by me.'

She had no plans to do anything else.

They descended into the cavern, with Ryan holding out his hands to help her down onto the cave floor. It was a decent size. About the size of her bathroom at home. Tall enough to stand up in. Ahead of them was a small crawlspace, lit with lamps.

Have I got to go in there?

'It shouldn't be far. Remember the mountain rescue guys are in the next cavern already.'

Addalyn nodded. Her mouth had gone incredibly dry, yet the rest of her was sweating, and her heart was hammering away in her chest. All she could feel was a sense of pressure all around her. The pressure that might be on the rock walls. The floor. The ceiling. And if she crawled into that space...

'Addalyn?'

She looked at Ryan.

'You can go back if you want.'

The temptation was immense. It would be so easy, wouldn't it? To just start climbing back in the other direction. Towards the surface. Towards the sunshine and the light and the fresh air. To space and freedom and peace.

But there was a man in trouble who needed her. A man who needed her medical expertise. She couldn't walk away from him, no matter what.

'No. I'm doing this.'

He nodded, a slight smile playing around his beautiful mouth, and that smile was enough. That smile said, *I believe in you. I'm proud of you.*

She thought of her father. Her brother. She was not going to die like they had. 'Let's do this.'

Ryan grinned. 'All right.'

He got down on his hands and knees and began to crawl into the tunnel. As his feet disappeared into the shadows she sucked in a determined breath and followed after him, trying to ignore all that she felt digging into the soft flesh of her belly, or the way her helmet would knock into the rock above her head. Her clothes were wet and dirty and her kit bag, being dragged behind her, must be in a terrible state.

They crawled for what seemed like an age, towards the lights and noises ahead, and then suddenly, in front of her, Ryan was getting to his feet and turning to help her up. His hand reaching for her. She ignored how it felt to take it. Then they were in the second cavern with two of the mountain rescue team.

'Ryan. Addalyn.' Ryan made the introductions.

'Raj. Max,' said one of the men, doing likewise. 'And this lovely gent down here, in need of your help, is John. John Faraday.'

John lay on his back on the cavern floor, his left leg trapped under an immense rock and some rubble. Around him sat the other cavers, two men and a woman. They all looked scuffed and dirty, muddy and frightened. John was pale, but conscious. He lifted a hand in greeting.

'We didn't want to leave him,' the woman said. 'We come down together. We go up together. That's our motto.'

'Sounds good to me,' said Addalyn. 'Now, let's see how we can do this. Ryan? Would you check these guys over whilst I look at John?'

'Sure.'

She knelt by John, took his hand and squeezed it. 'Hey, how are you doing?'

'I've had better days.'

'I bet. On a scale of one to horrible, do you want to tell me how much it hurts?'

'Surprisingly, not much.'

That was probably the adrenaline, keeping him numb.

'I'm going to get a line in to give you some painkillers anyway, just in case. You allergic to anything, John?'

It helped her to focus on her patient. It stopped her being aware of what was all around her, pressing down.

'Just my ex-wife.'

She smiled. She liked him. It took a lot to remain upbeat in a situation such as this.

'This should help.'

She gave him a shot of painkiller, then hooked up a bag of intravenous fluids.

Ryan knelt beside her. 'Just cuts and bruises on the others. They missed the worst of it because John, here, pushed them out of the way.'

'Hero, huh? We need them to go to the surface.'

He nodded. 'Agreed. What do we know about the three trapped behind the rubble?'

One of the mountain rescue guys spoke. 'They're okay. Just John got badly hurt.'

'Okay.' Addalyn stood, stretched her legs. 'I know these guys want to stay and help John, but we need them to go up. That way we can work better on getting John out and opening up the tunnel for the others too. Besides...' her voice dropped low '...I'm not sure they're going to want to see what comes next.'

Mountain rescue nodded. 'I'll get them out.'

Addy knelt back down to John, her gaze taking in his position, his leg beneath the rock, his foot sticking out on the other side. 'Can you wiggle your toes for me?'

'I'll try.' John concentrated and looked up at her hopefully. 'Did my foot move?'

'No. I'm afraid not.' Grim, she reached past him, squeezing past the boulder. 'Can you feel me touching you?' She stroked just above his ankle.

'No.'

The boulder was massive. His leg beneath it had to be crushed and there would be no way to save it.

Loosening his boot, she tried to feel for a pedal foot pulse, but nothing would register and the foot was cold. She sat back on her haunches.

'John, what kind of support do you have at home?'

'I live with my girlfriend. She's a nurse. She's gonna be so angry with me about this.'

Addy gave him a sympathetic smile, then turned to Ryan. 'Any chance this boulder could be lifted quickly?'

'We could get equipment in, to either remove it or break it up into smaller manageable pieces, but it would take time.'

'How much time?'

Ryan shrugged. 'As much as I'd like to say it could be done quickly, in these conditions it might take time to manoeuvre it through those crawl spaces before we could get set up. But even if we removed it, wouldn't he be at risk for compartment syndrome?'

She was impressed that he would know about it. Compartment syndrome was a condition that occurred in incidents like these, when pressure within the muscles built to dangerous levels. That pressure could lead to decreased blood flow and prevent nourishment and oxygen reaching the tissues. Which, in turn, could lead to a build-up of toxins, so that when the pressure was removed, those toxins would flood the heart and cause the patient to go into cardiac arrest.

'I could do a fasciotomy, but that would just prolong the agony long term.'

A fasciotomy was an emergency procedure performed to try to prevent compartment syndrome. It involved making an incision along the fascia to relieve tension and pressure in tissue.

'Addalyn? You don't have to whisper. Just tell me straight,' said John.

She knelt beside him once again. 'Your leg isn't great, John. It has a severe crush injury with a lot of soft tissue avulsion and high levels of contamination. Your foot has no pulse, and it is also cold and does not move. Your blood pressure is low and you're the wrong side of fifty.'

Her patient swallowed. 'None of that sounds good.'

'It isn't. I'm sorry, but I'm pretty sure a doctor is going to want to perform an expedient procedure on your lower leg.'

She watched his face carefully, having avoided the word amputation, but knowing it was implied. No medic liked telling a patient bad news. But it was something she'd hardened herself to. She couldn't allow doubts and recriminations any room in her mind these days. She already had enough to deal with. So she steeled herself.

'Will it hurt?'

'No. The doctor would put you under. You won't feel a thing.

And me and Ryan are going to help take care of you and get you back up to the surface afterwards.'

John looked at Ryan, then back to Addy. 'Have you seen many of these before?'

'Yes.' He didn't need details. He just needed to know this wasn't her first time. 'Everyone is going to do their best for you, John, okay?'

He nodded. 'Before they put me under...can I ask you to tell my girlfriend something? Just in case.'

'You'll be able to tell her yourself when you wake up in hospital. But sure... Just in case.' She leaned in to hear.

'Tell her that I love her and that she made my life the best that it ever could be.'

She looked him in the eyes. 'I will. But everyone's got you, okay?'

'Okay.'

Just then more of Ryan's fire crew arrived, this time with a doctor in tow. Addalyn apprised Dr Barrow of the situation, he confirmed the necessity for the procedure, and made quick work of removing John from his left leg, bandaging him and stabilising him for removal back up to the surface.

Dr Barrow went first, then Ryan took the front of John's stretcher, whilst his crew mate Tom took the rear. Addalyn followed them up, keeping an eye on the monitoring equipment and hoping that John didn't choose to have a further medical crisis whilst stuck in a small tunnel. Thankfully, he remained stable all the way, and they all emerged on the surface, dirtied, muddied and relieved, before passing John off to an ambulance that would take him to hospital.

Addalyn turned to see Ryan heading back into Finnegan's Hole. 'Where are you going?'

'There are still people down there.'

'I know, but surely it's someone else's turn to go down?'

'That's not how this works.' He smiled, disappearing into the earth a second time.

Addy called through to Control and apprised them of the situation. 'One patient has been medically evacuated, but there are still three trapped behind the collapse. I've been informed that they don't have any serious injuries, but as this is still a multi-operational job, I'd like to stay on scene and be of some help, over.'

'Thank you, three one four. Received. Stay safe out there.'

'I will. Over and out.'

CHAPTER TWO

IT TOOK THREE hours to dig out the tunnel safely and free the rest of the potholers, who were mightily relieved to see some friendly, helpful faces on the other side of the rubble.

Their cuts and bruises were as to be expected, though one of the potholers, a young woman, had a suspected fractured forearm. Ryan splinted it and then followed the others out through the tunnels and into the fresh air, where the sky was blue and the air was warm and welcome.

'Addy? I've splinted this lady's arm. I think she might have a fracture.'

'I'll take a look.'

He was glad to see Addalyn was still there, waiting for him to come out. There'd been no need for her to stay. After all the main casualty, John, had been evacuated many hours before, and the other patients had only mild injuries that wouldn't even require a visit to hospital. And there were other paramedics here. Other ambulances.

She could have left.

But she hadn't.

And he had to admit it felt quite good to see someone looking so relieved when he emerged safe and sound.

He barely knew Addy. Had met her only today. But they'd been through something dangerous together and that bonded people in a way that no one else would be able to understand, so he knew he'd look forward to working with her in the future.

Finnegan's Hole would now be closed to the public until the tunnels and caverns could be confirmed as stable and safe.

Ryan checked in with his chief, then headed over towards Addy to thank her before he left. She was helping the lady with the injured arm into an ambulance, standing back as the doors closed.

'Thanks for staying.'

She turned to smile at him. A beautiful smile.

'It was my job.'

'Yes, it was, but even so… I appreciate you still being here now we've got everyone out.'

'*"We come down together, we go up together."* I think I heard that somewhere,' she said with a smile, repeating the words of one of the potholers. 'Besides, I have this thing about keeping an eye on firefighters.'

'Oh?' He gave an amused raise of one eyebrow.

She smiled at him. 'Long story.'

'Best ones are. Listen, I've just spoken to the chief and we're all heading to the Castle and Crow for an evening of decompressing, fine ales and a trivia quiz. You and your team are all welcome to join us.'

He thought she'd say no. He thought she'd say she'd think about it. Or she'd try to make it. Any of those excuses. But it wasn't as if he was asking her out on a date. This was a group thing. It had been a long day, and this last job had been a tough and exhausting one. All he wanted was to have a shower, some food and then an early night, but he also knew of the restorative power of a night out with his crewmates. Decompressing, destressing, having fun and laughing was crucial to help deal with their long hard days on the job. And tonight was a good night to do it. His daughter, Carys, was with his parents for a sleepover.

To his surprise, she said, 'Sounds great! I'll ask the others.'

'Perfect. I'll see you later, then.'

She gave him a nod and turned to head back to her rapid response vehicle. She was still in the clothes she'd been in when she'd gone below with him. The mud had dried out.

'Hey, listen…' He hadn't known he was going to say anything else until his mouth had opened up and begun to spurt sounds. He thought rapidly as she turned to face him again, a look of query on her face. 'You did great down there today. I know you weren't exactly fond of being in such a confined space.'

She smiled and nodded. 'I wasn't, but…thanks.'

He wasn't sure exactly how to end the conversation now. Nod? Say goodbye again? Give her a little wave?

No, that would be weird. Why does it matter? What's got into you? Just walk away, Ryan.

Why had he suddenly become tongue-tied? The last time he'd been tongue-tied had been ages ago. When, exactly?

He frowned, and when the memory came he felt bad.

He'd been tongue-tied when he'd watched his bride, Angharad, walk down the aisle towards him. She'd looked so beautiful in her stunning white gown, holding that bouquet of summer flowers before her as she'd walked to the sound of the 'Wedding March', and just seeing her had seemed to stop all his normal bodily functions from working. His mouth had gone dry, his brain had emptied of all possible thought and reason, and all he'd been able to get himself to do was continue to breathe and try not to cry.

Addy looked nothing like Angharad. She was muddy, rumpled, her hair sprouting loose tendrils around her tired face,

but there was something about her…something that called to
him. What was it?

*It doesn't matter. She's just a colleague. I probably won't see
her again for a while after tonight. I can just enjoy her company and not think too hard about it.*

'I'll see you tonight, then?'

Another nod. Another smile. Her eyes were *stunning*.

'You can count on it.'

'Great. I'll…er…' He pointed in the direction of the fire engine. Saw the amusement in her gaze and laughed at himself
as he walked away.

Addy pushed open the doors to the Castle and Crow. It was one
of Derbyshire's tiniest pubs, situated in what had used to be
the gatehouse to a castle that now stood in ruins. She'd been,
oh, so glad to get the invitation—anything to keep her out of
that empty and now silent house.

She wasn't a fan of that silence. It felt thick and heavy. It
made the house seem…lifeless. And somehow, though she was
the only one living, she felt like a ghost, haunting its rooms,
looking for life to latch on to. She missed her dad. She missed
Ricky. The empty spaces where they'd usually sat felt cru-
elly difficult. Dad by the window in the recliner he'd loved so
much. Ricky stretched out on the couch, playing video games.

Gone.

Taken from her so quickly.

They'd been her whole world, her security blanket, her soft
place to fall after all that horrible business with Nathan, and
just as she'd begun to shine again…just as she'd begun to smile
and laugh again…life had snatched them both away.

It hurt to be in the house.

Music greeted her as she pushed through the doors and then
smiles and cheers as some of the ambulance and fire crew

greeted her, insisting she join them at their table. She made the international gesture that said *I'll just grab a drink...anyone else want one?* by pointing at the bar before making her way back over to them armed with a gin and tonic.

Chrissie and Jools had a seat open next to them, so she sat there. 'Hi, guys.'

Chrissie was a paramedic and Jools was an emergency care assistant. On the table next to them were some of the fire crew guys. Paolo, Brewster, Tom and—her heart thudded quicker—Ryan.

She raised her glass to them all. 'So, what are we doing?'

'Pub quiz,' said Chrissie. 'Ambulance versus Fire versus everyone else, I guess. Thatch is in the loo, but he's going to help make up our four.'

Thatch was one of the 999 call takers who worked at Control.

'Great.' Addy took a sip of her drink. 'I always knew all that trivia Dad used to give me would come in handy one day.'

It had been her dad's thing. Every day at dinner he would present her and Ricky with a fun fact for the day. Even when she'd moved back in with them after her split with Nathan. Sometimes it would be hilarious, sometimes intriguing, but it always sparked conversation, and dinner times Chez Snow had quickly become her favourite time of the day.

Nowadays dinner was a ready meal heated in the microwave and eaten in silence in front of the TV. Addy would do her best and watch a quiz shows if she could, whilst eating, but it never quite took away the fact that she was eating alone and that the two seats that would normally be filled with two strong, hearty men were actually empty.

Paolo nodded. 'Ah, yes, Vic knew a thing or two. Where did he get his facts, Addy? Novelty toilet paper?' He laughed and took a sip of his pint, raising his glass in a mock salute to the dead and the lost.

She smiled. 'I don't know. He picked them up from somewhere.'

'Victor Snow?' Ryan asked.

Addy nodded.

'I've seen his picture in the fire station. Ricky's too. I didn't realise you were related. I'm sorry for your loss.'

'Thank you.'

A strange atmosphere settled around the table, with no one quite sure what to say to change the subject, or even if changing the subject was the right thing to do. They all knew what had happened. They all knew what she'd gone through. With maybe the exception of Ryan.

Thankfully it was broken by the return of Thatch from the toilets.

'I'd give the restroom a miss for five minutes, guys. I think I had a dodgy kebab at midday.'

Everyone burst into laughter and Thatch looked around him, not quite sure that his joke had been that funny, or original, but appreciative all the same.

Behind them, at the bar, one of the barmen switched on a microphone and notified them that the quiz would start in ten minutes and that someone would come round with paper and pens momentarily.

Addy took a moment to catch up with Chrissie and Jools. She'd not seen them since the job at Finnegan's Hole that afternoon, and she asked them if they'd had any other interesting shouts.

'A guy who thought he was about to go into a diabetic coma.'

'You got to him in time?'

'He wasn't even a diabetic, Addy! Not been diagnosed—nothing. His blood sugars were fine, but when we looked up his deets on the tablet we could see the guy is constantly visiting his doctor, day after day after day.'

'Health anxiety?'

She nodded. 'We had to check him over, though. The only thing we found wrong was a slightly elevated heart rate, but that was probably down to his stress.'

'Poor guy. Must be hard to live with a condition like that.'

'I think he's lonely, too. Lives alone. Has done for years. The place had a feeling of neglect, you know?'

Addy could sympathise. When she'd lost Dad and Ricky, she'd found it hard to keep up with maintaining the house. Especially because she'd worked as many hours as she could so that she didn't have to be in that empty house. And the more and more things piled up, the worse she felt. But this last year, on New Year's Eve, she'd made a resolution to get on top of things with the house. She'd put on some music, or listen to a podcast, or an audiobook, she'd told herself, and work for fifteen minutes.

Today I'm going to tidy and sort that corner by Dad's chair.

This time I'm going to go through that wardrobe and get rid of the clutter at the bottom.

It was easier in short, manageable bursts. Not so overwhelming. And there'd even been a moment, when the house had begun to look better, brighter, when she'd been proud of herself. The depression and the grief had lifted enough for her to see good things in life again.

It still didn't make it any easier to be home alone, though. She wasn't sure she'd ever get used to living that way.

'Welcome, everyone, to the Castle and Crow quiz night! We've got some amazing prizes for our winners and our runners up. For the team that places second there is a lovely prize of six bottles of wine, donated by the Tutbury Vineyard, along with tickets to a wine-tasting evening. But for our winners— drumroll, please…'

The clientele all began a low drumming on their tables,

building to a crescendo and stopping only when Natalie, the pub landlady, who had the microphone, raised her hands, laughing.

'For our winning team there is a prize kindly donated by the local zoo. Free tickets for six people alongside a zookeeper experience and a meal, drinks included, at their onsite restaurant, Reservation!'

Addy's friend Chrissie leaned in. 'A zoo? No, thanks. I get itchy just thinking about fur.'

Addy smiled.

'So, get your pens and pencils ready!'

Addalyn grabbed her pen and then happened to look up at the fire crew's table. Her gaze met Ryan's and she smiled at him before looking away. She would have quite happily sat at their table. The fire crew had long been a part of her family because of her dad and Ricky. And Ryan seemed nice. Dangerously nice. But he was a fireman, so that made him off-limits.

'First question! What is considered the most dangerous bird in the world?'

Most dangerous bird…? thought Addy.

Chrissie leaned in and whispered, 'Would that be a bird of prey, do you think?'

Addy didn't think so. It might be the obvious choice, but she felt sure she knew the right answer. She just couldn't think of it.

Jools added, 'An emu? They can hurt you if they kick you.'

And then the answer came like a bolt of lightning. 'It's the cassowary,' Addy whispered.

'The what?' Chrissie frowned.

'Lives in Australia. Claws like daggers. Trust me, it's the cassowary.'

'Okay, but if you're wrong, you owe me a glass of wine.'

Addy knew she wasn't wrong. She remembered her dad telling her. One of his fun facts for the day. They'd been discussing flightless birds, and the only ones she and Ricky had been able to come up with had been penguins and kiwis. The cassowary was apparently bigger and stronger and infinitely more dangerous to humans.

'Question two… Which planet has a pink sky?'

Addy looked blankly at Thatch, Jools and Chrissie.

'Mars is the red planet,' said Thatch. 'Could be that.'

'We don't have any other answer. Let's write it down.'

They continued on through the questions, with the quiz pausing at half-time for people to use the loo and order more drinks. Addy was waiting at the bar when Ryan came alongside her.

'Hey,' he said.

'Hey, yourself. How are your team getting on?'

'Not bad, I think. We may be in with a chance of winning.'

'Confident! I like it.'

He laughed. 'It's either confidence or arrogance. Take your pick.'

'Well, you seem like a nice guy to me, so I'll say confidence to be kind.'

'How's your team doing?'

'Good. Though Chrissie has to leave in ten minutes, because her babysitter is on a school night, and Thatch is too busy chatting up that girl in the green dress over there by the pool table, so I think the second half might be just me and Jools.'

'Ah. The fickleness of friends. Who knew the promise of a day at the zoo wouldn't be enough to hold people in their place?'

She laughed. 'A day at the zoo sounds amazing to me. I love animals.'

'Me too.'

He turned to smile at her. A genuinely warm smile. His eyes were bright with happiness and she felt it again. That punch to the gut…that pull in his direction. It disturbed her, so she distracted herself by trying to get the barman's attention to ask for an extra packet of crisps.

'Well, good luck for the second half.'

She grabbed her and Jools's drinks, gripped the crisp packet corners between her teeth, and walked back to her table, her heart still fluttering from having been in Ryan's presence.

He was easy to be with. Easy to talk to. He made her nervous, yes, but it was a *good* nervous. An exciting nervous. It was something she would have to be in control of, but she knew she couldn't avoid him. They worked in the field of emergency response—they would most likely meet lots of times now that he was with Blue Watch.

'Everybody ready? Okay... Question number sixteen... What object will a male penguin give a female penguin to try and romance her?'

There was some muted chuckling and whispered answers. One team shouted out a rude one, to a chorus of giggles, but Addy simply smiled and wrote down the answer—a pebble.

'How long are elephants pregnant?'

The questions got more and more intense, and when the quiz was done the answer sheets were collected in for marking.

Jools grabbed her coat and stood up. 'Well, I've got to go.'

Addy looked up at her in surprise. 'But we've not got the results yet! You can't leave me here alone.'

'You've got the fabulous men and women of Blue Watch to sit with.'

'They're the enemy!' she said, with a laugh.

'They love you. They're your family. Sit next to Ryan. There's space there. Ryan? You don't mind if Addy sits next to you, do you?'

He looked at her. Smiled. 'Of course not.'

That smile was everything. Drawing her in until her anxiety put up a wall.

'But what if we win?' she asked Jools. 'I think we're in with a good chance.'

'Then you go to the zoo and have your meal at Reservation! Zoos aren't my thing. They always leave me feeling sad. But, hey, if we're runners up I wouldn't mind having one of those bottles of wine.'

And with that Jools slung her bag over her shoulder, dropped a kiss on Addy's cheek and sauntered out through the door.

Flabbergasted, Addy turned and looked at Blue Watch, who made welcoming motions with their arms and invited her to sit with them. Nervously, she took her drink over to their table and settled into the seat next to Ryan.

'Thanks.'

'You're one of us by all accounts, anyway. An honorary fire crew member.'

Addy blushed even though he was right. She did still feel that these guys were her family. Paolo, the chief, had worked with her father for a long time. He had served with him and was now near retirement. He'd also been chief to Ricky. They'd all been close. She thought nothing of calling into the station to say hi, if she was passing by.

Nervously, she glanced at Ryan, and caught him looking at her. 'How long have you been a fireman?' she asked, knowing she needed to say something, and that was the only question that popped into her brain.

'About four years.'

'But you were in the army before—is that right?' she asked, recalling what Paolo had told her at Finnegan's Hole.

'Yes, I was.'

'What made you leave the army, if you don't mind my asking?'

'Not at all. I was married and my wife didn't like it. Said she felt isolated. Like she was a single woman. She didn't want to feel like a single parent when she learned that she was expecting.'

'Oh, you have a child?'

She could almost feel herself relaxing. If he was married with a child, then she didn't have to worry about whether he was attracted to her or not.

He smiled. 'Carys. She's five.' He reached into his back pocket and pulled out his phone and showed her a picture.

The little girl was the spitting image of her father. Same dark hair, same chocolate eyes. A wide smile. 'She's beautiful.'

'I think so, but then I'm biased.'

'Is your wife looking after her this evening?'

His eyes darkened slightly. 'No, she's with her grandparents for a sleepover.'

'Oh. Your wife didn't want to come out tonight?'

He shook his head, a grim smile upon his face. 'I'm no longer married to Angharad.'

Single?

'Oh?' She felt nervous again. 'I'm sorry to hear that.'

'She…er…wasn't cut out for motherhood. She thought it was something she wanted, but when Carys arrived she realised that being a parent was harder than it looked and that it required a significant amount of personal sacrifice that she wasn't willing to make. So she left.'

Addy stared at him in surprise. She couldn't imagine walking away from her own child. Being a mother was all that she'd ever wanted. Something she'd chased with singular determination at one point in her life. But nature had let it be known that she would probably never get her dream. She had been unable to get pregnant when she'd been with Nathan, and tests had not shown why. Unexplained infertility had placed a huge toll on their relationship and Nathan had sought solace in the arms of another. Someone who would give him the child that he wanted, leaving Addy alone and desolate and having to move back in with her father and brother.

'I'm sorry. How old was Carys when her mother…?' She didn't want to say *left*.

'About sixteen months.'

'Oh. That must have been difficult…'

How did any woman walk away from her child? Her own flesh and blood…made with the man that she'd loved? She tried to understand. Tried to imagine what might have made her leave. It could have been anything, and she was in no place to judge.

'It was. But I got through it, and Carys and I are good.'

'Does she ask about her mother?'

'Sometimes. She misses having one—I know that. I try to be everything that she needs, but…it's not the same.'

Addy wanted to offer him some comfort. Maybe place her hand on his in a show of compassion. But she was scared to do so. Her life might have been in his hands this afternoon, but she still felt unable to reach out and let him know that she understood his pain, and that she was sorry he was experiencing it.

'I'm sure she'll be fine.'

They were stopped from talking any more when Natalie switched the microphone back on and it made a high-pitched sound. Everyone winced.

'Whoa! Sorry everyone!' she laughed. 'The results are in!'

Addy took a sip of her drink. All of her team were gone except for Thatch, who was technically still there in the pub, just not with her. He seemed to have been successful in his wooing of the woman in the green dress, as they were now sitting together, drinking and flirting with one another.

'It was a close-run thing, ladies and gentlemen, with just one point separating first and second place!'

The crowd whooped and cheered, and when the noise had settled down Natalie gripped the microphone and said, 'In third place, with twenty-one points, we have Team Eclipse!'

There was another cheer and applause.

'And in second place, with twenty-five points, and winning the six bottles of wine with a wine-tasting experience at the Tutbury Vineyard, we have Team Blue Watch!'

Addy clapped hard and beamed a smile at them all.

'And in first place, with twenty-six points, and winning the family zoo ticket, the zookeeper experience and dinner and drinks at Reservation restaurant, we have Team 999!'

Addy gasped in joy and surprise as everyone began to applaud. Briefly she stood and took a bow, this way, then that, before Natalie came over and presented her with an envelope containing her prize.

'Has to be redeemed by the end of this month, I'm afraid,' Natalie whispered, before smiling and walking away, back to the bar.

'Well done, Addy!' said Paolo.

'Yeah, well done,' said the others in chorus, including Ryan.

'It was a team thing,' she said graciously, wondering what on earth she'd do with a family ticket to the zoo when she didn't have a family. Well, she had Blue Watch... Paolo had four grown-up kids, but the others were single. Except Ryan...

She held out the envelope to him. 'You should have this. You and Carys.'

Ryan looked at her in surprise. 'But you won.'

'I don't have a family to take to the zoo. You do.'

Hesitantly, he reached for the envelope, but as he held it he looked at her. 'On one condition.'

'What's that?'

'You come with us.'

CHAPTER THREE

It HAD BEEN the right thing to do, hadn't it? Asking Addalyn to go with them to the zoo?

It was a question that kept rattling through his brain the day before they were due to go, as he and Blue Watch raced towards a road traffic incident on the motorway.

The call had come through eight minutes ago. A multi-vehicle pile-up, after a tree had come down in the strong winds they were having.

Would Addy be there? She might be, if she was on duty today. He'd not seen her since the Castle and Crow pub quiz, when she'd very kindly gifted himself and Carys the family ticket to the zoo.

Carys had been so happy when he'd told her about the day out they were going to have at the zoo. His daughter loved animals! She particularly had an affinity for tigers, and had two cuddly toy versions that slept in her bed with her—Tigger and Joey. And if there was a nature documentary on the television she'd much rather watch that than any cartoon or movie. He loved her confidence and thirst for knowledge, and nurtured it at every turn. So to be offered tickets to the zoo, where Carys could see tigers in real life and pretend to be a zookeeper...? Of course he'd accepted!

It had felt only right to invite the real winner of the prize along. Addy had said she had no family, but from what he understood she was an honorary member of Blue Watch because of her father and brother. So of course he'd insisted she go with them.

But it would only be as friends, even though he did feel attracted to her. How could he not? She was beautiful, inside and out. Dark, almost black, straight hair. Large chocolate-brown eyes, underlined by darker shadows that hinted at bad sleep patterns, and full, soft pink lips in a very pale face. The kind of pale that if you saw it in a movie, you'd imagine her as a vampire. Because even though she had an outdoorsy job, she looked as if she'd never gone out in the sunlight. Yet she was strong and funny and kind. Generous, clearly. Warm-hearted. And clever—he couldn't forget that.

She looked as if she needed a good day out, and he knew Carys was chatty and confident enough with strangers for it to not be awkward.

'We're going to have a lady with us,' he'd told her. *'Her name is Addalyn.'*

'Addalyn? She sounds like a princess.'

'I guess she is, in a way. She looks after people. She's a paramedic, but her daddy and her brother were firefighters like me.'

'Is she pretty?'

'I guess so.'

'Is she your girlfriend?'

He'd smiled at his daughter's questioning, before shaking his head.

'Do you want her to be your girlfriend?'

Carys had chuckled and snuggled into him on the couch, leaving him with a question that had been on his mind lately. When Angharad had left, he'd sworn never to be with a woman ever again. Especially one who wasn't committed. But would he one day be ready for a relationship? With his daughter in tow? He refused to expose Carys to any woman who wouldn't love his daughter as much as she loved him, and he just wasn't sure there were any woman like that out there. Or, more truthfully, any that he could trust. He'd already been burned, and he wouldn't do so again.

'Coming up on the site. Game mode, guys,' said Paolo from the driving seat of the fire engine.

Ryan looked through the windscreen to the accident site up ahead. Police were already there, blocking off traffic and sending it down the outside lane only, to help ease some of the tailback. Lights flashed, and on the side of the motorway he could see one or two people from various vehicles, clearly unhurt. Behind them he heard more sirens as ambulances approached, but he had no time to look as he fastened his helmet and clambered from the vehicle to receive instructions from Paolo.

He was to go and help secure a white transit van that was on its roof, teetering in the gale-force winds that were still blowing. Steam was issuing from its underside, where a radiator must have been broken, and the driver was still trapped inside. The vehicle needed securing so that the patient could be safely extracted without causing further harm to himself or to the other rescuers that were turning up on-scene.

He collected the wedges that would provide primary stabilisation for the vehicle, whilst his colleague Matt began to attach the struts. The winds were strong, and they didn't need the vehicle moving whilst they attempted an extraction.

And then he heard her voice.

Addalyn.

He turned to look, saw her with Paolo, organising the scene. She was saying who should go where, and triaging the remaining drivers and passengers with injuries as she strode towards the vehicle he was working on. She knelt down by the driver, who was unconscious and had a lot of blood dripping from his head onto the roof of his car. He was held in place by his seatbelt. She checked his pulse and called for a head collar from the paramedic who had rushed to her side to assist. Ryan watched her carefully attach the collar, talking all the time to her patient, explaining everything she was doing even though the man was unconscious.

He respected her for that. The trapped, injured man wasn't just a piece of meat, but a person, and whether he could hear her or not she clearly wanted him to know what was happening to him, just in case. Who knew what the unconscious mind retained? This man, if he survived, might have dreams years into the future of a woman's voice reassuring him in disturbing times and might later wonder what his dreams meant.

'Ryan? We need you to cover the spill from that motorhome and secure the gas canisters inside.'

He saluted Paolo and ran to attend to his next job. The motorhome was on its side, all passengers and the driver having escaped the vehicle. But these motorhomes had kitchens, with little gas stoves in them, and they needed to be fed from pressurised gas canisters.

Some motorhomes carried only one, others two.

And they were an explosive hazard that needed to be removed.

Addy looked up from her patient and watched as Ryan ran to contain the gas. A part of her wanted to reach out, grab his arm and haul him back. Say, *No, not you. You have a daughter. Let someone else go. I need you.*

She was shocking herself with her thoughts.

Someone had to go and contain the danger, and if it wasn't Ryan it would be another of the fire crew, so which one was more expendable if it were all to go wrong?

None of them! I can't lose any more people.

Ryan was a father. To a little girl who had already lost her mother. She didn't need to lose her dad too. And that was all this was, right? Concern for a little girl she'd never met?

But she had no time to think more deeply about it, because she needed to do a primary survey on this driver, trapped right in front of her. He had a large laceration to his scalp, many cuts embedded with glass on his face and hands, and a rapidly expanding forearm with distortion that spoke of a broken bone or two. The arm could wait to be splinted. It was his left arm, and she couldn't reach it from the roadside. But she could get his head bandaged to help control the blood loss whilst she performed her primary survey.

'Chrissie, can you get this?'

Chrissie, the paramedic with her and one of her team mates from the pub quiz, nodded and got to work.

Addy used her stethoscope to listen to the man's chest. He sounded a little bradycardic, but there were equal lung sounds, so that was good. She couldn't feel any depressed skull fractures and there was no way to ask the patient where he had pain.

She stood up as Chrissie placed an oxygen mask on the man's face and got the attention of Paolo. 'We need to get this man out as quickly as possible so he can be more fully assessed.'

'On it.'

Paolo got the attention of two of his crew mates and they began to cut open the vehicle after placing a protective blanket over her patient.

It was hard sometimes to stand back and wait. As a paramedic the urge to action was strong, but it was imperative that they do this right. This man's ability to walk and even have a future relied on their knowledge and training to know when it was right to stand back and wait and when to treat. When to go slow and when to act fast.

She looked up briefly, over to the motorhome. Where was Ryan? She couldn't see him, and felt some anxiety, but then he appeared as he came around the back of the vehicle and she felt a palpable sense of relief. Felt a smile appear on her face. Felt some of her tension leave her.

How strange that she should feel this way. And why? She barely knew him.

He kept me safe underground.

That was all it had to be, right? She owed him—that was all. And he'd been kind at the quiz night, even walking her to her car in the dark when she'd decided to go home.

They'd walked quietly, side by side, and she'd felt nervous about saying anything so had kept quiet before pointing her key fob at her car and hearing it unlock.

'Well, this is me,' she'd said.

'Thanks for a great night. And for being so generous about the prize.'

'It was my pleasure.'

And it had been. She'd felt good about offering him the tickets. A little girl would get more out of a zoo experience than she would. A family deserved the ticket and she didn't have one. She was alone, and most probably always would be.

Ryan had leaned in and opened her car door for her, like a gentleman. It had been nice. Thoughtful.

She'd clambered in. Put her key in the ignition.

'Well, goodnight, Ryan. Get home safe.'

'You too.'

And he'd let go of the car door.

She'd closed it, wound down the window.

'See you at work, maybe?'

'And if not Saturday. Ten a.m. At the zoo.'

'I'll meet you there.'

She was kind of looking forward to it. Having someone to go with. Spending some time with him. Him and his daughter. It would be nice. It meant not having to be at home alone, waiting for her next shift, trying to fill the hours with something, anything, so as not to be reminded that the house was so quiet because she was the only one in it.

The driver was out now. On a backboard. Addalyn let one of the other paramedics splint his arm, then assess him and whisk him away, so she could deal with the next trauma. There were a few lacerations. A degloving incident with a motorcyclist, who was sitting on the side of the motorway, cradling his bad hand. He'd worn a helmet and leathers, but not gloves.

'Let me look at that.' She examined him quickly. It would need surgery—that was for sure. She glanced behind her to quickly assess his bike. It was crumpled at the front. 'You ran into someone?' she asked.

'The red car. Threw me over the top.'

'Wait—you were thrown? Sit still.' She clambered behind him and held his head in place, whilst calling out for assistance.

Ryan came running over. 'You okay?'

'This motorcyclist was thrown over a car. He got up and walked over here, but I want him properly assessed in case of shock. Could you fetch me a neck collar and grab a couple more paramedics for me?'

'Sure thing.' And he ran off to do her bidding.

'I'm okay. It's just my hand,' the motorcyclist said. 'Nothing's broken. I just walked.'

'Your legs might be fine, but what about your neck? Your back? You were in a collision.'

'I don't feel anything else wrong but my hand, and even that doesn't hurt much.'

'Because you've not got any nerve-endings left, that's why. It doesn't mean it's good. And it could be only adrenaline keeping you upright right now.'

'Honestly… I'm fine.'

'What's your name?'

'Miguel. Miguel Aguila.'

'Where's your helmet, Miguel? And don't move your head.'

'I have it.'

One of the women nearby showed it to her. The helmet had significant scuff marks across it that showed Miguel had slid across the road on his head, and there was even a crack. He might have a closed head injury.

'Can you tell me what day it is, Miguel?'

'Friday.'

Correct. 'And who's our king or queen?'

Miguel paused. 'Charles?'

'Are you asking me or telling me?'

'Telling you.'

'Who's the prime minister?'

There was silence. 'I don't know. But I don't follow politics if I can help it.'

'Wise man. What did you eat for lunch?'

'That's easy. I ate…' Miguel's voice trailed off and then Addy's sixth sense kicked in as she felt a shift in Miguel's condition. He slowly began to lose consciousness and keeled over, with her guiding him down as much as she could.

At that moment Ryan arrived with two more paramedics, Cindy and Emma, pushing a trolley and carrying a head collar.

'LOC just moments ago. Helmet shows evidence of a substantial impact. Let's get him on the trolley. Em, can you get the oxygen on him, please? I'll do the collar.'

Miguel was still breathing. He had simply lost consciousness. The question was, why?

Addy examined his head and felt the shift of bone beneath her fingers in the occipital area. 'Damn. Let's get him blue-lighted immediately.'

As Emma and Cindy whisked Miguel away, Addalyn looked at the frightened onlookers who had gathered at the roadside.

'Has anyone else sustained any injuries at all?'

They shook their heads. They looked as if they were shocked at having been involved in something so momentous, and were hugely relieved to have escaped without significant harm. That tree might have come down on a car roof. Instead it had hit the road, causing the nearest car to swerve immediately, another to hit its brakes and then, like a domino rally, cars had shunted each other, spun each other and, in the case of the transit, flipped over, most probably due to an uneven load in the back.

'You okay?' Ryan asked.

'Of course. You?'

'I'm good.'

'Good.' She gave him a brief smile. 'I'd better check in with Paolo. See if there's anyone else in need.'

'I think we were lucky. The rest of these people will probably get away with a bit of whiplash.'

'They'll feel it tomorrow.'

'Police have already started mapping out the site, and we're about to do clean-up so we can get the motorway flowing again. Life never stops, does it?' he asked.

'It can do. And for some people life is never the same again.'

Ryan nodded, understanding on his face.

She hadn't meant to be maudlin. Life might continue, but when tragedy struck, those affected often felt in limbo, marvelling at those around them who just seemed to carry on as if nothing significant had happened.

Time had stood still when she'd lost her father and Ricky in one fell swoop. One moment they were alive. Her father. Her brother. Two people who loved her and cared for her. Her inability to have children didn't matter to them. And then they were gone, in an instant, and she was left alone in a hospital waiting room with her father's wedding band in a small plastic bag and her brother's St Christopher medallion in another.

That was all that was left of their presence here on earth—a couple of bits of metal that had sentimental value.

And memories.

And the knowledge that she would never get to speak to them again.

What had been their last words to one another? She couldn't recall.

'I'll see you tomorrow.'

Ryan laid a hand on her arm and rested it there for just long enough before he disappeared for her to register how reassured and comforted his touch made her feel.

Acknowledged. Seen. Appreciated.

Yes. But also liked and cared for.

His touch had surprised her. Pleased her. Made her yearn for more.

She felt a little bereft when he ran back to help his crew, and she admired his form as he did so. He didn't shirk the gruelling work. He mucked in with his team to help clear the road of debris.

He's a good guy.

But she knew she couldn't get involved with him. And that tomorrow she would have to be careful. Keep her distance. Maybe focus on Carys? Make sure the little girl had a good day out?

Then she wouldn't have to worry about having any little moments with Ryan.

Seems good to me.

CHAPTER FOUR

CARYS HAD WANTED to wear a pretty dress so that Addalyn would like her.

'She's going to like you no matter what you wear,' Ryan had told her that morning before they drove out.

'I still want to look pretty.'

'But you're going to get a zookeeper experience. It might be better for you to wear your jeans and a nice tee shirt instead.'

But Carys had insisted. And so here they were, waiting by the zoo entrance, with Ryan in jeans and a nice tee shirt and Carys in one of her party frocks—a beautiful pale green dress with soft white polka dots on it. She wore strappy white sandals and had even tried to paint her toenails, he noticed. In bright, bubblegum-pink.

He smiled, having managed to bribe her to wear a cardigan, too, and had bent down to kiss her on the top of her head when he heard a voice.

'Good morning! You must be Carys?'

And he watched as Addalyn knelt to be face to face with Carys and shake her hand, her face full of smiles.

Addalyn had chosen to wear a dress, too. A denim shirt dress, belted at the waist with a bright red belt. And her hair was down for the first time. Waves and waves of black hair that shimmered blue and indigo in the sunlight.

She looked beautiful.

'Hi, Addalyn,' said Carys, smiling. 'Thank you for winning the prize and sharing it with us.'

Ryan smiled. They'd practised that sentence in the car, with him telling his daughter it was a polite thing to say and do.

'Oh, you're very welcome. But you must call me Addy. All my friends do.'

Carys grinned. 'Addy.'

She stood and bestowed a smile upon him that gladdened his heart.

'Shall we go in?' she asked.

He nodded and stepped back, indicating that she should go first.

They entered the zoo and showed their prize ticket at the gate. The girl behind the desk beamed a smile at them and asked them to make their way to the giraffe house, where they would be met by the head keeper in fifteen minutes' time. She handed them a small map, pointed out where they were at the moment and showed them which path to take to find the location they needed.

'Thanks.'

Exiting the entrance building, they stepped out into sunlight. It was going to be a lovely day. Blue skies. A gentle breeze. Not a cloud to be seen.

'Did you drive here?' he asked Addy.

'No, I took the bus. My car's at the garage, having a service. I drove it there and caught the bus from the stop outside.'

'They didn't offer you a courtesy car?'

'They did, but I don't mind taking the bus.'

Carys had noticed an enclosure coming up on their left and ran over to look at it. As they got closer, they saw it was full of meerkats, and that there was a group of meerkats perched on top of a fallen tree trunk, staring back at the crowds.

'Daddy, can you see them? They're so cute!'

Ryan laughed and nodded, lifting her up onto his hip for a better look. There appeared to be Perspex domes inside the enclosure, so that people could go underneath the ground and pop their heads up and be closer to the meerkats.

'Can we do that, Dad?' asked Carys excitedly.

'Maybe later, honey. We need to get to the giraffe house, remember?'

She nodded and slid back to the ground, looking for the next exciting enclosure and finding it when she saw chimpanzees playing on some ropes. She squealed with excitement.

'She loves animals,' he said, feeling he ought to explain to Addy.

'I do, too. I don't blame her.'

'What's your favourite?' he asked.

'I like tigers.'

'They're Carys's favourites, too.'

'Really? Then she and I are going to get on!'

He laughed, and watched as Addy followed his daughter to the chimpanzee enclosure and stood beside her, helping to point out the animals, watching them play.

Carys was being Carys. Chatty. Sociable. Laughing. Smiling. Talking to Addy as if she'd known her her entire lifetime, even though they'd only known each other for ten minutes. But his daughter was like that. Everyone said so. When she'd started nursery the teachers had said that she was a confident, clever and happy girl, who wasn't afraid to talk to anyone. And when she'd started reception year her teacher had been so impressed with her she'd awarded her a Buddy Badge, which meant that she was the girl anyone could go to if they felt lonely or had no one to talk to. Carys would make them her friend and find them more.

She got that quality from her mother. Angharad had always been a social butterfly, loving life and going to all the parties and events where they'd lived. She loved being with people. Becoming a mother had placed limitations on that, she'd said, when she'd left. It had kept her at home and she hadn't liked how that had made her feel. As if life was passing her by and all she could do was look after a crying, squalling baby that wouldn't settle when she tried to comfort her.

That had been a huge thing in their relationship. Angharad had had difficulty comforting Carys when she was a baby, and yet Ryan would come home, pick up his daughter and she'd stop crying instantly. He'd tried telling Angharad that she just needed to relax. That Carys could pick up on her mother's frustrations and fears. But his wife hadn't liked him telling her that, either.

He'd thought he was helping. He'd just made it worse. Angharad had thought he was criticising her, but he hadn't been. He'd been trying to give her some advice. Trying to help her bond with Carys, because he'd seen how apart from her Angharad was feeling.

It had been strange, because Angharad had loved being pregnant. Had sailed through her pregnancy. Had blossomed, in fact. And yet when Carys was born, his wife had changed. She hadn't been the mother he'd thought she would be.

So it was nice to see Carys interacting so well with Addalyn.

They made their way to the giraffe house and saw a sign for the zookeeper experience participants, telling them to stand by and wait. So they did.

'Have you ever seen a giraffe in real life, Carys?' Addy asked.

'No. They're meant to be really tall. Like really, *really* tall!'

Addy laughed. 'Taller than me?'

'Taller than a house!'

'Taller than a castle?'

'Taller than the moon!' Carys beamed and slipped her hand effortlessly into Addy's.

He watched as a look of pleasant surprise crossed Addy's face, and then a warm, happy smile.

It was nice to see. Very, very nice.

The door opened and a young woman stood there, in a khaki shirt and shorts and boots.

'Hello, everyone! My name is Macy and I'm going to get you to help me feed the giraffes today. So, who's going to be my special helper?'

'Me, me, me!' said Carys, her hand in the air, practically bouncing up and down on the spot.

'And what's your name?'

'Carys.'

'Well, Carys, that's a very pretty dress you've got on. We won't want to get it dirty, so we'll have to be extra-careful. Why don't you and your mum and dad follow me?'

Addy glanced at him when Macy said *'mum and dad'*, but Ryan simply shrugged and let the assumption stay. What did it matter if it was wrong? What would be the point in explaining to Macy? It didn't matter. Not really. It was nice, actually. Because he'd never had that. That feeling of being a complete family unit. And if he wanted to pretend for a bit, then why not? Who was it harming? Carys certainly seemed happy about it, and was holding on to Addy as if she never wanted to let go.

They climbed some metal steps, their shoes clanking, and came out onto a platform with a metal safety rail. The aroma of giraffe was pretty strong, and now he understood why. There were three giraffes looking directly at them. At head level! And off to one side was a big pile of leaves and branches.

Macy stood in front of them. 'Giraffes are traditionally found in Africa, and they are the tallest living mammals on the planet.

Giraffes are considered to be ruminants. Do you know what that means, Carys?'

His daughter shook her head.

'It means that they're animals that get their food from grazing plants, such as grasses and leaves from trees. They then ferment that food in a special stomach before they can digest it.' Macy turned to scratch the head of one of the giraffes. 'This is Mabel. Next to her is her sister Ethel, and the slightly smaller one is Ethel's daughter, Clara.'

'Can I touch one?' asked Carys, her face filled with wonder.

'Why don't you grab a branch and offer it to one of them? She'll reach for it with her tongue and when she takes the branch you can stroke her.'

Carys chose a branch and held it out and the giraffe called Clara came forward to take it, her long, dark tongue wrapping around the branch to strip it of leaves.

Carys let go of Addy's hand to reach out and stroke the giraffe. 'She's so soft!' she exclaimed.

Macy smiled. 'These are what we call reticulated giraffes. They have quite a distinctive coat pattern with polygon markings. Do you know what polygon means?'

Carys shook her head.

'It means five-sided. If you look at the dark markings on her coat, you'll see each of them is five sided, separated by white fur—do you see?'

Carys nodded, her face awash with wonder and joy.

They all stepped forward with branches to feed the giraffes. Ethel, Mabel and Clara were clearly used to being fed this way by humans. They took a great interest in what was being offered to them and were not afraid to interact with them at all.

'Why do they have horns?' asked Addy.

'Both male and female giraffes have them, but you can tell the sex of a giraffe from their horns. If they are thin, and have tufts of hair, then you're looking at a female giraffe. If they're bald, then it's a male. They use them in combat, when they're fighting over food sources or females.'

'Oh...'

It was fun to feed the giraffes. They were quite gentle, with wide brown eyes and long, black tongues that they used almost like a tool.

'We have seven giraffes here in Tutbury Zoo, but Clara will be leaving us soon to become part of a new breeding pair down in Devon.'

'Won't she be sad without her mummy?' asked Carys.

Ryan felt his heart ache when he heard her ask the question. She often asked him what mummies were like, and why she didn't have one, and although he'd tried to answer her questions as truthfully as he could, they often made him feel he was failing her somehow.

How did you tell your own daughter that her mummy had felt tied down by being a mother? That she'd lost her freedom? That looking after a child who cried all the time had made Angharad feel that she wasn't cut out to be a mother? It would make Carys feel it was her fault, when it totally wasn't! Angharad's leaving had all been about Angharad, but Carys wouldn't see it that way.

And so he did his best. Told Carys that her mummy hadn't been able to stay. That some people thought they could be parents, but then found out that they just couldn't.

'She might be a little scared,' said Macy now. 'Especially with the travelling down to Devon. But then she'll be excited to be somewhere new, and to meet different giraffes and make a new family of her own.'

He could see that Carys was sceptical about this.

Addy crouched beside her. 'I'm sure her mummy will be sad to see her go, but that's what happens when you grow up sometimes. You move out and make a family of your own. I'm sure you'll do it one day.'

'And Daddy will be sad when I leave?'

Addy nodded. 'But you'll still be able to see him and you might not even move very far away.'

'What if I don't want to make a new family of my own?'

'Then that's absolutely fine, too. There's nothing in this world that says you have to. Lots of people don't have children.'

He looked at her then, and wondered. Addy was in her mid-thirties, if he had to guess, and she didn't have any kids. Was that a choice she'd made? He didn't want to ask.

But she seemed to like kids. Or she seemed to like Carys, anyhow.

'You can stay with me however long you like,' he said, to reassure his daughter.

Carys turned and smiled at him.

'Do you want to help me let them out into the main yard?' Macy asked.

Carys nodded.

'Okay. Follow me.'

They followed Macy back down the steps to a series of gates and levers. Macy showed Carys which lever to pull to open up the giraffes' enclosure to the outside yard. His daughter took a hold of the lever and pulled it down, and as she did so the metal doors slid open, revealing the zoo outside and the out-door giraffe enclosure, and Ethel, Mabel and Clara turned to look, before slowly heading out.

'Okay! Now I'm going to take you over to the ape house, where I believe you're all going to help prepare their food and clean the house.'

'Are we going to see tigers today?' asked Carys.

'That's the last step on the tour,' said Macy.

'You like tigers, too?' Addy asked Carys.

'I *love* tigers!'

'Me too!'

'Yay!' Carys threw her arms around Addy and gave her a big hug.

Addy hugged her back, squeezing her tight, and Ryan couldn't help it. He felt great about how the two of them were getting on. He'd known it was going to be good, but he'd not imagined the two of them would click so well. Addy was giving his daughter her full attention. Listening to her. Interacting with her. Holding her hand as they walked and pointing out interesting things. Clearly Addy was having a great time, too.

At the ape house they went into a kitchen area where there were huge piles of produce waiting to be prepped. They spent a good half an hour chopping fruit, leaves, seeds, bark and eggs, and then mixed it with some special monkey pellets which looked like small biscuits. The keeper added an insect mix afterwards.

'We like to try and reflect what they might eat in the wild,' he said.

'I thought monkeys only ate bananas,' said Carys.

The keeper, Ian, nodded. 'Lots of people think that. They do eat fruit—as you can see here—but we don't give them too much of it. We've found that by reducing fruit we can improve an ape's dental health as well as their physical fitness. Fruit that has been commercially grown for human consumption is different to the fruit available to primates in the wild, so we're very careful with the amount they consume.'

Carys looked lost.

'They're just trying to keep the monkeys healthy,' said Ryan, realising that Ian might not know how to simplify some of the terms he used so that younger kids could follow. Perhaps he was new?

'Oh, okay… Like Miss Roberts tells me not to eat too many sweets?'

Miss Roberts was the family dentist.

'Exactly!'

'And the fruit here is like sweeties for the monkeys?'

'That's right.'

'Oh…'

They headed out into an empty enclosure and Ian told them that they should all try to hide the food around the compound as it would 'enrich the apes' living experience'.

Again, Ryan had to explain. 'It's like a game for them…so they don't get bored.'

Carys had great fun stuffing food inside a rubber tyre. She even climbed a rope onto a platform and balanced half a watermelon on a pole there. Addy held her arms out to help Carys down. Once they were done, they were able to go out to the viewing area and watch as Ian released some orangutans out into the open for them to go and forage.

'Look, Addy! They found my food!'

'They did! Aren't they clever?'

Ryan started taking pictures on his phone. Carys was pointing at the apes. Addy was kneeling down next to Carys, with her arm around her shoulder. He took one of Addy and Carys laughing so hard and so genuinely it almost looked like a mother and daughter photo. He stared at the photo, his heart captured by the sheer joy on their faces.

Was this what Carys needed? A connection with a mother figure? She certainly seemed to be enjoying it. Revelling in it, actually. And Addalyn seemed genuinely happy, too.

He looked up from his phone at the two of them, deciding to put his phone away and enjoy this moment with them. Stepping forward, he laid a hand on Carys's back and pointed at a mother orangutan with her fluffy-haired baby.

'Aww! They're so cute!' squealed Carys.

'Having fun?' he asked Addy.

'I really am. I wasn't sure how this was going to go, but I am loving it. Carys is great, you know?'

'Thanks. I think so, too, but I am biased.'

'It must be difficult, raising her alone and having to work, too?'

'It's been a juggling act, but it's easier now that she's at school full time.' He looked at her carefully, before he said, 'I love being a dad. And you're great with kids. You're clearly a natural.'

She smiled at his comment. 'Thanks.'

But she looked a little sad. He was going to ask her if she was all right, but she spoke before he could.

'Hey, Carys, have you seen that one up at the top of the platform? He's huge!'

Clearly she wanted to change the subject, which was fine. The subject of whether people wanted children or not could be tricky to navigate. You couldn't assume that every woman wanted to have a child. You couldn't know if someone had had problems trying to conceive. It wasn't a conversation that you just blundered into, and he didn't want to upset Addy. They were all having a good day.

They fed the penguins next, actually getting to go into the enclosure with buckets of tiny nutrient-rich fish that were loaded with vitamins. The keepers made them wear overalls and boots and gloves, so that afterwards they wouldn't smell of fish, and it was great fun feeding them, watching them dive into the water or waddle on land. They were quite noisy too!

After that they went into the elephant house and helped to give the elephants a bath, spraying them with water from hoses after using what looked like a garden broom to give them a scrub.

The two elephants they were working with—Achilles and Bindu—loved their baths and playfully squirted water over themselves and their keepers, and in turn Addy, Ryan and Carys! They tried to stay as dry as they could, but it didn't really matter because they were all having so much fun! After the elephants' baths they were able to hand-feed them, and Bindu in particular was most enamoured with Carys, using his trunk to constantly sniff the little girl, making Carys giggle continuously at his antics.

And then came the moment that he knew Carys and Addy had waited for and looked forward to the most. The big cats. There wouldn't be the chance for any personal interaction, but they were given a behind-the-scenes tour and were able to help clean out a couple of pens.

'This is Sierra. She's a Sumatran tiger—a species which is critically endangered. But we are very proud to say that she is expecting two cubs, and has only about another month before she delivers.'

'She's going to be a mummy?' Carys asked in awe and wonder.

'That's right,' said Sally, the keeper. 'Sumatran tigers are usually smaller in size than the other tigers you might know about, and can you see those white spots on the backs of her ears?'

They all nodded.

'They act as false eyes and make other animals think that they have been spotted from behind.'

'Nature's so clever!' said Addy.

'Their coats are unique to each animal, so when Sierra has her two cubs they will each have their own pattern. Sumatran tigers usually have stripes that are closer together and more orange and black than other tigers'. They also have webbed paws, which makes them very good swimmers.'

'It's not true that cats don't like water, is it?' asked Carys.

'That's definitely not true! Sierra loves sitting or bathing in her pond out in her enclosure.'

'Where's the daddy?'

'The father is Loki, but you can't see him today, because he's currently with the vet, having a dental procedure.'

'Does he need a filling?'

Sally smiled at Carys. 'Kind of. He broke a tooth and developed a little abscess. It's being cleaned out, so it doesn't make him ill. We try to keep high levels of good health for our animals as we want them all to survive and work within our breeding programme.'

'She looks so majestic,' said Addy, gazing at the tiger as she panted away on her bed.

'She is a beauty,' agreed Sally.

The tiger wasn't the only beautiful creature he could see, Ryan thought.

'Tigers are meant to hunt and kill other animals to survive, so…what do you feed them?' asked Carys.

'You're absolutely right. Tigers do like to hunt—usually at night—so we feed them a variety of meat that we hide in their enclosure, so they have to hunt for it, or climb, or work out how to get the meat that's hanging from the trees.'

Sally knelt down and looked his daughter right in the eyes.

'Have you ever touched a tiger tooth?' she asked.

Carys shook her head.

'Want to see one?'

'Yes, please!'

Sally pulled a real-life tiger fang from her pocket and handed it to Carys. 'This came from a male Amur tiger called Colossus. Do you know where Amur tigers live?'

'No…' Carys took the tooth and gazed at it in wonder.

'They come from Russia. They used to be called Siberian tigers.'

'I've heard of those! I've seen them on the telly.'

'You have? Then do you know how many are left?'

Carys looked sad. 'Not many.'

'That's why tigers such as Sierra are precious. We not only try to keep up their numbers here in captivity, we also work around the world helping to educate people about tigers, their habitats, and how we humans can help them survive in the wild.'

'How can we?'

'Well, we work with the communities near tigers. The people there help us watch them and count them. And because the locals take an active part in monitoring them, it helps us reduce poaching. Do you know what poaching is?'

Carys shrugged.

'It's when someone illegally hunts an animal and kills it.'

'Oh. That's bad…'

'It is.'

'Why do people kill tigers?'

'That's a very good question. Some people want their fur. Others believe that parts of the tiger can be used in medicine.'

'Can it?'

Sally shook her head.

'I want to help a tiger. How can I?'

The keeper smiled. 'You're so sweet to want to help. We offer adoptions here, where you can adopt any animal in the zoo. Or you can get your mum and dad to help you look online and see if there's an animal charity you want to support instead.'

Sally was the second person to mistake them for a family. The idea that he and Addy were married, was… Well, Ryan could see the flush on her cheeks, too.

'I'll think about it.'

Sally smiled. 'Good idea. You don't want to rush into anything. I think you're a very wise little girl.'

'I'm going to be a vet when I'm older.'

'Sounds perfect for you. Now, let me show you the ocelots.'

They had a great time looking around the zoo, learning a lot about all the animals, and when the morning was over they headed to Reservation, the zoo's restaurant.

The restaurant was very elegant. Soft grey decor, crisp white tablecloths and hyper-realistic animal art in graphite pencil all over the walls. It was like a mural of a jungle, lit by wall sconces and candlelight. Greenery cascaded down from multitudes of baskets above their heads, and the soft scent of hibiscus was barely there.

Ryan, Addy and Carys were seated at a table in a bay window that overlooked the flamingo enclosure. Lots of salmon-pink birds stood in the water, occasionally dipping their beaks to try and feed on whatever it was flamingos fed on.

Ryan would bet Carys knew what they ate.

'What are you going to have, Carys? Do you need any help with reading the menu?' Addy asked.

She was sitting next to his daughter and opposite him.

'What's this?' Carys pointed to the menu.

'Vegetable lasagne.'

'Oh, I love lasagne! Can I have that?'

'Sure,' said Ryan. 'What do you fancy, Addy?'

'I don't know. Having seen all those animals, I'm kind of glad that this restaurant doesn't serve any animal products at all. I'd feel weird eating them after that.'

'I agree. All of this sounds lovely, but I'm not sure what to pick.'

'I think I might start with the gazpacho…'

'I'll join you. What about a main course?'

'Erm… I think maybe the vegetable chana with pilau rice?'

'Hmm... I think I'll go for the Brazilian black bean chilli.'

They gave their choices to the waitress, who took their menus from them and then provided Carys with a tablet to play animal games on whilst she waited.

'This is so nice... I can't remember the last time I sat in a restaurant,' Addalyn said.

'Really?'

'Really. I think the last time was before I lost Dad and Ricky.'

'What was the occasion?'

Addy frowned.

'Why were you in a restaurant?'

'Oh! Hen night for a group of friends.'

'You don't have a significant other who takes you out for a meal? Just the two of you?'

'There was Nathan... But that was so long ago I can't even remember.'

'Nathan?'

'My ex. Obviously. We did go out to restaurants in the early days, but then our lives became so consumed with other stuff I guess we forgot to remember we were actually a couple.'

He could understand that. When he and Angharad had first met, everything had been wonderful. A whirlwind of romance and nights out on the town. But then, after they'd been together for a while, living together, then married, work had become a priority for him—especially after he'd begun to feel that he was failing her as a husband. Angharad had never seemed happy. No matter what he'd tried. And then she'd got pregnant with Carys.

Yes, it had been unplanned, but she'd seemed to love being pregnant, and he'd thought, briefly, that everything would be all right between them again. But it hadn't worked out.

'Life can get like that, sometimes,' he said.

'Maybe. But I often blame myself.'

'Why?'

She glanced at Carys, but his daughter was absorbed in a game where she could chase butterflies with a net.

'Maybe I neglected him.'

'Did he tell you he felt neglected?'

'No. Not directly. But eventually his actions spoke louder than any words he might have used.'

Ryan frowned, unsure what she meant.

'He met someone else,' she said in a low voice, looking awkward.

Oh. He hadn't meant to make her feel bad. Because they'd been having a lovely time here today and the day wasn't over yet! The obvious hurt in her eyes pained him.

'I'm sorry. I didn't mean to pry.'

She shrugged. 'It's fine.'

'No, it's not. You must have been hurt.'

Were those tears he could see forming in her eyes? He had tissues in his pocket. He always carried them. For Carys. But now he passed one to her and felt his heart soften at the way she thankfully took it and dabbed at her eyes.

'A little.'

He wanted to reach for her hand. To comfort her. But he felt that he couldn't with Carys right there next to them. He didn't want to confuse his daughter with what was going on between them. He'd already told her that they were just friends who happened to work together, and that was all.

Instead, he tried to show it on his face. With his concern for her. His apology. 'I know what it's like to lose someone you once loved. To have them walk away and choose somebody or something else other than you.'

Addy gazed back at him. And then at Carys. She nodded.

CHAPTER FIVE

SHE DIDN'T WANT to talk about Nathan. She'd closed that episode in her life long ago. One huge painful episode, locked away in a box. She'd once believed it would be the only painful episode in her life, and then she'd lost Dad and Ricky, further breaking her heart…

Now she had lots of pain locked away in the dark recesses of her soul, and she never intended to examine it again. She was trying to reclaim her enjoyment of life. Find meaning in her work. Saving lives. Keeping people safe. Giving other people a future. It gave her some meaning. A reason for being here.

She intended to find her life's purpose in serving others, because that was all she could foresee. Stealing moments for herself that she would savour in private and hope that it would be enough.

But today? So far she was loving her time with Ryan and Carys. Carys was the sweetest little girl. Enthusiastic, warm, clever. And best of all Carys had kept on holding her hand, wherever they'd been that morning. They'd shared some lovely moments feeding the animals, and washing the elephants had been so funny. Especially when that one elephant had trumpeted water everywhere. They'd got a little wet, but Addy hadn't minded at all. Her dress had dried quickly in the lovely sunshine and so had Carys's.

They'd all been laughing, especially Ryan, and just for a

moment…for one brief second…she had allowed herself to imagine they were her family. That Ryan was her boyfriend or her husband, just the way Sally and the other keeper had clearly thought. That Carys was her daughter and that this was what love and family would look like. What it would *feel* like.

When had she last truly laughed like that? When had she last truly *belonged*?

And then that brief moment of joy had been followed by such a long, extended moment of hollow grief, in which she'd known that she was just borrowing someone else's family. That she was pretending and that none of this belonged to her. What was she doing? Believing in it? If she believed in it and enjoyed it too much, it would just make going home alone even harder than it normally was.

The tigers had perked her up somewhat. Getting so close to such magnificent animals. To Sierra, who was carrying the hope of two new precious lives.

Was she jealous of a tiger?

Having a baby had once been her entire reason for being. Having Nathan's baby was all she'd ever wanted at one time in her life…

'I only lost a boyfriend. It must have been harder for you. Losing not only your partner, but the mother of your child,' she replied.

'It was a shock, yes, but that doesn't mean my pain was greater than yours. Everyone deals with pain, grief and loss in different ways. What could bring one person to their knees might not even upset another.'

'I guess…' She looked at Carys, still absorbed in her game. 'What was she like as a baby?'

'I have pictures.' Ryan got out his phone and scrolled back through a photo album before passing the phone to her. 'Just keep swiping left.'

Her fingers brushed his as he passed the phone, and she felt a frisson of something race up her arm and smack her squarely in the gut. Trying vainly to ignore it, she began to scroll through and saw the first picture was of Carys as a baby, being held by her mother, Angharad, in the hospital. Angharad looked tired, but happy. There was a BP cuff around her upper arm, a cannula in the back of her left hand.

Angharad was pretty. The kind of woman who didn't need make-up. She had long, luxurious hair. Honey-blonde. Elegant hands and long thin fingers and she wore a doozy of an engagement ring. It must have cost a fortune. Carys was scrunched up, tiny, with chubby fists and a shock of dark, fluffy hair. She looked perfect. They both did.

'She's beautiful.'

'She was eight pounds two ounces of perfection,' Ryan said with a smile at his daughter.

Addy loved the way he looked at Carys then. Full of love and adoration.

'Was she a good baby?'

She scrolled through many more pictures. One of Ryan holding Carys. One of the three of them together, as if a midwife had taken the photo for them, or maybe a visiting friend or family member. Carys swaddled in her cot at home. Carys having a bath. Carys crying as water was poured over her head to wash her fluffy hair. One of her lying on a changing mat. And then a swathe of professional baby shots, all artfully done in black and white as Carys slept. Swaddled within a circle of daisies. In a basket. On a pretend cloud...

And then there was a shot that almost stopped her swiping. Made her want to peruse the image a little more closely. Another black and white arty shot. Ryan and Carys. But Ryan had no top on. He was doing skin to skin, cradling his daughter, and all she could see apart from a perfect baby was a perfect guy. Muscled and fit, with flat abs and a small military tattoo on his upper arm.

She wanted to study him. Absorb him. But she also didn't want to be caught staring at him, so she swiped on and began to notice that Angharad was in hardly any of the photos now, and when she was she looked distant, as if she weren't truly present in the moment.

Did Angharad not know what a gift she'd truly been given with this perfect baby and wonderful man? How had she walked away from all of that?

'She was very good. The kind of well-behaved baby that makes you think you've cracked parenting and could easily have another.'

'You wanted another?'

'Of course I did! I always wanted lots of kids.'

Another reason she could not have him. Because she could never give him what he wanted.

'Wanted? Past tense?'

He shrugged. 'I *do* want more kids. Being a dad is the greatest thing in the whole world. But finding the right person who wants that too is hard.'

'I guess…'

'Plus, it's going to take a lot of time, you know? Meeting someone that's right for you. Meeting someone that's not only right for me, but someone who's also right for Carys. I mean, I don't think I've ever asked her if she would want to have a baby brother or sister one day.'

'I want a sister,' Carys said, having clearly been listening.

Addy smiled and glanced up at Ryan. 'See? You have your answer.'

He grinned. 'Maybe one day, honey.'

'If I get a sister, that means I also get a mummy, right?'

'That's true—though technically she'd be your step-mum,' Ryan answered.

'Ooh. Would I help choose her?'

'Er…actually, yes, I think you will help me. When that day comes.' Ryan managed to look a little uncomfortable.

'I'll help you too,' said Addy, leaning in towards Carys. 'It's going to take a strong woman to take on a fireman.'

'Why?'

'Because a fireman has a dangerous job and that can put a lot of strain on a relationship. It's got to be someone who will go into it knowing she could get a phone call at any time to tell her that her husband has been in an accident and is hurt.'

She didn't want to say *or worse*.

'Does that mean that I'm strong?' Carys asked.

Addalyn nodded. 'It does. You're very strong.'

'Cool. Then maybe I could teach my new mummy how to be like me.' Carys pressed 'play' on her game again and became absorbed, as Addy looked up at Ryan and smiled.

'You see? It's easy.'

'Is it?'

Ryan raised an eyebrow as the waitress arrived at their table with their starters—gazpacho for both Ryan and Addy and a small green salad with croutons for Carys.

The food was delicious, and after such a busy morning they'd worked up quite an appetite. The gazpacho was sweet and re-freshing, a little peppery, and gone much too soon. But then their main courses arrived and Addalyn tucked into her chili hungrily.

'I wonder what we'll be doing this afternoon?' said Carys.

'I think we're free to roam around the zoo on our own now,' said Addy. 'Anything you want to see in particular?'

'I don't mind. How about you, Daddy?'

Ryan shrugged. 'I'm happy to just see where the path

takes us. So, Addy, what do you normally do on your time off from work?'

The question surprised her, and she wasn't sure how to answer.

This and that… I stay out of the house as much as I can… I waste time sitting in cafés or bookshops…

'I guess it depends. Erm… I like going and looking around bookshops. I…er…do a little dressmaking on occasion.'

'Really?'

'Yes. I made what I'm wearing now.'

'You made that?'

She blushed as his gaze swept over her body. Clearly he was looking at her handiwork, the dress, but it felt as if he was looking at her body.

'Is it difficult?'

Her mouth was dry. 'It can be, sometimes. But I've been doing it for so long now I kind of know what to do.'

'Well, I think that's pretty amazing. I tried to make an outfit for Carys's Christmas show once. She was an angel, so all I had to do was sew a sheet and tie her waist with some tinsel, but I couldn't even do that.' He laughed.

'Maybe Addy could help you make my Halloween costume!' Carys piped up eagerly.

'What's this?'

Ryan groaned. 'Oh, she's been on at me to make her the costume of one of her favourite book characters. No one seems to sell it, as it's a little obscure, but I've told her I'll do my best.'

'What's the character?'

Addy was interested. It might be fun to make something for Carys, and it would give her something to do when she had to be at home. Plus, as a bonus, she would have to keep seeing Carys for fittings, and that meant also seeing Ryan. Whom she liked. A lot. Despite his being a fireman and totally on her list of forbidden things.

'She's a princess,' said Carys.

Addy frowned. 'That doesn't sound too hard.'

'And…?' urged Ryan, raising his eyebrows at his daughter.

'And the captain of a space fleet. Her name's Hattie.'

'A princess space captain? Hmm… Does this book of yours have pictures?'

Carys nodded.

'Then you'll have to show me, so I can get some sort of idea.'

'Okay!' Carys seemed thrilled.

'You don't have to. It's going to be a lot of work,' said Ryan, obviously trying to give her a way out.

'It's no problem. I'd be happy to help out. I've got, like, six weeks? That should be plenty of time to work around shifts and school.'

'Carys? Say thank you to Addy.'

'Thank you, Addy!' Carys threw her arms around Addy and gave her a big squeeze.

Addy laughed and hugged her back. 'You're very welcome.'

Seriously… Was there anything better than this?

Their second to last stop was the gorilla enclosure. Addy wanted to see the big silverback and there he was, in all his magnificent, muscled glory. Sitting in the middle of the enclosure, with his back against a tree, he surveyed his group of females and their babies. There were one or two juveniles playing around, swinging from ropes and tyres and chasing each other, but most of them were basically just enjoying the September sunshine.

The crowds were thick around this enclosure, watching from up high, looking down at the gorillas below. Plenty of people were taking pictures of the big silverback, especially when he opened his mouth to yawn and revealed an impressive set of sharp, dangerous-looking fangs. He was a proud beast, and Addy was impressed by his presence. The way he just seemed to know he was the most important of all and that he owned all that he surveyed. It was his territory, through and through, and no intruders were going to come after his near and dear ones.

Which made it so incredibly shocking when someone in the crowd suddenly screamed, off to the left. Addy looked to see what was going on and realised someone had fallen.

A child had fallen into the enclosure.

Instantly she whipped her head back to check on the silverback. He was already up and slowly making his way across the grass as his females scattered with their babies and ran to the other side of the enclosure, away from the child.

The child's mother was screaming, yelling, trying to distract the big silverback, and so was everyone else.

Addy looked at Ryan. Hoping her gaze told him everything. *We need to move. We need to help.*

'Carys? Come with us.'

They began to run away from the enclosure, pushing through the crowds that had begun to gather to see what all the commotion was about.

'He's going to kill him!' Addy heard someone scream, and she hoped that it wasn't true. That they wouldn't be too late.

They burst into the welcome centre and Addy grabbed a woman from behind the desk. 'Please look after her!' She knelt in front of Carys. 'Your daddy and I have some work to do, okay? We'll be back. I promise. Just stay with this lady.'

Carys nodded, looking frightened.

Addy saw a rush of employees heading to a door marked *Staff Only* and followed them, with Ryan close behind. Once through, they found a room with a bank of screens overlooking the situation. The silverback was just sitting there, only once lifting his hand to prod at the small child that lay motionless beside him on the grass.

Addy and Ryan identified themselves to the staff.

'We have the Dangerous Animal Response Team formulating a plan now,' they were told.

'And how long will that take?' asked Addy. 'You need to disperse the crowd around the enclosure, because all the screaming and noise could cause that silverback to react badly.'

'Thank you, but we know what we're doing.'

'Do you? Because I don't see anyone trying to control the situation. You need to disperse the crowd and then either tranquilise the silverback or see if he can be called back to his indoor enclosure. Will he do that?'

One of the men looked at her. 'Maybe. If we got Garrett to do it.'

'Where's Garrett?' asked Ryan.

'I'm Garrett.' A young man with a straggly beard stepped forward. 'Kitaana seems to like me.'

'We need to get all the gorillas out of there so we can attend to that child. Have you called for an ambulance?'

'Yes, of course we have.'

'Then you need to get those gorillas out of there. Get the females inside with the babies—that might bring Kitaana in, yes?'

'It might be safer to dart him,' said another zoo employee. 'It's policy if the public become endangered.'

'Get the dart ready, but let's try the other way first. There's no reason Kitaana should suffer because a member of the public made an error.'

They moved quickly, and Addy watched the staff as they began opening up the doors that would allow the gorillas to return to their inside enclosures. The females ran in quickly, holding their babies and looking panicked. Addy could see that they were frightened by this event, too, not understanding what had happened. They were used to being watched by the public. To having humans nearby every single day. But they'd never come up close to one who wasn't a keeper. They'd never come into contact with people whose faces and scents they didn't know.

And now one was with them, lying motionless on their grass.

'Kitaana! Hey, boy!'

Addy and Ryan stood behind the tempered glass, watching as Garrett tried to get the silverback away from the boy.

The boy still lay face-down on the grass, with Kitaana beside him. The silverback had made no aggressive moves at all.

Kitaana looked to Garrett, then back at the boy.

'Bedtime, Kitaana. Come on, now!'

The silverback looked around his enclosure. He saw that the rest of his group had gone inside and slowly stood up, leaning over the boy. He made a low rumbling noise, and then slowly began to walk towards the enclosure doors.

Addy felt a surge of relief that this seemed to be working, and that no further harm would be done to the boy by the gorilla, but that still didn't mean it was over. The boy had suffered a significant fall and might have all manner of injuries. He did look as if he was breathing, but that was all they knew about his condition.

'That's it, Kitaana. Good boy. That's it...'

The silverback entered his enclosure and Garrett slid the door shut. As soon as it was closed Addy grabbed the basic first aid kit that was kept next to it and, with Ryan, ran out into the gorilla enclosure.

It felt weird, knowing that moments ago a huge, powerful animal had been present but that they were now safe. Rule one in any emergency was that before you ran into an accident site yourself, you checked that it was safe to do so.

'Get the rest of these people away—it's not a spectator sport!' Ryan ordered the staff as he followed her into the enclosure.

Addy settled herself beside the boy, glancing up briefly and meeting the gaze of the boy's mother before giving the boy a visual assessment. He had some cuts and grazes, and his left leg looked longer than the right, which suggested either a fracture or a dislocation. His right arm was bent in a way it shouldn't be, and she had no idea if he had any broken ribs puncturing organs inside. He could be bleeding internally. Every second was precious.

'What's his name?' she called out to the mother, up above.

'Leo!'

'Okay. Leo? Can you hear me? You're okay. We've got you. But if you can hear me, I need you to open your eyes. Can you do that for me?'

Leo's eyelids flickered, but didn't fully open.

So he was near consciousness. Maybe...

She ran her hands over him, checking his skull for any visible signs of deformity, feeling for the tell-tale signs of a possible skull fracture. Leo was unconscious, but he wasn't vomiting, and there was no bleeding from his nose or ears. There was no bruising behind his ears or beneath his eyes, so maybe he was just concussed? No one would know for sure unless he had a CT scan of his head, which wouldn't happen until he was in hospital.

Addy checked his neck. Ideally, she needed a cervical collar, but there wasn't one in the first aid kit and they were still waiting for the paramedics to arrive. His airway was clear, and without equipment she was reluctant to move him.

Leo groaned and began to cry. A good sign. In fact, it was a relief. Leo looked to be about five, maybe six years old. Skinny, though, so not much padding. When he'd fallen, he would have fallen hard.

'What should we do?' Ryan asked.

'Nothing until the paramedics get here with a collar and board. They'll get him on oxygen and insert an IV. Let's just keep him talking and awake, and be ready to roll him if he stops breathing.'

'You think he will?'

She shook her head. 'Children are strong. Resilient. And they can compensate for their injuries a lot longer than adults can. Leo? Sweetheart? My name's Addalyn and I'm a paramedic. This is Ryan and he's a fireman. You've had a fall, and I know you must be hurting, but try to stay still for me, all right? That's very important.'

Leo nodded his head.

'Don't move, sweetie. Don't nod your head. Just say yes or no, okay?'

'Okay...' Leo sounded incredibly frightened.

'Don't worry. We're going to look after you and you're safe. There are no animals here. All the gorillas are inside. It's just us and we're waiting for the ambulance to arrive.'

As if on cue, the sound of sirens could be heard as Addy finished speaking.

She looked at Ryan with relief. It was at times such as these that she realised just how much she depended on the equipment she usually had with her. She had nothing right now except for the few bandages and antiseptic wipes that existed in the first aid kit. It was designed for basic cuts and scrapes, not catastrophic falls. But having Ryan by her side was calming.

'They're nearly here. Tell me, Leo, what's your favourite animal?'

'G-G-Gorillas.'

She smiled. 'Well, the gorillas that you were with looked after you when you fell. They didn't hurt you. They were just curious. Even the big fella. The silverback. He sat with you and watched over you until we got here, so I want you to keep them as your favourite animal, okay?'

'O-Okay.'

'Good lad.' She stroked the side of his face gently, trying to provide comfort, keeping him talking until the arrival of the paramedics.

Apparently, he didn't like football, so couldn't tell her his favourite team. He preferred playing tennis. His favourite colour was blue, and his favourite ice cream flavour was triple chocolate chip.

She recognised the paramedics when they came running into the enclosure. Mikey and Jones. Good guys. Addy explained what had happened, and the results of her primary survey. She watched as together they splinted Leo's arm and leg, then gave him some painkillers, IV fluids, an oxygen mask and a collar, before they carefully, with perfect choreography, manoeuvred Leo onto a backboard. He cried out as they moved him, so they upped the painkiller before they got him on the trolley and wheeled him to the ambulance.

His mother was running alongside, crying and apologising as she went.

'I was filming the gorilla! I didn't see Leo climbing over the barrier to get a better look! I didn't see! I'm so sorry!'

Addy said nothing. She could feel the mother's distress and understood her position. You couldn't watch a child twenty-four-seven, and who wouldn't want to capture the perfect picture of that magnificent silverback? But at the same time she was meant to be responsible for her child. Her maternal guilt would beat her up about this incident more than anyone else could. Something like this would make the evening news, or at least the local newspaper, and plenty of people would have judgments to make. This mother did not need Addy's judgment. She and Ryan had simply been there to help.

With the ambulance gone, they were thanked by the zoo staff for their assistance and offered tea and coffee, which they turned down. They wanted to get back to Carys, who had to be frightened by events.

When they went to find her they found her in the staff room, munching on a biscuit and playing with someone's phone.

'Daddy!' She ran to her father and Ryan gave her a big squeeze. 'Is that little boy okay?'

'He will be, honey. He's at the hospital now, getting all the help he needs.'

Carys smiled, then looked up at Addy. 'Did you put him back together again? That's what Daddy says you do.'

'He was still in one piece, thankfully. I didn't have to do much mending.'

She didn't need to tell Carys about all the possible injuries Leo might have. Why frighten her?

'So, can we go home now?'

Addy looked at Ryan and he nodded.

'I think we've all had enough adventure for today.'

Ryan got Carys fastened into her car seat, then checked and double-checked the seatbelt before he stood up and closed the car door. Addy was standing there, waiting to say goodbye.

'Well, it's certainly been a day to remember,' she said, with a glorious smile.

'It certainly has. Can we give you a lift home?'

'I can take the bus.'

'Let me give you a lift. I know Carys would like it.'

Addy looked uncertain, but then she smiled again. 'Well, if Carys would like it...okay, then.'

She began to open the rear door.

'You can sit up front with me.'

'It's okay. I'd like to sit with Carys. Make sure she's okay.'

'All right.'

He got into the driving seat and started the engine, glancing into the rear-view mirror to check that Addy was seat-belted up. He couldn't help but notice the way Carys leant into Addy, looping her arm through hers and resting her head against Addy's arm. And he also couldn't help but notice the way Addy smiled. Her face was full of contentment and joy as she laid her head against Carys's.

The two of them had clearly bonded, and he wondered if he had held Carys's happiness back by not letting any women into their lives. He'd thought he was doing a good thing, not having a string of women coming and going through their lives. He'd certainly not been ready. He'd been afraid of how it might make his daughter feel, but also of how it might make him feel.

When he'd stood in that church and sworn to spend his life with Angharad he'd meant it. And he'd fought for his marriage. Fought to keep Angharad with them. His daughter had needed her mother. He'd wanted his wife. When she'd walked away, leaving them behind, he'd never felt pain like it. But he'd had to push it aside to look after Carys. There'd been no time for him to collapse, to wallow in depression. He had a daughter. And she'd needed her daddy more than ever now that she didn't have a mother.

The idea of letting another woman into his life when he'd so clearly failed with Angharad had left him doubting himself. Left him worrying about just what he had to offer a partner. He wasn't simple. He came with baggage. A child whom another woman would have to take on if their relationship ever got serious.

He'd often thought, even though Carys was confident and outgoing, that maybe she'd be different with a mummy figure—but look at her!

'Everything okay?' Addy asked, having caught him staring at them.

'Just thinking about how happy you both look.'

Addy smiled. 'She makes it easy. You must be very proud that you have such a wonderful little girl. You're doing a good job.'

'You think so?' He felt a warmth in his chest. Her words made him feel good. 'I often have my doubts.'

'Don't.'

He gave her a nod and then began to pull out of the car parking space. 'So, the big question is…where do you live?'

'Union Road. You know it?'

He raised his eyebrows. 'I do. It's two streets over from us.'

'Is it? Which road are you?'

'Thatcher Lane.'

'I know it well.'

'I can't believe we live so close to you.'

'Did you move into that small house on the corner?' she asked. 'The one with the large hydrangea bush in the front garden?'

'That's the one!'

Addy laughed. 'Wow. Okay…'

'Does that mean I can come round to your house and play?' Carys asked.

'Carys! You don't invite yourself to people's houses. You wait to be invited,' Ryan interrupted.

Addy raised a hand in protest. 'That's okay. I'd love you to come round one day. I don't have any toys or anything, though.'

'That's okay. I can bring mine. What do you like to play?'

'I don't know.'

'Do you like jigsaw puzzles?'

'I love jigsaws! I haven't done one in such a long time, though. I might not be any good.'

'That's okay. I can help you. Daddy has just bought me a five-hundred-piece one with tigers on it. I think it's going to be hard, but it would be fun to do together.'

'Okay! You're on.'

Ryan smiled and pulled out into the traffic. 'Beware, though...five hundred pieces...might take some time.'

Addy nodded and laughed. 'Sounds perfect. How about next weekend? Saturday?'

Carys beamed.

'She won't forget,' he warned Addy, with a smile.

'Neither will I,' said Addy, hugging the little girl once more.

It had been such a long time since he'd felt so content. Since he'd felt he was with someone to whom he could trust his heart. He could, couldn't he? He was wary of rushing into anything. And he didn't want to get hurt again. But the way Addy was holding on to Carys and enjoying her company reminded him of what he'd thought it might have been like if everything had worked out with Angharad. He'd hoped for these moments. Wished for them. Imagined them. And now he could see it in a woman with whom he worked. A woman who was not Angharad.

Was he ready to face these feelings? This overload of emotions?

One last glance in the rear-view mirror showed him that Carys had her eyes closed. Was she falling asleep? Snuggled into Addy like that? Most times he didn't mind her falling asleep in the car. He'd simply carry her out at the other end and place her in her bed. But they'd be dropping Addalyn off first.

'Which number Union Road?' he asked quietly.

'Four.'

'Okay.'

She gave him such a smile then, and it did even more crazy things to his insides. Today had been incredible. Crazy and scary at times, but he'd face any gorilla, any day, rather than have to figure out how Addalyn was making him feel.

Because what if this was serious?

He felt as if he was on a precipice and about to fall.

Did she feel the same way? He wasn't sure she did, because she looked so secure in herself. So happy. So content. Maybe he was reading too much into this? Maybe this was just a fun day for her? She'd bonded more with Carys than she had with him, and apart from her beautiful smiles he'd not noticed her sending him any signals.

I'm wrong. I have to be.

CHAPTER SIX

THE CAR RIDE came to an end much too soon, and before Addy knew it Ryan was pulling up outside of her house.

It seemed to stare at her knowingly. Taunting her.

When you come back in you're going to be alone. All alone! Again!

Her day with Ryan and Carys was at an end. Her unexpected day. Her gift from the win at the Castle and Crow. And what a wonderful day it had been. Apart from the little boy, Leo, falling into that enclosure, the day had been wonderful and dreamy. Just the sort of day she would have imagined for herself if she'd ever been so lucky as to have created a family of her own.

It was so easy to imagine Ryan as her partner. So easy to imagine Carys as her daughter.

But they couldn't be.

Ryan was a firefighter, and she simply would not attach herself to another man who put his life at risk every day. She'd worried enough about her dad and Ricky and rightfully so, losing them both in one fell swoop in that building collapse. She could not be with Ryan and go through that kind of worry again.

Besides, he'd told her today that ideally he wanted more children, and she couldn't give him that. It hadn't worked with Nathan, and Nathan had left her, finding himself a woman who could give him the children he'd so desperately wanted.

And Carys? She wasn't her daughter. And she couldn't deny that precious little girl the chance to have a brother or sister. But she could pretend, at least for a day, that she was her mother.

'Here we are,' Ryan said, coming to a halt outside her property and pulling on the handbrake.

Addy glanced at the house one more time. She could envisage its empty rooms. Its quietness. The living space with its empty chairs. Dad's empty spot. Ricky's. Their faces smiling down at her from the photos she had framed and lined up on the mantelpiece, to keep them with her as much as she could. The neat, tidy kitchen, without the crumbs that her dad would leave behind every time he made himself a cheese sandwich. Without the knife perched over the edge of the sink in case he decided to make himself another. The empty bedrooms. The wardrobes still filled with their clothes. Clothes that, on occasion, she would still press her face into, to inhale their scent that was fading now.

Time was slowly erasing all evidence of them and only her memories remained. Memories that could quite often be haunting.

'Thank you for giving me a lift.'

'You said your car's having a service?'

'Yes. It should be ready on Monday.'

'Need a lift to pick it up?'

'You're very kind, but I can walk it.'

Addy looked down at Carys, still slumped against her, fast asleep. She didn't want to wake her. Didn't want to move her at all. If she could stay here for the rest of her life in this bubble, pretending, then she would. Very happily.

'She looks so content. I don't want to disturb her,' she said quietly, stroking Carys's hair.

'She'll be okay.'

Addy nodded, trying to draw out the moment, but knowing she shouldn't. So, she leant down and kissed the top of Carys's head.

'Hey, sleepyhead. I've got to go.'

Carys mumbled and stirred, but didn't wake up as Addy moved away and undid her seatbelt. Every movement was torture, because she knew every movement was a return to her loneliness. Her solitude. It was probably a good thing that Carys didn't wake up, because it would have made it so hard to say goodbye. Even though they did have a jigsaw date next weekend.

Addy opened the car door and got out, closing it behind her gently, but firmly. Still the little girl didn't stir.

Ryan got out too. 'Nice house!'

She turned to look at it, forcing a smile. 'It's all right. I'll give you a tour when Carys brings over her jigsaw.'

'You know you don't have to honour that promise, right? A five-hundred-piece jigsaw? That's not something that gets completed in one visit.'

'I don't mind. She can come over as often as she wants. I like her. I like her a lot. And it's not a hardship to spend time in her company.'

'What about spending time in mine?' he asked.

Addy looked at him, her heart pounding in her ears. How to answer? Should she tell him the truth? That she liked him enormously? That she found him attractive? That she longed for more? For human contact? To be loved? But that he terrified her all at the same time?

'You're okay. Not as great as Carys, but...' She laughed.

Ryan laughed too. 'Of course not. Who is?'

'Honestly, it's fine. Besides, I made her a promise and I don't break my promises to children.'

Ryan nodded appreciatively. 'You're amazing. You know that, right?'

Addy laughed nervously. 'Thanks. Erm…so are you.'

For a moment they just continued to stare at one another. The air in the gap between them was taut as a bow, and neither of them seemed to know what to say or do next.

Would he step forward and drop a kiss on her cheek?

Would he step away and simply say goodbye, giving her a cheery wave?

Which would she prefer? The heat and excitement and danger of the kiss? Or the disappointment of him simply walking away from her? If he kissed her, what would it mean? A simple friendly thank-you? Or something more?

If he walked away that would mean he didn't see her as anything other than a colleague or a friend. And somehow, in that moment anyway, she really didn't want to be just a colleague or a friend, no matter what job he had. She wanted the excitement and danger of a kiss on the cheek. She wanted the wonder. She wanted the thrill.

She wanted to be seen and acknowledged.

'Well, I guess I'd better go…'

'Yes.'

'Thank you for today. It was an adventure.'

She nodded. 'It was.'

'You're back at work on Monday?'

'Yes.'

'Me too.'

'Great. Maybe I'll see you?'

'Yes. If not, what time would you want me to bring Carys around next Saturday?'

'Around eleven? I could do lunch, and then we can jigsaw in the afternoon?'

'Sounds great.'

'Great.'

Another moment of tension, and then suddenly he stepped

forward, placed his hands on her upper arms and leaned in to drop a kiss to her cheek.

She sucked in a breath and closed her eyes, trying to absorb every exciting moment as his lips brushed against the side of her face. He was close enough for her to hold. To touch. To kiss back if only she turned and faced him.

But she wasn't brave enough.

Because she was much too scared to let this become something else.

To let Ryan become something else.

And then he was stepping away, walking back to the driver's side of the car, and Addy looked down and saw Carys looking at them both.

She was smiling.

CHAPTER SEVEN

'Is ADDY YOUR girlfriend now?' Carys asked as he got into the car.

Carys had tricked them both. Making them both think that she was asleep. Or had she just been fortunate and woken to see her father kiss a woman?

He was so bamboozled by the question that he just laughed awkwardly and shook his head. 'No, of course not! We're just friends. That's what you do when you say goodbye to friends. You give them a quick hug or a kiss goodbye.'

'I don't say goodbye to my friends like that.'

'No? Well, that's because you're little. You will when you're older.'

'Why?'

'I don't know. You just do.'

He started the engine and glanced out of his window at Addalyn. She wasn't going in, but was standing there, waiting for him to drive away. To wave goodbye.

Kissing her goodbye had felt good. He'd dithered about doing it. About how to leave her. Not sure what they were. But at the core of his feelings was the fact that after today they were definitely good friends, and so he'd chosen to do what he always did with his female friends—politely kissed her cheek, thank her for her time and walk away.

Only it hadn't worked that way with Addy. It hadn't felt as

casual as that. He'd sensed in her a yearning for a connection. As if she was a solitary castaway on an island who needed the comfort of another person, loaded with need. Her eyes had said it all, almost like she didn't want him to go.

The softness of her skin, her alluring scent and the sensual caress of her long dark hair as he'd pressed his lips to her cheek had sent his senses into overdrive. His mind had gone blank. He'd almost forgotten what he was doing...had allowed himself to pause as he breathed her in... And just before he'd pulled back slightly, tempted by the idea of a full-on kiss—one his daughter wouldn't witness because she was asleep, so maybe it would be okay—his logic and higher reasoning had jumped in to protect him and he'd stepped away completely.

I'm not ready. I might not be good enough for her. What if she doesn't feel that way?

And now he was back in the car with a curious daughter and he had to drive away.

Why isn't she going inside her house?

Addy continued to stand by her front gate, watching them drive away, one hand raised in a wave. From this distance she looked like a ghost, with her pale face and dark hair. He felt drawn to keep looking at her, to keep wondering. And then he knew he couldn't do it any more, so he took a turning he didn't need, just so he didn't have to keep looking back. To keep regretting. To keep being annoyed at himself for being so cowardly.

When she was out of sight he still didn't relax, feeling he would have handled himself better if given a second chance.

'Daddy?'

'Yes, baby?'

'Are you okay?'

He pulled over and stopped the car to turn and look at her. She'd never asked him that question before.

'I'm fine.'

'You look sad.'

He tried to laugh it off. 'I'm not sad.'

'Are you lonely? Madison, at school, she only has a mummy and no daddy, and she says that her mummy gets sad sometimes because she's on her own.'

'I'm not on my own. I have you. You're my everything. I don't need anybody else.'

Carys smiled. 'But don't you sometimes wish? Because sometimes I wish for a mummy.'

Her words touched his heart. 'I know you do. And sure… We all wish sometimes.'

'I like Addy.'

'I do, too.'

The house felt so empty when she went inside. Quiet. Much too quiet. Devoid of life and warmth and joy. She dropped her bag by the bottom of the staircase and with a heavy sigh made her way out to the back garden, unlocking the French doors and swinging them wide, so that she could stay outside for just a moment longer and breathe freely. She felt stifled inside. The warmth of the day had made the house seem fusty on her return.

Addy gazed at the trees, their branches softly moving in the gentle breeze. At the flowers turned up to the fading sun. At next door's cat, George, perched on the fence.

Life was beautiful. It could be beautiful. But why did she only allow herself to enjoy it when she was with others? Why did she insist on beating herself up about coming back to this place? Would it be best if she moved?

No. Their memories are here. If I moved away, I'd feel like I was losing them all over again.

Addy knew she needed to find a way to deal with her solitude. To find a way to enjoy being in this house again. Perhaps she needed to decorate it? Make it more her own now that it was no longer her father's?

She turned to look back into the kitchen. It hadn't been updated or remodelled for at least a decade. Maybe if she breathed new life into it, she might feel better? If she worked on the house as much as she was trying to work on herself maybe that would make her feel better about being here?

She stepped back inside and walked through the kitchen to the lounge. She looked at the wallpaper on the feature wall. It was a soft mushroom colour, with a tree effect on it. It looked a little sad, but maybe she could change that? She went over and looked at it. Down at the bottom, a piece was curling free. She took hold of it in her fingers and gave it a big rip, tearing a huge strip away.

And she felt a real buzz of excitement, and a rush…as if more and more of the past was being ripped away.

A fire had broken out in a small marina. Originally a cooking fire, on one barge, the flames had spread to three other boats and now the thick black smoke billowed up into the sky.

Addy saw it as she raced towards the scene in her rapid response vehicle. There were two known casualties, suffering burns and smoke inhalation, but she had no idea if there were others.

On the scene, she quickly appraised the casualties and handed them over to the paramedics when they arrived. They'd get them to the local burns unit quickly. Then she began a conversation with the fire chief, Paolo. Blue Watch were on duty, which meant that maybe Ryan was here, too.

'What have we got?' she asked.

'Pan burning on the hob on this boat.' He pointed at the burnt-out shell. 'Left by the first female casualty, who is suspected to have dementia. The second female casualty had left her for a moment, to deal with a mechanical issue down below. The fire then spread to boat two, where we think it rapidly burnt its way up the sail and mast, which collapsed onto boats three and four, causing considerable damage.'

'Any other casualties?'

'My crew are sweeping the boats now.'

'Any hazardous materials?'

'Gas canisters. Boat fuel. The usual. All have been secured.'

'Have we established a perimeter?'

'Got the boys in blue on it.'

'Good. Keep me apprised.'

'Will do.'

She wanted to ask him if Ryan was one of the firemen she could see fighting back the flames. The blaze was furiously eating up the old wooden barges. This marina in particular, she knew, was an historic one, where tourists came to view the older boats that sometimes took people out on tours around the local canals. She'd been on one of them herself, with Dad and Ricky, and enjoyed it so much, she'd taken Nathan. But he'd hated what he called 'the faff' of the locks and the slow progress of everything. He'd hated that it took almost a day's sailing to get somewhere that would take fifteen minutes in a car.

She watched the firefighters as they slowly covered the flames with water and foam, making their way forward slowly but surely. A sudden bang had her flinching and cowering in shock, her arm raised to cover her face, her heart in her mouth. When she turned around, she saw that something they'd overlooked must have exploded in the heat. The firefighters all looked to be safe, though, and were continuing their push forward.

Her heart thudded painfully in her chest. It simply reminded her of the call with her dad and Ricky. Watching helplessly, unable to do anything. Worrying about the two men whom she loved so deeply and hoping that they would be okay.

What if the firefighters had been closer to that explosion? What if they'd been blown into the water? What if, God forbid, they'd been hurt? What if one of them had been Ryan?

She could easily ask Paolo who he had fighting the blaze. Could easily check. But she refused to do so. Because asking would mean something, wouldn't it? If she asked him it would reveal, not only to herself but to everyone else, that she cared about Ryan in particular. And she could not admit that to herself, never mind anyone else.

So she stood there and waited, biting her lip and keeping her torturous thoughts to herself.

With the blaze finally contained, Ryan pulled off his helmet and ran his hands through his sweaty hair as he made his way across the marina towards Paolo and, behind him, Addalyn.

'It's under control now, boss.'

'No further casualties?'

'Thankfully, no. Looks like all the boats were empty, as they usually are at this time of day.'

'Good. Finish off and then let's clear the area.'

'Will do.'

He peered past Paolo as his boss stalked down the grassy verge towards the carnage, and smiled at Addalyn.

'Hey.'

'Hey.'

She smiled back at him. A shy kind of smile. A sweet smile. One that seemed to say she was mightily relieved to see he was okay.

'How have you been?' he asked.

She paused for a moment. 'Good. You?'

'Yeah. A bit hot, but I'm okay.'

He pulled off a glove and examined his wrist. He'd felt that blast when it had gone off. He'd been incredibly close. But adrenaline had kept him going. Until now. Now he could feel hurt and pain, and he wondered if he'd been caught by something.

Instantly she was by his side. 'Let me look at that.'

She took his arm in her gentle, delicate hands, turning his wrist this way, then that. 'Can you feel me touch you here? And here?'

'Yes. It's sore, though. It's not a burn, is it?'

'No, it looks like something hit you when that blast went off. Did you feel anything?'

'Not in the moment.'

'You should get it properly looked at. You have good range of movement, but there are so many little bones in the wrist… You might have fractured one.'

'I'll get it checked.'

'I can splint it for you in the meantime.'

'No, that's okay.'

He had to pull his arm free. It was distracting him. Her touch. The way she held him.

It had been a long time since someone had taken care of him. When he'd married Angharad she hadn't taken any interest in his injuries. If it wasn't gushing blood, or broken, then she didn't get alarmed or worried. And she hadn't thought he should. He wasn't a dainty snowflake. He was a strong guy who worked out. Who looked after himself. He had to, working for the fire service.

And all the scrapes he'd got into in the army meant he didn't worry about the little things either. Army medics in particular didn't mollycoddle you. They patched you up and sent you back out if it wasn't anything deadly serious.

But to see the concern in Addy's gaze now, the intensity of her examination and the soft way she touched him, as if she really cared about him, was disturbing.

'You need to get it checked, Ryan.'

'I will.'

'When?'

'Later.'

'You can't work with a broken wrist. You could jeopardise a rescue if it decided to give out on you during a shout.'

She was right. And he hated it that she was right.

'I'll report it to Paolo as a possible injury,' she insisted, but she was smiling, trying to show him that she was only doing this for him so that he didn't get into trouble, and not just because she wanted to be a thorn in his side.

He laughed. 'Okay, okay... Thank you for checking it out.'

'You're welcome. Are you still coming on Saturday with Carys? I thought I could get the measurements for her Halloween costume whilst she's there.'

'Sure. But only if you're still happy to do that?'

'Of course! Why wouldn't I be?'

He had no way to answer. Because he was very happy to go and spend time with her. He knew Carys would be happy, too. But it felt like something scary.

I mean, what am I doing? What am I pursuing here? A friendship? Something more?

He'd always known that someday there might be someone else. In fact, he'd hoped for it, not wanting the rest of his days to be spent in solitude once Carys moved out and started a family of her own.

But this soon?

His head was a mess. His logic was confused. The only thing that was perfectly clear was how attracted he felt to Addalyn Snow.

* * *

It took Addy four days to complete her renovation of the living room.

The old wallpaper had come off easily with a steamer. She'd sanded the walls and filled in the cracks, then bought new wallpaper in a soft duck-egg-blue and applied it to the walls after watching a few how-to videos online. It turned out she had quite a knack for wallpapering.

Next, she'd repainted, covering her doors and skirting boards in a fresh coat of glossy white paint and her ceiling in a matt white. Yesterday a new pair of curtains had arrived in the post, and she'd taken down her father's old brown ones and put up her own to match the wallpaper. She'd rearranged a few photo frames, added candlesticks, put a new rug over the wooden floors and added some potted ferns she'd bought from the local garden centre and now the living space felt fully transformed.

She was happy with it, and proud to show it off when Carys and Ryan arrived.

'This is what you've been working on?' Ryan asked as he came in and admired her work.

'Yes. Just this room so far. Next, I plan to work on the bedrooms.'

'I can't believe you did all this in one week.'

'It's amazing what you can do when you put your mind to it,' she replied, not wishing to add it was also amazing what could be achieved when you had nothing else in your life and no one to help you procrastinate.

'Well, it looks fabulous.'

'Thank you.'

It felt strange to be proud of the house. For a long time she'd only felt haunted by it. Burdened. Now she was looking at it in a different light, and she had to admit she was already beginning to feel a little better about being here, with all her plans to modernise and make the house work *for* her instead of against her.

'So, what can I get the two of you to drink?'

'Whatever you're having is fine,' Ryan said.

'Could I have juice?' asked Carys.

'Sure. What kind? I have apple or orange and mango.'

'Orange and mango, please.'

'No problem. I'll just get that for you. Why don't you get the jigsaw set up on that table over there and I'll be right back in.'

Addy headed into the kitchen and Ryan followed.

'She's been driving me crazy all week, going on about today. She couldn't wait to come here and be with you again,' Ryan said, leaning against a counter, smiling.

And him? Had he been waiting to be with her again?

His casual presence here with her felt strangely exciting. She grabbed two mugs from the cupboard and began to make tea, before she grabbed a glass and filled it with juice from the fridge.

'I've been looking forward to it, too,' she said.

'There's not many people who'd look forward to spending time with an excitable five-year-old.'

'Well, then, there must be something wrong with the rest of them. Besides, Carys is great, so it's not like it's any hardship on my part. And kids in general are fun! They remind you of what life was like before you had any grown-up responsibilities.'

'Life certainly is easier when you're a kid.'

'Exactly! The world hasn't hurt you yet, or tainted your vision of life.'

Ryan nodded. 'It does do that… I'm not exactly sure if I remember being a kid all that much.'

'You don't? I do. My dad and Ricky were my whole world growing up. My brother and I used to play in this area of green belt land, making dens and bows and arrows, or paddling in the brook trying to catch sticklebacks, or making rope swings on the trees. When I think back all I remember is an endless summer…' She paused. 'With maybe one heavy snowfall.'

'Snowball fights? Making snowmen?' He smiled.

She nodded, her memories reminding her of happier times. Times when she'd felt surrounded by love. Never alone. Even without a mother she had never felt that something was missing, because her dad and Ricky had made sure that she didn't. They'd involved her with everything. Made huge deals of her birthday and Christmas.

In fact, the only time she'd wished she could have a mother had been when her periods had begun and she'd been scared. But, again, her dad had come to the rescue, sitting her down, providing her with the products she needed, explaining everything. Not once had she felt embarrassed about it. Plus, she'd had her friends at school…

But she'd ached for her mother at that point. Realising that all those other important milestones she might have as a woman— puberty, marriage, pregnancy, giving birth—would pass by without her mother at her side.

When she'd struggled with her fertility with Nathan, undergoing all that IVF, she'd wondered what it might have been like to have faced it with her mother to talk to.

That was why she identified so closely with Carys. Wanted to spend time with her. Because she knew, deep in her heart, that even if Carys didn't say anything to her father, maybe she missed her mother anyway. Maybe not too much yet, but as she approached puberty she would. No doubt about it. She'd grown up without a mother by her side and she knew how it felt. And Carys had no brother to carry her through it. Just her dad. Another fireman. And who knew if that spelt doom for her as it had for Addy?

'We made the best snowman, Ricky and me. We went full

out. Borrowed one of Dad's hats, one of our grandad's old pipes. Stick arms. Carrot nose. Scarf!'

Ryan laughed.

'Has Carys ever made a snowman?'

'I don't think it's snowed enough yet. But one day we will. Maybe I'll take her skiing one year, or to Lapland at Christmas. Who knows?'

'You should do that. Before she gets too old to want to build snowmen.'

'Does anyone ever get too old to want to build snowmen?'

Addy thought about it and laughed. 'Probably not.'

She'd never been skiing. Or to Lapland. She'd dreamed, with Nathan, that when she got pregnant—when they finally had a baby—they would do all the fun things. Lapland for Christmas. America for all the theme parks. The Caribbean for the beaches. They would explore and have fun and live life after all the rounds of drugs and injections and procedures she'd had and being made to feel like their lives were not their own, but something owned by the fertility specialists who'd kept her on strict regimens.

Maybe they shouldn't have waited? Maybe if they'd had more fun together then Nathan wouldn't have left?

'How strong do you like your tea?'

'I don't mind.'

'Okay. Strong it is, then.'

She passed him his cup and poured some juice for Carys, eager to get back into the next room and spend some time with her.

They walked through into the living area and spotted Carys at the table, patiently holding on to her box.

'So, what is this jigsaw, then?' Addy slid into the seat opposite her and Ryan sat beside his daughter.

'The tiger one!'

'Oh, wow.'

It was a very pretty jigsaw. Three tigers, lying together among lots of brown savannah grass. The pieces were all going to look the same…this was going to be a challenge.

'You don't pick easy ones, do you?'

'If it was easy then we'd finish it too fast,' Carys said.

'Well, we wouldn't want that to happen,' laughed Ryan.

Carys opened the box and spilled out the pieces onto the table.

'Shall we pick out edges and corners first? Try and build the outline?'

'Let's do it.'

They began sorting the pieces. It was a slow process and took them a good half an hour, even with three of them, as occasionally someone would miss one and throw an edge into the middle pile, from where it had to be retrieved and found by someone else. But eventually they'd sorted them all and began constructing the edges.

Addy couldn't help but notice Ryan's hands. His fine fingers. Occasionally they reached for the same piece and would laugh, embarrassed.

'I can't remember the last time I did a jigsaw,' Addy said. 'When *do* adults stop playing games?' she mused.

'I'm not sure all of them do.'

She laughed. 'No. I guess not. But I meant like this. Board games. Jigsaw puzzles. Video games. Whatever it is they loved as a child, when do they drift away from all that and why?'

'I guess other pressures step in. Work. Bills. Socialising. Relationships.'

'Maybe…'

'Do you have a boyfriend?' Carys suddenly asked Addy, stopping to look up at her with a smile.

'Do I...? Erm...well...no, I don't,' she answered, feeling her cheeks fill with colour.

'Do you want one?'

Addy laughed nervously. 'Well, maybe one day. I did have one, but things didn't work out, so I'm taking care that whoever I choose next is the right one.'

'What was wrong with the last one?'

'Carys, we don't ask our friends questions like that,' said Ryan, trying to give her an out.

But Addy wanted to answer. She didn't want to evade the little girl's questions. Felt it was vital to be as honest with her as she could.

'Well, Nathan and I were happy for a while, but then we had a falling out.'

'When I fell out with Ruby, our teacher Mrs Graves said we had to shake hands and make up.'

Addy smiled. 'Mrs Graves sounds like a very sensible person. But adult relationships can be a lot more complicated than that.'

'Why?'

'They just are. You'll discover that as you get older.'

'So you didn't shake hands and say sorry to one another?'

Addy shook her head. 'No.'

'Oh.'

She looked at Ryan and he gave her a look back that said *sorry*. He had nothing to apologise for. And she did feel she'd answered Carys truthfully, so that was good.

Soon Carys found the last corner piece, and then they were able to attach two longer edge strips to form a bigger corner. The jigsaw was going well, and now they were beginning to find pieces to work on the tigers' faces.

'Here's a piece of fang!' Carys said, with a huge smile.

'Anyone want another drink?' Addy asked, grateful for

Carys being there, distracting her, keeping her focused, so that she didn't have to worry about being alone with Ryan.

'I'm fine. But maybe we should stretch our legs for a bit? Go for a walk?' Ryan suggested.

Addy looked to Carys, to see what she thought of that idea. A walk with Ryan would be wonderful! Alone, it would be risky. Too intimate. But with Carys there…? Easier.

'Okay!' said Carys.

It was beautiful out. Sunny, but not very warm. Lots of people were out, to take advantage of the late summer they seemed to be having as September wore on.

'When we get back to the house, Carys, I'll take your measurements and show you some of the fabric I have. You can pick what you want for your Halloween costume.'

'You must let me know how much it costs, though. You're not doing this for free,' Ryan said.

'Nonsense! It's a pleasure.'

'Pleasure or not, I know fabric isn't cheap. I'll pay for what you use.'

She smiled, knowing he wouldn't win that one. She had had no intention of taking payment for making Carys's costume. It was going to be fun. Something she would enjoy doing. Something for someone else. It would give her a purpose.

'I don't want to be that space princess any more,' Carys said.

'You don't? What do you want to be?'

'I want to be a tiger.'

'Oh. Well, I'm not sure I have any tiger fabric…'

'Let's go and buy some, then,' said Ryan. 'I'll pay.'

Decision made, they headed through the park towards the row of shops on the road that led towards the town centre. Halfway down was a fabric and haberdashery shop that Addalyn often used. When they walked in, it was busy, but Carys's face lit up at the sight of all the pretty fabrics on show.

'Ooh, Addy! Look at this one!'

Carys had lifted a corner of soft tulle, delicately embroidered with dainty flowers in pale blues, pinks and mint-greens.

'Gorgeous!'

Addy pulled out a longer strip of the fabric to look at the pattern and see how it repeated. Ideas were whirling in her head as to what she might use it for.

'You won't look like a tiger in that,' Ryan said.

Carys nodded and looked around for animal prints, spotting some at the far end of the shop. They made their way there.

'Now, do you want a cotton print, or fleece, or fur?' asked Addy. 'Bearing in mind that when you wear this it will be the end of October, so it could be cold.'

Carys was touching all the fabric, but seemed most enamoured by the fur.

'This one! It's nice and soft.'

'Hmm…'

Addy tested it with her fingers to see if the many layers might be too much for her sewing machine to deal with. But it seemed light and thin enough not to be a problem, yet thick enough to keep Carys warm. And if it wasn't, then Carys could always wear some clothes beneath it.

'This could work.'

'How much will you need?' Ryan asked.

'Two metres? To be on the safe side. And— Ooh, what about this?' Addy pointed at some lace trim that she knew would work well as teeth.

'Get whatever you need.'

The lady who owned the shop wound out two metres of fabric and half a metre of trim, folded it all and placed it in a bag for them as Ryan got out his card and paid.

They headed back outside.

'Where to next?' asked Ryan.

'Can we see if my magazine is in the shop?' Carys asked.

Addy looked to Ryan. 'Magazine?'

'She gets this partwork… It's about all the birds in the world. I think she's got about twelve issues. At the moment they're doing birds of the UK.'

'You like birds?' she asked his daughter.

'Yes! I do! My favourite is the robin redbreast.'

'They are sweet. They're pretty tame, you know? You can get them to feed out of your hand if you're patient enough.'

'Can you?'

This piece of information seemed to blow Carys's mind.

Laughing, Addy allowed Carys to slip her hand into hers and they headed over to the newsagent to see if they had Carys's magazine. They did, so they bought it and headed back towards the park.

'You know, I've got a few bits and pieces in,' said Addy. 'We could easily make up a small picnic in the back garden.'

'Oh, we wouldn't want to put you out.'

'You wouldn't be! It would be a pleasure,' she said, smiling, hoping Ryan would say yes.

She didn't know what it was. She knew she ought to be not getting as involved with them as she was. But she simply couldn't help it. She loved their company. Loved the way it felt to be with them. Loved the way she felt she was a part of something. And she didn't want it to end now that they were here.

At home, they did a bit more on the jigsaw and then, when they'd all begun to feel that they truly couldn't see any of the pieces any more, and progress began to be severely stunted, Addalyn went into the kitchen and began making sandwiches and putting little snacky things like sausage rolls and cocktail sausages in the oven to warm through.

'Please don't go to too much trouble. Carys and I will be happy with a sandwich.'

'It's no trouble. In fact, I like it! It's been such a long time since I got to take care of anybody.'

Ryan looked at her for a moment, then turned around to check to see where Carys was. The little girl was giving the jigsaw one last attempt.

'You miss your dad? And your brother?'

'More than words can say,' she said, feeling a wave of sadness creep over her.

'Do you want to talk about them?'

She did. And maybe he would understand? Being a fireman himself...

'You must have heard what happened to them?'

'I know there was a building collapse.'

Addy nodded. 'They got called to a fire in a block of flats. Twenty floors that needed evacuation due to what turned out to be a faulty electric bike charger. Someone had been trying to charge their battery overnight, but the item was faulty and it started the blaze. We didn't know that until after...'

She paused in her chopping of the strawberries she was working her way through and turned to face him.

'I was there too, helping co-ordinate resources and the rescue with Paolo, who was newly in charge of Blue Watch.'

'My chief Paolo?'

She nodded. 'He'd worked hard to get his promotion. Had earned it. He and my dad were best friends, and though they'd both gone for the post my dad couldn't have been prouder that his friend got it.'

'He sounds like a good guy.'

'He was the best. Ricky and Dad were tasked with trying to get as many people out as they could. They were using the stairwells, because they were concrete and weren't burning, and for a while it was working. They rescued forty-one people that night, before the heat and the fire became too much.

The fire grew out of control, despite their measures to contain and dampen it. Dad and Ricky were in flat twenty-three when a roof gave way and trapped them both. Ricky's leg was trapped beneath some masonry and Dad attempted to pull him out. But then the top of the building began to collapse and they got trapped in the rubble. They burned to death before anyone could rescue them.'

Ryan stared at her in silence. 'You watched it happen? You were there?'

She nodded, wiping a silent tear from her eye. 'I was.'

Suddenly he moved from his spot opposite her and embraced her, holding her tight. It was sudden and unexpected, and she forgot to breathe for a moment, so shocked was she to be in his arms and to be held. But then she let go of the breath she was holding and relaxed into him. She squeezed him back and just allowed herself to be comforted. Breathing in his unique, wonderful scent.

Ryan felt so good. So strong. She could feel the musculature of his body against hers and realised that for the first time in years she felt safe. Protected. Cared for.

It was a heady moment, and one that she didn't want to end.

'Can I have some more juice?' Carys's voice piped up behind them, and suddenly Ryan let her go.

Addy stepped away, wiping her eyes rapidly before turning to smile at Carys. 'Of course you can! Have you got your glass from before?'

She refilled the glass with juice and handed it to her. 'Why don't you go out into the garden with that blanket over there and pick a spot for our picnic?'

'Okay!' But then Carys paused and looked at them both. 'What were you doing?'

Addy froze, not sure how to respond.

Ryan came to the rescue. 'Addy was a little upset. She was

telling me about how she lost her dad and her brother. I was comforting her, that's all.'

'Oh. Okay!' And Carys grabbed the blanket and headed out.

Addy looked over at Ryan. 'Thank you.'

'It was the truth.'

'No. For the hug. I hadn't realised just how much I needed that.'

He smiled back at her. 'You're very welcome.'

CHAPTER EIGHT

HE'D HEARD THE story of the loss of Victor and Ricky Snow. How could he not have? He worked in their station. Their pictures and their names and their years of service were up on the memorial wall with the others who had been lost over the decades. But he'd not heard it from her point of view and he hadn't known that she had watched it happen.

He couldn't imagine how that must have felt. To lose a father and a brother at the same time was awful enough, but to be there, helpless, watching it happen, knowing she could do nothing to reach them, must have been an agony he could only hope never to experience. Would he have been able to hold himself together? He wasn't sure of it.

Addalyn Snow was a remarkable woman. Stronger than she knew. And being able to hold her in his arms like that and comfort her had meant more than she knew. He'd longed to hold her. Longed to make her feel better and take away some of her pain. But the feel of her in his arms...the heat of her...her softness... He'd longed to do more. Kiss her. Tell her she was special. Keep her in his embrace and never let go.

Only he couldn't do that.

He helped her carry out the food she'd been preparing and together they assembled their picnic. He felt as if he wanted to give her a reason to smile again. To be happy. Because he felt that he was the one who had reminded her of her sad past and he felt responsible. It had been eye-opening to hear her version of events, that was for sure. And now he wanted her to think of happier times, so he would make her smile.

Losing a crew mate at a rescue was a risk of the job. They all knew that. They all knew the danger, but did it anyway. And they honoured those they'd lost. Honoured their sacrifice in trying to rescue others or to stop a fire from claiming any lives. Lost crew were heroes. Addy's father and her brother were heroes.

'I'm starving!' Carys tucked into a sandwich and opened up a packet of crisps.

'You should try one of these,' Addy said, offering Carys a halloumi stick wrapped in streaky bacon.

'What is it?'

'A special kind of cheese. It doesn't melt when you cook it.'

Carys took a bite. 'Yum!'

Addy laughed.

This was nice, thought Ryan. Sitting in her back garden, in the sunshine, eating a picnic together. A simple pleasure. This was what it was all about, right? Spending time with family. Enjoying being together.

Addy was going to make someone a wonderful mother one day.

'You ever thought about having kids?' he asked, feeling relaxed and casual.

He felt he could ask her now. They knew each other so much better, and he now knew she'd been in a relationship before, with Nathan, so surely she must have thought about it. Or they must. And he only asked because Addy got on so well with Carys that he couldn't imagine her *not* being a mother.

But he saw a cloud cross her face and realised his error much too late.

'Of course I have. I've always wanted kids. But… I can't have them.'

He stared at her, shocked and surprised.

And feeling guilty. Again.

He should never have pried. 'I'm sorry.'

'It's okay!' she said, clearly trying to say it with a smile. 'I've accepted it.'

'Are you…? I mean, have you seen a doctor about it? Or…?'

'Nathan and I were trying for a long time. We tried naturally, and when nothing happened after a couple of years we went for testing. They couldn't find anything wrong with us, so we began IVF. I had four rounds. Three on the NHS and a fourth that we paid for ourselves, using all our savings. But it didn't work.'

'I'm so sorry.'

'It's not your fault.'

'I know, but… That's twice now I've brought up something sad for you and I'm beginning to feel paranoid.' He tried to laugh it off, to make her feel more comfortable, and he could see that she appreciated that.

'Honestly, it's fine. It's good for me to talk about it. People should talk about infertility openly, so it's seen as natural.'

'I guess…'

'We did have some hope on the second round. I did a home pregnancy test and it was positive, and we were over the moon. But when the clinic did a blood test the HCG levels were so low. Not where they ought to have been. And a second blood test a few days later showed that the levels had dropped even more. So…that was a no-go too.'

'That must have been devastating.'

'It was. All those treatments. The drugs, the injections… You begin to feel like a human experiment, you know? Your life becomes ruled by it all. You can think of nothing else. And as a couple you either turn towards each other after each failure, or you go looking for comfort elsewhere. Like Nathan did.'

'How long have you been apart?'

'Four years now. Four and a half… Something like that. I came back here to live with Ricky and Dad and then I lost them, too. It's been a hard few years.'

'I'm sorry. And I know I keep saying that, but I really mean it.'

'I know. And thank you. It's fine. That's life. Bad stuff happens. We just have to go with it.'

'Of course—but maybe this means that you've had your share of the bad stuff and from now on it's only good stuff all the way.'

Addy smiled and nodded. 'Let's hope!'

They finished their picnic and sat in the sun. Then Addy remembered she had ice creams in the freezer, so they had those. He liked watching her laugh. Loved watching her smile. But more than anything he adored the way she interacted with Carys.

Carys had been his whole world for years, and he would give his life for his daughter. To see Addy loving and having fun with his little girl meant everything.

It made him think about the future. It made him think about what sort of happiness he might find some day. Would it be with Addy? They got on so well together.

But…

He wanted more kids. He always had. And if Addy couldn't have children, then…

There's more than one way to have a family.

Addy looked at him as she laughed with his daughter, and he felt, deep down, that he would be able to pursue those other alternatives if Addy was by his side. Suddenly his heart began to pound as he realised he was thinking about what it would be like to have a family with Addalyn! It scared him. Terrified him. Made him realise that maybe he thought more of Addy than he ought to.

But he simply couldn't tear his eyes away from her as his thoughts raced ahead. Because when he'd held her, comforted her earlier, there'd been a response. He'd felt the way she'd sunk into him. She'd even made a soft sound of gratitude…of affection, and neither of them had really wanted to let go. And she was spending all this time with him. With his daughter. And sometimes he saw a look in her eyes. Of query. Of hope. Of fear.

But mostly he felt she was as attracted to him as he was to her.

Boy, we are both in so much trouble here!

CHAPTER NINE

ADDY RACED THROUGH the streets, sirens blaring, as she navigated the traffic towards her latest shout. An industrial accident… All she knew was that there were a number of workers involved with some sort of chemical spillage.

As she drove, she tried to think of all the things she'd need to be aware of upon entering the site. Getting details from whoever was in charge. Establishing safety protocols. Keeping herself and the other rescuers safe, so that there wouldn't inadvertently be even more casualties than there already were.

It was the number one rule as a first responder—make sure it's safe for *you* before you proceed to assist a casualty.

It was a thought that had been running through her mind a lot just lately. Keeping herself safe. Keeping her heart safe, especially. Because spending time with Ryan and Carys was wonderful and she didn't want anything to spoil it. It had been a long time since she'd felt this happy. And the last few times she'd felt happy life had thrown spanners into the works and ruined everything, taking away the source of her happiness.

Maybe Ryan was right? Maybe it *was* now her turn to have happiness?

She wanted to believe that, but she was scared of not holding back. Not giving her absolute all seemed to be the only defence she had, and if she kept it in the back of her head at all times that she could lose Ryan and Carys at any moment, then maybe she'd be prepared for it, if it ever happened? Just thinking about it even now, as she raced towards someone else's tragedy, made her stomach churn.

She'd only known them such a short time and they already meant so much.

She'd been having dreams of kissing Ryan. A couple of times they'd come close. Both times they said goodbye to each other after spending time together Ryan would kiss her cheek, but she'd been yearning to have him kiss her on the lips.

He had not. Because each time Carys had been there.

At least, she thought that was the reason why. Maybe at the weekend he'd not kissed her on the lips because she'd told him that she couldn't have children. She knew he wanted more. He'd told her that. He probably thought there was no point in pursuing anything with her.

But she dreamed of his lips. Of his mouth. The way it smiled. The way it might feel. All the possible things it could do and how they might feel. And she loved to listen to him talk. He was funny and kind. Empathetic and genuine. That was what she loved about him the most. You got what you saw. He put on no airs or graces. There was no pretence about Ryan. And she liked the way he looked at her. Interested. Content. Warm. He seemed happy in her company and she was very happy in his.

But it was all so difficult, because of what he was—a fireman. Maybe if he was still in the army it would be easier? Or if he was a travelling salesman? Or a postman or a truck driver?

Why did he have to be a fireman?

As she got closer to the location she became aware of more sirens, more blue lights, as other first responders raced towards the scene. It was on an industrial site, and as she weaved her way down the road she became aware of workers in high-vis vests and hard hats exiting the site in an orderly manner, as their own buildings' sirens sounded to indicate that an evacuation needed to take place. Up ahead was a singular fire engine, and behind her came two more.

She felt herself switch into full-on work mode as she searched for a place to park that was safe.

'What are we dealing with?' she asked as she got out of her vehicle, slipping on her own high-vis vest and attracting the attention of what looked like a supervisor from inside the building.

'Acetone production. Somehow a fire started in Block B. We've evacuated, but we're still doing a headcount.'

'Get those numbers to the fire crew as soon as, please. Any casualties?'

'A couple over there. Robert, I think. And Wendy.'

Addy turned to look at two people sitting on a grass verge, both with their hands wrapped in gauze. She used her personal radio to contact ambulance control, update them on the situation and order more ambulance crews. This could be incredibly serious. Then she headed off towards the first fire engine to liaise with Paolo.

'We've got an acetone fire.'

'I've just heard. I've ordered all the men to use their breathing apparatus. Do we have a number?'

'Supervisor is doing a headcount right now. I'm going to check on those two over there and establish a triage tent. Get any casualties brought to me after decontamination procedures, yes?'

They needed to be cleaned of any acetone before they got to Addy as a preventative. To stop any more issues.

Paolo saluted her and ran off to issue orders to his men.

She didn't have time to look for Ryan. Her mind was on her patients.

As she got to their side, she set down her bag and evaluated them. 'Hi, my name's Addy. Can you tell me what happened?'

She started with questions because they were both conscious and breathing. Robert staring at his hands. Wendy looking away into the distance. A cursory glance told her they did not appear to have any blood-loss or broken bones. They were the walking wounded, and getting them to answer her questions would give her a good idea about their respirations and their ability to talk, and whether she needed to check their airways.

She would do that anyway. It was something always checked after a chemical spill. Some chemicals could burn throats and airways if inhaled, and though her knowledge of acetone itself was sketchy, she did know that high amounts could cause irritation to the mucus membranes.

'We don't know,' said the man, Robert. 'One of the machines had been making funny noises all morning, and we were waiting for Engineering to take a look. We were going to shut it down, but our boss Gregori told us to keep it moving. There was a flash. Sudden. Blinding. And we heard a bang. Next thing we know the room is on fire.'

'You have injuries?' Abby asked, indicating his hands as she slipped on her gloves.

'Burns. My hands hurt like hell, but Wendy says hers feel fine.'

That wasn't good. When burns didn't hurt, it usually meant that the thickness of the burns was deep and had destroyed the nerve-endings.

'How did the burns happen?'

'We tried to stop the fire. Used the extinguishers. But we got too close. My clothes caught fire and Wendy tried to put me out...rolled me on the floor.'

'And then I slipped and fell into the flames,' said Wendy. 'I think I've burnt my hair too.'

Wendy turned to look at her. All this time she'd been turned away, as if staring off into the distance. She tried to smile. And that was when Addy saw the burns on her face.

Damn.

They went halfway up her face. Reddened and painful-looking. Some of her hair was gone, as were her eyebrows and no doubt her eyelashes. It looked bad enough that she might need a skin graft.

'Did you go through a decontamination procedure?' she asked as she rummaged in her bag to set up for a cannula. She needed to get fluids and painkillers into Wendy immediately.

'I don't think so...'

She couldn't let Wendy or Robert sit there with acetone still burning into their wounds. It might hurt, but she needed to wash the chemical off their skin before she applied new coverings.

Technically, she needed soap and some warm water to wash it off fully, but she didn't have soap, and nor could she get them to rub their wounds. All she could do was rinse and dilute the acetone as much as possible.

Chrissie had arrived, along with her partner Jake, to assist. Addy explained the situation and after she'd rinsed the wounds Jake and Chrissie began applying dressings, so Robert and Wendy could be transferred to hospital.

'How are you doing, Wendy?' Addalyn asked, feeling the woman was in a state of shock and disbelief.

'I'm okay, I think. Is my face all right?'

Addalyn took in her visage. No, it wasn't all right. But it would be. One day.

'You'll get the best doctors and sort it out in no time.'

'But I'm getting married in two months.'

Addy's heart sank. 'You are? Congratulations.'

'Thanks. Me and Brian are soul mates. Knew each other at school, but then went our separate ways. He got married, so did I, and then we both got divorced for differing reasons. We met each other again a year ago and it was like life said to me, *Here you go. Have some happiness after all*.' Wendy tried to smile. 'Do you have a mirror? I want to see.'

'I don't. But there's no point in looking at it right now.'

'Is it bad?'

How to answer?

'It looks very sore.'

'Brian loves my face. Tells me every day I'm beautiful. Will he still do that, do you think?'

Addy hoped so. She hoped that, whoever this Brian was, he was the type of kind, loving man who would see past the burns and the scars that might remain and still want to marry the Wendy he'd fallen in love with.

'I'm sure he will.'

'This is our second chance at happiness. If he doesn't… Well…' Wendy blinked slowly, her eyes starting to glaze over.

Addalyn looked up in time to realise that Wendy was about to pass out. She called to Chrissie for help and they caught Wendy and lowered her to the ground, placing her in the recovery position and applying an oxygen mask to her face. She might have just fainted. It might just be shock. But they would monitor her blood sugar, her BP and her airway, just in case.

Addy was pushing the fluids, squeezing the bag, when something exploded. Instinctively, protectively, she covered Wendy's body with her own.

The boom was deafening, and smoke and a horrific stench filled the air. Blinking, cowering slightly, she turned to check on her colleagues. They were fine, but shocked. All of them were as they turned to look behind them. Part of the factory had gone up in smoke and the fire crews were trying to beat back the fire.

Ryan.

But she had no time to worry about him. No time to run

and make sure he was safe. She had her priorities. Robert and Wendy... Chrissie and Jake.

Wendy was slowly coming round, having missed the explosion completely. She groaned as she came to. 'I feel sick...'

'You passed out. But you're okay. Stay lying there. We're going to transfer you to a trolley and get you off to hospital.'

'Can you call Brian?'

'Of course. Once you're safely in the ambulance.'

'Is he okay?'

'I'm sure he is. Where does he work?'

'In the admin office.'

Addy was soon transferring Wendy onto a trolley, getting her strapped in for the switch to the ambulance.

'Whereabouts?' It was best to keep her patient chatting. It was also a good way to keep an eye on any neural issues.

'The admin office here.'

Addy stopped briefly. 'Here? Where you work?'

'Yes.'

Addy turned to look at the building. Half of it was a blackened wreck, with smoke and flame billowing from all window cavities. Was that the admin office? Or part of the factory? No point in worrying Wendy until she had to.

'Give me his number and I'll pass it on to the paramedics. They can give it to the hospital, and they'll try to contact him for you, okay?'

'Okay.' Wendy smiled, her gaze content and dreamy.

Clearly the strong painkillers were working well.

Painkillers and anaesthesia were a blessing. They took the pain away. The hurt. The grief. For a while you were blissfully unaware. Reality would always come crashing back in at some point, but in that moment they would feel fine.

Addy had no idea if Wendy's future had been eliminated or not. She hoped it hadn't been. She hoped that Brian had escaped the fire and that he would meet Wendy at the hospital and hold her hand through all her painful debridement and surgeries. That he would stand by her side at their wedding and tell her she was beautiful, as he always had.

But she couldn't know for sure.

In her peripheral vision, she saw someone waving madly. She turned to see Paolo, flanked by two other fire crew, carrying an unconscious fireman away from the smoke and flame.

Her stomach flipped and churned.

And she ran towards the casualty.

CHAPTER TEN

THE FIREMAN STILL wore his oxygen mask, so she couldn't see who it was. She raced towards them, watched as they got clear of the danger and laid the man down on the pavement.

Addy fell to her knees at his side and wrenched off the mask, her heart thumping crazily.

Please don't let it be Ryan. Please don't let it be Ryan!

It wasn't Ryan.

Relief hit her like a tsunami—and then immense guilt. It shouldn't matter who it was. One of Blue Watch was hurt. Hank Couzens. She didn't know him all that well, but she did know he had a wife. Three kids. Two boys and a newborn baby girl. Any of Blue Watch or any first responder getting hurt was horrible.

But still, relief was her overriding feeling as she placed the oxygen mask back over Hank's face and began a primary survey.

'What happened?'

'He was caught in the blast. Got knocked backwards into a wall. He banged his head pretty bad.'

She examined his head and his neck. She couldn't feel any depressions, nor any movements that might indicate a fractured skull, and Hank wasn't conscious to tell her if anything hurt. But she had to assume there were injuries she wasn't aware of, and so she wrapped a cervical collar around his neck to immobilise his head and spine in case of hidden injury.

Addy checked his arms and legs. Nothing seemed broken. His abdomen was soft, as it should be. Hopefully, he was just concussed. She radioed for one of the ambulance crews to make its way to her position and when it came helped get him onto a spinal board and into the vehicle that soon roared away, sirens blaring.

She let her gaze fall upon the burning building. The fire crews were still aiming their water hoses at it and she wondered which one of them was Ryan. How many more times would she have to stand there and wonder if he was okay? This wasn't meant to be happening to her any more. He was only meant to be a friend. And yet already she cared for him deeply.

Maybe I need to put up bigger walls?

Maybe I need to cut off contact altogether?

It had been a fierce blaze and Ryan was sweating thoroughly by the time he emerged from the site, his job done. All the flames were out and the site had been doused with enough water that no spark would survive, no matter what.

Wearily, he pulled off his helmet and lifted his face to the waning sun, grateful for the small measure of cool breeze upon his face. He stood there for a moment before moving forward towards Paolo, towards the rest of his waiting crew.

He saw Addalyn there, too, nervously biting on her fingers.

He couldn't imagine how difficult this shout must have been for her. It had been no picnic for those inside, tackling the blaze, but knowing now what she had gone through with her brother and Ricky, he knew watching any fire get out of control must be difficult for her.

'You okay?' Paolo asked as he got closer.

'Yeah. All done and dusted. I think the source of the fire was in the east wing of the building, but Investigative Services will figure that out for sure.'

With any big fire like this, the fire service investigated the cause and origins of the fire. It was useful in criminal or arson prosecutions to have their evidence and skill.

'Okay. There's water over there—get it down you and then we'll head back.'

'Cheers, boss.' He gave Paolo a small salute and grabbed a bottle of water, necking half of it before he drew level with Addy. 'Hey.'

She didn't look happy. She looked nervous. On edge.

'You're all right?'

'Yeah. Just tired. Smelly. Looking forward to a good shower.' He tried to laugh. To make light of the situation.

She nodded. 'I bet.'

'I hope you weren't too worried about me.'

'About you? I was worried about all of you! I had to send Hank off to the hospital.'

'Hank? Damn. Is he okay?'

'He was unconscious. Caught in the blast.'

'I didn't know.' He felt bad then. Before, all he'd wanted was a shower. Now all he wanted was to go and visit his friend. Make sure he was okay.

'I thought it was you. When they brought him out he had his mask on. For one minute…' she breathed in, then out, steadying her voice '…I thought it was you.'

He stared at her, realising in that moment that she cared for him as deeply as he cared for her and how scary that must be for her. He felt guilty. As if he was somehow torturing her because of his choice of job. But what could he do? He'd never been the kind of guy to want to work in an office. He liked jobs that required the use of adrenaline. The army. The fire service. He couldn't imagine any other life. That wasn't who he was.

'It wasn't. I'm fine.'

She nodded again, not actually looking at him, and he could

see in that moment that she was fighting tears. That she was fighting a huge torrent of emotion.

'I like you, Ryan. I do. And I adore your daughter. But... I can't do this again. I can't stand there and watch and wait for you to be brought out on a stretcher or in a body bag. I just can't.'

'Addy—'

'No. I can't. I'm sorry. I have to protect myself here.'

And she turned and walked away from him.

He watched her go, shocked. They were hardly in a relationship with one another—they were just friends. Very good friends. Maybe this job had been too much? Any of his callouts had the potential to be fatal and some people couldn't handle that.

But what about *her*? What about *her* job? She was a HART paramedic—she put herself in danger, too! She might lose her life one day, doing the job she loved, and then *he* would be the one left without *her*!

Did she ever think about that?

Because he thought about it all the time. And being left alone again did not appeal at all!

CHAPTER ELEVEN

LIFE WAS SO much better without Ryan.

At least that was what Addy kept telling herself every time she felt her thoughts wandering to him. Perhaps if she told herself enough times then it would be true. It would be like when someone kept telling you that you were ugly. After enough times, you'd begin to believe it. This had to work in a similar fashion.

I don't need Ryan and life is so much better without him.

So why was she sitting at her sewing machine, missing him like crazy, and working on Carys's tiger costume? The headpiece was like a hood, but she was trying to put ears in, and eyes, and create some teeth, so it looked perfect, and it just wasn't working.

It's because I need to fit it on Carys. See exactly where the eyes and ears need to go.

But she couldn't go to their house. Couldn't visit. Because she needed this space from him. It was better this way. Before either of them got in too deep. Addy had sensed where their relationship was going. Yes, they were fine as work colleagues, and great friends, but her own feelings had been heading in a totally different direction when it came to Ryan and his daughter. They were like the little family she'd always dreamed of having. The almost perfect guy and the perfect little girl. Of course she'd begun to fall in love with them. Put water in front of a thirsty person and eventually they'd drink it even if they were told the water could hurt them.

So she'd had to separate herself from the water.

Tell herself she didn't need it.

If only I could get these ears right!

She wondered briefly if Ryan took his daughter to the park often. Maybe if she saw them she could pull the little girl to one side so that she could get her to try on the outfit, mark where the ears and eyes ought to be, and then scurry off back home?

Did I just even think that? Stalking a little girl in a public park and pulling her away to some bushes? I'm losing it here.

Addy got up from her sewing machine and began to pace the room. Maybe she should give up making the costume entirely? After all, she didn't owe it to anyone.

Except I made Carys a promise.

And that meant something.

Just because she couldn't be with Ryan, that did not mean she could let down that wonderful little girl!

I'll just march around there, knock on the door and ask for a fitting.

Ryan was standing in the kitchen, busy making pancakes, pouring his mix into the frying pan, allowing it to spread, and then getting Carys to count to three before he would try and flip them. So far, one had fallen to the floor, the second one had caught on the edge of the pan and ripped, and now he was on the third.

'Are we ready? One…two…'

The doorbell rang.

'Three!'

He flipped the pancake and it landed perfectly. Typical. But he didn't want to leave it on the heat, where it would burn, so he shifted the pan off to one side and pointed at his daughter.

'Don't touch it, okay? I'll be back in a minute.'

He wiped his hands on a tea towel and threw it over his shoulder as he headed towards the front door. He had no idea who was calling, but he was waiting for a parcel delivery. Maybe it was that and he needed to sign for it? He'd ordered Carys a scooter—a special treat. He needed to feel good about himself, and maybe get out of the house more. Stop moping about Addalyn walking away from their friendship.

Okay, so maybe it had become more than a friendship. Even though, technically, they hadn't done anything romantic. But the thoughts and the feelings had been there. The wishes. The yearnings. The whole shebang.

He'd felt strangely upset after that factory fire, when she'd told him she couldn't be his friend any more. He'd understood why, but spending time with Addy had begun to bring him out of his shell again. He'd not been able to remember the last time he'd felt so happy. As if he were part of something special.

And damn straight they'd had something special—even if they hadn't kissed. Not on the lips, anyway. He'd kissed her cheek, and each and every time he'd wondered what she might do if he turned and kissed her on the mouth. But he'd not done it. Afraid to ruin what they had. That fledgling relationship. Both of them still cautious…both of them teetering on the edge of taking flight, not wanting to fall.

But fall he had. He'd fallen big time.

Buying his daughter a scooter was something he hoped would take his mind off the fact that he wouldn't get to see Addy again except at work.

He yanked open the door.

And his mouth dropped open.

Addalyn.

She stood there looking beautiful, despite the furrow in her brows, and despite the hardened, determined look in her eyes.

She held a bag at her side and looked not at him but somewhere just over his left shoulder.

'I need to borrow Carys.'

Borrow Carys? Right. Of course. That seemed perfectly natural.

'Addalyn… Borrow her for what?'

'For a fitting. For her tiger costume.'

'Oh… Oh! You're still making that?'

'Of course! I'm not going to let her down when I promised.'

'She's just inside.'

He stepped back and watched in confused admiration as she stalked past him, then paused, awaiting instruction.

'She's in the kitchen,' he added helpfully, not sure how to proceed with what was clearly a tetchy woman completely on the edge.

'Thank you.'

'You're welcome.'

He followed her through to the kitchen, pausing a few steps behind her as she paused in the kitchen doorway.

'Hey, you.'

He watched as her entire demeanour changed when she saw his daughter. A wide smile crept across her face, and when Carys looked up and saw who it was she barrelled into Addy with an enthusiasm that made him smile from ear to ear.

Just as Addy did.

Addy scooped her up and hefted her onto a hip. 'You are getting bigger every day! It's a good thing I came round to check!'

'Are you here to play with me?'

'I'm here to measure you up for your tiger costume. I've made a start on it, but I need to keep checking it on you, just so I don't go wrong.'

'Okay! Can I see it?'

'Of course you can!'

Addy and Carys headed off towards the lounge and Ryan followed, not sure how to act or how to proceed.

'Can I...er...make you a drink?' he asked, feeling that hot beverages were safe ground to tread.

She looked up at him, her face losing its smile. 'I'm not stopping that long, so no. Thank you.'

He gave a nod and realised that he was not needed there, and that Addy would probably be much more comfortable if he disappeared and left them to it.

It was hard to leave them be. Especially since he'd been missing her. It had only been a couple of days, but already he'd begun to feel it. And Carys had been asking repeatedly when they could go back to Addy's house to continue with the jigsaw.

He hadn't wanted to lie to his daughter, so he'd simply said that he didn't know as he hadn't had a chance to ask Addy about it. Which was kind of true! He'd just not mentioned the other part.

The pancake lay cooling in the pan and he turned the cooker off and began to tidy up. Clearly Addy was more important to his daughter than her lunch. He didn't want to interrupt them, but it was agony not being able to be with her. Just in the next room!

How quickly Addalyn has become important to me.

But this was what happened to him, wasn't it? He'd not been able to keep Angharad, either. She'd walked away. For different reasons, maybe, but if their love for one another had been stronger, would she have been able to walk away so easily? Maybe he'd not given her enough space? Maybe he'd not loved her as fiercely as he ought to have done? Maybe he'd put Carys first too much and she'd felt neglected?

But wasn't that what you were supposed to do as a father? Put your child first?

The feeling of failure as a man had hit him hard when his

wife had left. He'd always thought of himself as a relatively good catch. A decent guy. Hard-working. Dedicated. Loyal. But maybe he'd given too much to his job and his daughter? Had Angharad felt neglected? She'd not been too thrilled about him being a fireman, either, though in the beginning of their relationship she'd viewed it as sort of a cool thing. Maybe when the reality of life with a fireman had hit, replacing the image of a hunky, half-naked man cuddling puppies for a charity calendar, she hadn't been able to handle it?

Like Addy.

But Addy had known the reality from the start. She'd never seen him or viewed him as anything else. He'd always been a risk to her, and maybe that was why she'd never got too close?

He pottered about in the kitchen for some time. Cleaning. Tidying away. Sitting at the table with his head in his hands until he got fed up.

In the next room he could hear laughter. Carys's perfect giggling. Addy's too.

He wanted to know what was going on. He felt left out.

This is my home. Why am I hiding away in the kitchen?

So he decided to make his presence felt.

Addy was so glad she'd come to do a fitting on Carys, because clearly she'd sewed one of the main seams on the outfit wrong and it was much too big, drowning Carys in reams and folds of tiger fleece so that the little girl could barely be seen beneath it.

'Grr! Roar!'

Carys tried to sound like a tiger from within the folds of fabric as Addy tried to locate the neckline, and when she did, and Carys's head popped out through the top, they both giggled with fits of laughter.

And then the door opened.

Addy swallowed and sucked in a breath when she saw Ryan standing there.

'How's everything going? It all sounds fun.'

She gave a polite smile, trying to control her breathing and her heart rate around him. It hadn't got any easier. In fact, since she'd walked away from him and told him she couldn't do this with him any more, it had seemed harder!

'I just need to take a few more measurements.'

'Great.' Ryan settled down onto the couch and picked up a magazine that happened to be lying there.

She glanced at it. It was a kids' magazine. Brightly coloured. It looked odd to see him reading it—because surely that wasn't his reading material of choice? Was he trying to act casual and normal around her?

Addy smiled at Carys encouragingly as she positioned her this way, then that, marking out her seams with carefully placed pins. 'That's it. Don't move for a minute.'

'When can I come round to yours to do more of the jigsaw?'

'Erm… I'm not sure.'

'What about this weekend?'

'Er…'

Ryan put down the comic. 'You're off to your grandparents' house this weekend, remember? They're taking you to visit Lara and Jacob, your cousins.'

'Oh.' Carys sounded as if that was the last thing she wanted to do.

Addy smiled at her. 'Sleeping at your grandparents' house will be fun! Think of how much they can spoil you! I remember going to my grandparents' house as a child and I loved it. Nan used to make this egg custard tart that was better than you'd get in any shop. And I remember she had this horse and carriage ornament that sat in their bay window… It was actually a music box, and I would sit and play with it, and open up its secret compartment, and every time my nan would have put something inside—like fifty pence, or a sweetie, or something else for me to find.'

Carys smiled.

'And they had this cute little white poodle called Toby. He was a bit smelly, but I used to love him anyway. Do your grandparents have any pets for you to play with?'

'They have a cat.'

'What's his name?'

'Munchkin.'

Now it was Addy's turn to smile. 'What colour is he?'

'Kind of black and brown.'

'He's a tortoiseshell,' Ryan added, drawing her eye. 'He's very rare, apparently. Most torties are female, so it probably means that...' He stopped talking, looking kind of afraid to say more.

'Means that what?' she asked.

Ryan looked away from her briefly, before closing the magazine and putting it back down on the table. 'It means that he's probably sterile.'

Addy stared at him.

'What's sterile?' asked Carys.

Now she looked at his little girl. At her curious face. 'It means he won't be able to give a female cat any babies.'

Carys thought for a moment. 'Aww! That's sad. Poor Munchkin. He'd have very pretty babies. Hey, Dad, can we have a kitten?'

And the subject was changed as fast as that.

Ryan was clearly blindsided. 'Er...not just yet, sweetie. A kitten takes a lot of looking after, and it wouldn't be fair to get a cat whilst I'm at work most days and you're at school. It would be all alone.'

He was right. Addy had often thought about getting a pet, to help her deal with being alone in the house, but it just wouldn't be fair. Unless she got a rescue cat? One that was older and already housebroken? A cat looking for somewhere to spend its golden years?

'You know, Carys, I've been thinking about getting a cat,' she told her. 'I couldn't have a kitten, for the same reasons as you and your dad, but I've thought about getting an older one. Maybe bringing it home when I've got a week off or something. I do have some holiday due. That way I could use the week to help it settle in, and after that it would be fine on its own. Maybe… I don't know.'

'Could I come and visit if you do?'

Addy glanced at Ryan. His face was impassive.

'Sure. I'll let you know if I ever do it.'

She helped Carys off with her outfit, making sure she didn't get pricked with any errant pins.

'Right. Well, I'd better be off. I should be able to make some headway with this now.'

'I'll walk you out,' Ryan said.

'Oh. Thanks,' she muttered, gathering her things and heading to the front door.

She stopped there and turned to face him. Looked past him to make sure he was alone.

'I'm sorry if I was a bit abrupt earlier. I didn't mean to be. I just felt awkward. But I hope—I really, really hope—that we can get along with each other if we meet at work or anything.'

She felt awkward. Felt as if she was rambling. But she knew she'd been harsh before, and that it was only because of how Ryan made her feel.

She was hoping that, with distance, it would get easier. But standing here, right now, in this moment, staring into his beautiful chocolate eyes and looking at his soft mouth and the slight hint of stubble, made her feel that maybe she was making a mistake. He looked so good in his dark jeans and white tee. Those arms... That chest... And his hair! So perfect... I've-Just-Got-Out-of-Bed messy hair, that made her want to run her hands through it, and touch him, and stroke him, and pull him close and smell him, and...

But Ryan represented everything that was dangerous to her emotional wellbeing. Ryan was a firefighter, and he had a child. He needed someone stable to be in his life. Someone who could give him future children. She was none of these things, and yet...

'We'll always be friends,' he said now. 'No matter what.'

He had a lovely voice. Soft. Gentle. Understanding.

I want to kiss him. I want to kiss him so much!

'I really do.'

'What?' Ryan frowned.

She felt her cheeks colour. Flush with heat. 'I mean thank you. Sorry. I was...er...thinking of two conversations at once. You know how your mind drifts sometimes?' She laughed nervously.

'Mine does it all the time,' he said sincerely, staring straight back at her.

'I ought to go. Say goodbye to Carys for me.'

'I will.'

He held open the door and let her step through.

'She's welcome to come and finish her jigsaw any time.'

'And...am I allowed to come with her? Stay?'

How would she be able to concentrate on anything with him there? But how could she say no, without being rude?

'It's okay if not. I could drop her off for an hour or two and then you could call me when you want her to be picked up.'

She was grateful that he'd given her a way out. 'Or I could just walk her back,' she told him. 'Seeing as we live so close to one another?'

'Sure! She's away this weekend, though, as I said, so maybe the weekend after that?'

'Great. Sounds great. I'd love that. I could do another fitting for her then as well.'

'Or take her with you to get a cat if you choose to. She'd love that. Though it might be dangerous for me, allowing her near all those animals that desperately need homes.'

He laughed good-naturedly.

'Yeah…anyway, I'd better go.'

She pointed at the pathway, as if it wasn't clear which direction she'd be taking as she moved away from him. It was wholly unnecessary, but her brain didn't seem to be functioning very well around him.

'Of course. I'll see you around.'

'Absolutely. Yes. At work.' She nodded.

'At work. Work only.'

'Mmm…'

She stared at him a moment longer, clinging to her last vestiges of hope that if she were just brave enough all it would take would be two steps towards him to plant a kiss on his lips. After all, what harm would that kiss, in that moment, do?

Terrify him? Embarrass him? Send me down a path that I would regret afterwards?

That last one was the reason that made her pause and reconsider. Because she didn't want any more regrets in her life. She had enough to deal with. She'd lost her boyfriend because she couldn't give him children. Lost her father and brother in a tragic accident. Did she really want to lose Ryan too?

By resisting—by not kissing him, not letting this attraction thing she had going on proceed any further—she could stop any more regrets right now. They could remain friends. And that was enough, right?

'Goodbye, Ryan.'

She gave a slight smile and, using all her strength, she walked away.

CHAPTER TWELVE

WATER RUSHED FROM the hose towards the flames as Ryan held it steady, grimacing inside his helmet as his gaze took in the blackened walls, the blooms of soot, the curtains that seemed to dance as the fire consumed them from the floor upwards, the way some of the ornaments that had been in the window had either exploded from the heat or melted.

The source of the fire was the sofa. Someone had not noticed their cigarette falling from the ashtray that was perched on the arm, and it had fallen into the innards of the upholstery and started a fire.

Smoke had been the first sign. Luckily the owners had been in the kitchen when they'd noticed it, and had been able to get everybody out of the house before smoke inhalation had become a problem. But they would still need to be checked over by an ambulance crew, just in case.

There was no one to rescue here, which was great.

Their job was to extinguish the flames and stop the fire spreading to the houses on either side, as this one was mid-terrace.

Paolo had made sure those homes had been evacuated, too, just to be safe.

Smoke billowed all around and another window shattered, allowing in more oxygen to fan any remaining embers.

The heat was incredible, but Ryan kept the hose aimed at

the source until the flames began to die down and the living room became sodden.

Black licks of soot patterned the ceiling in a kaleidoscope of marks, and one part of the roof had begun to burn through. He kept an eye on it, aware of the possibility of collapse, but he had no reason to move further into the room from where he was. They had control now. They had it beaten.

Ryan grabbed the hose lock and turned off the water, bracing himself for the drop in pressure that would affect his balance. When only drips dropped from the hose-end he and his crewmate Jonno, who'd been behind him holding the hose too, began to make their way out of the devastated and ruined building.

'Fire origin was definitely the sofa in the lounge, boss,' he told Paolo.

Paolo nodded. 'At least everyone got out. That's the main thing. You can replace bricks and mortar; you can't replace people.'

Ryan nodded. Paolo was right. You couldn't replace people, even if you tried. Because everyone was different. When Angharad had first left him he'd never imagined wanting to replace her. He'd been too hurt. But lately he'd often thought about what it might be like to meet someone new.

Like Addalyn.

Carys adored her, and he did too. But she would never replace Angharad. He would always remember his wife. Always try to remember the good times they'd shared. Because life was too short to keep on remembering the pain.

Addy, in turn, could never replace her father or her brother. Or that guy she'd hoped to have babies with. In fact, she didn't seem interested in replacing anyone. Almost as if she was too scared to—which he understood. She was still in the scared phase. It would pass. One day. He hoped he would still be around when it happened. Because he believed that if she ever got brave enough, then his life with her could be something amazing!

But her fear, her hesitation, her need to flee…that worried him. Because if he was going to be with someone else—someone who would be part of his daughter's life—then he needed someone who was strong. Not someone who was a flight risk. He couldn't let Carys hope that Addy would be in their lives for good if Addy was going to run each time things got difficult or terrifying.

'Get the hoses back and pack up,' Paolo ordered.

'Will do.'

Ryan glanced over at the two ambulances that had turned up to treat the family in case of injury, hoping to see Addy. But she wasn't there. She only got sent to the really serious jobs. And even though this had been a potentially hazardous rescue, the information that had come in before the shout had told Control that there was no danger to human life. Everyone was out. A HART paramedic had not been needed on this occasion.

Maybe she was on a shout somewhere else? Maybe she was on a day off? Maybe she'd finally taken that holiday she'd said she would?

I miss her.

That was the pervading feeling. He'd got used to seeing her at work. He'd finish a job and look up to see her there. It always made him feel good, knowing that she was by his side. Knowing that she was safe. Taking care of her patients. But also knowing that she had one eye for him as well. For all of Blue Watch.

Her family.

The Tutbury cat rescue centre was practically overflowing with cats. Kittens, pregnant females, feral cats that had been captured and were being trained to get used to humans and, of course, the older, senior cats, which were kept in a different, quieter building. A retirement home of a kind.

That was where Addy had asked to go. She'd spent some time being interviewed at the front desk—about her home, her lifestyle and what sort of cat she was looking for. She'd told them about her job and her hours, and fully expected the manager to say *I'm sorry, but you're just not suitable.* But then Addy had explained that she'd got a couple of weeks' holiday booked soon, and she wasn't actually going to go away, but wanted to use that time to help a senior cat settle in. After that she'd be out for eight or nine hours each day. Sometimes more, if a job ran over, because accidents and emergencies didn't run to a neat schedule.

'But I grew up with cats,' she'd told the manager. 'My family always had them. Mostly moggies, but I do remember we once had a Russian Blue.'

'I think one of our senior cats will be perfect for you,' Letty, the manager, had said.

So she'd been escorted to the senior cats' housing unit and allowed to look around on her own. The majority of them were curled up fast asleep, as classical music played softly in the background. Each unit had a single cat in it, or sometimes two, if there was a brother and a sister, or a bonded pair that couldn't be split up. Cats of all colours. Of all types. One had an eye missing. The card attached to its cage said that Poppy had been injured in a fight with another cat and an infection had caused her to lose the eye.

There were so many sad stories. One cat had feline FIV. Another only had three legs after a traffic accident. One had been diagnosed as having cerebellar hypoplasia—a neurological condition that made it wobbly and have issues with its balance. This one was a black cat.

'Black cats are often not chosen for rehoming. People can

be terribly superstitious,' Letty had said, as if apologising for the quantity of black cats she was about to see.

And there were a lot of black cats.

Addalyn was not superstitious, and as she perused the cards she also looked at the dates, wanting to know which cat had been there the longest.

And then she found him. In the last unit. Sitting in his soft bed, washing his face. Curly.

Curly had been born with anophthalmia, his card said. Which meant he'd been born with no eyes. And he'd been at the home the longest.

Seven years.

Addy couldn't imagine a cat being stuck inside this place for seven years. Seven years of classical music. Seven years of listening to people come and go, never being chosen.

He was a pure black cat, thirteen years old, and he'd come to the rescue centre after his previous owner had died.

It was a long time to be here.

A long time to go without someone to love.

A long time to go without affection.

Even though she felt sure the caretakers here would have done their absolute best for him, she felt an affinity for Curly. She'd lost the person she loved too. She'd been left alone with no home until her father and brother had taken her in, and then she'd lost them too. And she had spent a few years without affection. Blind to love.

'We're made for each other, you and I,' she whispered, putting her fingers through the bars and making noises to try and entice Curly to the front of the cage.

Clearly he'd heard her. His other senses must be heightened because of his blindness. He came forward to sniff at her fingers, and then rubbed himself along her hand and the side of the cage, his tail in the air.

Addy smiled.

She'd found her cat.

'I'm going to take you home with me, Curly. Would you like that?'

Curly purred in response.

She spent some time with him in a special room along with Letty, who was thrilled that Curly had been chosen by her.

'He's such a special cat. We've all become so fond of him. In a way it'll be sad to see him go, but he's going for all the right reasons.'

'My time off doesn't start for another week,' said Addy. 'Can I collect him then?'

'Of course! And you're welcome to visit him as often as you'd like in the meantime.'

'Really? That's great. I'll try to pop in every day after work—if I have the time and you're still open.'

'Perfect. Shall we do the paperwork?'

'Let's do it.'

It was a mere formality. Addalyn had to promise to send the rescue centre pictures of Curly in his new home, and agree that if for any reason she couldn't keep Curly she would return him.

'I don't think that's ever going to happen, let me tell you now,' she said.

Letty smiled. 'I'm sure it won't, but it does happen on occasion, so we ask everyone.'

'Okay. I feel like he's mine already. It's going to be hard to walk away right now,' she said, stroking his soft fur. 'But I need to get the house ready for him. Get bowls and toys and a litter tray…'

'Exactly. You want to be ready when you invite someone new into your life.'

Addy looked up at Letty. She meant the cat, clearly, but she was right in other ways too. If you went into a new relationship without being ready then it was likely to fail at the first hurdle. Life was difficult enough without plunging headfirst into emotional turmoil.

She thought of Ryan and Carys. She missed them so much—which was crazy! Staying away was hard when you knew the person you'd like to spend time with was just around the corner. Literally two streets away.

When the paperwork was done, she gave Curly one last hug and then turned to leave the building. She pulled open the door and walked smack-bang into a man's chest.

'Oh! I'm so sorry! I…'

She looked up and saw Ryan. Of all the places… She'd never expected to find him *here*.

'Ryan! What are you doing here?'

He looked embarrassed, and shocked to find her there.

'Same thing as you, I'm guessing.'

'You're adopting a cat?'

'After you spoke about it Carys and I talked a lot, and we decided that it was something we both really wanted to do. Give a cat another chance at life. Give it something better than what it has right now.'

'You do have love to give,' she said with a smile, knowing the feelings he was talking about.

He stared her right in the eyes. 'Yeah… We do.'

She stared back. Taking in the beautiful darkness of his soft, chocolatey eyes. The intensity of his gaze.

'Have you chosen one, or…?'

He broke eye contact—reluctantly, she thought.

'Yeah! Curly. He's back there. Last cage on the left.' She pointed behind her.

'Mind if I take a look?'

'Sure!'

She walked with him over to the pen, smiling at Curly as

he settled himself back in his cat bed, plumping the soft pillow with his paws, purring away.

'He's cute.'

'He was born without eyes, so I think people might have overlooked him because of it.'

'Bless him… He looks sweet. He'll make you a very good pet. What other guys have we got in here?'

Addy decided to walk around with him as he considered the senior cats, even though she'd been on her way out. It seemed right to do so—and besides, Letty was still there, so it wasn't as is anything was going to happen.

'Who's this guy?'

'Girl,' Addy said, looking at the card. 'It's a female. Molly.'

Molly was a striped tabby cat. Twelve years of age.

'She has six toes on one front paw, it says here!'

'I can't see…'

Molly was curled up in her bed, slowly blinking at them. Probably wondering why there were suddenly so many people in the centre, looking at her.

'Perhaps she only shows them to people who are special?' Addy said with a smile, then laughed as Molly stood and stretched, front legs low, back end high in the air, showing off her six-toed foot after all.

'Hey, there…' Ryan put his finger though the bars so that Molly could sniff him. 'What do you think, Addy? Will Carys like her?'

'She'll love her! She looks like a little tiger.'

'With huge feet.'

'With huge feet!' she echoed, laughing, letting Molly sniff her fingers too.

'Molly gets on very well with Curly, actually. We think they love one another,' said Letty, coming to stand behind them.

'When we let them out into the outdoor runs for some fresh air, they snuggle up all the time.'

Addy looked up at Ryan. 'That's sweet, isn't it?'

'It is.' He turned to Letty. 'Could I get Molly out to see how she reacts to me?'

'Sure.'

And so they sat on the floor and let Molly explore them. The cat sniffed here and there, intrigued by the other pens, but eventually she came over to Ryan and Addalyn, walking between them, tail held high, as they stroked her and she began to purr.

'She's perfect,' said Ryan.

'You're made for each other,' agreed Addy, feeling a mixture of emotions. She was happy for Ryan and Carys that they would have a cat so perfect for their home, but also strangely jealous of Molly. Because she would get to spend so much time with her favourite people. People she herself was trying to train herself to stay away from.

Ryan arranged with Letty that he would call again when he knew his shift pattern and would have a decent break to help settle his new pet. He filled in the paperwork, and Addy listened as Letty asked him the same questions and had him agree to bring Molly back if she got too much for any reason.

As they left the centre, Ryan walked next to her through the car park towards her car.

'Well, this is me,' she said, pulling her car keys from her bag. 'Where's yours?'

'I walked.'

'You *walked*?'

He laughed. 'This is going to sound silly, but the house is so quiet without Carys there. It feels strange being there on my own.'

'I understand that feeling.'

'I thought it would take up more time if I walked.'

'Less time home alone?' she asked, smiling.

'Yeah!'

She knew, intimately, how that felt. It had been her life for years, and she could see he was struggling with it.

'Do you fancy going for ice cream?'

The question was out of her mouth before she could think about the dangers. And after she had asked it she told herself it would be fine. They would be in public. Nothing would happen. They were just friends. That was all.

'Oh!' he said. 'You don't have to…'

'No. I mean it. We're okay, aren't we? We can have an ice cream. A walk in the park. It doesn't have to mean anything. Besides, we're going to be like in-laws.'

'In-laws?'

'Because of our cats. They're in love. Or whatever,' she said, with a hint of embarrassment.

She could not quite believe what she had just said. She looked at him and shrugged, as if to say *You know what I mean*.

'That's as good a reason as any,' he said.

Addalyn drove them to the high street and parked near the fancy ice cream parlour that had opened up there. She'd been meaning to try it for ages. It was called One Scoop or Two? and as usual it had a queue out through the door, despite the time of the year.

Addy had heard nothing but good things about the place. Apparently it was owned by an Italian whose grandfather had begun a gelato shop in Naples. It had become two shops, then three, then four. She'd heard people say the flavours and the texture of the ice cream was out of this world!

She'd not had an ice cream for years. She'd used to go out for ice-cream all the time with Nathan. He'd loved nothing better than a raspberry ripple every weekend. More often than not she wouldn't have one herself, preferring a sorbet or nothing at all, but right now she wanted to have an ice cream with Ryan and go for a walk in the park. Spend time with him now that she'd run into him. It was as if this moment was an unexpected gift and she didn't want it to end. Not yet.

As they got closer, they spotted a board listing the flavours— all the usual suspects, but also butterscotch, cake batter, green tea, maple, watermelon and bubblegum. Lots of unexpected things.

'Do we try something new or stick with a favourite?' Ryan asked, turning to smile at her.

His smile made her feel special.

'Go for whatever you fancy,' she told him.

His look, with a raised eyebrow, made her blush slightly.

When they got to the front of the queue, Ryan ordered one scoop of matcha tea ice cream, with a second scoop of maple. Addy ordered cake batter and butterscotch.

They were delicious! Smooth, and not too overpowering in flavour. Sweet, without being sickly.

'Want to try mine?' Ryan offered his cone to her.

She looked directly into his eyes as she leaned in, took hold of the cone and licked it. The matcha was amazing! Slightly bitter, but sweetened enough that it wasn't off-putting. She offered her own cone and he tried her flavours, looking directly at her as he licked the ice cream.

There was something almost sexual about it. Almost hypnotic. Addy couldn't tear her eyes away from his gaze. And then he mentioned he liked the cake batter more than the butterscotch and she remembered they were sharing ice cream in a public space.

'It's good, isn't it?' she said.

'It can be scary, trying something new, but sometimes you can find something that you don't ever want to let go of,' he said.

She nodded. He was right. In, oh, so many ways.

With food.

Experiences.

People.

Ryan was like a drug at this point. She wanted to be with him so much. To experience him. To taste him. Smell him. Envelop herself with him. But he was dangerous. He represented a threat to her mental and emotional wellbeing. He could hurt her. Not intentionally. But it might happen anyway.

Could you experience someone like that in moderation and not go mad?

People in the park were enjoying the last of the warm days. There were families, couples, people jogging or walking their dogs. Here in the park, surrounded by greenery, unable to see the town, it felt as if they were in a small bubble of peace and serenity. It was nice. Soothing. And she understood completely why people liked being surrounded by nature.

Here she could forget. For a moment, at least. Pretend that all was right with the world and that being here with Ryan was fine. Meant to be. A gift that she should cherish, because soon it would be over. Soon he would go home and she'd be alone again. Without him. But right now, at this moment, it was perfect—because he was here by her side.

'I love it here,' she said, as their steps carried them past the lake.

'It's very peaceful.'

'Makes a change from our jobs, doesn't it? We're so frenetic there. Running on adrenaline, with a million thoughts and possibilities and prospective dangers rushing through our heads…lives on the line…other people relying on our life-or-death decisions…'

'We can be like everyone else here. Normal.'

'Yeah…'

A dog raced past them and leapt into the lake, sending a group of ducks quacking in all directions as the owner bemoaned the fact that her dog was now wet and would stink up the car.

They both smiled as the dog came trotting out of the lake, pleased as punch, its tongue hanging out of its mouth.

'When does Carys get back?' she asked.

'Sunday evening.'

'Not long to go, then?'

He glanced at his watch. 'Too long. I always think it'll be good to have a break from being Dad. Nice for Carys to spend some dedicated time with her grandparents, being spoilt, but I always miss her when she's gone.'

'Do her other grandparents ever see her? Angharad's parents?'

Ryan shook his head. 'They did once. Had her for the day. But…it didn't work out. They said it was too stressful—that they were too old to look after a little one. Which didn't make any sense as they were only sixty-something, and in very good health. Maybe it was too stressful for Angharad? Having the daughter she gave up on spending time with her parents?'

'I'm sorry. Carys has lost more than a mother…she's lost grandparents too.'

'You can't change other people's decisions. If they've decided they can't have you in their lives, then that's how it's got to be.'

She pondered on his words. She had made a decision not to have Ryan in her life because of her deep growing feelings for him. Yet here she was. Walking through the park with him. Sharing ice creams and not yet ready to walk away.

Because every time I walk away I think it won't hurt this way. But it does. It does.

'Do you ever wonder if she thinks she made a mistake?'

'Angharad? No. If she did, I would have heard from her.

Texts. Calls. Maybe even emails. But I get nothing—so, no, I don't think she has ever doubted herself.'

Addy doubted herself. She yearned to protect herself, but she also yearned to be with Ryan.

What am I doing?

'Hey, look, the boat place is still open! Fancy sharing a rowing boat with me? I'll row,' Ryan offered.

She'd finished her ice cream, so…

'Sure!'

She still wasn't ready to walk away. Today was a gift.

The rowing boats were all lined up alongside the small lake, and after they'd paid the boat guy took them over to one that had faded red paint on the hull, and held it steady as they both clambered in.

Ryan began rowing and took them out onto the water, dark green and cloudy. She tried not to notice the muscles flexing in his forearms as he rowed.

'Wow. This is so peaceful,' she said. 'I don't think I've been out on a rowing boat before.'

'You haven't?'

'No. I've been on a cruise ship, though.'

'Exactly the same.' He smiled. 'This is your captain speaking. We have just left port and we'll be making our way around the local lake today. Conditions are sunny and warm. Wind is blowing at a slow two knots and the onboard entertainment for today is…er…me.'

Addy laughed at him and he laughed back.

'You're silly.'

'I am. One hundred percent.'

'I like you, Ryan Baker.'

He paused as if to consider her. 'I like you, too. A lot.'

Her heart beat a little faster at his words and she felt her cheeks grow hot, so she looked away, at the people walking in the park, not knowing what to say next.

The fact that he liked her too…it meant something. It meant that what she was feeling wasn't stupid. She wasn't imagining this attraction between them. They both felt it. It was a war they were fighting, both not sure which tactic to use next to ensure they both survived and came out of it relatively unharmed.

Because being hurt was scary.

Being hurt was difficult and hard.

Painful.

The recovery process could be long and arduous, and she'd been injured so much already. She wasn't sure how many more injuries her heart could take. Which was why she tried to eke out small moments in which she could be happy.

Like today.

Like now.

With Ryan.

There was a small island in the centre of the lake, thickly populated with trees and bushes, and Ryan headed towards it. 'There's a folly on it somewhere. Want to go and find it?'

'Why not?'

He rowed their boat towards the island, looking for a small bay or inlet they could use, and on the far side of the lake they found one. A small nook, barely noticeable behind a weeping willow that overhung the shoreline. As they approached Ryan slowed, so that they could move aside the curtain of overhanging branches. It was like being transported into a new world. A hidden world. With the willow muffling the sounds from the lake. After he'd moored up, Ryan pulled the boat higher onto the shore and then proffered Addalyn a hand so she could disembark.

She took his hand delicately, her skin electrified by his touch and guidance as she stepped onto dry land.

It was quiet here. Darkened beneath the canopy of trees.

'Are we allowed to be here?'

'Probably not.'

'How do you know there's a folly?'

'I read about it once. When we moved here. This lake, and the land around it, used to belong to a duke or something.'

'I didn't know that. I've lived here all these years and never knew.'

He smiled at her and reached for her hand as they walked along the narrow path through greenery that was waist height.

'He built the folly for his wife. In remembrance of her.'

'Sounds like he loved her very much.'

'She died young, I think, and he pined for her for the rest of his life.'

Addy felt his pain.

'Can you imagine that?' he asked, stopping to turn to her.

'Which part?'

'Being so overwhelmed by grief that you couldn't enjoy life any more?'

She stared into his eyes. 'Perhaps he didn't know how to?'

'Perhaps he never met the right person who could help him.'

Addy didn't know what to say. She didn't have a folly for her father and Ricky, but there was kind of a shrine in the fire station. She didn't want to be like this duke! Pining for those she had lost for her entire life. Because what kind of life would that be? She still had to find happiness. She still had to find the thing or the person that would give her joy. And right now the people who did that for her were Carys and Ryan.

And what would her dad say if he could see her acting this way?

Take the chance, love! You can't live a life alone.

'Ryan, I...' Her voice faltered.

She wanted to tell him, to let him know that she hadn't

walked away before because it was his fault in any way. But for some reason the words wouldn't come. They caught in her throat. She wanted to say how much he meant to her, how he made her feel, and just how she wished she could be what he needed her to be.

'It's okay. I know,' he said, smiling at her. 'You make me feel that way too.'

She sucked in a breath. What he was saying…what he was admitting… This was more than friendship. This was scary territory. But territory that she just might be brave enough to enter all the same. With him.

The folly emerged up ahead. A stone building once white, but now cobwebbed and grey, with moss, lichen and ivy creeping over its old bones. Parts of it had crumbled away, proving time was not a kind mistress to memories either.

Was Addy going to make a lifetime of grieving?

Or create something new?

Something to celebrate?

Ryan led her up the two stone steps and turned to face her. She held her breath. Afraid and terrified of what he might say or do. And yet at the same time eager and keen for something to happen. Because this was a magical place. She could feel it in her bones. In her blood. In her heart.

'Addalyn…'

'Yes?'

'You mean the world to me… I want you to know that.'

'You're important to me, too.'

'I think we could have something amazing together if we let it happen.'

She nodded, unable to speak now. He was saying all the right things. The things she'd dreamed of him saying. But it was scary stuff. Heady stuff.

'Will you let it happen?' he asked. 'I won't do it unless you want me to.'

Consent. He wanted her consent. He knew she'd be scared and, despite how much he wanted her, he needed to make sure that she was happy. Was determined that she should be the one to decide if this proceeded or not.

She'd tried walking away and it had hurt.

What would happen if she allowed him to take his pleasure with her?

Surely the world wouldn't be cruel enough to take away a *third* firefighter from her life?

She gazed deeply into his dark eyes. Stared intently at his lips. Imagined them on her own.

They were hidden from the rest of the world here. In this spot that symbolised a lost love. Maybe they could find love here? Change the significance of this place even if it was just for them?

'Kiss me, Ryan. Kiss me.'

A slight smile curved the edges of his lips as his head lowered to her hers and the rest of the world drifted away.

CHAPTER THIRTEEN

HE'D NOT INTENDED to bring her to this island. He'd not intended to run into her at all! Discovering her at the Tutbury cat rescue centre had simply been lucky. Right place. Right time. And now they were both looking forward to rehoming Molly and Curly.

Getting to spend time with Addalyn was an unexpected bonus. First ice creams, then a rowing boat, and now this.

He knew she was scared, and he'd refused to kiss her without her consent. Because there was no way in hell he was going to do anything that would send her scurrying for safety again. He didn't want to represent danger to her. He didn't want her to view him as some sort of risk. He needed her to see him as who he was. Ryan Baker. A man who could offer her happiness and joy if she let him.

The kiss deepened.

He felt her sink against him, heard almost a purr or a growl of pleasure in her throat, and it was enough to stir his senses and make him giddy.

His hands sank into the hair at the nape of her neck as hers came to rest at his waist. He couldn't remember the last time he'd kissed a woman in this way. There'd been no one since Angharad, and their relationship had been dying a slow death since the birth of Carys. She'd not wanted him near her. He'd felt confused. Rejected. All he'd wanted to do was love her.

Protect her. Revel in the tiny person that they had made together. But she'd pushed him away, and for a long time he'd felt unworthy. Unworthy of another's love. Unworthy of another's attraction.

Until Addalyn Snow had come into his life.

She loved his daughter almost as much as he did, and he had to be careful not to let that sway his feelings for her. But it was hard not to. She was sexy, brave, clever, beautiful, funny, loving… His desire for her was a powerful thing, and having been told once to stay away when he had feelings for her had been one of the most difficult things he'd had to deal with. And it had come just as he'd been beginning to accept that Angharad's behaviour and desertion from their marriage was more about Angharad than it had ever been about him.

It wasn't my fault.

That had been a huge thing for him to accept. To realise that he did have something to offer a woman, but it was about finding the right woman.

And Addalyn, he felt, could be the one.

He needed to let her know just how much she meant to him. This wasn't just a snog…this wasn't a mere attraction. This was more. Ryan wasn't playing games. He was serious. All his life was serious. Personally and professionally. And Addalyn got that, because hers was too.

Maybe she was the only one who could ever understood him?

When he came up for air, he gazed into her eyes, noted her full, soft lips and knew he wanted more.

'Are you all right?'

She shook her head. 'No.'

That startled him slightly. Had he misread the signals? She'd wanted this, hadn't she?

'I don't understand…'

She smiled. 'I want more. I want all of you. Here. Now. In this place.'

'I don't have protection.'

She turned her head, kissed his hand. 'I can't get pregnant, and I haven't been with anyone since Nathan.'

'I've not been with anyone since Angharad... Are you sure about this?'

'I'm the most sure I've ever been about anything. *You* make me sure.'

He stared deeply into her eyes. Into her soul. She wanted this as much as he did.

'All right then.'

He kissed her again, but this time he released the chains and did not hold back the way he had a moment before.

His fingertips found the buttons of her blouse and began to undo them.

One by one.

Until his fingertips found flesh and heat.

And after that...?

He wasn't sure he could think straight.

Being with Ryan was everything and more. Her senses were firing as if they were being electrocuted. Short-circuited. Her entire system was in a frenzy of pleasure and ecstasy. He was gentle, yet strong. With the right amount of rough and the perfect amount of dirty.

She'd never made love outside before. She would never have imagined that being out in the open, during the day, in the middle of a public park, with no soft beds or soft lighting, would be anything but uncomfortable. But in actuality she felt no discomfort at all. Because being with Ryan felt so right that it would never feel wrong.

Afterwards, she lay in his arms, feeling so relaxed, so sated, so happy… She found herself wondering what she'd been worrying about. Nothing this amazing could be bad. Her thoughts from before, her entire rationale for staying away from Ryan, were faulty.

They had to be.

She curled into him, her head upon his chest. 'I don't think I ever want to move from this space.'

She felt his smile. Heard it in his voice.

'Nor me. But we only get an hour on the boat, so…'

Addy laughed. 'They can bill us. I'll split the charge with you.'

'Let's stay out here all day, then.'

He gave her a small squeeze and pressed his lips to the top of her head. A little gesture, but it meant so much. Their relationship had taken a step forward and now they were on uncharted ground. But that little kiss told her that whatever waters they waded into next he would be by her side. That they would do it together.

'I wish we could…'

A small gentle breeze blew over her skin and she shivered.

'Cold?'

'It's getting cooler.'

They agreed to go and both stood up, straightening their clothes and making themselves presentable again. Ryan held her hand as they made their way back to the boat, and he helped her into it before pushing it back into the water and hopping in himself.

The boat rocked slightly, then settled as he rowed them out from beneath the weeping willow and back into the sunshine. The goosebumps on her arms dissipated beneath the last warming rays of the sun as he took them back to the boat house, apologising for being late. The guy was fine with it, and they soon got back onto dry land and headed towards the car park.

At her car, they got in together and looked at one another.

'Want me to drop you off at your place?' she asked.

Ryan smiled. 'You could. Or…'

'Or?' she asked with a smile.

'Or you could come back to mine and stay the night. Carys is away, so she won't know, and I rather like the idea of getting you into a hot shower. What do you say?'

Ryan. Naked and wet. In a shower.

'Sounds perfect.'

'Then let's go.'

Addalyn came padding downstairs in her bare feet, her hair wrapped in a towel, wearing his bathrobe. Never before had he ever considered his bathrobe sexy, but with a naked Addalyn in it… It sure the hell was!

He put down the knife that he was using to chop peppers and turned to greet her, pulling her into his arms and kissing her deeply. He simply could not get enough of her.

They'd made love all day. In the shower. In his bedroom. Once against the wall and a second time in the actual bed, where he'd taken his time to take her in and marvel at how she responded to his touch, how she tasted, how she felt… He'd almost forgotten about his own pleasure. He'd just wanted to see her enjoy hers—until she'd rolled him onto his back and trailed her lips down his body, and then he hadn't been able to think at all.

'Can we stay in this bubble?' she asked.

'At least until tomorrow we can. Carys comes back in the evening.'

'You want me to be gone by then?'

'Of course not! But I don't want to give Carys the wrong idea about us.'

'That's fair. I don't want to confuse her either. Best wait until there's something to tell her.'

'Do I tell her that I've seen you?'

'I don't mind that.' She smiled.

'Okay. I'll tell her we chose cats together. That's a cute story.'

'I'd miss out the island chapter, though,' she said.

'And the shower one? And the bedroom one?'

She laughed. 'Of course! Mmm…something smells good. What are you making?'

'A sauce to go with pasta.'

'You don't just use something out of a jar?'

'Carys isn't the biggest fan of tomatoes, so I usually make my own.'

'Can I help?'

They spent a merry hour in the kitchen. They nearly got derailed when he spoon-fed her a taste of his pasta sauce and his thoughts ran away with him slightly, but their hungry bellies kept them back on track and eventually they sat down to eat in front of the television and watched a movie. An adventure flick about art thieves and a heist.

When had he last sat down and watched a movie with a beautiful woman in his arms? Ryan wondered. When had he last felt this content? He couldn't remember. Even with Angharad there had always been an *edge*. A slight nervousness. A feeling of never being fully relaxed.

But with Addalyn he felt as if he could be himself. Totally. Wholeheartedly.

Why was that?

Actually, he didn't need to question why. He knew. His feelings for Addalyn ran deep. He cared for her. Adored her. Maybe he even loved her?

But he wouldn't say so. Not yet. Because he didn't want to scare her away—not when they'd just spent practically all day and evening in each other's arms. A declaration of love now might be too much!

He smiled to himself and laid his head against hers. 'Happy?'

'Very much so.'

Her answer was all he needed.

CHAPTER FOURTEEN

ADDALYN WAS PACKING up the car, going through her checklist to ensure the vehicle was ready for her shift, when a call came over the radio—a fire at a four-storey building. Multiple casualties, residents trapped inside.

Her blood ran cold, as it always did, as she listened to Control reel off information. There was a possibility that the incident had begun after some kids had been found mucking about with fireworks in one of the flats. She recalled going to that building once before, as a fledgling paramedic. It was always overcrowded, meaning many lives could possibly be at risk.

'Roger, Control. ETA six minutes.'

She turned to look at the town and saw grey-black smoke beginning to billow up into the sky over on the western side. It was rush hour, too. So the roads would be busy. Already she'd calculated the fastest route in her head, and thought about any shortcuts she could take to maybe get there quicker to liaise with the fire crews and the police.

And to think she'd come to work this morning floating on cloud nine…

Her weekend with Ryan, though short, had been the most wonderful couple of days and the most amazing, mind-blowing night. When she'd left him she'd practically skipped away from his house, and for the first time ever had returned to her own home without that feeling of dread, that sense of isolation, she usually felt.

She'd gone home, taken a shower, sewn a bit more of Carys's costume and then spent the rest of Sunday evening retiling the backsplash in her kitchen. She'd changed so much in the house now and made it her own. The repairs and decorations had really helped with the sense of comfort she felt there now. It was as if she'd given the place a new lease of life. The way Ryan was making her feel like a new person. And Addy liked who he had helped her become.

But now they were back to reality—and their reality was that their jobs were to assist with the accidents and emergencies of life. Life or death situations.

Addalyn raced through the traffic, her lights flashing and her siren blaring as she weaved through parked cars and the vehicles that had come to a standstill to let her pass. She forged her way down the centre of one road as cars pulled over to each side, and had to perform an emergency stop when an old lady stepped off the kerb, thinking the traffic had stopped to let her cross.

Maybe the lady couldn't hear or see very well, but she almost jumped out of her skin to see Addy sitting there, waiting in her car, lights circling red and blue.

And then she was going again—always aware, always on the lookout for dangers as she drove. It would be no good if she got into an accident herself when she was needed somewhere else. She glanced at the dashboard clock. Two minutes down. At least another four, maybe three, if the traffic lightened somewhat.

'Scene update. Fire services now on site. Police are cordoning off Bart Road.'

'Thanks, Control.'

Ryan was working today—she knew that. Day shift. He was probably already there, along with Paolo and the others.

She tried not to think about him having to go inside a building that was aflame. It was his job. He knew what he was doing. They all did. They were trained for these situations. They practised. People like Ryan and the rest of Blue Watch, they kept calm and steady. They knew what they had to do and how. Knew that fires were tackled in certain ways.

'The best-known method is something we call direct attack,' she remembered her brother saying. *'We aim to suffocate the flames at the base of the fire. To do this effectively we must have a clear line of sight to the fire. Then there's the combination attack method, where we use direct and indirect attacks on the fire to help fight the overhead gases and the flames as well. Or we have the two-line-in method, when we have to deal with a fire in high winds. A solid stream and a fog nozzle work best with those.'*

She could see her brother now, sitting at the breakfast table, trying to show her using the salt and pepper shakers as props and the cereal boxes on the table to represent a building.

That very day he and her father had been killed. She remembered because afterwards, when she'd raged and screamed and cried, someone had patted her on the back, trying to soothe her with words.

'They knew what they were doing. It was just an accident.'

There were high winds today, so maybe the two-line-in method, then?

Traffic began to back up and clog as she got closer and closer to the site. She had to honk her horn a couple of times, to get people to move, and slowly but surely she crept her way up the road.

Bart Road sat at an intersection with Williams Street, and now she could see what she was responding to. One of the blocks of flats—a four-storey building called Nelson House—was billowing thick, black, choking smoke from almost every window. The outer walls were darkened with soot and orange flames roared furiously out of the ground-floor and second-floor flats, moving upwards.

'Holy hell...' she muttered, looking for a place to pull over and park.

Her gaze was caught by a couple of firemen helping two people away from the building. Probably residents, they were coughing and choking furiously, their skin smoke-stained, and one of them, she could see from her position, had burns to the back of one hand.

Addy leapt into action, slinging on her high-vis vest and getting the attention of two other paramedics to attend to the burn victims.

The fire crews behind her had many hoses pointed at the building, jets of water streaming in through the broken windows to the flames within. Around the site sat many people, shocked, stunned, coughing—residents who had escaped.

But how many were still left inside? Trapped? Terrified?

'Sit rep?' she asked Paolo as she reached his side.

They spoke a shorthand that might seem strange to others, but it was something they knew well, and he brought her up to speed.

There were still people trapped inside and he'd sent in some men to rescue them.

Addy looked at the building, at the fire that still seemed to be out of control and raging inside, and tried to imagine having to walk into that. How had her dad done it? Her brother? How did Ryan do that?

'Who have you sent in?'

'Ryan and George. White Watch have sent in two, as well.'

Ryan was inside.

She tried not to focus on that one piece of information. It would not do her any good to imagine him inside that hell on earth.

'How many do we think are still trapped?'

Paolo looked at her with a frown. 'Unknown.'

'So how will they know when to stop looking?' she asked with concern.

It was a question she had never asked before, and she'd only asked it because she knew Ryan was inside. She didn't want him in there any longer than was necessary. She wanted him *out*.

Paolo glanced at her with a raised eyebrow. In all the time they'd worked together she'd never sounded worried, because she'd always slip into work mode. Businesslike. Stoic. Calm. She'd never shown fear before, and he'd clearly heard it in her voice.

'When the fire gets too great or the building becomes unstable.'

Unstable.

Immediately she saw in her mind's eye the building that had collapsed right in front of her, killing her father and brother in an instant.

Addy felt sick.

'Right.'

Paolo turned to her. 'Addy? If this is too much, then maybe you should—'

'It's not. Too much. I'm fine. I have a job to do.'

And she walked away from him towards the gathering patients to assess and triage quickly, so that the other paramedics knew who to attend first, who were walking wounded and who were fine.

It was odd that even with something like this there were people who could walk away without a scratch. It had happened when Ricky and her father had died. People had lost their lives that day. Firefighters and residents alike. But some had escaped without even a cough.

She tried to concentrate. Tried to do her job. But with every shout, every yell, every call, she looked up, distracted, often needing to pull her focus back to her patients with grim determination and fight the desire to stand in front of the flames and yell Ryan's name.

Addy dealt with burns and smoke inhalation. A broken wrist from a fall. A fractured femur in someone who had leapt out of their second-storey window. And then she heard it. A rumble, a crash. And she turned to see a new cloud of thick, black smoke puff up into the air as the roof of the building collapsed and flames leapt into the air.

'Ryan!'

The heat was unbearable. Ryan was sweating non-stop, and he could barely see anything through the thick smoke as he emerged from the stairwell to check for anyone stranded on the top floor. People had told him there were others still up there. Residents trapped in their rooms. They'd heard the screams.

The stairwell was the safest place in the building. Made of concrete, it couldn't burn—not like the rest of the place, which had seemed to go up like dry tinder. It was an old building. Built during the sixties. No doubt with cheap materials and the work contracted out to save money. And this was the result. A highly flammable building, overflowing with families and children. Pets.

He'd already guided out three families. Saved over twenty lives.

'You must get Mustafa! He lives in flat forty-two. He's bedbound and blind!' someone had told him.

He'd promised he would, sending the families down the

stairwell and out into the fresh air to be treated whilst he remained and surged upwards. George trailed behind him. George was a seasoned firefighter and they worked well together. He trusted his life to him.

The fire was working its way up through the ceiling of each flat now, and when he emerged onto the fourth-floor corridor the smoke was thick and black and flames licked from beneath the doors of one or two flats. Yes, they would check flat forty-two—but they had to check *all* the flats, just in case.

He kicked down a door and called out to see if anyone could hear him over the noise of the consuming flames.

'Is there anyone in here?'

He looked in the narrow kitchen, the living space, the bedrooms, the tiny bathroom, edging along the sides, avoiding the gaping holes in the burnt-through floor. He knew lots of people would hide in bathtubs, after soaking themselves with water. But this flat was empty.

Eventually they got to number forty-two. Smoke poured out from beneath the door and Ryan burst it open, calling out.

And he heard a voice.

It was weak. Croaky. Scared. Coming from the bedroom.

'Stay where you are! We're coming for you!' he yelled, unsure if the old man would hear him.

Fire had burst through a hole in the floor in the main hall and the smoke was thick and dark, billowing like steam from a kettle.

George followed behind him.

'Let's maintain our exit!' Ryan shouted.

George nodded as he checked through a doorway to find a small storage area, cluttered with towels and cleaning equipment.

He watched as George grabbed the towels and took them

into the bathroom to douse them with water. If they reached
Mustafa in time, they might help in getting him out.

There was the sound of something breaking. They paused
their advance long enough to check it was nothing in their immediate vicinity and then continued on down the hall to the
bedroom at the end.

The hall was cluttered. Filled with newspapers and scientific
journals. It would all go up like tinder if the flames reached
them, effectively blocking their exit. They had no time to lose.

Ryan surged forward and checked the bedroom door, to
make sure it wasn't hot before he opened it, and when he did
he saw an old man, huddled in bed, coughing and afraid.

'Mustafa?'

'That's me.'

'I'm Ryan, and I've got my friend George with me. We're
with the fire service and we're going to get you out of here,
okay?'

'That would be wonderful, my friend.' He coughed again.
'COPD.'

'Or maybe just smoke.'

Ryan smiled as he wrapped Mustafa in the wet towels, apologising for how they might feel.

'I would rather be wet and cold than dry and burnt.'

'Good attitude. Right. Let's get out of here. Can you walk?'

'No.'

'Then we'll carry you—but we must be quick. We're losing
flooring with every second.'

'Do what you must.'

Ryan hefted Mustafa into his arms. He barely weighed
anything—all skin and bone. The wet towelling seemed to
weigh more. He checked their exit, saw that it was still vi-
able, and began to thunder his way back down the corridor.
There was another crash behind him and he turned to check

on George. He was right behind them, but the flames that had begun licking up through the floor had reached the pile of papers and magazines and was beginning to feed.

And that was when he saw it. Down at the bottom of the pile, leaning up against the wall, almost hidden by the journals, was the top of a gas canister. A canister of oxygen.

Mustafa's COPD.

'Damn. Let's go!'

He practically ran from the hall, out of flat forty two and into the stairwell, and then began running down the stairs as quickly as he could.

When the whole building was rocked by an explosion Ryan fell to his knees, rolling expertly to protect Mustafa from the concrete steps, and all around him the world went black. A high-pitched ringing noise was the only thing he could hear after he briefly banged his head against the floor and came to a stop.

And then all vision was lost as thick plumes of dust and dirt and soot filled the air.

CHAPTER FIFTEEN

THE TOP FLOOR collapsed in on itself, it seemed, and Addy couldn't stop herself from screaming out Ryan's name.

'Ryan! *Ryan!*'

She surged forward, only to be held back by Paolo.

'No, Addy. You can't go in there!'

'But Ryan's in there. It can't happen again! It can't!'

Paolo wrenched her back and stood in front of her, staring into her eyes until she made eye contact with him.

'Stay. Out. Here. Let us deal with this.'

Addy began to shake, shudder and cry. She couldn't think. She couldn't deal with this. It was just so awful, so horrible…

Ryan could be in there—could be trapped. Maybe pinned down by a concrete pillar or a beam? Maybe knocked unconscious somewhere, unaware of the flames getting closer? Or maybe he was dead already? Killed by smoke inhalation so severe that he had been completely asphyxiated.

She sank to her knees, realising that she was of no help now. She couldn't help anyone. That wasn't what she was there for. All she could do was stare at the building and feel such pain that…

She blinked. Were those figures coming out of the flames? Or were her eyes just so watery from her tears that she was imagining things?

It looked like two figures. One was misshapen and blackened...the other looked like a fireman...

And then the smoke cleared as they got closer and she realised it was two firemen, but one was carrying a man wrapped in towelling. He lowered the man to the ground, once they were clear, and pulled off his helmet.

Ryan!

Addy surged forward and ran to him, almost knocking him over when she reached him.

'You're safe!'

He was bleeding. Blood had trickled down his scalp and dried on his face, which was riddled with sweat and soot.

'This is Mustafa. Registered blind and with a history of COPD.'

Ryan staggered to his feet to give her room to treat him and she literally had to force her brain to go into medical mode. She didn't want to treat anyone. She wanted to make sure that Ryan was okay. He looked so pale...he looked as if he was going to pass out.

'Ryan, are you okay?'

'I'm fine. I'm just...' And then he sank down to his knees and keeled over, his eyes rolling into the back of his head.

She wanted to go to him, but couldn't. Other paramedics rushed forward to treat Ryan as she dealt with Mustafa, getting him further away from the burning hazard that was his home and towards the ambulances.

She knew she couldn't give him full-flow oxygen as that might be damaging to someone with COPD and could cause hypoventilation. But Addy almost couldn't concentrate. Couldn't do her job. Her mind was focused on Ryan and whether he was okay. He had a head injury—that was clear.

She managed to get the attention of another paramedic and passed the care of Mustafa on to him. He deserved the best medical attention he could get and she was distracted. Couldn't think. Was panicking.

And that made her useless.

She could not do her job because of how she felt.

Addalyn sat in one of the horrible plastic chairs that hospitals always provided in their waiting areas. It was green, with a questionable bleaching stain on the seat, but that didn't matter. She sank into it gratefully, her mind awhirl, as she tried to gather her thoughts and think straight for the first time since the fire.

She had a decision to make. Maintain her relationship with Ryan or walk away. And, as much as she loved him—for she knew now that she did—she knew that being his girlfriend, or whatever she'd be classed as, meant facing days like today. Over and over again.

Did she have the strength?

Or she could walk away. End it now. Create distance between them. Go back to being just colleagues and try to forget the last couple of days of bliss. Consider them a gift. A cherished memory. Walk away to keep her sanity and what remained of her heart intact.

But first she needed to know that he was all right. His head injury meant that he'd been taken to Accident and Emergency. He'd probably be needing stitches or glue for his scalp laceration, and maybe an X-ray to check for any skull fractures— though he hadn't shown any signs of anything as horrific as that.

He'd been lucky.

They'd been lucky.

But was it lucky to have gone through what she had?

Because to her it had felt like hell. That building's top two floors had slowly collapsed, as if in slow motion, and the horror of losing her dad and her brother had come rushing back. The feeling it had engendered in her—hopelessness…impotence… pain—was not something she wished to experience ever again.

A doctor holding a patient's file came into the waiting area. 'Addalyn Snow?'

She stood, felt her mouth dry. 'Yes?'

'I'm Dr Barclay. Come with me, please. Ryan is asking for you.'

That meant he was okay, right? Conscious. Capable of forming sensible sentences.

She followed Dr Barclay to a cubicle where a dirtied, smoke-stained Ryan sat on a bed, having a gauze patch taped to his head by a nurse.

'Eight stitches and no broken bones,' she explained as Addy looked at her in fear. 'He's got a tough skull, this one.'

'Numbskull, more like.' Ryan grimaced, giving a half-smile.

His eyes had lit up at seeing her approach, but she could see in his face that he didn't know what she was going to say.

'I'm sorry if I scared you.'

Sorry. He was sorry. But it wasn't his fault. He'd been doing his job, after all, and he'd saved that old man. Risked his own life for it. He didn't have to apologise.

She did.

'I've never been so scared in my life.'

She stared at him, wanting to say more, but the nurse was still there, and the doctor, so she turned to them.

'Would you mind if I have a moment alone with him, please?'

'He's all yours,' Dr Barclay said. 'He can go home. You're a hero,' he said to Ryan, turning and shaking his hand before he and the nurse left.

Alone in the cubicle with him, Addy felt terrified all over again. 'I'm glad you're all right.'

He smiled. 'So am I.'

He held out his hand to her, as if he wanted her to be nearer. To hold her. Touch her.

And she wanted that too… But she couldn't do it.

Addalyn took a step back—a hint at what was to come.

'I'm very glad that you're all right. More than you could ever know. But—'

'Addalyn, you don't have to do this.'

'Don't I? I had to stand there and watch again—*again, Ryan!*—as a building collapsed into itself with someone I love inside.' She laughed bitterly, feeling tears burn her eyes. 'Losing one person in a fire is a tragedy, two is ridiculous—but three? Do you know what it does to a person to stand there and feel helpless? To watch as their world crumbles before them, knowing that they can't do a thing about it?'

'It must have been awful.'

'It was. Words aren't enough to explain how I felt in that moment when I thought you might be dead. How much I hated Paolo for holding me back from running into a burning building. And how relieved I felt when I saw you emerge from the flames.'

'But I'm okay, Addy. I'm okay!'

'I know. And I'm glad. But I can't keep doing that to myself, Ryan. I can't keep putting myself through that. We work in the same field; we know the risks. I couldn't do my job!'

'What?'

'My job. I needed to help Mustafa and I *couldn't*—because you'd collapsed and my fear for you stopped me from doing the one thing in this life that I can do well! I love you. I do. But being in love with you is painful, Ryan. It hurts. It burns me. And I can't be burned any more.'

Ryan looked down at his shoes. 'I'm sorry.'

'Don't be. You did your job. As the doctor said, you're a hero. And I'm so glad that you get to go home to Carys tonight.'

'I'd love to come home to you too.'

She smiled sadly as tears dripped down her face. 'Me too. Goodbye, Ryan.'

And she turned and walked away, her heart breaking as she walked away from the man she loved.

The man who caused her too much pain to be with.

CHAPTER SIXTEEN

LIFE WASN'T THE same after Addy walked away. At first he'd felt shock, then anger. He couldn't help what he was! He was a firefighter and she'd known that from the get-go. He was not going to change the job he loved. And with the anger had come the thought that maybe he and Carys were better off. His daughter had already experienced a flaky mother—she did not need to experience her dad's new girlfriend not being dependable either.

Because that was what he knew he needed. Someone he could rely on. Someone who would love him no matter what. Who would accept what he did for a living and not ask him to change. He'd never ask Addy to stop being a paramedic. Stop doing her job! He would be better off finding someone who was strong enough to be by his side for all of life's little foibles. Not someone who was going to run every time life got hard.

But even though he kept telling himself that he didn't need Addalyn in his life, and even managed—sometimes—to convince himself of this, every time he saw her at work it was hard. He tried to not be around when she was on the scene, avoided her as much as he could, but today was one occasion when he'd just got his timings wrong.

'Addalyn.'

He gave her a nod of acknowledgement, hardening his heart, telling himself that being polite was more than she deserved.

But ye gods, it was hard. Seeing her was a torture. He might have told himself he no longer needed her, but he wished somehow he could make his body and his heart understand that. He wanted to stand by her. Touch her. Let their fingers intertwine and share a smile with her. Just to see a smile on her face when she looked at him would be enough…

'Ryan! I didn't know you were on today.'

They'd been called to a small village where, after a particularly heavy amount of rain, there'd been a flood from the local river. It had broken its banks and flooded streets and homes and many people had had to be evacuated.

'I think most of us are here,' he managed to say, knowing that fire services from many local areas had sent in teams of rescuers.

'Of course. And…you're well?'

'Very.'

'No problems since the head injury?'

'No.'

'That's good.' She nodded, all businesslike. 'I'm very pleased to hear it. Don't let me stop you. I'm sure there's plenty you need to be doing.'

'We've finished evacuations. I think we're going to try pumping some of the water out of the infant school.'

She nodded and turned away from him. Dismissing him? She was discussing her plans with Paolo, as she often did when she arrived on scene.

He hated it that she'd made him feel as if he was surplus to her requirements. That he was nothing.

'That's it?'

Addy turned to look at him, alarm showing on her face. She glanced at Paolo, before looking back at him. 'I'm sorry?'

'That's all you have to say to me?'

'I'm not sure there's anything else to say, Ryan. We've said everything.'

Paolo took a step between them. 'Baker. You're needed at the school.'

He gave Ryan a look that said *You don't want to do this*. And, no, he didn't. But he couldn't help himself.

'Did you ever think about *me*?'

She looked shocked.

'Did you ever think about how much *I* worry about *you*? *Your* job? You're a HART paramedic! You could be hurt! You could die! And I'd be the one left behind. Me and Carys. And I can't let my daughter be abandoned again.'

Ryan stalked away, feeling a fire in his blood that took some time to douse. He occupied himself in pumping out the water from the school and focused hard on the job. By the time he'd done everything he could, Addalyn was gone.

He knew he should have handled it better, but things had still felt so tense between them.

When he got home he tried to be present for Carys, who was happily chatting about a project she was doing at school with her best friend Tiffany. Something about a poster... But it was hard to concentrate.

'Dad?'

'Huh?'

'I asked you a question and you didn't answer me.'

'Sorry, honey. I was miles away. What was the question?'

'When can we go back to Addy's house? I haven't finished my jigsaw,' she said.

'Um…that might be difficult for a little while. I think she's busy.'

'Oh. Can we knock on her door and ask?'

'Er…maybe. Not tonight, though.'

'Of course not! I'm in my jammies, silly.'

She began to giggle and carried on playing with a doll that appeared to be having a tea party with some teddy bears.

'But we can go and see her new cat when she gets it, can't we?'

He nodded. 'I'll have to ask. She'll want it to have time to settle in, I should think, and get used to its new home before strangers can come in and cuddle it. It might be scared.'

'Like Molly might be when we get her?'

'That's right. She'll need time.'

He thought about what he'd said. Did Addy need time because *she* was scared? And, if so, time for what? To process? To understand? To change her mind? Had he been too hasty in judging her? She'd been through a lot.

He tried to imagine how she must have felt when he was trapped in that building. She'd lost her father and brother the same way. Watching from outside. And that day she'd known it could happen again, with him inside. No wonder she had panicked! She must have felt awful!

Guilt filled him at the way he'd raged at her earlier, and he wondered if it might be too much to give her a ring and ask for a chat? Clear the air a little? Maybe let her know that he would still be there for her if she needed him?

But he didn't get time to ring.

Because the doorbell did.

Addy stood on the doorstep and tried to calm down, her nerves doing nothing to still the trembling in her body. She'd thought long and hard about her decision back at home, sitting there and staring at Carys's completed Halloween costume. She wanted Ryan's little girl to have it. After all, a promise was a promise, and she would never, ever want to let Carys down. But also she felt she needed to talk to Ryan. Clear the air.

His lights were on, and she thought she could hear the TV, so they were definitely in.

She raised her hand and pressed the button for the bell again, hearing it ring inside.

Oh, God, what am I doing?

Through the patterned glass she saw Ryan walk towards the door. Her heart began to hammer even faster and her mouth went dry.

I won't be able to speak.

Ryan pulled the door open and stood there, looking gorgeous as he always did. He wore a black crew neck jumper and blue jeans. His feet were bare.

He stared at her in surprise. 'Addalyn. We were just talking about you.'

Oh. Okay.

'You were? Nice things, I hope?'

Her voice lilted upwards at the end of her question.

I sound Australian.

'Carys was asking about coming to see Curly and working on her jigsaw—but don't worry… I told her you were busy and that Curly would need time to settle in.'

'Oh. Right. Okay.'

He seemed calmer than earlier.

They stood there for a moment, staring at each other.

'What's that?' He pointed at the parcel under her arm, wrapped in rose-pink tissue paper and tied with a pretty bow.

'It's Carys's Halloween costume. I thought I'd bring it round. A promise is a promise, after all.'

He nodded. 'Want me to call her?'

'I would like to see her. I've missed her.'

He turned and shouted behind him. 'Carys! There's someone here for you.'

Someone.

'And I'd like the chance to talk to you also, if I may?' she added.

Now he turned back to look at her, confused, but he didn't get a moment to say anything because Carys barrelled past, straight into Addalyn's arms, and clung on like a limpet.

'Addy! I've missed you! Can I come round soon?'

Addy laughed and gave her a squeeze. 'Of course you can! You're always welcome in my house.'

'We're getting a cat called Molly!'

'I know you are.' She playfully tapped Carys on the nose and set her down on the ground. 'Listen, I need to talk to your dad. Why don't you take this?'

She passed Carys the now crumpled tissue-wrapped gift.

'For me?'

'For you,' she said with a smile, watching with joy as Carys ripped it open to gasp in delight and awe at her tiger costume.

'It's got a tail, Dad—look! And teeth!'

'I can see! Carys, honey…why don't you head upstairs and try it on for size?'

'Okay!'

Carys dashed up the stairs, her little feet thudding so hard it sounded as if a herd of wildebeest was passing through.

Ryan stepped back and invited her in.

She passed by him and headed to the lounge, feeling apprehensive. The easy bit was done. The hard part might just be impossible…but she had to try.

'Thank you for letting me speak to you.'

'I wasn't sure you'd ever want to speak to me again.'

'Of course I would. I would always want you in my life. I've just had to deal with some pretty strong emotions. Ones that I wasn't ready for. Or didn't think I was ready for.'

He nodded and she took a seat, whilst he settled onto the couch opposite her.

From upstairs there came a thump.

'I'm okay!' they heard Carys yell, causing them both to smile.

Addy sucked in a breath. 'I panicked. Before. At the fire when I thought you were trapped, and then again afterwards when you made it out.'

'You panicked when I made it *out*?'

'Yes. Because I knew in that moment that if I stayed with you I would have to experience that feeling over and over again.'

'Right. Of course.'

He looked disappointed. But she needed to lay the ground-work before beginning her explanation. 'I've taken a long time to think about things. Work through my emotions. I even went to a couple of therapy sessions. And that stuff's not cheap.'

She tried to make a joke. Lighten the mood.

'We all could probably do with therapy,' said Ryan. 'No matter who we are. What did you learn?'

'That I felt like a nobody.'

'A nobody?'

'I don't like feeling helpless. Or out of control. I've had it all my life, Ryan. I couldn't have children, no matter what I tried, and I lost the chance of having the family I'd always dreamed of. I thought getting pregnant, having a baby, would be easy. Natural. It wasn't. And when Nathan left me for someone who could give him the family he craved, it made me feel like...'

Her emotions threatened to overwhelm her in that moment.

'A nobody?'

She nodded. 'Like I was worthless. Useless. That I had nothing to offer anyone. That's why my job has always been so important to me. Because I make a difference! I save lives!'

'So do I.'

'Yes. You do. And that's why I know I could never ask you

to change who you are—because it's important. Very important. Both our jobs are.'

'I'm glad you agree.'

'When I lost my father and my brother I felt so incredibly alone. I felt so incredibly unseen. All I did was work. I told myself that I couldn't get close to anyone. That I couldn't love anyone. Because everyone I loved left me alone and hurting and in pain. It seemed simpler to be alone.'

'And then I came along…'

She smiled. 'You came along. You brought life and warmth back into my life. I was scared of it. Scared of what you'd made me feel for the first time in ages. I felt like I mattered. Like I wasn't alone. And you brought me so much joy! So when I thought I'd lost you, I felt like I was going to lose myself all over again…when I was just beginning to live.'

He reached across for her hand. Squeezed it.

'In that moment when I thought I'd lost you I felt like the world was trying to tell me that it would take everyone from me, and I stupidly thought that if I stayed with you then I would lose not only you, but Carys, too. That something horrible might befall you. And I didn't want to be responsible for that.'

'It wouldn't be your fault.'

'I know. The therapist said the same thing. She made me realise that my life alone was more painful than my life with those I love. That I cannot control what might happen to anyone and that's okay. I'm not meant to be in control of that. But that doesn't mean I need to punish myself by staying away from people. I deserve love, and I deserve to feel like I matter. And, more than anything in the world, I really, really want to matter to you and Carys.'

'What are you saying, Addy?'

'I'm saying that… I love you. And that terrifies the hell out of me. But what terrifies me more is being alone. I feel we have something that could be amazing and beautiful if we let it. If you're willing to forgive me.'

She let out a shuddering breath. Had she said it the way she'd wanted to? No. Even though she'd practised her speech in the car, and at home, and on the walk over she'd forgotten bits. Missed bits out. Got confused. But she had spoken from her heart, and she hoped that he would appreciate that even if he sent her packing. Because she'd had to try. Had to say sorry. Even if he wouldn't allow them to be together.

'Thank you. For all you've said.'

He paused for a moment. Was he practising his own speech? she wondered.

'I was hurt when you walked away. Confused and angry. Which I want to apologise for. I should never have shouted at you like that. In front of Paolo, too. I thought it might make me feel better to blurt it all out, and it did for about a second, but afterwards...?' He frowned. 'Every time I try to love a woman she walks away from me. So I know how you feel!'

He smiled ruefully, before his face grew serious again.

'I vowed to never bring a woman into my daughter's life unless I knew I could depend upon her—because it's not just me that's had someone walk away from them. It's Carys too. She had a mother who one day may make *her* need therapy. *Why wasn't I good enough for her to stay for?* I didn't want her to think that you'd done the same thing, so she doesn't actually know that we fell out.'

'Oh. Well, that's good. But I would never have stopped contact with Carys. I would have asked you to consider letting me stay in her life even if I couldn't be in yours.'

'Really?'

'Yes! Absolutely! I could never imagine walking away from her. Her mother doesn't know what she's missing...what a wonderful person she is.'

Ryan smiled. 'I knew in my heart that you would never abandon her, whatever happened. But I have to know you're serious, Addy. Because my job is going to continue to make you feel helpless, and I don't want to be the cause of any more emotional pain for you.'

'I am serious. Relationships aren't easy, Ryan. None of them. They're difficult and they're painful and they're upsetting at times. But people get through because they're a family. I've lost my family twice now, but being with you and Carys has shown me what it's like to be in one again, and I'd rather be there, in a family, loving one another and being terrified, than not be in one. Love is worth the risk. *You* are worth the risk. Carys is worth the risk. I want to love you both. I want to spend my days with you. My nights. I want to soak up every minute with you and enjoy it. Even the difficult parts. I won't run. I won't hide. Because I can't leave you. And even if you do one day have to leave me I will be there. For our daughter.'

He smiled. '*Our* daughter?'

'She feels like mine. I can't stop thinking about her. Worrying about her. This time away from her has been torture.'

Ryan moved from his seat opposite to the one next to her. He stroked away her tears and tucked a strand of hair behind her ear.

'You're amazingly strong—you know that?'

'I've been cowardly.'

'No.' He shook his head. 'You've been incredibly brave. All that you've been through… It would break some people.'

'It almost broke me.'

'But it didn't. You *fought*. For yourself. For us.'

'Us? Is there going to be an us? I can't give you any more children.'

He smiled again. Broadly. 'Yes. There is an us. There has *always* been an us. And there is more than one way to make a family.' He kissed her. Lightly. 'I have always loved you, Addalyn Snow. And I'm going to continue to love you until the end of our days.'

Her heart soared. 'I love you too.'

At that moment Carys jumped into the room with a roar, her tiger tail swinging behind her.

They both laughed, and Ryan swooped her up into his arms.

Addy moved to stand beside them. 'You look amazing. It fits perfectly.'

'We all fit perfectly,' said Ryan.

And he leant in and kissed Addalyn on the lips.

'You kissed! Does that mean you're my daddy's girlfriend now, Addy?'

'Only if you say it's okay,' she answered.

They both looked at Carys.

'Yay!'

And Carys pulled them both in for a hug.

EPILOGUE

THIS WAS THE perfect place. Now was the perfect time. Addy stood waiting in the bathroom on the morning of her wedding day. Waiting and staring suspiciously and hopefully at a small piece of plastic perched on the back of the loo.

She'd never dared to hope. Never dared believe that the happiness she already had could actually *increase*. Because life with Ryan and Carys, making her new family, had been *everything*.

Of course there'd been moments. Scary moments every time she'd got called to a shout that she knew Ryan was on, knowing that at each job he would be running towards danger, whereas she and anyone who wasn't a fireman would be staying away from it.

But she'd dealt with it. Grown accustomed to the fear and now called it her *'old friend'*. Because that fear only existed because *love* existed. And she was going to hold on to that love for as long as she could. She trusted in Ryan's training. In his skills. He'd survived the army. He'd survive the fire service. And if he didn't—if he got injured or, worse, killed—then she would be devastated, of course. But she would still have had their love, she would still have the many memories that they'd made, and she would still have Carys.

And maybe—just maybe—if this pregnancy test confirmed

what she already suspected, she would have someone else to love and care for, too.

The doctors had never found a reason for her infertility, but she'd just accepted that she was infertile. But these last few weeks she'd become tired…occasionally had some tension headaches. And she'd felt bloated, sometimes nauseous. But she had put all that down to the stress of planning her wedding. To sampling lots of cakes—red velvet, lemon and poppyseed, fruit, sponge, chocolate… They'd tried them all.

And then her period hadn't come. It had to be stress, right?

But her period had continued not to come, and yesterday she'd gone out and secretly bought a pregnancy testing kit to use today, on the morning of her wedding.

It seemed right.

It seemed perfect.

Only what if it was negative?

Would it spoil her day?

Their day?

Today was a day for unadulterated happiness, and she didn't want anything to mar that!

But she had to know. She couldn't wait another minute.

Addy picked up the test, squeezing her eyes shut and praying to whatever gods there were that this test would be positive. That just for once life would work out for her and give her every iota of happiness it could. That things would go right. That she might go from being no one to being a beloved girlfriend and a beloved fiancée, to being a stepmother, and then to an actual *real* mother to her own child.

It didn't matter that Carys wasn't hers. That she wasn't her biological child. Addy felt that she was hers and always would. She loved Ryan's daughter as if she was her own, and grieved for the fact that she'd never known Carys as a baby. Never held her in her arms and rocked her to sleep.

Please. Please. Please!

Her wedding dress was hanging from the shower rail, having been steamed the night before. Her make-up lay waiting for her to apply it. Her hair, wrapped in a towel on her head, awaited the stylist.

And Addy waited too. Fear lingered for one last moment, pausing her hand, before she finally found the strength to open her eyes and look at the result.

Addalyn gasped, putting her hand to her mouth in shocked disbelief.

Pregnant.

Laughing, crying, she looked at her reflection in the mirror. She was going to have a baby! Ryan's baby! A sister or brother for Carys! The family she had always longed for.

Everything was perfect.

Addalyn felt happy. Serene.

Not calm. But buzzing!

How to tell Ryan?

When to tell Ryan?

After the service?

At the wedding dinner?

As they danced their first dance?

She tried to imagine his face when she told him. When they told Carys.

They would have picnics. With their children chasing one another as Ryan and Addy sat on blankets on the grass and held hands, watching them.

Happiness and joy were now hers for the taking.

Life only got better and better.

* * * * *

MILLS & BOON MODERN IS
HAVING A MAKEOVER!

The same great stories you love,
a stylish new look!

Look out for our brand new look
COMING JUNE 2024

MILLS & BOON

COMING SOON!

We really hope you enjoyed reading this book.
If you're looking for more romance
be sure to head to the shops when
new books are available on

Thursday 20th
June

To see which titles are coming soon, please visit
millsandboon.co.uk/nextmonth

MILLS & BOON®

Coming next month

ER DOC'S MIRACLE TRIPLETS
Tina Beckett

'There's something I need you to know.'

Seb sat in silence, staring at her face as if he didn't want her to say another word. But she had to. He deserved to hear the words so that he could make whatever decision he felt he needed to. So she pushed forward. 'I'm pregnant.'

'Pregnant.' A series of emotions crossed his face. Emotions that she couldn't read. Or maybe she was too afraid of trying to figure them out. 'But the last attempt failed.'

Even as his words faded away, an awful twist of his mouth gave evidence to what he was thinking. That the babies weren't his. She hurried to correct him. 'But it didn't. I assumed when I started spotting that I'd lost the pregnancy, because it was the pattern with the other IVF attempts. And I didn't go to have it checked out right away because of all the stress. I waited until you were gone to try to sort through things.'

'So you didn't lose the baby?'

His words were tentative, as if he was afraid that even saying them out loud might jinx everything. She got it. She'd felt the same way when they'd done the ultrasound on her and told her the wonderful news.

'Babies. I didn't lose the babies…plural.'

He sat up in his chair. He was shocked. Obviously. But was he also happy? Dismayed? Angry? She could no longer read him the way she'd once been able to.

'You're carrying twins?'

She slowly shook her head, unable to prevent a smile from reaching her lips. 'There are three of them.'

Continue reading
ER DOC'S MIRACLE TRIPLETS
Tina Beckett

Available next month
millsandboon.co.uk

LET'S TALK

Romance

For exclusive extracts, competitions and special offers, find us online:

- **f** MillsandBoon
- **X** @MillsandBoon
- **O** @MillsandBoonUK
- **d** @MillsandBoonUK

Get in touch on 01413 063 232

MILLS & BOON

THE HEART OF ROMANCE

A ROMANCE FOR EVERY READER

MODERN
Prepare to be swept off your feet by sophisticated, sexy and seductive heroes, in some of the world's most glamourous and romantic locations, where power and passion collide.

HISTORICAL
Escape with historical heroes from time gone by. Whether yc passion is for wicked Regency Rakes, muscled Vikings or rugg Highlanders, awaken the romance of the past.

MEDICAL
Set your pulse racing with dedicated, delectable doctors in the high-pressure world of medicine, where emotions run high and passion, comfort and love are the best medicine.

True Love
Celebrate true love with tender stories of heartfelt romance, from the rush of falling in love to the joy a new baby can bring and a focus on the emotional heart of a relationship.

HEROES
The excitement of a gripping thriller, with intense romance at its heart. Resourceful, true-to-life women and strong, fearless men face danger and desire - a killer combination!

From showing up to glowing up, these characters are on the path to leading their best lives and finding romance along the way – with plenty of sizzling spice!

To see which titles are coming soon, please visit

millsandboon.co.uk/nextmonth